Entertaining Angels

Joanna Bell is a GP who lives in a Suffolk cottage with her husband, six children and a vast number of thatch spiders. She was one of the first women at Caius College Cambridge, but has also worked as a night porter and a topless dancer. She spends her spare time giving lifts to her children. She is afraid of nothing but, even so, her husband deals with the spiders.

Also by Joanna Bell

Pillars of Salt

Entertaining Angels

❦

JOANNA BELL

ARROW

Published by Arrow Books in 2002

1 3 5 7 9 10 8 6 4 2

First published in the United Kingdom in 2002 by William Heinemann

Arrow Books
The Random House Group Limited
20 Vauxhall Bridge Road, London, SW1V 2SA

Random House Australia (Pty) Limited
20 Alfred Street, Milsons Point, Sydney,
New South Wales 2061, Australia

Random House New Zealand Limited
18 Poland Road, Glenfield
Auckland 10, New Zealand

Random House (Pty) Limited
Endulini, 5a Jubilee Road, Parktown 2193, South Africa

The Random House Group Limited Reg. No. 954009

www.randomhouse.co.uk

A CIP catalogue record for this book is
available from the British Library

Papers used by Random House
are natural, recyclable products made from wood grown in
sustainable forests. The manufacturing processes conform to
the environmental regulations of the country of origin

ISBN 0 09 941697 2

Typeset by SX Composing DTP, Rayleigh, Essex
Printed and bound in Great Britain by
Cox & Wyman Ltd, Reading, Berkshire

To Anastasia Hebe Rose Selby

Acknowledgements

To my sister, Alex, for reading this and to my husband and children for everything.

'Be not forgetful to entertain strangers: for thereby some have entertained angels unawares.'

Hebrews 13 : 2.13

Prologue

Some people say that every place has an angel, and every angel a place. Foxbarton's angel was left to Foxbarton church by Mackenzie Brown, a sculptress born in the village, who achieved fortune and glory before dying old and rich and bequeathing all her other worldly wealth to her disreputable family (who promptly spent the lot). The angel was only eighteen inches high but it was Foxbarton's pride and joy, attracting visitors to St Gregory's from as far afield as America and Japan. It was also, however, a millstone around the Church's neck, for it had been bequeathed with the condition that it must always be on public display in the village. In practical terms this meant the vicar opening the church at any time of the day or night, in any weather and without question, to anybody who wished to see the statue. The very minute anyone tried to restrict viewing times, ownership of the angel would revert back to the Browns.

The remaining Browns were an impecunious lot, known for turning up in Foxbarton and banging on the vicar's door at all hours in the hope that he would have a virus and thus be rendered unable to open the church. The moment this occurred they would be able to claim the statue back for posterity and the restoration of family pride (and to sell, obviously).

The statue, meanwhile, increased in value at an alarming rate, until the church's insurance premiums became impossible to afford. In the year when the angel disappeared the church treasurer had simply not had enough money in the

1

bank to pay for both the insurance and the vicar, and she chose to fund the vicar, leaving the statue uninsured.

Afterwards, of course, there were plenty of people who said that she chose unwisely, particularly as it was widely held to be the vicar's fault that the angel was stolen. There were, on the other hand, one or two people who said that it was a jolly good thing that the angel had gone, since St Gregory's was a church, not an art gallery, and surely the money was better spent on commendable things, like prayer books, rather than nebulous things, like insurance premiums. Most, though, did feel they had lost something rather special, something that could never be replaced.

It was in the early hours of the morning on a hot summer night that the angel disappeared. It was still there just after the pubs closed the previous evening, as James Brown turned up at half-past eleven, fresh from the Fox and Hound via the curry house in Haverhill, breathed vindaloo all over the vicar and demanded to be shown his inheritance. The vicar let him into St Gregory's, the two of them observed the statue, then the vicar was called urgently to sit with a dying woman and so escorted James Brown out again and locked up behind them. That was the last time they saw the angel.

The police thought the vicar must have failed to lock the church door after leaving, because the only other way in was the window that ventilated the vestry, and that was ten feet up and not big enough to admit a fairy. The angel could have flown out of it, people said, but no one could possibly have got in.

No one had seen anything suspicious, even though no one had slept very much that night. Foxbarton Grange, which was the nearest house to the church, had been full of people, as Simon and Merrill Gilfoyle had been having a party to celebrate Merrill's thirtieth birthday. Virtually the whole village had been there, so every inhabitant had almost everyone else as an alibi. The vicar himself had not been at the party but had spent from midnight till five a.m.

at the bedside of Mrs Braithwaite, widely known as the village witch, who had supposedly been dying that night of extreme old age. She had mysteriously recovered by the following morning after dismissing the vicar abruptly at five a.m. with the words, 'I've been called back, Vicar, so you might as well go.' She was still going strong four years on in her house in the woods, where she made herbal remedies to sell and drank them herself if they didn't.

The gypsy-traveller contingent who had turned up to camp in a woodland clearing ready for the annual Foxbarton Horse Fair (actually now largely a car boot sale, but the more romantic name persisted) were, of course, widely suspected of the theft, as travellers always are, and the police searched their small but homely caravans very thoroughly before muttering that the angel had probably already flown off to a South London pub to be traded for cash. Since the travellers did not, on principle, speak to the police (other than to tell them where to go and how to get there) this view stood, largely undefended, and four years passed swiftly on.

The angel never surfaced despite nationwide publicity about its disappearance. The pedestal where it once stood remained empty, and the church's insurance premium was relatively affordable again. The tourists went elsewhere and the vicar of Foxbarton retired, leaving his successor to a life that featured just as many night calls as before – but none of them, these days, concerning angels. At least not usually.

Chapter One

Illumination comes in many colours. When Joshua Gilfoyle gazed out at the familiar skyline of the City of London on his last night as Chairman of Gilfoyles, it was lit both by moonlight, and by the streetlights which gleamed sulphurously off wet pavements, making them look as if they really were paved with gold. The Gilfoyles building was also floodlit in blue, the first choice for City institutions who wanted to say publicly that they had recently employed an architect to do their lighting because their interim financial report was so bloody good – but Joshua's eye was drawn by the white light that illuminated the great dome of St Paul's Cathedral some fifty yards away. He could see the gold cross on the top from where he stood, representing the path to glory or, perhaps, the unattainable. It made him think of the lost Foxbarton angel, and he wondered how that artist he'd employed was getting on with the new one. Slowly, probably, given that she was an artist and therefore clearly incapable of a properly disciplined day's work. He felt this was the last time he would stand in this place. Life is a series of phases; the next one for him would be the last and he no longer wanted to spend any of it here.

Far below he could see a man in the street, staggering. Drunk. Probably one of these loonies who live in shop doorways, thought Joshua, who did not hold with mental illness of any kind. They should be sterilised, these people. There were enough of them about as it was, without them breeding. They turned up everywhere. Like that loony child he had inadvertently installed in Foxbarton, the artist's daughter. He had seen her staring in at him the other day when he was working in his study. Just staring, with great big vacant eyes like pools of darkness, tunnels into another world. She ought to be sent away somewhere. That mother of hers shouldn't force her upon people like that. He had bloody well told her so and she had had the effrontery to tell him to piss off with his prejudices. No one had told Joshua Gilfoyle to piss off since he was at school, and he had been so taken aback that he had found he quite admired the mother for her guts. (And her breasts, of course. Great breasts.) So he had said the child could stay, even though he had only wanted the mother there, definitely not the child. He wanted the mother as Foxbarton's artist in residence. She was a sculptress of reputation. She had won prizes. She was the kind of artist he wanted to make something lasting to stand on that plinth in the church now that he knew he himself was not invincible.

The fool doctor had said he could have years – prostate cancer was a slow-growing thing, might not kill him for a decade even if it killed him at all – but then you never could tell. They were all the same, doctors, never telling you anything, covering themselves. How he managed to father a bloody doctor himself he'd never know. What damn use was it to know the bomb was ticking if you couldn't measure the fuse? His days were clearly numbered, and he would respect the warning and prepare.

The new Foxbarton angel would be his legacy, would ensure his immortality. Well, that and his grandchildren – both, thankfully, intelligent and normal. You didn't want trouble of that sort in the Gilfoyles. But they were Simon's children, and that was only half of the hand fate had dealt him. He had once had another son, a lost son, and he wanted to be sure of him too.

He turned back to face the room, the white walls, the Hockney, the small chair in which he had spent so many hours, days, weeks, commanding the pieces of his empire like chess. The empire his elder son should have commanded after him . . .

He looked at the company lawyer in the expensive suit sitting in the chair by his desk. 'Mark, I suppose you haven't come to tell me you've found him?'

Mark Smythe sighed. 'I've looked everywhere, Joshua, followed every trail. He's out there, I'm sure of it. I can only imagine he doesn't want to be found. I'm sure people are holding out on me. Perhaps it would be better to let me engage a private detective agency on your behalf after all?'

Joshua Gilfoyle was not accustomed to being questioned by people who worked for him, but since hearing his diagnosis he had mellowed a little. 'I've told you, Mark, I want this kept within the company. Keep trying. I just know he's still alive. I would know if he weren't. I want him found – and when you do find him, you tell him he has his inheritance back – with those conditions, of course. Half the company will be his if he complies. He'll come back.'

The younger man hesitated. 'Don't you think the directors might feel . . .?' He could imagine what it must have cost Joshua to backtrack on that. Everyone knew Gabriel had been disinherited after he –

'Dammit, Mark, this is my company, I made it and I'll give it to whomever I like, make whatever conditions I like.' He had to. It wasn't bad for the son of a Suffolk farmer whose father had started a small city company as a London hobby – particularly when he also had to his name a five-thousand-acre estate, a grand house, a fair chunk of Cambridge property and a former mistress, now his wife, named Sonja, of Norse extraction. It was called diversifying. Joshua had never limited himself to only one of anything. Not even wives, now that he'd married Sonja.

Mark looked awkward. 'Of course. Joshua, I'm really very sorry to hear about your . . . illness.'

'My cancer, you mean? Then say cancer, Mark. For God's sake, don't start beating around the bush with me now.

Don't you know how bloody common prostate cancer is? You have a forty per cent chance of getting it yourself before you're seventy-five. Don't waste your pity on me, you may need it one day for yourself.'

That was Joshua through and through, thought Mark, as he let himself out of the building and headed home – a hard, unpleasant old man, tough as a walnut and infinitely more bitter. Yet it was hard to imagine Gilfoyles without the man who had single-handedly built a company of such standing, such immensity, from the small thing it had been when he took it on.

Mark glanced up as he walked round the edge of the cathedral. The great dome towered above him, celestial and pale, older than any man living, reducing men and their hopes, dreams, lives and deaths, he reflected, to small matters. Would the impending death of Joshua Gilfoyle matter enough to his son Gabriel to bring him home when the welcome was so qualified by Joshua's unwavering prejudices?

Frowning at the view from the window, Joshua picked up the phone and called for his driver. He had had enough of this place. It was time for home. He was tired, his bones ached. The bloody doctor wanted to scan him again. If they scanned him every time his bones ached he'd never be out of the bloody scanning machine. Well, he would go home and let the local quacks take care of him now. As long as they put him down if he went potty they could do whatever else they liked. Leave the City to its squabbling – he'd done what he set out to do and that was it. Now he wanted to extract the remaining juice out of the rest of his life. What was the point of having married your mistress if you spent your energy shouting at accountants? You got all the costs and none of the benefits. He frowned at the moon's gentle face and wondered if you could see it from Heaven.

*

By nature's trick the moon showed her same face to Foxbarton, competing there not with streetlights but with the incredible brightness of stars which shine properly in those places where man has only placed a few of his feet at any one time and hasn't left a rash of yellow streetlights in his wake. Foxbarton lay south-east of Cambridge in that great splash of rural Suffolk that remains almost feudal in its loyalty to wealth, where squat thatched cottages are painted white, cream, pink and yellow at the whim of their owners, and children still swim in the rivers. Here, where Boudicca once fought, and countless generations tilled the land and tolled the bells, the huge and rambling Foxbarton Grange nestled snug in the hollow of its own creation. Behind it were its neat lawns and less neat orchard, and a meadow where a small but very obstinate llama grazed a field of lush grass. Beside it began the vast and sprawling Foxbarton Woods, where canny foxes were fed oven ready chickens through the winter to keep them fit for occasional pursuit by the unspeakable in the time-honoured tradition. Beyond it stood the church of St Gregory the Illuminator, into which generations of wealthy landowners had poured a little of their largesse, making it grander by far than most village churches of its size and congregation. And within which an angel had once stood.

At the edge of the woods Woodcutter's Cottage was just visible, a light glowing late in one bedroom. Hebe Fitzgerald was looking at the moon, and the moon, for all her pretended interest in London streets and tower blocks, in cathedral domes and flashing stars, was actually looking at Hebe, shining solely for Hebe. Nothing else interested the moon. It was Hebe's moon and hers entirely. It was part of the cleverness of nature that no one but Hebe should realise this to be true. But then Hebe didn't see things as other people did. Sometimes she saw the same things differently, and sometimes she saw different things all together. In the years of her adulthood this might be her blessing or it might be her burden – but for now, as she was only eight, it was her gift. And as her pale face glowed with a moonlit intensity unmarred by understanding that there was any way to see things other than her way, her mother, Julia, in the next room, fiddled with her long blonde plait and tried not to think of any of it at all. She stared at the page beneath her hands in dissatisfaction. This was still not going well.

For three months now Julia Fitzgerald had lived in this cottage, half employee, half guest, since she had accepted the offer from Joshua Gilfoyle, the father-in-law of her older sister, Merrill, to become artist in residence in Foxbarton. Her payment was not only remuneration for her work, but also the tenancy of this cottage for as long as she chose to be here. Her task was to produce Joshua's bequest to St Gregory's church, to immortalise his memory for ever in the place he had claimed for his own. Joshua Gilfoyle wanted his own Foxbarton angel, and he wanted Julia Fitzgerald to make it. Julia – who had achieved national fame nine years before, when her final-year piece had won the Turner prize and a substantial cheque. That was why he wanted Julia – he thought she was one of the best.

But that was nine years ago. And that had been a bold construction entitled *Being*, which all sorts of people had imbued with religious significance but was actually a representation of someone she had once spent the night with without ever knowing his name. Someone who she had once hoped she would find again, but never had. A lover and a man. Not at all the kind of being that had once stood on a plinth in Foxbarton church.

But as far as Joshua Gilfoyle had been concerned, she was famous for making something people had assumed was an angel, and that qualified her to make another one. And Julia had so very much needed a way out of London for Hebe that she had accepted the assignment and come to Foxbarton.

But how can you hope to make an angel when you don't believe in them? At least, not in winged things that hang around in clouds, playing harps and simpering at passing souls, haloed products of the mishmash of hope and wishful thinking that was, in Julia's view, the Christian Church. To Julia, angels, if anything, were spirits without form, clouds of energy which touch the lives of those who least expect it and most need it – and how do you represent that in cast bronze? Particularly, thought Julia, biting her lip and taking another sip of the dandelion wine that old Mrs Braithwaite had given her, particularly when you haven't actually managed to produce a single truly original piece of art work since your daughter was born. Particularly when the essential part of the last sculpture you made was its penis. They wouldn't want a penis on this one – absolutely not.

She sighed softly to herself and downed the last of the dandelion wine. Mrs Braithwaite had said it was a marvellous treatment for the vapours. Julia wasn't sure that she was having what Mrs Braithwaite called the vapours, but the absence of a man in her bed for some years now was certainly doing something to her and it wasn't good. She stretched out one bare foot idly and looked at it. It was a perfect foot – Julia loved feet, and was rather proud of her own, which were large and square and, in her view, beautiful. Not beautiful in the vain sense of women's magazines but in an artist's sense of being a fabulously perfect creation. It was her particular weakness – or had been in the days when she had had the opportunity to express it – to have her feet stroked. If only there was someone free to tickle her feet now. What a waste of feet to be celibate for all these years. 'Poor feet, poor celibate feet,' she told them, and realised that the latest angel she had sketched now had enormous feet. Feet of clay.

Bored, she stood and paced the cottage, swinging the plait, looking for distraction.

Julia didn't have a TV. She didn't believe in TV, thought it mindless and boring, but there was the odd night – like tonight – when she felt mindless and boring herself, and would secretly have liked to sit down in front of one of those programmes where publicity-seeking interior designers turn suburban living rooms into visions of Egyptian tombs and everyone pretends to love it. She screwed up the picture she had been doodling. It looked like a child in a Nativity play wearing her father's wellingtons, and she realised she had drawn Hebe.

'Does it have to be an angel?' she had asked Joshua Gilfoyle when he had told her what he wanted. 'I mean, I could do you a tree, or a star, or a heron.'

But Joshua Gilfoyle had lowered his eyebrows and she had watched them in fascination, for they seemed to have a life of their own, winged and matted like small grey rodents glued to his face. 'I don't want a bloody heron in the bloody church. D'you think I want to be remembered down the centuries for a bloody matchstick bird? I want an angel.'

'Well, maybe I'm not the right person for the commission . . .' I've accepted the house from the old sod now, she had thought even as she said it. I've brought Hebe here out of London, uprooted her like a flower. I can't just throw in the towel.

Joshua was having none of it. 'They tell me you're a sculptress – so bloody well get on and sculpt. I don't want one of these namby-pamby types coming here to chop up dead things and pickle them. I've seen what goes on at those art exhibitions. Death and pornography – pah! It may suit the Saatchis but it doesn't suit me. An angel to sit on that plinth, that's what I want. And bloody well get a move on before I'm dead.'

'Don't give me that. You're not going to be dead for years,' retorted Julia, who, unlike her sister, Merrill, was not at all intimidated by Joshua.

'How would you know, woman? I've got cancer in my bones. Until you've got cancer in your bones don't presume to tell me about mine.'

Julia remembered how she had turned her back and

marched off in protest, but underneath she had known then as she knew now that she couldn't give up. Not this time – and not because of Joshua Gilfoyle. No, this was the test, to see if she actually had any artistic impulse left in her at all, or if she was merely basking in the reflection of her former reputation.

Her inspiration had been missing since Hebe was born – actually, since Hebe was conceived. She had been exhibiting throughout her pregnancy, but the work, crucially, had all been thought of well before her hormones started rising. She might have sculpted since then, but it was all from sketches she had done before . . . Then when Hebe was little there had been no time. She had taken a year out – to be a proper mother, she had told herself – and then the year had become two. Then Hebe's autism was diagnosed, and two years had become three, and then four. By the time of Merrill's thirtieth birthday party, the night when the Foxbarton angel disappeared, Julia had begun to realise she was just making excuses to herself. After all, Hebe was so peculiarly self-contained that there was still plenty of time to create. True, Hebe was a brilliant escape artist and you had to have an ear and an eye on her absolutely all the time . . . Julia had even taken to sleeping with Hebe's bedroom doorknob tied to a bell beside her bed – but it wasn't enough of an excuse. How much time can one child occupy, even one who had turned out to be less of a child than a fairy?

It all boiled down to one thing. If she couldn't make the replacement for the Foxbarton angel then she couldn't call herself an artist. This was the test to see if Julia Fitzgerald was actually still a sculptress at all, or if Julia Fitzgerald was a rather zany woman with sexy feet who had given birth to a fairy child, who made decidedly unoriginal garden ornaments out of willow and wire to supplement her income and who had once been to art college and done a bit of sculpting, long ago.

She sighed and tried not to remember that there had been

a time when inspiration surged through her veins like champagne, when she would wake in the morning so full of it that she had to get to fresh clay before she could even dress. It had peaked on that morning, the day when she had sculpted *Being* – she had done so stark naked, and it had been a full two hours before she had even realised that her lover, the unknowing model for *Being*, who had gone out for croissants for breakfast, had simply not returned. That day she had been inspired. But now she was struggling to do anything at all.

She climbed the stairs quietly and went into Hebe's room. Hebe was kneeling at the window, her pale face made luminous by the moon. Hebe's hair was pale, almost white blonde, so that she looked as if a light was upon her even when there was no light, but now the moon gave her a silver halo. She did not react to her mother's presence and Julia went over and kneeled beside her.

Hebe sighed loudly.

'What are you looking at?' Julia asked.

'The angel in the moon,' said Hebe. 'It's singing.'

'What does it sing?'

'I don't know,' said Hebe, and began to cry, suddenly, tearlessly into the night.

Julia put her arm around her, knowing that you couldn't understand Hebe's moods on a rational level. 'What's wrong? Is the angel in the moon sad?'

'It's nine sevens,' said Hebe through her tears, still staring at the moon. 'They're sixty-three.'

'That's right, darling. Are you counting the stars again?' And, when Hebe nodded, 'Why is that sad?'

'I don't know,' said Hebe, and began to howl like a lost wolf.

Julia was used to this – what Hebe said bore no resemblance to what she was actually feeling, to what worried her. She couldn't express that so she said whatever came first into her head. Counting stars was her joy and her pain.

'Come on,' Julia said. 'Let's go to bed.'

Hebe wrapped herself round her mother and clung on tight, still howling. 'Can I sleep with you?'

'Of course you can,' said Julia, thinking, it's not as if anyone else is likely to want to. Her friend Lisa from London, who wrote her long vulgar letters every week or two, had suggested she bought one of those dreadful vibrating toys they sell in sex shops but Julia had been deeply appalled at the idea. It wasn't that she was a prude, it was just that she believed in nature. Sex was part of nature. Being naked in the woods was part of nature. Ravishing a handsome stranger for hours because it seemed to please him and it was that time of the month was nature. Giving birth – well, that wasn't quite the orgasm that the Kitzinger book had promised her but it was still nature. Boy, was it nature. But plastic things that vibrate? Those were crap. If her sister's theory was correct and her artistic integrity needed regular orgasms to function, well, that was crap too. A woman without a man is like a fish without a bicycle. Isn't that what they said at the single parents' group she had been to in Islington? Mind you, they had all been lesbians so what did you expect? I do miss sex, she thought. I really do.

A hundred yards away, in the east wing of Foxbarton Grange, Merrill and Simon Gilfoyle sat companionably together on a large sofa trying not to watch TV. William had insisted they all sat down to watch this programme, and it was perfectly vile.

'The trouble is,' whispered Merrill to her husband, 'he's obsessed by the revolting.'

'It's not revolting, Mum,' said William, overhearing because he had ears that were tuned to respond to non-audible speech when his name was involved, 'it's nature.'

'It may be nature,' said his twin sister, Matilda, who had also been forced to watch, 'but it's still disgusting. I can see

its intestines. If God had wanted us to see spiders dis-
embowelling centipedes on TV He'd have given us aerials
on our heads in the first place.'

'You'll never be an explorer if you don't watch *Wildlife on
One*,' said William critically, forgetting momentarily that
the only one who wanted to be an explorer was him.

'Well, I don't want to be an explorer, do I? Charlotte
Church is on BBC2,' said Matilda darkly. 'I bet they're not
showing any intestines on BBC2.'

William sniffed. 'It might be more interesting if they did.
She's *so* girlie.'

'She is a girl,' said Matilda. 'I mean, on the inside as well
as on the outside. You're only a boy on the outside. I think
you're a beetle in the middle.'

Merrill giggled and tried to turn it into a cough but
William rounded on her critically. 'Mum, you shouldn't
laugh. When I've got my own series on TV you'll be sorry
you laughed.'

'Sorry, William.' Merrill looked suitably ashamed. 'I'm
going to make cocoa. Anyone want some?'

'I'll help.' Her daughter and her husband both followed
her into the kitchen with alacrity, leaving William alone
with the wildlife.

'Philistines,' he muttered. He wasn't sure if that was the
right word for what they were but it was what the school
music teacher called his class when none of them wanted to
learn about opera. Opera, I mean, I ask you. What was the
point?

'Why did your father go to London today?' asked Merrill
as she stirred mugs. 'Is everything OK?'

'Everything's fine,' said Simon. 'And even if it weren't,
Father doesn't really have to do anything these days. The
Board runs Gilfoyles.'

'Why did he go then?' The business worried Merrill, the
endless fear that since his brother, Gabriel, disappeared
from their lives, Simon would get sucked into Gilfoyles and

its Board in his place, turning him into a stranger and her into a corporate wife.

Simon sighed and glanced at Matilda, who was piling crackers and cheese on a plate with the appetite of one who has not yet become aware that there is such a thing as cellulite. 'I think he was meeting Mark about his will. Sonja said he had some loose ends to tie up.'

'Oh . . .' Merrill put her hand on his arm, not wanting to say 'the Norwegian tart', but thinking it anyway. Simon knew what she thought but said nothing. He had fancied Sonja for far too long to let it slip out how. Ever since he first saw her, in fact – but, considering the circumstances, it perhaps wasn't so surprising. It was still appalling, though – there was something pathetic about men who fancied their father's mistresses, particularly when they lived in the West wing of the same house. Not a mistress any more, either, not since Joshua's shock announcement last month that he had finally married her once and for all.

Matilda wandered back towards the living room muttering, 'Time for more gore.'

After she had gone Merrill said, 'I know they don't know how long he has . . . but you're a doctor. You must have an idea.'

Simon sighed. 'He has prostate cancer, Merrill. It will probably kill him eventually, but that doesn't mean he's dying.'

'How do you mean, not dying? How much more dying than that is there?'

'His is a slow cancer, not very aggressive. It could have been spreading for years. He could just as easily live ten years and die of something else.'

'So why don't they take it out?'

'It wouldn't make any difference now. It doesn't in prostate cancer. Anyway, the surgery is pretty major – it could make him impotent. Look, we have to accept we don't really know.'

'So why's he saying goodbye to his life? That is what he's doing.'

'I agree with you, he is. He's planning for the worst, I suppose. He won't talk to me about it. You know what he's like. He doesn't get close like that. He never talked to Mum when she was alive either. She despaired of him. D'you know he once sent her a faxed memo cancelling their anniversary dinner?'

'I certainly do.' Merrill replied. 'He doesn't talk to me at all. He's never liked me, always preferred the other sister.'

'Don't be silly. That isn't true.'

She frowned. 'The minute he set eyes on Julia he told you you'd picked the wrong sister, don't you remember?'

'He was joking; she was only seventeen. Mind you, I've never seen that much cleavage on a bridesmaid. There you were, as demure as a virgin, and your sister looking like Goethe's Lust, following you down the aisle a good twelve inches behind her nipples.'

'I don't like to hear you say nipples in the same breath as my sister.'

'Oh, you are such a prude, even after thirteen years of marriage. What do you think, that I've fancied your sister all this time?'

'Of course not.' It had never occurred to Merrill that Simon might fancy Julia – it was bad enough that he fancied Sonja. Would it be better if he fancied dozens of women rather than just one? 'It's just mean to go on about her boobs as if she was a character on a naughty postcard. She couldn't help it. She got unexpectedly hit by puberty when she thought it had more or less missed her.'

'Hit by it? She was jolly well inflated by it. I've never seen anything like it.'

'Oh, don't be mean, she *was* seventeen. It's jolly late for puberty. She thought she'd stay skinny and boobless for ever, then her hormones arrived all in a rush. She grew three cup sizes between having the dress fitted and actually wearing it.'

'Well, the vicar had to turn his pacemaker down.'

'Don't be silly, you don't turn pacemakers down.'

Simon laughed. 'You're learning. All these years married to a doctor are rubbing off on you.'

'Rubbing off? I was a properly qualified nurse, thank you very much, before you turned me into a boring housewife. I haven't forgotten my stuff.' Merrill looked at him with anxiety. 'You are going to stay a doctor, aren't you? I mean, you're made for it.'

'Of course I am.' Simon ran a hand through the tuft of brown hair that stuck up endearingly on the top of his head. 'I wouldn't miss all those sessions trying to tell people how to look after their health whilst they point their ears at the answers and wonder if they can afford an extra packet of fags. I live for the times when people bring me pots of poo and threaten to tear my head off if I don't prescribe their first choice of drug of addiction. I love it when the Government tell me all doctors are crap and I must work harder for longer hours and less money if I expect anyone to ever ask me to sign a passport photograph in my own time again. How could I do any other job?'

Merrill ignored the complaints, as she had heard them all before. 'I mean, you're not going to try and run Gilfoyles? I know he'd like you to. Whenever he goes rushing off there I worry it'll be followed by one of those family conferences we used to have when he told you it was your responsibility now that Gabriel had gone.'

Simon shook his head. 'I won the argument back then, Merrill. I haven't got to have it again. Gilfoyles doesn't need me – it has the Board to run it. I'll have to go to meetings occasionally but none of them would take any notice of me if I asked them to. I'm a GP – I know about infected toenails and swollen tonsils, not interim figures and City gossip. Father knows that. Gabriel was the one who was supposed to take over the business. He was groomed for it from day one. I was the one that was free to choose.'

'Oh sure, that's why we came here to live in his house with his mistress and his Peeping Tom gardeners.'

'Come on, Merrill. Sonja's his wife now, you can't keep on with that – you were just as keen to come here as I was. We didn't want to bring the children up in central London.'

'I sometimes miss it, though,' said Merrill wistfully, remembering parties and theatres and trips to Hampstead Heath. 'Do you remember how we used to swim in Hampstead ponds?'

'I remember you going in wearing your bra and knickers one baking hot day and coming out to find that the twins had thrown the rest of your clothes in after you.'

'I know. God, we've been here nearly nine years. And we were still in London the last time we saw Gabriel. Nine years and not a single word.'

'I didn't see him. You only *thought* you saw him. Like Banquo's ghost peering in through the window.'

'I'm sure it was him,' said Merrill, 'but when I went outside he'd gone. I wonder where he is.'

'I wonder that every day,' said Simon wistfully, remembering years of having a brother. Years of games in Foxbarton Woods; of cricket on the lawn and swimming in the river; the time Gabriel climbed the church tower with a melon and put it on top of the weather vane; the time the fire brigade had to be called to get them both down off the roof of the Grange. 'Father's had people looking for him for years. They'd have found him long ago unless he didn't want to be found. He'll turn up one day, I'm sure of it. Come on, I think there's a half-eaten centipede waiting for us.'

At the other end of Foxbarton Grange, Joshua Gilfoyle, back from London, relaxed at last.

Sonja stroked his forehead. 'You're tired.'

'Of course I'm tired, woman. I've got bloody cancer.'

20

'Now, Joshua, do not be a pig. Did Mark Smythe find anything?'

'Pah,' said Joshua. 'Mark Smythe has all the imagination of a roll of packing tape, but at least he agrees Gabriel is still alive, even if he only does it to keep the payments coming.'

'You worry Gabriel is not all right?'

'No, he's alive. Marjorie always said we'd know if he died. I used to think that was more of her barmy talk – seemed a reasonable assumption seeing as she went completely crackers the day she started that bloody HRT – but now I think she was right. No son of mine could die without me knowing it. That boy will come crawling back when he hears about my will, mark my words.'

'He won't,' said Sonja darkly, shaking her head.

'What was that?'

'I said he won't, you silly old fool. Gabriel left you because he was as proud as you are. And he won't come back because he's as stubborn as you are too.'

Joshua glared. 'What would you know, you animated Barbie doll?'

Sonja laughed good-naturedly. 'Don't think you can rile me, Joshua Gilfoyle. I heard worse insults than that in primary school. We were all Barbie dolls in Tromsø, you know – it's in the genes. Simon told me about Gabriel. You've told me about Gabriel. He leaves the company and you never forgive him, you tell him he causes his mother's death and you call the police to take him away from her funeral. You can't expect him to forgive it now.'

'Him forgive me? What rubbish! The boy just pissed off because he couldn't hack the responsibility of being my son. He didn't deserve to be at her funeral and he didn't deserve an inheritance.'

'So why d'you want to leave it all to him now?'

'Why d'you think? He's a Gilfoyle.'

'You love him and you want him back.'

'Crap and nonsense. Do Mills & Boon® in Norse, do they?

Obviously. I want him back here. He belongs here, not bringing me into disrepute somewhere else.'

Sonja shrugged. 'Please yourself, old man. I see right through you.'

'I will,' said Joshua, 'so don't think you'll get your hands on my fortune, you Scandinavian tart.'

'I don't want your stupid fortune,' said Sonja, tossing her strawberry-blonde hair back from her face and suddenly looking rattled. 'I don't want a bloody penny of your bloody millions.'

'You'll get your trust fund, don't you worry.'

'Don't be a fool.' She started to cry. 'I don't want anything. I want you to be well.'

'Shh, I'm sorry, don't . . .' He put his arms around her, stroked her hair.

She wept into his shirt, her freckles standing out golden on her pale face. 'To have found you too late. It's just not fair.'

'Life,' said Joshua, 'never promised to be fair, but at least it's been interesting.'

Chapter Two

They were cutting the lawns around Woodcutter's Cottage early the following morning, although it probably had more to do with the view from the ride-on mower than the length of the grass. The gardeners knew they really didn't need to mow there every day – but none of them wanted to miss out. You never knew when you might get a glimpse of Julia Fitzgerald in her kitchen and they were driven by the hope that one day soon, when she flung open her curtains as they chugged noisily by, she would be stark naked.

Julia had become tolerant of the endless mowing. True, there was the occasional moment when she could not quite raise her usual cheery wave – and there had been that morning last week when, struck by a virus, she had flung open the back door and rushed forth to vomit on the grass as they approached to mow that very patch – but by and large it did no harm and it actually seemed to please Hebe. Since most things that pleased Hebe were invisible to everyone else, Julia found it reassuring that she noticed at least some physical aspect of the world.

Now Julia waved cheerily at the mower as she pulled on her wellies and walked down the path to the shed where she kept her sculpting willow. It had been soaking for quite long enough and she had an order of four herons to make before the weekend. She told herself it wasn't just another way of putting off making the angel, it was essential to earn some extra cash. But she knew it was exactly that – a means of postponing the long-overdue confrontation with the stubborn artist's block.

Stewart Barlow waved back and made a mark in the exercise book they kept on the tractor mower. Laboriously, under the heading 'Sightings of Julia', he scrawled one tick. After a minor hesitation he added, 'naked' after the tick. He glanced at the pages Charlie and Matt had filled in. Almost every one of their entries was also accompanied by a scrawled 'naked', too. He didn't believe them, nor they him, but there was preservation of face involved.

He gazed rather woefully at the lawn, which did not, not by any stretch of the imagination, need any more mowing today, then turned the mower reluctantly away. Julia watched him go, pushing blonde hair out of her eyes and shielding them against the bright early summer sun. One day, she thought, I'll wander out there in front of him stark naked and then we'll see if he manages to steer his tractor mower round the tree stump. She dragged the willow pieces into the centre of the rather bald lawn, humming tunelessly as she did so, and eyed them slightly wearily. It had seemed like a good idea at the time, making willow herons. Willow herons were rather trendy in the villages round Foxbarton and they were simple to make. But they weren't interesting, in the end. And whilst you could spend day after day bending willow into the shape of herons, there is only so much artistic mileage in a willow heron. The first one might have been vaguely original, but was the twenty-fifth just a mass-produced garden artefact? And surely an artist should keep creating.

If only I could remember how to create, get back the spark. After all, it's not just me I have to worry about . . . Inadvertently she looked up at the bedroom window, but there was no movement. Hebe was not up yet.

Hebe's day did not begin when other people's days began, neither did it end when theirs ended – but since she no longer attended school Julia found it perfectly reasonable that she should set her own waking hours. The woman from the education department who was supposed to monitor

Hebe's home learning always had a lot to say about that, but Julia, who had spent much of her own life not conforming, could not see why it mattered. School had failed Hebe, they were all in agreement with that – schools and autistic children weren't always compatible. They couldn't teach her anything and they couldn't keep her safe. Julia had always said so – and after Hebe had climbed in through an upstairs storeroom window at her primary school, after shinning up a rusty drainpipe one break time when they were meant to be watching her, eaten the entire school supply of batteries and had to go to hospital to have them removed, the education authority had been forced to agree.

Julia sighed. So, she thought, I gave up teaching art to bored schoolchildren and moving things I had already made between galleries and agreed to come here. It had clearly been the sensible choice, once she had been offered the cottage and the commission by Joshua Gilfoyle. Hebe needed to be out of the city, needed to be with Julia somewhere where she wouldn't endlessly climb out of windows and get herself lost in dark alleys. And Julia needed to get out of London, to get out and start again – with art, with fun, with life. Merrill might have this odd idea that she was burdened with a handicapped child – but it wasn't like that. She was simply entrusted with the responsibility of caring for a child who couldn't understand people, and who was not understood by them, a child who might not use her senses it quite the way other children did, but a child who saw other things, things other people don't see, like angels and fairies and the colour of music. A child who counted stars.

Julia pulled out a handful of willow strips and began to weave. Her own plans and desires just had to wait, that was all. Hebe had been granted to her by the fertility gods purely as a consequence of those needs, and now Hebe took priority.

As she wove the bird swiftly took shape – an arched beak

and neck, a twist here and there. Julia's hands had become calloused by the work and Hebe loved the rough patches, liked to feel them stroking her forearm, as though it produced some heightened sensation of reality that pulled her into the world.

'Good morning,' came a voice from over the fence, and Julia was slightly irritated to see Jonathan Doyle, the vicar, stopping to talk. He stopped to talk often, but she should expect this as it was his parish and he perhaps therefore saw her as his responsibility even though she was about as Christian as Genghis Khan (and considerably less likely to turn up in church, even taking into consideration his being dead, as she liked to remind Merrill when she got all godly).

'Hello, Jonathan,' she said now – thinking, he is a good man, after all, and moderately handsome too. Perhaps he can't be solely blamed for joining in with the greatest mass delusion of all time. 'How are you?'

'Very well.' He lingered and Julia's spirits sank. He had that look of a man who wanted a cup of tea and wasn't going anywhere till he got one. He'd not want tea if he knew I was ovulating, she thought. Still, with a bit of luck Hebe would come downstairs and do something dreadful and he'd go. When that plumber had come in pretending thirst but obviously hoping for a closer look at Julia's cleavage, Hebe had dropped her latest dead insect collection into his tea. Three dead beetles, a wasp and half a centipede.

'Would you like a cup of tea?'

'Do you know, I think I would.' He hopped over the fence with considerable alacrity – but then, Julia thought, he's only about forty. Why shouldn't he hop with verve? He might make love with verve too, but imagine what the village would say if she deflowered their vicar.

She suppressed a smile and, leaving the heron a quarter-completed, led him into the small cottage kitchen, cosy with cups and pots and assorted bunches of other people's garden flowers that Hebe had gathered the previous day when she had escaped from the watchful eye of her mother and gone marauding. Some of them were definitely Merrill's lupins, but Merrill wouldn't complain, not about Hebe. Actually no one had said too much about Hebe's foibles so far – they didn't like to criticise the Gilfoyles' sister-in-law. And they probably know I'd break their noses, Julia thought with characteristic fierceness, even though she was aware that having Hebe loose in the village was rather like being sacked by the Gauls (you just didn't know if anything at all would be left when she'd finished).

Jonathan Doyle watched her as she brewed tea, watched her strong long-fingered hands measuring out the leaves into the pot, watched the muscles of her forearm move as she lifted the kettle from the stove, watched the way she brushed back loose blonde hair from her cheek and tucked it behind her ear, observed the fine freckles and the rose-pink cheeks, the clear skin and the strong green eyes, the small dark mole just next to her upper lip, the curtain of thick blonde tresses which fell down her back, caught only by a piece of elastic with a green bobble on it which must surely be Hebe's. She looked, he believed, like Isolde the fair, of Arthurian legend, whose thick curtain of golden hair and healing hands captivated the hero Tristan. Her hands fascinated him – she had such strong hands, the hands of a sculptress. He knew they were lightly calloused – remembered like an imprint on his palm the feel of those rough patches when he took her hand in his the first time they'd met. The sort of hands you would want to feel again, stroking your skin . . . were you not her vicar and therefore thoroughly able to suppress such deeply inappropriate thoughts.

'Is Hebe up and about?' he asked as Julia poured tea dark enough to stand a spoon in. It somehow went with the passion implicit in her bones, the sensuality of her every move, that her tea would be strong, colourful and full-flavoured. Just like her. He liked his own tea rather weaker than this, but vicars acquire the ability to drink all sorts of tea at a very early stage in their ministries.

Julia heaped sugar into her own cup, eschewing the milk completely. Tea, she felt, should be black as night, sweet as love and hot as hell. 'Not yet. She was up late watching the moon so she's still in bed.'

'She's an extraordinarily beautiful child,' he said, trying to think of something complimentary that would sound neither ridiculous nor pitying.

Julia suppressed a sigh, resenting the very fact that he felt he needed to make an observation about Hebe at all. You didn't go making observations about people's normal children when you came to tea, did you? Or maybe you did. I've never had a normal child, thought Julia, surprising herself, so how would I know?

'It's been said,' she said slightly tersely. Hebe's beauty worried her as much as it pleased her. Whilst she need never fear that Hebe would be rejected on grounds of appearance alone – rejection would be delayed until her tantrums began, her hyena laughter grated, her screams of distress at minor infringements of what she required of the world became inappropriate – there was always the fear that Hebe's beauty might bring her the wrong sort of attention. 'Beautiful children are vulnerable,' she added. 'Like those tiny purple orchids in Foxbarton Woods; there's always the fear that someone will grab them and make off with them.'

'Isn't that every parent's deepest fear?' asked Jonathan, accepting his tea and hoping to draw her into greater intimacy than she had offered previously.

But Julia flushed slightly, her pride disliking the suggestion that every other parent and she had anything in common. In a strange way, she knew, she took pride in Hebe's condition. After all, if Julia Fitzgerald was to have a child it would have to be an extraordinary child. Not just gifted, like her nephew, William, with his extraordinary cleverness and his encyclopaedic knowledge of insects. Not just beautiful, like her niece, Matilda, William's twin, with red hair she could sit on and the voice of an angel. Not just captain of the school cricket team, like the son of the deeply competitive Kate Coleman, who lived in Foxbarton's old schoolhouse and whose husband had left her years ago for a secretary whose own thickset and uninspiring children did not turn his life into the ringside seat in a perpetual child-achievement competition. No, Hebe had to be completely different, one-in-ten-thousand-children different, how-could-this-have-happened-to-me? different. Autism was as different as it got.

Jonathan saw her bristle – it was unusual, as she rarely gave anything away. Instead he felt she wore armour which kept things in as well as keeping things out. She was like a hedgehog with reinforced spikes. 'Of course,' she said, 'but some are more vulnerable than others. Hebe has an extra vulnerability. She doesn't see people the same way we do.'

'And yet you hate her being labelled.'

Julia was defensive. 'Just because she's autistic doesn't mean she'll be anything like the last autistic child you met or the next one you see. And to start trying to define it, to say, oh, she's high-functioning this and a bit like that – well it makes her sound like a scientific specimen. No one should be labelled.'

Jonathan raised his eyebrows, spotting a chink. 'You've labelled me, though, I think.'

'You label yourself,' said Julia curtly, 'with that silly collar.'

Jonathan's biscuit dissolved smoothly into his tea. He blushed and Julia was embarrassed by guilt. 'I'm sorry, Jonathan. I didn't mean it like that. I know you're on duty. I suppose I don't quite know why you're trying to save my soul. It's not saveable. I'm happily heathen.'

'I'm not trying to save your soul, I stopped for a cup of tea, that's all. I don't save souls constantly, you know. I am allowed time off for good behaviour.'

Julia shrugged. 'So if I were to tell you I was thinking of extramarital fornication you wouldn't try to talk me out of it?'

He swallowed. 'Well, of course I . . . Why, are you?' *With me*? he wondered suddenly and sinfully.

'No, of course I'm damn well not,' she lied without guilt (well, the truth would only upset him). 'I'm just trying to point out to you that I can't just talk to you as if you weren't a vicar, because the minute you think I'm heading for mortal sin you'll come charging after me with a bloody fiery sword.'

'I think you're confusing me with Justice,' said Jonathan mildly, and Julia smiled suddenly. It was like light illuminating darkness.

'Sorry, I get a bit heavy. You know the Church just isn't my thing. I tried going in there to think about the angel and it just made me laugh. I find more inspiration sitting at the bedroom window staring at the moon.'

'The church is a very peaceful building. It's a good place to reflect.'

'I found myself looking at the stone effigies of Simon's ancestors staring grimly at the bat-infested ceiling and thinking that they must wonder why, after a lifetime of good and generous works, they were destined to be crapped upon for all eternity by winged rodents. It seemed too funny to be conducive to the artistic spark of creation. Pax?'

'Pax.' Jonathan stood up to leave. 'And I think contemplating angels is a start, even if you laugh. I'm sure angels laugh all the time.'

'It's a work of art I'm making, not a religious icon,' said Julia. 'The Church can't lay claim to me just because I'm making an angel, and you don't have to be Christian to believe in angels.'

Jonathan smiled. 'Most people who do basically are, though.'

'D'you think they have an advantage, then, when it comes to angels?'

'I don't know. I've never seen one. Have you?'

Julia was surprised. 'Not as far as I know. I didn't think Anglican vicars set much store by that sort of thing. It's all a bit New Age.'

'Well, the Anglican Church is perhaps more about faith than visions, but it doesn't mean I don't believe some people see things others don't. I wish I had seen an angel. Sorry about the biscuit in my cup. It's made a slurry.'

He put it down and her attention was caught suddenly by the very hint of a five o'clock shadow. She had a sudden urge to touch it with the back of her hand, nearly did. Touch is such a wonderful thing. She remembered the touch of unshaved cheek against her, long ago, and flushed suddenly. 'Er – that's OK,' she said, appalled at herself.

He stood. 'I must get on.'

Julia got up hastily. *Get him out*, said the warning bells in her head, *before you pin him to the floor*. God, she thought, who needs temperature charts? They ought to put a warning on the road outside: 'Danger, woman on heat. Avert your eyes and do not in any circumstances remove your truss.'

She showed Jonathan out and he resisted the temptation to take her hand to say goodbye. It would be inappropriate because he would be *doing* it inappropriately, not to be polite but to feel the calluses on her skin. The bishop wouldn't approve of him lusting after a parishioner, particularly an unmarried mother. Mind you, the current bishop didn't approve of anything other than virgins and nuns, and you had to live in the real world. He wondered who Hebe's father was – but then, if village gossip was anything to go by, her family had been wondering that ever since Hebe was born, and no one was any the wiser. Whoever he was, thought Jonathan, he's been luckier than I'll ever be.

Upstairs Hebe awoke and started to sing. He heard her voice as he walked down the lane. It was, he suddenly realised, quite arrestingly beautiful. He couldn't tell what she was singing, but it stayed in his mind for the rest of the morning.

A short distance away in Foxbarton Grange, Julia's sister, Merrill, glared at the telephone, then, looking up, swore mentally at the llama which she could see stretching over the hedge to eat her delphiniums. Where was William, her llama-loving son? It was his blooming llama, his stupid idea that if he let it on to the lawn once a week they would save lawnmower petrol and thus, consequentially, the natural world. Whoever heard of a llama called Brian?

'Mum,' he had said, when she'd tried to suggest that the contents of the fuel tank of one lawnmower did not a greenhouse effect make, 'that's what George Bush said when he backed out of the Kyoto agreement.'

'How the hell do you know about that? You're eleven,' she had said.

'We do world stuff at school,' he had replied scornfully. 'It's not just sums and skipping these days, you know. We're citizens of the planet.' And then he had slouched off to collect insects from tree stumps as usual.

Now Merrill hung up the phone and stared at Brian despairingly.

'Bugger. I don't know anyone who'll cook at this sort of notice.'

She could cook herself, she thought, but she had realised her limitations in that department some time ago, and knew the result would almost certainly resemble something heated on a bonfire by a foundry worker with no sense of smell. Joshua would swear and mutter, whilst Sonja would sniff and pick daintily, then be caught later in the kitchen eating pickled herrings straight out of the jar.

Merrill found Mrs Barker polishing things in the hall.

'Mrs Barker, I know you were meant to be off this evening, but do you think you could cook? Fiona has just called in to say she's ill and we're having a family dinner this evening.'

'Well, I don't think I can, Mrs Gilfoyle. My daughter is coming over from Cambridge for the weekend and Mr Barker has got a Bruce Willis video in.'

Merrill sighed. 'We'd pay overtime, obviously, and you could have a day off in lieu.'

'I'm sorry, Mrs Gilfoyle, but Mr B and I particularly look forward to our Fridays off,' said Mrs Barker. 'It's the only night he stays sober for his conjugal rights, if you get my drift. Now if you'll excuse me, I'll just clear up the kitchen, then I'll be off.'

'Of course, absolutely,' said Merrill weakly, as Mrs Barker disappeared. The thought of Mr and Mrs Barker cavorting on a Friday night was really quite daunting. Mrs Barker was enormous and wobbled in places you wouldn't think a person could wobble, like the backs of her ankles and the skin of her wrists. Simon had once said, rather uncharitably, that if she wobbled at the right frequency she could trigger enough low-frequency seismic waves to demolish half the buildings in Suffolk. William had said he thought that made her a biological weapon.

Gazing out of the window Merrill spotted William coming across the lawn – he appeared to have been chest-deep in mud in the very recent past. Dammit, one day he'd drown in that lake and they'd never even know about it. She rushed to the window to yell at him about his offending llama, but the window was double glazed and had both locks and the kind of stiffly ancient catches that even Houdini couldn't have managed in under half an hour, so getting the thing open in time to shriek at a passing child was a bit ambitious. Merrill resorted instead to beating on the window at him and trying to assume a questioning but disapproving glare. It didn't work. William waved cheerfully and disappeared round the corner of the house. And in a house this size there was no telling which door he'd come in through. Mind you, this was William – he sought proximity to food at every available opportunity . . . Merrill made determinedly for the kitchen.

In the kitchen Mrs Barker was waving her polishing cloth and lecturing Matilda, who was eating chocolate cake at a rate that seemed to make death by chocolate a very real possibility.

'Your mother thinks we don't have a life, Mr B and me, but all married folk need their private time,' Mrs Barker was saying. 'You mark my works, Miss Matilda Gilfoyle, the way to keep your man interested is to feed him well and be available for his every whim at least once a week. If you do that you can bend him round your little finger the rest of the time.'

Matilda pulled a face. 'I don't want to get married,' she said. 'I mean, Charlotte Church isn't married and she's the greatest choirgirl that ever lived.'

'You do go on,' said William, coming in through the kitchen door. 'You're eleven. You can't just become a choirgirl now, just like that.'

'You're only jealous because I'm in the church choir with you.'

'I wish you could be in it instead of me, but singing "All Things Bright and Beautiful" with me and Oscar Coleman and all the warbly ladies doesn't make you Charlotte Church.'

Matilda shrugged and shook her long red plaits. 'I'm waiting to be discovered.'

'You'll have a long wait,' said William.

Matilda ignored the taunt, sure that when she got her recording contract he would be utterly humbled. 'Anyway, what happened to you? You look as if you met Godzilla in the lake.'

'I was watching this really unusual toad and it swam off.'

Mrs Barker rolled her eyes. 'One day you'll drown in that lake, young William, mark my words.'

William sighed patiently. 'Mrs Barker, I am eleven years old, you know, and by the time I'm twenty-two I shall be stalking tarantulas in the darkest Amazon with no one but my trusty monkey, Matilda, for company.'

Matilda stuck her tongue out at him. 'Don't you dare call your monkey Matilda.'

'Why not? It's a jolly good name for a monkey. Some of the stupidest monkeys I know are called Matilda . . .'

Matilda spotted the trap and recovered her dignity. 'You can't goad me,' she said. 'I'm just as eleven as you are.'

There was no arguing with that, William felt, given that he was ten minutes younger. 'Nightmare,' he said. 'I'm twinned with the missing link. Mrs Barker, I could eat a horse. There must be food somewhere.'

'Ooh my,' said Mrs Barker tolerantly, 'you do say such things, young William. I remember when you were three years old and you'd just got here from London and you ate a whole worm. I don't think you'd ever seen a worm before.'

William looked hurt. 'I do wish you wouldn't keep on about that, Mrs Barker. I wouldn't eat a worm now; they're part of natural history.'

'So are sausages,' said Matilda, who was vegetarian, 'and you eat them.'

'When did you last see a living sausage in its natural *habitat*? Anyway, look what I found.'

'Ugh, for goodness' sake,' said Matilda, as he put a large toad on the kitchen table, 'do you have to bring things like that in here?'

'Of course,' said William, genuinely puzzled. 'I have to draw him properly before he goes back. Why did Tigger look down the loo?'

'Ugh, I don't know and I don't –'

'To look for Pooh. Ha ha. Mrs Barker, can I have some biscuits?'

It was a rhetorical question as he grabbed a whole packet of digestives from the larder and disappeared upstairs just as his mother, who had been sidetracked by finding an unexpected stag beetle on the hall floor, tried to stop his shoes making contact with the pale yellow carpet. She sighed as the series of footprints followed William across the hall and up the stairs, then picked up the telephone. Once upon a time, she thought, I didn't care a hoot about carpets. Now I'm Boring Woman.

'Julia? Listen, I really really need a favour, and don't say no because I know you're not out. Well, because you're never out. And Matilda would love to have Hebe to sleep over. Just don't be too way out. Please.'

William Gilfoyle had spent the last eight and a half years of his life in Foxbarton but there was still a lot to discover about Foxbarton Woods. When you considered the sheer number of microclimates and ecological niches there were in a single tree you could spend for ever in there just trying to work out if the woodlice from one end of the wood were any different from those at the other.

Even so, he had a good *sense* of the woods, huge as they were. If boys from the nearby town of Haverhill came out in the night to crash about in the undergrowth with girls and cigarettes, William could always tell. They dropped things where things were not usually dropped. They disturbed things where things were not usually disturbed. They made little bits of mess that were actually quite significant if you were a beetle and had to walk round them. They left their mark.

Someone had obviously been around recently because there were signs of a wood fire over on the far side of the lake. He had noticed it when he had fallen in after the toad. Moreover, someone had been fishing there – and filleting their catch with some skill. There were neatly cleaned bones and small heaps of scales in a little pile at the edge of the water.

William frowned to himself. It wouldn't normally matter – it wasn't as if they were his woods, even if they were his grandfather's. As a boy who regularly trespassed on everyone else's land, he saw no reason why others should not trespass here. It was just that this particular mess was going to ruin his experiment. He had been working on this experiment for some weeks now. It was entitled 'Experiment to see if deep forest beetles react differently to people from those at the edge'. It involved catching beetles at various forest locations and assessing them in terms of how nervous they were of people (to be judged by what they did when Matilda found them in her underwear drawer) and how they adapted to human habitats (to be judged by letting them loose in the hall at home and watching how long it took them to get outside). So far the experiment was going well – he had lost only three stag beetles and a woodlouse in the house, and the woodlouse shouldn't have been in the experiment anyway as it was the wrong species. But the discovery that the beetles in his deep woodland site might already have been exposed to man could completely throw his results, setting scientific knowledge back by decades.

So William did what he always did when he wanted information about the woods – he went to see old Mrs Braithwaite, who lived in them. First he had stored his toad safely in a small plastic aquarium he had prepared for the purpose, complete with water, mossy stones and a small plastic house called Toad Hall in case it should have aspirations. Now, slipping out of the house again by a back door so as not to disturb his mad mother (who would only feel that washing his ears and doing his piano practice was somehow more important – I mean, how bizarre was that?), he made his way towards the trees.

There were a number of woodland cottages on the Foxbarton estate, and one of them had been home to Mrs Braithwaite for all of her life – or at least, since her life had apparently been longer than anyone else's in the village, for as long as anyone could remember. Although Joshua Gilfoyle had insisted on piping electricity to her house twenty years earlier, and sent her a box of groceries every Friday, she still lived by candlelight, heated her home with a wood fire, and lived off a combination of her pension and the money she made selling her herbal remedies in the village. Local people called her, rather fondly, the village witch, although as far as anyone knew she had never done anyone any harm. William thought she was the wisest person he had ever met.

'You should be at home with your mother,' she said now when she saw him strabbaging through the undergrowth towards her cottage. 'Midsummer's coming up. You don't know what might be about.'

William shrugged and accepted a seat. 'Mrs Braithwaite, have you seen someone making a fire in the woods on the far side of the lake?'

Mrs Braithwaite twitched her exceptional black eyebrows and wrinkled her rather hooked nose. 'That might have been the gypsies,' she said slightly mysteriously. 'They've been here a few days, you know.' Since she always spoke slightly mysteriously William took her to mean it *was* the gypsies. He knew they would be camped in the clearing over behind the lake towards the far edge of the woods – they always camped there for the Foxbarton Horse Fair.

'Oh no,' he said, 'it won't be them – they don't do any fishing. Last year they got Tesco to deliver to them. The man was ever so cross when he had to walk up the track in the rain with all their stuff. So I thought maybe there was an escaped convict in the woods or something.'

'There's always someone up to something,' said Mrs Braithwaite eerily, 'in woods.'

William eyed her thoughtfully. 'I was doing my experiment on the far side of the lake,' he said, 'on undisturbed beetles, except that they're disturbed now.'

Mrs Braithwaite whistled through her teeth. William listened fascinated – he longed to do the same but his mother insisted on regular visits to the dentist, which seemed to have resulted in annoyingly even teeth that resolutely refused to whistle. 'An interesting place,' Mrs Braithwaite said, 'the far side of the lake. Famous for the restless headless highwayman who rides around the lake, of course.'

'I don't believe there's a headless highwayman. You're always pulling my leg,' said William, who believed firmly in the world of science and could not accept that anything headless, however restless, could possibly ride around anywhere. 'It's all rubbish.'

'Ah,' said Mrs Braithwaite, 'there's more on heaven and earth than you can see, young William. I was born over five hundred years ago, and I remember when there were highwaymen between here and Haverhill. A miserable hungry lot they were too – the main road to London was sixty miles west and they could never work out why no one came their way. Low IQ, you see. Got themselves hanged in Cambridge in the end, after robbing a judge of his beer money. Headless George was their leader. He met with an unfortunate accident.'

'Can't have been much of a highwayman,' said William, who had heard some of this before, 'what with having no head. It's no wonder he got caught.'

Mrs Braithwaite cackled delightedly. 'You're as good as Angus Deayton,' she said, slapping her legs and proving that her refusal of most of the modern conveniences of life in her cottage had not prevented her from eagerly embracing the TV. 'You may be a sceptic, young William Gilfoyle, but I'm a wise old woman, there's not a lot passes me by.'

'Exactly,' said William, 'which is why I wanted to know if someone was trying to spoil my experiment. You know, someone about my age, living in the village. Someone like

Oscar Coleman? All the great scientists have people trying to ruin their experiments, you know.'

'There's no one here in these woods who shouldn't be,' said Mrs Braithwaite, and William had the strong feeling she was holding out on him. Still, when you're a boy of eleven you get used to that, so he strabbaged off again in the hope of finding another toad before supper.

'Well,' said Julia to Hebe, 'I've landed us in it now. Do you want to sleep at Matilda's house tonight?' Another day to postpone thinking about the angel, she thought. I'll have to plan this meal instead.

Hebe rushed to her and hugged her ecstatically. 'Yes please. Can I stay all night?'

'Yes, you can. I can collect you in the morning.'

Hebe frowned. 'What about the stars?'

'The stars will come with us. You know the stars are always there.'

'OK,' said Hebe cheerfully. 'We can go.'

'Come on, let's brush your hair . . .'

It was long and thick, just like her own, and wavy because of the plaits it lived in. It's another of my vanities, thought Julia, keeping Hebe's hair long. Hebe wouldn't care either way. Perhaps Hebe herself is one of my vanities. She frowned suddenly. 'You do know I love you more than life itself, don't you, Hebe?'

'Why do you?' asked Hebe.

'Because.'

'What's because?'

'It's what you say when there isn't a reason.'

'OK. Can we go now?'

'No, we're going this evening. What shall we do now?'

'Can we go to the woods? I like the woods.'

'I know you do. Hebe, you mustn't go into the woods on your own, you know.'

'I know. Can we go and see the witch?'

Julia smiled. 'All right, but you mustn't call her that.'

'OK.'

They set out a few minutes later, neither having any reason to delay, and found Mary Braithwaite brewing something green in a pot. Hebe flung herself upon the old lady with her customary excess of everything and rubbed her smooth pale cheek on Mary's old brown one.

Mary smiled and looked thoughtfully at Julia. 'Ovulating, are you?'

Julia frowned. 'No, I'm jolly well . . . Well, yes, actually. How do you know?'

'Been a woman a lot longer than you have, my dear. Moon's up and it gets them all in Foxbarton.'

'You don't mean we're all synchronised?' asked Julia in fascinated horror. 'How many of us? God, how gothic!'

'Ah, well, only those who're in tune with it all. Midsummer moons are the worse, you know. Tea?'

Julia peered at the green stuff, wondering if perhaps you got closer to nature in all sorts of ways when you came to live in the country. Mind you, she thought, I've been like this every fourth week since I was eighteen, and I didn't live in the country then. Perhaps I'm just in tune. It was an attractive thought. 'Oh, yes, please. Is it camomile? I'm cooking at the Grange tonight for Merrill and the family. I'm after some nettles for soup.'

Mrs Braithwaite cackled heartily. 'It's vervain – one of the twelve herbs of grace, you know. They call it verbena these days. Nettles, hey? Love to see their faces. There are plenty behind my cottage – I don't let them mow there, those boys. They come and mow my clearing every week.'

'They mow around me every day,' said Julia.

'I can imagine. That's why you've no nettles,' said Mrs Braithwaite blandly. 'You pick some whilst I brew up. Hebe, you come in here and help me cut cake.'

'You shouldn't give us cake,' said Julia. 'Hebe doesn't eat enough proper food as it is.'

'Of course she does, she just sometimes wants something different from the rest of us. Fairies are like that.'

Julia smiled and left Hebe to the cake – which she was sure would be excellent, even if some of the ingredients were sometimes rather curious. She'd trust Mrs Braithwaite to know what was safe to eat in these woods, though. It must be wonderful to know woods like that. Julia, who had grown up in a town, had always secretly wanted to be a kind of child of the greenwoods. Behind the cottage she grasped a few nettle stalks, managing not to be stung by seizing them firmly. The trees beyond the cottage were silent, green, beckoning. If I didn't have stuff to do, thought Julia, I could wander into there and let it swallow me up for a while. Perhaps Hebe and I should just go and live in a tree for a few days. Or even for ever – she'd love that. If only life were that simple.

She went back round the front of the house to find Hebe happily munching an enormous slice of something green and orange.

'Borage, potato and carrot cake,' said Mrs Braithwaite, catching her look. 'She'll not get tooth caries from me. I've all my own teeth, you know.' She bared them. 'See? Here, drink your tea.'

Julia was impressed. 'They're very white. Hebe hates the dentist. She has to be anaesthetised if anything needs doing, or she bites and won't let go.'

'You're just not approaching her the right way.'

'Through the mouth is the usual, with teeth,' said Julia thinking, all this wisdom is all very well but you don't have to stand there when the dentist is screaming and dripping blood.

Mary scratched her head, her extraordinary black crew cut standing on end even more than usual. 'Just tell her exactly what he's going to do and she'll be fine. She has a gift, you know. She sees the angel that watches her.'

'I wish I could see it,' said Julia, who had heard this before and assumed it to be the kind of thing Mary Braithwaite said to everyone. 'I wish I could see any old angel, for that matter. I don't know what they look like, you see, and I really need to work it out.'

'It'll come to you, angels always do. Here, have some vegetable cake. Hebe, d'you want some more cake?'

Hebe beamed. 'Can I have jam on it?'

'Of course you can. Best crab apple and rose geranium jelly. Made it myself.'

Julia grinned. 'I don't suppose you could let me have a jar? I thought of doing something complicated with pork. Perhaps it'll take my mind off lust and the moon.'

'Of course I could. Tell me, my dear, is that where you think you get your inspiration?'

Julia couldn't follow the conversational leap. 'Is what where I think I get my inspiration?'

'Lust and the moon. Men.'

'God,' said Julia, embarrassed, 'I do hope not.'

'No shame in it if you did,' said Mary. 'It's part of nature. We all find it in different places. If you're happy with yourself and you're happy with what you believe then you're all right. Your inspiration is wherever you think it is, and it doesn't matter where that is. That's all.'

Julia was curious. 'Where do you think yours is?'

'You'd never believe me if I told you,' said Mary. 'Now I'm off to see a gypsy. Do finish your tea.' And she was up and gone, disappearing into the trees, Julia thought, with remarkable speed, as if she were part of the greenwoods herself rather than someone who just lived in them.

Julia eyed Hebe warily – it could be very difficult to get her to move once she was happy in a particular spot but she had nearly finished her carrot cake with crab apple jelly, and there was no denying it was nourishing, if a little strange. 'Come on, we should go back.'

But Hebe beamed. 'Good cake,' she said. 'Can I see the Grandpa tonight?'

'I don't think so,' said Julia, well aware that if Joshua Gilfoyle discovered that Hebe called him the Grandpa he might blow a fuse and throw them both out. Silly old bugger. He owed Hebe hundreds of apologies for his nasty attitude.

Hebe beamed. 'You're nice, mummy.'

Julia smiled. 'Do you know,' she said, 'it's a good job you think so, because if I wasn't nice I'd spit in his soup. What a shame we don't have any crow; I could have made a nice crow pie. I don't suppose he's ever eaten crow in his whole life.'

'Why?'

'Oh, because he's a grumpy old grandpa. Shall we go back round the pond? We could climb a tree.' That would have been something, she thought, as Hebe skipped along in front of her, betraying a strangely instinctive knowledge of the way through the woods – to see Joshua Gilfoyle eat crow without even knowing about it. She smiled to herself. Merrill might not react well when she discovered they were having nettle soup and crap apple and rose geranium jelly, but if you ask the mad hippy artist to cook your food, well, you have to expect mad hippy food. It's true what Merrill says, thought Julia, I do like being a way-out woman with a way-out child. And that's fine. There's nothing wrong with that at all.

'There must have been someone else we could have asked,' said Simon a few hours later as he put in his silver cufflinks and glanced over his shoulder at Merrill. 'I mean, getting Julia to cook for us – it seems awful. You know she and Father spark each other off.'

Merrill shook her head, feeling uncomfortable enough already. 'Julia promised not to have a go at him. I know she's fiery but she does hang on to her temper when she has to.'

'Fiery? You could ignite the North Pole with her when she starts.'

44

'Don't be silly, you do exaggerate. Anyhow, what else could I do at ten minutes' notice?'

'We could have managed something,' said Simon placatingly. 'You know how Father likes simple things – kedgeree, shepherd's pie . . . You could have rustled something up. Matilda could have helped.'

'Oh, ha ha. Matilda thinks the kitchen is for singing in. If you so much as ask her to peel a potato you get a rendering of "Panis Angelicus" whilst she shreds the whole thing, then feeds it to that blooming llama, so I don't see her being any good. As for me – well, the last time I made shepherd's pie it made poor Mozart vomit. I've always told you, if you wanted decent cooking you should have married Delia bloody Smith.'

Simon sighed and put his arms around her. 'That cat was ill anyway, you know that. He's never got over being named after a dead composer.'

She shrugged him off. 'Not as ill as he was after my shepherd's pie. You heard the vet. He asked what we'd been feeding him and said Burmese have delicate stomachs.'

'I'm sorry, darling, I'm sure that was only because William insisted on taking the vomit to show him. I think even vets have some sensitivity.'

'Well, I can't cook, whatever you say, and I've done my best.'

'OK. Pax . . . but I'm still not happy about tonight. Your sister shouldn't wait on Father and particularly not on Sonja. It isn't right.' And it's not because I fancy Sonja, he thought rather defensively, not in the slightest.

'So you do mind Sonja's graciously married presence? Thank God for that. You know, Simon, when your seventy-year-old father moves a twenty-eight-year-old blonde into his home – or at least, his bit of your home – and then *marries* her, surely you're entitled to *mind* a bit? You know, sometimes I feel you're on his side all the time. It's as if you're trying to make up for Gabriel leaving, even though it was your father's bloody fault he went.'

'Rubbish,' said Simon, feeling she had touched a nerve. Because it was just as much his fault that Gabriel had left. If he had tried harder . . . 'He's just trying to feel young again. You can't blame him – not many seventy-year-olds get a chance with a twenty-eight-year-old Scandinavian goddess.'

'Is that how you think of her? A goddess? And I suppose I'm just the old bag in the sensible knickers?'

'No, of course not. You know what I mean. Just because it makes me uncomfortable doesn't mean I don't understand it. If I was him I'd probably have done the same. I don't know, Merrill, he's so disappointed in everything else.'

'Not in you, Simon.'

'Yes, in me too. He didn't want a doctor for a son. He tolerated it when he thought Gabriel would take over the business, now he's stuck with it. The least I can do now is allow my father his consolation prize, even if it is a goddess.'

'Oh, that *does* make me feel better,' said Merrill, thinking, I *so* hate it that he thinks she's a goddess.

'I don't mean *I* think she's a goddess . . . and, anyway, even if she were seventy and ugly as sin, having your sister serving her supper *still* takes the welcome a bit too far.'

'Well, it's done now,' said Merrill. 'It would all have been fine if Mrs Barker didn't want to have sex.'

'What?'

'You don't want to think about it – believe me.'

'I think I'd better. So look, can we trust Julia around Father?'

'What? You mean not to tip his soup into his lap and with that one gesture write off the main driving force of his life?'

'No, I mean I don't want some argument about single parents again. The last time they started you could hear them across the road.'

'Well, what do you expect? She won't take criticism from him. Her private life is none of his concern.'

'I know. It just bugs him, the single parent thing, the idea that she really doesn't know who Hebe's father is. I mean, the carelessness of it.'

Merrill shook her head. 'It's a bit of a sore point, actually. You know how Julia was then. She was forever taking men home for the night and using them, but she's far too clever to stick with something that isn't right. And far too stubborn to take stick from your father about it.'

Simon straightened his tie. 'I just hope they both keep their cool tonight. And, Merrill, please do try to be pleasant to Sonja. I know what you think, but Father does seem to love her.'

'Love her? He doesn't see further than those inflatables she's got glued to her chest wall.'

'You can't blame her for those – he bought them for her.'

'Well, the Nordic races don't have very much to boast of naturally,' said Merrill, slightly smugly. She might not be quite as well-endowed as Julia, but she could give even an enhanced Norwegian a run for her money in the cup-size stakes.

Julia carried Hebe piggyback over to the Grange from Woodcutter's Cottage, ready to cook, thoughts of angels revolving in her mind. Thoughts but, sadly, no visions. Joshua might think her well qualified to make an angel because of her prize-winning 'Being'. Yet 'Being' had been the direct result of a night of properly fulfilled lust, and that was all. Lust can always be reproduced – it's not a rare thing, there had been nothing particularly special about *him*. True, she had had hopes that he might come back the next morning – preferably with the croissants he had gone out to fetch – but he hadn't, he had simply taken off with her ten-pound note. And that was the last morning she had felt that rush, that certainty that what she was creating was exactly right. At least, that was the last time that feeling had been applied to art. It had, of course, been applied to her pregnancy in even greater measure.

Still, it didn't help now, now that she was finally being put on the spot and told to stop prevaricating and prove she was still an artist of integrity.

She stopped as a small stone wedged itself between two of her bare toes – and Hebe clung on tightly as she bent down, her plaits dangling onto Julia's neck. Out of that night, reflected Julia as so often, came someone I love more than life itself. Maybe all that emotional energy, which once went to create art, now goes into Hebe.

Hebe leaned down carefully over Julia's shoulder as she fiddled with her feet and picked a daisy. 'For you, Mama,' she whispered in Julia's ear, and Julia smiled.

'I do love you, Hebe,' she said.

'I love you, Mama,' said Hebe, and ate the daisy with some satisfaction.

'It'll make you wet the bed,' said Julia.

Hebe shrugged. 'Mrs Braithwaite says daisies make me better.'

Julia was intrigued at the concept. 'Are you poorly, then?'

Hebe sniffed and spoke in a monotone. 'No, I'm a fairy, she says.'

Julia smiled. I'd rather have Hebe than anything else, she thought, even if it meant I never made another single thing in the whole of the rest of my life. On the other hand, maybe I just need a night of properly fulfilled lust. I could take Mary Braithwaite's view, she thought: that anything's OK if you honestly believe it is. Well, that wasn't quite what she said, but she definitely implied that it was OK to want sex once a month.

But no-strings lust is less acceptable when you're a mother. I owe it to Hebe to behave like an adult when it comes to sex. You can't always have exactly what you want exactly when you want it. Not sex or inspiration.

Something would come to her, though, she had to believe that. Things come to you when they have to. And if Julia had no other faith to sustain her through her multicoloured life, she had at least always stayed true to the fatalism that kept her calm when everyone around her was moaning about the past, the present and the future. It was why, Merrill always said, she had kept her dimples.

Admiring her feet for a moment more, she straightened up and strode on, enjoying the grass between her toes, enjoying the moment, wondering if Mrs Braithwaite had a potion to help you ignore your ovaries, aware that she wouldn't take it even if it were offered.

Hebe sang as they went. Not your average nursery rhyme for Hebe, either, but Shakespeare in her high, eerily beautiful voice, a voice which seemed suddenly to have appeared and blossomed since they moved to Foxbarton. She sang a little in London, thought Julia, but not this much – not nearly this much. Then, it was rare, occasional; now it's all the time. I don't know much about singing, but it sounds rather lovely to me.

> 'Where the bee sucks, there suck I;
> In a cowslip's bell I lie;
> There I couch when owls do cry.
> On the bat's back I do fly . . .'

Julia had sung it to her once, months ago, in her tuneless contralto, but Hebe had recently demonstrated an uncanny ability to remember things which she wanted to remember, and remember them in tune, even though they had not been demonstrated that way originally. She forgot all the other things, of course, the things she saw no use in, like how to put your knickers on and whether or not you needed salt on rice pudding. She laughed occasionally as she sang, a rather shrill laugh which didn't sound at all like the laugh a child should have. More like the noise a baby hyena would make if someone stole its chunk of impala.

'Shush, Hebe,' said Julia, jiggling her up, 'just sing. Uncle Simon will think you're a witch if you cackle.'

'I am a witch,' said Hebe in her singsong yet oddly expressionless voice. 'A small and clever witch. Did you know witches have no toes? Mrs Braithwaite has no toes and she's a witch and William says she knows everything. William knows everything about beetles did you know he's got a stag beetle in a matchbox? You mustn't play with matches the bear in the cave says you can set fire to the whole woods if you play with matches . . .'

'Just sing,' said Julia, who had long since ceased to try to follow Hebe's flights of ideas. 'Look, here's Matilda. Down you get.'

She watched Hebe go tearing off with Matilda whom she adored, and wondered what Merrill had in the fridge. Hopefully some nice pork, she thought. I'm in the mood for chopping up meat. It comes upon me at the same time as the rush from my ovaries. How peculiar is that?

Merrill was waiting for her at the kitchen door, her fawn hair that had once cascaded down to her bottom and rippled like a Pre-Raphaelite fantasy shaped into a neat doctor's-wife bob.

'Julia? Thanks so much for saving me. I thought smoked salmon and I've got these duck breasts from the game dealer.'

Julia glared at her, fluffed the hair with her hand. 'Grow it back, woman, and don't tell me what to cook.'

'OK. You do what you like, I won't interfere – but please, don't do that nettle stuff again. That woman GP who had applied to join Simon's practice had the trots all weekend.'

'That wasn't the nettle soup,' said Julia. 'There's nothing wrong with my nettle soup – you put a hex on her.'

'Don't be ridiculous,' said Merrill.

Julia shrugged. 'You will continue to deny your true self. It must give you terrible indigestion. I saw the way you looked at her, Merrill Gilfoyle. No one in their right mind wants a blonde bombshell working late with her husband, particularly not when he's heir to Gilfoyles. He might just as well have a huge great target painted on his penis and a sign saying "Jackpot".'

'Julia!'

'Oh, don't take offence, you know I'm joking. But at least after my nettle soup and your hex he got himself an ugly partner instead.'

'Barbara isn't ugly, and I wouldn't know how to hex.'

'Oh yes you would, and Barbara looks like your llama. You'd hex me if you thought I fancied Simon, and I'm your little sister – and, before you ask, of course I don't fancy him. He did my smear, for God's sake.'

Merrill shrugged. 'Plenty of women go to Simon for their smears because they fancy him. One turned up in purple suspenders last week.'

'How horrible. Well, I'm not that desperate.'

'Oh, thank you very much.' Merrill sighed inwardly. It didn't matter to her how many women fancied Simon, it was the lone one she knew he fancied that worried her.

'I didn't mean that. You're my sister, for goodness' sake. I'm not the sort of person who fancies her brother-in-law. Mind you, I'm so sex-crazed at the moment that I see all men as targets, even the vicar.'

'Oh, you couldn't have him. Kate Coleman's adored him for years. She'd eat your liver.'

'Are you serious?'

'No, she's vegetarian.'

'Oh, ha ha, she is not. Anyway, how do you know about this, oh Old Wise Woman?'

'Well, she gazes at him adoringly in church every week.'

'Mrs Padley gazes at him adoringly in the post office,' said Julia. 'I think it's because he's a vicar, not because he's a man.'

'You never know, with Mrs Padley,' said Merrill. 'She

can't have had sex for decades. Her first husband died of food poisoning, you know.'

'I'm not surprised. Did you know she puts peanut butter in her malt loaf? Speaking of food . . . Now, have you got any pork in that enormous fridge? Hebe would never forgive me for cooking duck. The ones down by the ford are her friends.'

'She wouldn't know,' said Merrill.

'You never know what Hebe knows,' said Julia. 'She makes up for not being able to do the things other children do by doing a whole assortment of things other children can't.'

Upstairs Matilda and Hebe sang on . . .

> *'Merrily, merrily shall I live now*
> *Under the blossom that hangs on the bough.'*

William appeared at Matilda's bedroom door. 'Was that you singing?'

'Me and Hebe.'

'She's got a brilliant voice, hasn't she?'

Matilda stared at Hebe. 'I suppose she has,' she said, a little reluctant to accept that anyone other than herself should have any voice at all. But this was Hebe – her cousin. It was obviously in the genes. Her mind worked fast. There was only one of Charlotte Church. What if she and Hebe were to be the incredible singing cousins? A trio would be even better. She looked at her brother wheedlingly, 'William, d'you remember in *The Sound of Music* when –'

William was telepathic where his twin was concerned. 'No,' he said, backing away. 'I am absolutely not going to join in. I've tree spiders about to hatch and it could be any minute.'

'Oh, do be an angel,' said Matilda, whose cello teacher said this to her all the time.

'Bog off,' said William, and disappeared.

Matilda shrugged and looked at Hebe, who was watching her intently. 'How do you be an angel?' Hebe asked.

Matilda shook her head. 'You can't. It's just something people say. Mind you, some people say if you sing beautifully that's like an angel.'

Hebe digested this. 'Angels live in trees,' she said. 'Singing.'

'Actually I think they live in clouds,' said Matilda. 'Tree fairies live in trees. Come on, I'm going to sing you something, then you do it. Like an angel would.'

'Angels live in trees.'

Matilda saw no point in arguing. Just along the corridor William listened as they started up the singing again, and was reluctantly impressed.

Chapter Three

✦

Julia pottered around in Merrill's enormous steel and granite kitchen steaming broccoli and seasoning soup and muttering, whilst Merrill watched her anxiously from the doorway.

'I'm not pandering to him, Julia. He's not well. One family dinner seems not a lot to ask.'

'Not a lot more to ask, you mean. He asks all the time. Actually, no, he demands. I suppose he's bringing the Norwegian tart?'

'Of course he is. She's married to him properly now, you know, has been for weeks.'

'Of course I know. You never shut up about it. Vile old man. She could be his granddaughter.'

'Julia, please. You mustn't provoke him. Promise? Simon wants a civilised meal.'

'Well, I shan't provoke him because I won't be there. I'll cook for him because it's for you, but I certainly won't sit and eat it with him.'

'Oh, please do. You can't cook it and not eat with us – you're not a servant, you're family.'

Julia frowned. 'I'm still just an employee as far as he's concerned. I'm not part of *his* family.' Uncomfortably Julia reflected on her lack of progress with Joshua's angel. Not much of an employee, she thought. I'm supposed to be making an angel and I haven't even started. Still, Joshua Gilfoyle was an undeserving old bugger – she hadn't forgiven him for his horrible attitude to Hebe; would have told him to stuff his commission if she didn't feel that Hebe

54

was a million times better here than she had been in London. And it was what she, Julia, needed too. It was time she confronted her lack of inspiration head-on and stopped hiding behind procrastination.

Merrill sighed. 'I need you to be there. When he starts on about posterity and The Family I get twitchy that this time he'll win Simon over to Gilfoyles' boardroom and I'll suddenly find myself married to Commuting City Man. It's bad enough being married to a GP – he's hardly ever home – but at least I know he's coming back at the end of the day and he'll be sober.'

'Oh, come on, Simon wouldn't give up medicine. It's what he is – and, anyway, you're a grown woman, you don't need me to defend you.'

Merrill looked defensive. 'It's not that . . . Joshua admires you.' Better than me, she thought. She tried not to mind, almost succeeded. 'You mellow him.'

'You could have fooled me. He's a prejudiced old fart,' said Julia, 'and about as mellow as pig iron. I'm cooking but I'm not eating with you. I never said I would.'

Merrill shrugged and sighed. 'What's the soup? It's very green.'

'Nettle and rosemary,' said Julia. 'Perhaps it will give Sonja the trots. She's far too cute. God, what a vile word cute is. Pass me the pepper, would you?'

'Here.' Merrill decided not to remind Julia that she had asked her not to do anything with nettle. She should have known Julia would do her own thing, anyway. She always had, even as a child. 'Sonja would never get the trots. She's like Snow White – totally perfect in every way, including her bowels. Don't you remember? Skin as white as snow, lips as red as blood, bowels as regular as clockwork.'

'Not sure I remember it quite like that.'

'Trust me – Sonja's straight out of a fairy tale. Speaking of which, Jules, I meant to say, have you heard Hebe sing?'

'Of course I have. What kind of a daft question is that?'

55

'A bloody daft one, obviously. It's just that I heard her earlier, singing with Matilda, and I was quite struck. She was singing that fairy song out of Shakespeare, you know, "Where the bee sucks", and I thought it sounded extraordinary. Maybe she ought to have lessons.'

Julia frowned. 'I can't afford it – and I don't want your charity, before you offer.'

'It's not charity. She's my niece *and* my goddaughter.'

'She is not your goddaughter – she was never christened.'

'She was too.'

'That was a naming ceremony,' said Julia icily. 'I don't think us getting pissed on elderberry wine next to the statue of Peter Pan in Kensington Gardens could possibly be viewed as a christening. And you are her sponsor, not her godmother.'

'Same thing,' said Merrill, undeterred. 'And Mrs Peel, Matilda's teacher would love to take Hebe. Come on, Julia, you can't deny her singing lessons out of pride.'

'I can.'

'Yes, but you won't. I know you better than that.'

'OK,' said Julia, lifting the potatoes from the cooker to drain them, 'but can I just say that for someone who's my sister you're a real cow.'

'Hi, Aunt Jules.' William appeared, to forage for food. 'What's for supper?'

'Nettle and rosemary soup, pork with sage and crab apple jelly and sweet potatoes, and rhubarb tart for the grownups,' said Julia. 'And assuming you can go and pick me some decent rhubarb right now, then I'll do you some hot dogs and beans.'

'I can't have beans,' said William, 'I'm on spider watch. They've been in labour for hours. If I fart it might put them off.'

'Don't be disgusting,' said his mother.

He shrugged. 'I'm a boy, Mum, I can't help being disgusting. They teach disgusting at boys' schools, we have double disgusting on Wednesdays and you get a black mark if you don't say fart at least once a day. So, you see, I'm a victim of my own chromosomes. I'm programmed.'

'Not in my kitchen you're not, and don't talk rot either – I know spiders lay eggs. You made me watch that whole horrible thing about tarantulas the other night, so I know they don't have to go through what I went through having you. Thirteen hours it took, and even then you had to be pulled out with a pair of salad servers, you and Matilda both. Just imagine that – they didn't deliver you, they served you up. I thought they were going to give me a couple of blooming lettuces.'

William looked aggrieved. 'You're not being fair. You should be pleased that I talk about chromosomes when I'm only eleven. I bet the mother spider goes through the same mental anguish you did, *and* she has to eat the dad. They need my moral support.' He disappeared out of the kitchen, calling back over his shoulder, 'Imagine if you'd had to eat *our* dad . . .'

'Where does that boy get his vocabulary?' asked Julia, 'I mean, "mental anguish" at the age of eleven? It's scary.'

Merrill laughed. 'He found one of my old childbirth books in the loft earlier this week – said he needed it to help him understand the spiders. He's probably gone back up there to tell them to pant. D'you want some help with that?'

'Here, you can mash these if you like, then we're ready. I can do the rhubarb whilst you're eating.'

'Oh Julia, please, you must eat with us. I can't have you serving up the food and hiding in here like a skivvy.'

'Well, you'll have to,' said Julia. 'You can't risk me in polite company when I'm ovulating. I can't help saying fuck all the time.'

'Yes, you can. You're being ridiculous.'

'I'm fucking not.'

'Oh, you're bloody impossible,' said Merrill, 'you and your nettle bloody soup.'

'Ha fucking ha,' said Julia.

About a quarter of a mile away Kate Coleman was also cooking supper, whilst her son, Oscar, played table tennis with the vicar. Kate had no idea that her cycle was synchronised with the full moon and, therefore, with Julia Fitzgerald's. Sometimes she missed her ex-husband, Martin, more than other times, but she had not twigged that this meant that it might be particularly dangerous to invite the vicar for supper on the third Friday in May.

Kate adored Jonathan, had adored him ever since he had come to Foxbarton, but, she told herself endlessly, she adored him in a chaste and acceptable manner, in a please-ask-me-out-on-a-date-and-touch-my-hand kind of manner, the kind of manner appropriate to one who believes sex should be reserved for after the wedding day and no decent woman ever looks at a penis.

It was hot – that was, of course, the perfectly good reason why she had worn such a flimsy shirt and unbuttoned it down to her cleavage. The kitchen was full of steam – that was why she had a faint gleam of perspiration on her brow. The pan of pasta was heavy – that was why her heart began thudding slightly when Jonathan Doyle came into the kitchen and lifted it from her hands with surprising chivalry. She had always blushed easily – that's why her face turned scarlet when his hand brushed the side of her breast as he reached past her for a towel.

'Oscar,' she called, over the clamour of her racing hormones, 'supper's ready.'

Jonathan Doyle did not notice a thing. He generally tried not to have sexual thoughts about his flock – true, he had failed once already today, with Julia Fitzgerald and her big bare feet and surprisingly shapely waist . . . But apart from this and other similar wholly inappropriate lapses Jonathan maintained a celibacy of thought which would have been admirable were it not so inconsistent.

'This is very kind,' he said now to Kate as she served up pasta and chicken in the big homely kitchen which had been her share of the divorce settlement (Martin's share had comprised the pension fund, the Jag and acute testicular bruising). 'I do so enjoy Italian food.'

'You should come to supper more often,' said Kate, thinking, please come live with me and be my love. You can even have oral sex. Oh, you hussy, Katharine Coleman, thinking that about the vicar. Go and wash your mind out with soap . . .

Jonathan smiled noncommittally. As a vicar he felt he had to share himself equally, and his penance for this pleasant supper with Kate and her son would be an evening with old Mrs Padley in the bungalow at the end of the village, eating sausages that weren't quite cooked in the middle. Jonathan had an iron digestion.

'Did you realise,' he said conversationally, 'that on Midsummer's Eve it will be four years exactly since the angel was stolen?'

'I know. The gypsies will soon be arriving for the horse fair,' said Kate, whose public disapproval of the gypsies was matched entirely by her deeply secret fantasy that one of the more handsome ones – lean, bearded, poetic and sporting a single gold earring – would drag her into the woods and ravish her within an inch of her life.

'I heard,' said Jonathan, 'although I gather since the foot-and-mouth outbreak there's been a bit of resistance to the fair from the Parish Council.'

Kate, who was Parish council secretary (one of her many local duties) nodded wisely. 'People have wondered whether we ought to be having a horse fair in Foxbarton any more. Foot-and-mouth was such a disaster for the country-side.' She tipped the pasta into a bowl and started to pile chicken and olives in on the top. 'I mean, do we really know that people can't carry it? Mrs Padley said the ulcers on her legs got really weepy right in the middle of the outbreak,

59

and you never know with gypsies' animals. They're not always inoculated, you know.'

'Sounds like an excuse to me,' said Jonathan, passing her the olive oil and blotting the thought of Mrs Padley's ulcers from his mind as Oscar sauntered in, having carefully judged his timing so that he wouldn't have to prepare anything but would not lose out on eating it. 'I mean, it's really become a sort of car boot sale, hasn't it? It would be a shame if the gypsies didn't come. They're the last real link with the old tradition that began it.'

'Thank you,' said Kate, taking the oil. 'It's the thin end of the wedge, Jonathan. But it's not as if they're real gypsies any more. They have satellite TV. And everyone thinks they stole the angel. Oscar, have you seen any gypsies around yet?'

Oscar nodded. 'Sort of. There was a fire down by the lake, and a load of fish bones. I thought it was William Gilfoyle but he thought it was me, then Mrs Braithwaite said it was gypsies.'

Kate shuddered and tossed all the pasta and chicken with a pair of huge wooden spoons. 'You see, Jonathan, they're here already. They come earlier every year. Soon they'll be permanent residents. Oscar, I wish you wouldn't go near that woman. She's a bad influence.'

'I think she's a proper witch,' said Oscar, sitting expectantly at the table. 'She makes her own medicines, you know. She does this thick green stuff for colds. Everyone buys it, and Mrs Padley says it's excellent for bronchitis.'

Kate shuddered. 'I can just imagine. It's probably snot. I hope you haven't been taking it, Oscar. It could do something awful to your hormones.'

'Couldn't be any more awful than what's happened already,' said Oscar, beaming at Jonathan. 'When my voice started breaking I sounded like a Dalek. D'you want to hear a God joke?'

'Er . . .' said Jonathan.

'No, he doesn't. Really, Oscar, you are just so . . . Here, help yourself – Jonathan, do sit.'

'What's wrong with Mrs Braithwaite's stuff?' Oscar was persistent. 'I thought you were in favour of alternative medicine, Mum. You said your body was a temple.'

'I did not,' said Kate, blushing scarlet, 'and Mrs Braithwaite's not alternative, she's the Other Side.'

'Honestly, you're so superstitious. Christians shouldn't be superstitious, should they, Vicar?' said Oscar who, at fourteen, liked to be right about absolutely everything.

'Er, hmm,' said Jonathan, not wanting to be drawn in and fired as ammunition. 'Indeed. Do you remember the angel disappearing, Oscar?'

'Of course I do. Everyone said it was the gypsies who took it but Mrs Braithwaite knew it wasn't them. They always get the blame for everything because they say fuck off a lot to the police. But so would you if the police were forever turning up and making you move on.'

'Oscar!'

'I was quoting, Mum. It strikes me that people *enjoy* blaming the gypsies. Anyway, Mrs Braithwaite says they're Roman Catholics and they'd never steal from a church. She says that some people think Gabriel Gilfoyle took it.'

'Oscar, honestly,' said Kate, 'you shouldn't spread such gossip. Gabriel Gilfoyle was long gone well before the angel disappeared, poor boy. Oscar, will you fill Jonathan's water glass? Jonathan, can I get you anything?' *Can I offer myself to you on a plate, surrounded by grapes and with a strawberry between my teeth?*

'I'm sorry?' He looked so startled that for a horrified moment Kate thought she had spoken her unexpected thought aloud.

'Er – would you like some grapes?' She asked, trying to cover, whilst Oscar stared at her as if she'd grown another head and then said pointedly, 'We haven't got any, so it's probably best to say no.'

'No, thank you . . . I mean, what was that you said about Gabriel?'

'I said he was a poor boy,' said Kate defensively. 'He was ill, you know.'

'In what way?'

'Well . . .' Kate was starting to fidget now. 'You know.'

'I don't know,' said Jonathan. 'I never met him – but I'd like to find the angel and if Gabriel Gilfoyle might have any clues . . .'

Kate sighed. 'I didn't really know Gabriel. It's all gossip. I mean, none of us knew him – he was never here. When we first moved here, when Oscar was a baby, Gabriel was virtually running Gilfoyles in London. I used to see Marjorie, his mother, in the post office. She was always worrying about him, said he should never have gone into the City, did it to please his father. She thought he was dreadfully unhappy, but Joshua didn't want to know, just wanted him to get on with it. He was always away – I remember she would say he was in Hong Kong, New York, Tokyo – he even missed his brother's wedding.

'Anyway, it was nearly ten years ago – Oscar was four or five at the time – that he suddenly dropped out of Gilfoyles and disappeared. Joshua was so angry, you couldn't say Gabriel's name in the post office without him appearing at the doorway and shouting at you. Marjorie became a shadow of herself. I used to see her every day, walking by the river . . . And then she got breast cancer. Or perhaps she already had it. It all seemed to happen awfully quickly. No one had realised she was even ill, so when she died it was a shock all over. I'd just thought she was pining over Gabriel.

'Anyhow Gabriel turned up at the Grange on the day of the funeral. He was very hairy and drunk, and absolutely distraught. Awful . . .' She shivered suddenly, remembering the scene, the sense of pain. 'I think he blamed himself. He had an enormous row with Joshua right there at the church, and then the police turned up and they took him away. I suppose it was to sober up and calm down, but it seemed so awful, being arrested at his mother's funeral. That was the last time he was here.'

'Did anyone keep in touch with him?'

'I don't know.' Kate looked embarrassed. 'It's easy to say afterwards, oh I could have tried – but I didn't know Gabriel, I was married, and my own life was, well, a little disrupted at the time.' She had been in the very middle of discovering Martin's riotous lunch hours with Penny Cellulite-Bottom on the walnut veneer executive desk, she remembered, flushing painfully.

Jonathan took her hand, sensing distress, surprising her, and she felt the warm reassurance of his palm against her skin; suddenly wished she could take the hand and place it, palm down, firmly on her quivering breast. 'You don't have to be guilty. I wasn't blaming anyone. I just meant, since he grew up here, you'd think someone would have kept in touch . . .'

Kate swallowed, resisting the urge to pull away guiltily in case he guessed how much she longed for him. She felt heat in her loins and blushed. 'I know. But you know, he'd been away at school, at university, at Harvard, he didn't really have any ties here. Anyway, we got on to this because of the angel. You see this was all several years before the angel disappeared.'

'I was ten when the angel disappeared,' said Oscar. 'Actually I was the youngest person to be interviewed by the police.'

'What made people say Gabriel took it, then?' Jonathan asked Oscar curiously.

Oscar shrugged. 'Mrs Braithwaite said the vicar would never have left the church door open, and she told me there's a tunnel in the woods somewhere that goes to the church vault. She says no one else would know about it except a Gilfoyle.'

Jonathan frowned. 'There's no tunnel mentioned in any

of the church documents. Where did Mrs Braithwaite hear about this tunnel?'

Oscar smirked. 'She says it was built four hundred years ago and she was there watching when they did it. It was secret and they did it in the dark, night after night for months.'

'Stuff and nonsense,' said Kate, 'an old woman's stories, like that one about headless George who haunts the lake.'

'Headless George?'

'The worst highwayman ever,' said Oscar cheerfully, 'owing to him having no head. All his accomplices were hanged but he fell off the cart on the way to the gallows and the wheels ran over him and chopped his head clean off.'

Jonathan suppressed a smile, and Kate frowned. 'You shouldn't take any notice of that nonsense. The vicar left the door open and the gypsies got in and stole the angel, and that's the end of it.'

'You're wrong, Mum,' insisted Oscar. 'The vicar went to see Mrs Braithwaite that night. She says the first thing he said was that he'd had to lock up the church because of the party at the Grange and the key had been really stiff. And Gabriel Gilfoyle could have come back and stolen the angel just to get his own back.'

'That's rubbish,' said Kate, who suddenly didn't like the thought of how they had all abandoned Gabriel Gilfoyle and were now allowing him to be a suitable scapegoat to carry responsibility for the lost angel. What's a village about if not to take care of everyone? That was why she sat on seven different committees and filed the minutes of the meetings in seven different cardboard boxes in the loft.

'Anyone could have taken it,' she said now. 'In any case, what would Gabriel have done with it? What would anyone want with an angel? It was never sold; there were dealers watching for it all over the world, yet it was never seen again.'

'Perhaps it was melted down,' said Oscar. 'It was gold.'

'It was only gold-plated,' said Kate, 'so it wouldn't have

been worth anything melted, and you couldn't sell it. It was no use to anyone.'

'It sounds to me that if anyone had use for an angel it was Gabriel,' said Jonathan, and Oscar gave his mother a crossed-eyed look. If he started to get all holy, she had agreed, he could clear off and listen to music.

'Where are you going?'

'I've finished, Mum. I don't want pudding. Bye, Vicar ...'

'Call me Jonathan,' he said as Oscar disappeared upstairs, leaving Kate looking at him with a hunger that would quite have unnerved his bishop but which he found peculiarly endearing. She was clearly lonely – his tutors at theological college had always said that women who looked at you lustily were either lonely or sad. They had not covered the possibility that they might, actually, be consumed by lust, as they knew very little about the resonant sexual power that synchronisation brings to rural villages on day fourteen. Neither had they ever discussed the simple fact that vicars sometimes, however unexpectedly and unintentionally, get erections.

'Tell me about your divorce,' he said to her, shifting slightly in his seat, and all Kate's warm feelings towards him evaporated as completely as snow in a desert.

At Foxbarton Grange an equally sudden silence had descended as Joshua made his announcement. Julia, in the process of clearing the plates, thought they all looked rather like muppets when their mouths dropped open like that. Especially Sonja. Julia had disliked Sonja without knowing her, purely on Merrill's behalf, and now it struck her guiltily that since Merrill disliked Sonja on Simon's behalf, and Simon did so on behalf of his mother, and his mother was dead and had never even known Sonja, it was rather fourth-hand dislike and impossible to excuse.

'You can't put that in your will,' Simon was saying. 'That's worse than cutting him out of it completely.'

Joshua Gilfoyle shrugged. 'I can put what I like in my will, and frankly, to put anything else would be hypocrisy. I promised my father I would keep this family strong and that boy had his mother's weak genes. Weak genes pollute families like this one. My father warned me about it and I won't let it happen.'

'That's nonsense, Father. There's nothing genetically wrong with Gabriel. He just didn't want to run the company. You forced him into it and in the end he couldn't bear it, so he walked away from Gilfoyles and he walked away from your money. He won't come back now.'

'Then he loses. Your mother was responsible for him leaving,' said Joshua. 'I blame her for turning him against me. Well, if he turns up back here and takes his place in the family he can have his inheritance – but if he has children he loses the lot. I'm not breeding weakness into the Gilfoyles. I've seen enough of it in my life, you know. It's all over the streets of London, littering the doorways. I'll not be responsible for more of it.'

'God, you sound like Grandfather. Gabriel wasn't weak, Father, he was just unhappy running Gilfoyles. Anyone can run into trouble with alcohol –'

'You're playing with words. He was a drunk and that's weak in my book. Anyway, I don't know why you're making such a fuss. This place is yours, together with your share of the company. Sonja has her trust fund, so do your children. You're all catered for.' Sonja took his hand and smiled at him. Merrill averted her eyes. It was disgusting, at his age. No wonder he hadn't wanted his prostate removed.

'Father, I'm making a fuss because he's my brother, and I want him back too – but he won't come back if you make conditions like that. It's positively gothic. Anyway, he may already have children. What then?'

'Then he gets nothing,' said Joshua stubbornly. 'It was your mother's genes, you know. At first she was as sane as anyone I ever met, but you should have seen her when your brother took off, pacing the house at night and forever crying in corners. That idiot GP gave her hormones made out of horses' urine but I knew she was going barmy.'

'Oh, come on,' said Simon. 'Now you're being ridiculous. Mother was as sane as I am. She was worried about Gabriel, that's what was –'

'Don't presume to pass comment on things you know nothing about,' said Joshua. 'You saw him at the funeral – my son, the man who had run Gilfoyles, drunk, shouting at me and crying like a girl. Mental weakness, madness, it's all the same, and that's what it was.'

'He was drunk, Father. For God's sake, he hadn't even known she was ill.'

'And whose fault was that? It's all the same thing – drunks, loonies, people sleeping in doorways . . . There are only two kinds of people on this earth, the weak and the strong. And I've said what I've said – I want no more weakness in the Gilfoyles. It was my father's greatest fear. Bad genes destroy dynasties, he said, and he was right. All that crap about the meek inheriting the earth is utter stuff and nonsense. They should put all the meek together with the loonies, if you ask me, and lock them all up somewhere so that the rest of us don't have to carry them along.'

'I can't believe I'm hearing this,' said Julia suddenly, angrily, from behind him. 'You stupid, prejudiced old bigot, you sound like bloody Hitler. How dare you say such vile things? What makes you think you're so genetically bloody perfect?' She stared at him, challenging. Her face was pale, her cheeks pink, her arms full of dirty dishes: she looked like Cinderella with attitude. Everyone fell silent. Sonja, who had picked at her food like a sparrow, fiddled with the remains of her bread roll. Julia resented her leftovers. There was more on Sonja's plate than before she started, she'd swear. Perhaps she didn't need food. Perhaps she was an alien species and capable of photosynthesis. It would certainly explain why her breasts pointed upwards – they were trying to phone home.

'Who the bloody hell asked you?' Joshua pushed his chair back and stood to face her. She was taller than he was, and a small portion of his mind admired that. Statuesque, she was, she had presence.

Julia glared at him, then turned on one heel and stormed out of the dining room, slamming the plates down on a sideboard as she left and shouting over her shoulder, 'No one needed to ask me. Your obscene prejudices forced their way into my two ears unasked . . . and you can find your own bloody rhubarb tart. I'm going home!' Merrill rushed out after her.

'Now look what you've done,' said Simon angrily. 'That was uncalled-for.'

Joshua shuffled his feet, slightly awkward in his stubbornness mingled with a hint of guilt. 'Julia Fitzgerald should mind her own business,' he said darkly. 'She's only here at my behest.'

'You should be careful what you say. Remember she has Hebe.'

'That retarded child? I never wanted *her* here. She should have been put in a home years ago. They always were, you know, when I was young. No one wants to see children like that. And what does she know anyway? Gabriel broke your mother's heart. That's what weakness does.'

'Father, for heaven's sake. Gabriel didn't break Mother's heart, she died of breast cancer.'

'He buggered off without a word, walked out of the company, chucked away his responsibility . . . What else d'you think broke her heart?'

'Oh, for God's sake, Father. There's no such thing as a broken heart. I should know, I am a doctor.'

'No son of mine should ever have been a bloody quack. What bloody good have they done me? You should be running the company.'

'I'm sorry, Father – but I am a doctor now. I can't change that, and I couldn't chair Gilfoyles. We had all this out long ago.'

'Someone's got to run it.'

'Not me,' said Simon. 'We agreed long ago. You agreed. I couldn't do it even if I wanted to. Gabriel had the training, not me.'

'You'll do as I ask.'

'No, Father, I will not. Merrill would never forgive me. I don't want to run it. Gabriel didn't want to either for that matter. You can't make people into what they're not. He didn't want to be a City whizz kid, and I am what I am. And, anyway, you must know him better than that after everything. You must know he won't come back for money.'

'Then he can bloody well stay away,' Joshua sighed and sat, deflating almost visibly. 'Top of his year at Harvard,' he said, 'what a bloody waste.'

Simon sighed. There was no reasoning with the old man sometimes. 'I'll go and get the rhubarb tart,' he said, and marched out of the room after his wife.

Joshua glared at Sonja. 'And what are you looking at?'

'A stupid, stubborn old man,' said Sonja, chewing her roll and fixing him with her unblinking dark blue gaze. Joshua tried not to wonder how such a beautiful creature could be his.

'You can piss off back to Tromsø if you feel like that.'

'And throw away your money? Hah, think again, Joshua Gilfoyle. I will not leave you, not even if you ask me to. When you married me you got more than you bargained for.'

'You can say that again. I never asked for an interfering cow.'

'I grew up in a cold place, old man, so you can forget the look of ice. My first grade teacher did better on a hot day. You are being a fool and only I will tell it as it is. It's time you appreciated your children instead of turning them against you. In Norway we say if you want to harness the sleigh-dog first you must put away the whip.'

'You made that up.'

'I did not. You need your family more than you want to say. You want to see your lost son because you love him, that is what this is, but you cannot bear to admit it. So you think to tempt him back by the offer of money and the rejection of his children. This is not the act of a clever man. You must hold out your hand, not your whip.'

'And what would you know?'

'More than you think. There's something behind this rubbish you talk about madness, Joshua Gilfoyle. This is not about the drunkness of Gabriel. A little drunkness and throwing in his job that you choose for him, that may hurt but it is not enough to make you so unhappy and afraid.'

'I'm not unhappy or afraid, I'm protecting the family name. Those are my terms. I promised my father I would see to it that the Gilfoyles were strong, that we stayed strong, and that's the end of it.'

'You talk like the crap now. You think this shows you are strong? I will get to the bottom of it, you see.'

'Talk crap,' said Joshua, suddenly impatient with her linguistic oddities. 'It's not "talk like the crap", it's talk crap.'

'What is? I don't understand what you say.'

'Are they all as thick as you in Norway? The correct phrase is I talk crap. I talk crap.'

'You said it,' said Sonja triumphantly. 'I go for the rhubarb now, one tart to fetch another.' And as she stalked past Joshua, leaving the faint scent of lilies that followed her wherever she went, he had the uncomfortable feeling that he had been outwitted, a feeling that had been entirely unfamiliar until he met her, and entirely familiar ever since.

Outside Matilda's room Merrill was trying to reason with Julia. 'Come on, Jules, don't go rushing off now. Let her stay over. You know how she loves sleeping with Matilda and they're quiet as mice. They must be fast asleep. Look, why don't you stop here too? I'll make up a bed for you.'

'What, and face Adolf down there over breakfast? No thank you.'

'He doesn't have breakfast with us, you know that. He and Sonja stick to their own wing of the house. Please,' Merrill put her hand on her sister's arm, 'I don't want you tearing off like this in a state.'

Julia sank down on to the thick-pile carpet, sliding her back down the wall, her shoulders sagging. 'He just . . . It's not him, Merrill. I don't care in the least what he thinks. It's just that he epitomises the worst that other people can think about Hebe. You know, I know, we all know there's going to be prejudice out there, that her life's not going to be easy – but when someone I actually *know* says things like that it gets to me.'

'Joshua's the worst,' said Merrill, 'but you know, he adored Gabriel, he was so proud of him, sang his praises from the rooftops. Joshua had so much to lose – he put all his hopes in Gabriel. It was a lot to live up to, I suppose – but that's why this has been so terrible for him. You should see the photos of the two of them in the family album. They're all your typical family shots – Joshua with Gabriel on his shoulders, Joshua throwing Gabriel in the air, Joshua and Gabriel in the boardroom at Gilfoyles . . .'

'He doesn't seem the type,' said Julia, wiping a tear from her cheek. 'Not fatherly.' She wished for a moment that there had been someone to swing Hebe in the air and put her on his shoulders too. 'Just because he lost his son doesn't mean he should be condemning people with mental illness.'

'Hebe hasn't got a mental illness,' said Merrill. 'Calm down.'

'No, but people like him think she has so it's the same thing.'

'Hebe will be fine. She's fantastic.'

'But she's only got me,' whispered Julia 'I deliberately, *deliberately* had her all alone, as if to prove to everyone I could take the consequences. It never occurred to me that *she* might not be able to take the consequences. I was so bloody selfish. I mean, what happens to her if I die? She'd have to come and live here with you and eugenics-man.'

'Julia, it's not like you to be so maudlin. Hebe's one of the happiest children I know . . . most of the time,' said Merrill, 'so stop feeling sorry for yourself. Come on. Let's go and have a look at them, all snugly sleeping.'

Julia shook her head and sniffed musically. 'Sorry, it's not me, it's Mrs Braithwaite's dandelion wine talking. I polished off nearly a whole bottle in the kitchen.'

'My God, you didn't! That stuff's lethal. Were you drinking it whilst you were cooking? I'm amazed you managed to carve the pork.'

'It was touch and go,' said Julia, grinning suddenly. 'You should see the rhubarb tart. It looks like something the cat dragged in. I was actually looking forward to seeing Joshua's face when I served it up.'

'Come on down then,' said Merrill. 'If we're quick you will.'

'They've gone,' whispered Matilda from her lookout post by the door. 'Come on, now's our chance . . . Hebe, what are you doing? You'll fall.'

'It's easy,' said Hebe, swinging her leg over the window ledge. 'I always go this way.'

'No you don't. You've never gone this way.'

'I have,' said Hebe, 'yesterday when the angel was singing. Come on. William's waiting,' and she disappeared out of sight.

'Oh, for goodness' sake,' said Matilda. 'Am I the only sensible one in this house? I never wanted to go badger-watching anyway. I'm a girl, nearly a teenager. I'm supposed to want to stay up late listening to boy bands and painting my toenails pink . . .' She was still muttering as she climbed cautiously down the trunk of the creeper that grew up her wall of the house. Hebe could climb like a tree frog, could climb down walls as well as trees, and suffered from a complete lack of even an appropriate sense of fear, and William had a genetic advantage, being a boy and therefore closer to the apes. That meant it was her job to be the sensible one and show them how they ought to have done it.

Hebe and William were waiting impatiently.

'Come on,' said William. 'By the time you get down here it'll be Christmas.'

'Don't be rude. I've got biscuits and cheese and a carton of milk. What have you got?'

'Gobstoppers,' said William, 'essential when you take girls out watching badgers. Right, follow me and not a word.'

They crept after William, into the shadows thrown by moon-silvered trees, the world a magical place of shades of grey and dark, dark green, the branches whispering, quietly but kindly . . .

'Hold my hand,' whispered Matilda to Hebe. 'You'll get lost.'

'We might be eaten,' said Hebe conversationally. 'There's a bear in the woods.'

'What do you mean?' Matilda glanced around nervously.

'Nothing,' said Hebe. '*Where the bee sucks, there suck I . . .*'

'Sssshhhh,' said William. 'You can't sing, you'll upset the badgers. Come on . . .'

It took them about ten minutes to reach the hide William had made with Oscar Coleman out of branches and ferns. It smelled damp and green, and they wriggled in carefully, for it was not a solid construction and barely held three.

'Now,' said William, 'we wait.'

Matilda awoke about an hour later, feeling cold and damp, after a dream in which she actually turned into a fern.

Someone was snoring, and to her disgust she discovered it was William and he was leaning on her. Something tickled her leg and she jumped violently, expecting a tarantula at the very least, sending William tumbling onto the ferns on the ground.

'Wha . . . what did you do that for?' William had been watching badgers in his sleep, dozens of them, playing, gambolling in the moonlight, filming them with a huge camera whose giant furry microphone had suddenly turned out to be . . . Matilda.

'You were asleep,' accused Matilda. 'You'll never be David Attenborough if you fall asleep the minute you sit down to watch something.'

'You can talk,' said William crossly. 'You told me you could stay awake all night.'

'I could if I wanted to,' said Matilda with dignity. 'I just didn't want to.'

'Well, Hebe fell asleep first. She –'

'Oh my God, where's Hebe?'

Matilda and William stared at one another and William's heart began to thud. 'Mum will go mad with us.'

Matilda felt the patch where Hebe had been. It was stone-cold. 'She could have been gone ages. Aunt Julia will murder us,' she said, her eyes round with alarm. 'Mrs Braithwaite will turn us into something really terrible. You know how she loves Hebe.' Fear was growing in her like a choking ivy; she could feel it coming up her windpipe.

'Don't be silly. Mrs Braithwaite wouldn't do that.' William didn't actually want to say she couldn't, just in case she did. In the bright light of day, in the safety of his own home, he was happy to say Mrs Braithwaite wasn't a witch. But here in the woods in the middle of the night, when she might be sitting on her broomstick directly overhead, well, the idea seemed far less ridiculous.

'Don't you be so sure,' said Matilda. 'Come on – we've got to find her. Give me the torch.' But as they crawled out

of the hide, all thoughts of badgers forgotten, they heard
her.

> *'Once a jolly swagman camped by a billabong*
> *Under the shade of a coolibah tree . . .'*

Matilda crawled outside, relief washing over her like the
tide. Hebe was lying on her stomach playing with a
hedgehog, which had curled into a ball to resist her
advances.

'Did you see?' she asked.

'What?' asked William. 'The badgers? Did you see the
badgers?'

Hebe shook her head. 'I saw an angel,' she said. 'Taller
than the sky,' she put her hand in the air to show them,
'taller than the stars in the trees.'

'Stars aren't in trees,' said William. 'They're in space,
floating.'

'Why?'

William frowned. He knew all there was to know about
astronomy, being a boy, but this wasn't a question he'd been
asked before. 'Just because,' he said, after some thought,
'that's all.'

Hebe nodded – she could accept that explanation – but
Matilda couldn't. 'That's not much good, is it? Just because
what? I mean, what sort of a reason is that?'

William glared. 'Well, why do you want to be a singer?'

'Because it's the best thing in the world,' said Matilda
triumphantly.

'Why is it?'

'Well, because I love singing.'

'Why?'

'Because it's the best thing in the world.'

'See,' said William, 'all the most important questions
don't have answers.'

*

The following morning Julia, back in her own kitchen, scooped Hebe's egg out and ate it. It was the second this morning that had not been quite right. The first had been double-yolked and had made Hebe scream and this one, Hebe said, was just too yellow.

'Where did you see the angel, then?' she asked her as she scooped.

Hebe looked blank. 'Singing,' she said, 'up high.'

Julia smiled and watched the water boiling. 'What was its name?'

'Angels,' said Hebe, drinking her orange juice and looking through Julia with her big blank eyes, 'are as tall as the stars.'

'Don't do that, darling,' said Julia, and Hebe frowned ever so slightly. It was a tiny frown but Julia knew it meant Hebe understood the request, understood that she had switched into a particular sort of detached and empty stare which needed to be opted out of again. Julia had gradually persuaded her not to defocus in this way quite so much, but she wasn't sure if this was real progress or just a cosmetic touch. 'Did Matilda see the angel?' she asked cheerfully.

'Matilda was asleep,' said Hebe, 'and there's a hairy bear in the woods with a string thing. *Waltzing Matilda, waltzing Matilda, You'll come a-waltzing Matilda with me . . .*' She was dancing around the kitchen in her nightdress. (She still could not dress herself – she found it just too overwhelming a task, requiring mental organisation on a scale she did not possess.)

Merrill appeared at the door, 'Morning, Julia. Thanks for last night . . . Hello, Hebe, are you a fairy?'

'That's stupid,' said Hebe, and sat on the floor and began to howl.

Merrill spread her hands apologetically at Julia, who shrugged. 'I think she had a funny dream. She says she saw an angel.'

'Maybe she really did,' said Merrill. 'You did when you were little.'

Julia kneeled beside Hebe and wound the child around her like ivy. Hebe continued to howl. 'I did? Are you serious? When was this?'

'Don't you remember? D'you know, it never occurred to me you might not. But then, I suppose you were only about three, or maybe four. You can't have been any older because Granny was still alive. You got lost somewhere, and when we found you, you said an angel had looked after you. A tall angel in a green dress, you said.'

'It was probably some kind passing stranger,' said Julia, smiling.

'Maybe so,' said Merrill, 'but you were very clear about the wings. Enormous wings, you said, all shining in the sky. I never forgot it. When I'm desperate about things I think of it and it gives me faith.'

'How extraordinary. I really don't remember.' I wish I did, thought Julia. Imagine that – I saw an angel when I was three and now, when I need to know what an angel looks like, I can't remember it. 'I expect I imagined it,' she said aloud.

'Wearing green? You were very insistent. They say children can see things we can't because they're open to joy.'

'Who says that?'

'It was probably Mary Braithwaite. She's always coming out with wise stuff like that. What was Hebe's angel like?'

'Tall and shiny,' said Hebe, between continuing but fewer sobs, 'high up high in the trees.'

Merrill hugged her and smiled. 'That sounds nice, Hebe. Julia, d'you need anything from Sainsbury's? I'm just off for supplies.'

'Get me one really good mood, for Hebe, and a packet of artistic originality for me. That'll do for now.' She stroked Hebe's hair. Hebe was quiet now, listening intently to the conversation. Julia had sat through *University Challenge*

77

with her once at the Grange, and afterwards she had recited all of the questions – and the answers. She was capable of extra-ordinary focus when she wanted it.

Merrill smiled. 'You'll be fine,' she said. 'You just have to have a little faith.'

'Faith is the one thing I don't have.'

Merrill shrugged. 'I meant in yourself.'

'It's not faith I need,' said Julia to the closing door, 'it's inspiration.'

Later, Hebe and Julia wandered into the woods picking wildflowers. Julia saw no harm in a minor gathering of the common and non-poisonous, and it was important to teach Hebe what bits of things she mustn't eat, especially as the belladonna was already flowering deeper in the woods. They had called in on Mrs Braithwaite, since all paths seemed to lead past her cottage, but she was out, so now they found themselves deep within the green mystery of the trees, lying on their backs in a small, round glade and contemplating the golden shafts of sunlight that bathed them.

'Where are the stars?' asked Hebe. 'Are they gone out?'

Julia shook her head, 'No, they're there, Hebe, you just can't see them.' She knew it worried Hebe terribly and Hebe frowned now.

'Why?'

'Because the sun is very bright. Look how it shines through the trees. If the sun went to sleep it would go dark and you could see the stars.'

'Angels live in trees,' said Hebe, and began to sing again, *'Waltzing Matilda, waltzing Matilda, You'll come a-waltzing Matilda with me.'* It sounded oddly at home in the English greenwood.

Julia stared up at the canopy, watching the way the branches curved over into a cathedral of vaults and arches, watching the way the sun sent shafts of green-stained brilliance down through leaves dancing to an impalpable breeze. It was suddenly easy to imagine the whole Host of Heaven singing in amongst that ethereal light. It was certainly the right place to look for an angel. Perhaps Hebe was right – perhaps there were angels in trees. What better place was there for angels to hang out, after all?

This, she thought, was surely where the idea for cathedrals began. Long ago, someone lay somewhere very like here, and looked up at the curves and the dappling light, then tried to reproduce it in stone and stained glass, to make it accessible, because not everyone can spend their days lying on their backs in the greenwoods staring up at the light.

That's what I need to do, she thought. Make the angel I saw accessible, because not everyone gets to see an angel. But I don't remember it, and now I don't see angels either. Perhaps Merrill was right and angels only appear to people who are open to joy. Children are open to joy, after all, but when you grow up you filter it out. You can't *be* truly happy without an awareness of the cost; so you can't see an angel because you can't accept it could be so. So perhaps angels appear all the time but most people just filter them out.

Hebe doesn't. Hebe doesn't filter anything out. Hebe is open to every emotion there is, sometimes all at once . . .

Beside her, as Hebe sang on, the sun caught her silver-gold hair and gave her a halo of her own. '*Up jumped the swagman, and sprang into the billabong. "You'll never take me alive," said he . . .*'

Julia felt strings around her heart constrict, as they did so often when she looked at Hebe. She took her hand, felt it nestle small and warm and trusting in her own large one.

'*And his ghost may be heard, as you pass by that billabong, "You'll come a-waltzing Matilda with me."*'

Julia closed her eyes, tried to remember what she might have seen as a child, couldn't. Have I filtered it out? Am I not open to joy? 'Hebe?'

Hebe looked through her and beamed at nothing. 'What, Mama?'

'Did you know the first word you ever said was "angel"?'

But Hebe frowned, her attention caught elsewhere. 'I can hear strings,' she said, 'singing.' Her ears must surely be sharper than Julia's, because Julia, although she strained hard and cupped her own ears to make them more like a rabbit's, heard nothing.

They lay together gazing up at the leaves for a little longer, holding hands and enjoying the woods, one of them hearing the distant sounds of a mandolin through the trees, the other not. Finally the dampness of the grassy clearing began to penetrate their clothes and they headed home for lunch.

Chapter Four

~~~~~~~~~~

The River Stour ran idly and thoughtfully through Foxbarton, crammed with fish fed on a variety of agricultural chemicals which seemed to do them no harm. William Gilfoyle loved the river, populated as it was by otters, kingfishers, and escaped Turkish crayfish, which had gradually worked their way up to Foxbarton from far down in the estuary and lay slothfully in the shallows, procreating and waiting for their food to come floating by. On summer days he and Matilda liked to dangle pieces of bacon on string from the bridge and see how many they could catch. The crayfish, like Aesop's monkey, would rise from the river clinging to the chunks of old breakfast by their impressive claws, thus demonstrating, as Kate Coleman had once rather moralistically informed them, that man did not invent the qualities of greed and lack of foresight, only refined them.

Kate did not love the river, but she was obliged to walk beside it most days wearing her wellingtons, which she felt were unbecoming, disguising as they did her ankles, her best feature, without doing anything to cover up her hips, which she detested utterly. Greed was not one of Kate's particular failings, but lack of foresight certainly was. In the flurry of loneliness which had immediately followed Martin's departure, she had acquired a puppy, a wonderful, endearing, lolloping grey puppy called Gwen, from a dog rescue. Unfortunately the warden had assumed Kate knew all about Irish wolfhounds and Kate had not bothered to disillusion him, so she now owned the biggest dog in the world. And she had to walk her herself as she could not possibly spare Oscar from his tennis lessons, violin lessons, drama lessons and extra maths lessons to walk a dog. Oscar's achievements – particularly now that Martin had acquired a pair of such dull and unimpressive stepchildren – were what Kate lived for, her only justification for the choices she had made.

Now, as Gwen dragged her along the footpath she wondered with uncharacteristic melancholia whether there was any point at all to her life in Foxbarton. Yet the Village Residents' Committee would never cope without her guiding voice reminding them of the standards they should all be maintaining in their flowerbeds, and if she didn't organise the Village Hall Committee they would be arguing even now about who ought to keep the key, rather than giving it to Kate, who was by far the best person to look after it. The Parish Council would fall apart if she weren't there to take the minutes. And then, of course, the horse fair would be chaos without her telling them all what to do. It was clearly her duty to stay. Her own longings and desires must remain in hibernation, as pale and silent as the Sleeping Beauty herself awaiting the kiss of a handsome –

'Good morning.'

Kate nearly shot out of her boots. She was not accustomed to meeting people down here. Particularly not strange bearded men with earrings. Well, one earring. She swallowed anxiously.

'Don't worry – I'm not a lurking rapist, I promise.'

Kate turned into a parody of a bluestocking, 'Oh, phew, great, I'm Kate Coleman . . .' What are you doing, introducing yourself to strange men by the side of the river? You know damn well what you're doing. He's lovely . . . He looks like Jesus in Renaissance art, all haunted and beautiful.

'John James. I'm staying in a caravan nearby. Pleased to meet you, Kate.' He took her hand and she thought he seemed slightly on edge. It was impossible to gauge his age with that beard . . . late thirties, maybe. The small gold earring somehow suggested he was under forty. She put her left hand rather ostentatiously on top of their two clasped right ones – just so he could see, should he wish to check it out, that there was no band of gold on her fourth finger.

'Are you here for long?'

'As long as it takes,' he said, and Kate felt her heart thud. A mystery man. *Oh God, I've fallen into a Mills & Boon® novel.*

'As long as what takes?'

'I'm a writer,' he said, 'of poetry.'

'Oh gosh, how marvellous. I run the village Literature Appreciation Group actually – we meet on the second Monday of the month . . . It would be wonderful if you would come and talk to us – maybe do a reading . . . ?'

He smiled, showing perfect teeth. 'I'm honoured to be asked, but to be honest I'm not a performer.'

'Oh, of course, I didn't mean to be pushy,' she flustered, thinking: I so wish you'd just ravish me, right here, right now. I could live off the memory for years.

'Not at all, you weren't pushy. If you'd like to hear some of my work, some time, I'd be delighted to read to you, but to you alone. I'm not the man for a gathering.'

'Oh, goodness, well, that would be lovely.'

'We could meet in the woods – tomorrow, perhaps? I have a caravan on the gypsy encampment.'

This is my fantasy, thought Kate. I'm obviously dreaming. She wondered if he would notice if she pinched her thigh, hard . . . 'Oh – er, I – no, I'm afraid tomorrow's a bad day. I, er . . . ' Suddenly Kate did not want to mention Oscar and his tennis lessons with Zack the coach, whose rippling hamstrings had once been the main object of her deeply repressed sexual fantasies, until replaced by the one involving Jonathan Doyle and an altar cloth that now she was sometimes forced to repress deeply during communion. 'How about the day after tomorrow?'

'I'll find you,' he said, 'same time, same place?' and Kate swallowed and nodded, finding herself dry-mouthed as he walked on the way she had come, wondering if he was actually real. If only I were younger, more attractive, if only Martin hadn't had the best years of my life. She sighed, then gasped as Gwen grew bored and leaped after a butterfly, nearly dragging her arm out of its socket and pulling her flat on her front onto the soft ground.

Julia was washing clothes and singing loudly but completely tunelessly when Kate turned up, covered in riverbank mud but with an unusual sparkle in her eye and a marked flush on her cheeks. Julia had strung a makeshift line between the wall of the cottage and her shed, and had constructed a washing machine out of half a barrel and her own feet. Now she was in the process of treading her whites load.

'Good morning. Oh dear, Julia, I knew someone who got terrible chilblains from being barefoot. Can't you get yourself a washing machine?'

Julia looked up from her bouncing rhythm, which involved rather more of her than one might usually expect as she wore no underwear on washing day, allowing the laundering of all of her bras at once.

'Have you looked at what they cost, Kate?'

Kate was offended. 'Of course I know what they cost, but for you to be out here trampling it like . . .'

'Like a washerwoman? I enjoy it, actually, and it's jolly good for the feet – keeps them really soft and subtle. No chilblains at all.' Julia privately thought Kate's need to interfere with other people's lives was the consequence of an absence of anything interesting in her own.

'Really?' Kate was intrigued, despite herself – she had noticed Julia's rather beautiful feet before now, envied them a little – 'Is it something in the water?'

'Absolutely. You should try it.'

'Oh, gosh no, I don't think . . .' Kate hesitated, rather pink, torn between finding the suggestion totally outrageous and really wanting beautiful feet.

'Come on, Kate, get your socks off.'

Jonathan Doyle was surprised – and rather puzzled – to see Julia and Kate stamping the smalls together ten minutes later as he took a young couple to show them the church where they planned to be married (more, he thought sadly, to check out its suitability for the wedding video than experience the atmosphere of devotion and godliness). He waved over the low hedge as he went by, firmly squashing his sudden urge to fling off his socks and merrily join them (for why should a vicar not have *fun?*), and from the upstairs window of the cottage heard a snatch of the most beautiful singing voice.

> *'Merrily, merrily shall I live now*
> *Under the blossom that hangs on the bough.'*

That was Hebe again. She got better every time you heard her. Jonathan shivered suddenly. Great talent could be such a two-edged sword. Yet that voice – it made you think of something not of this world.

Deep in the woods Mrs Braithwaite was also doing her washing, but as she had accepted the offer of a washing machine from Joshua Gilfoyle some years earlier, this was not as great a task as it might otherwise have been. She smiled when William and Oscar arrived, bearing a piece of rotten branch which was home to a particularly hairy caterpillar.

'We came to ask you,' William said, 'what this is. I think it might be poisonous and it isn't in my insect book. Did you know the most poisonous creature in the world is a caterpillar?'

Oscar sighed patronisingly. 'I keep telling you, Wills,

you've been reading too many SAS manuals. When you get to my age you start to realise that –'

William crossed his eyes. 'Anyone would think you were a hundred.' He waved the branch at Mrs Braithwaite. 'What d'you think, then? You know everything about nature.'

Mrs Braithwaite peered at the caterpillar short-sightedly and fished in her pocket. 'I need my glasses, dear.'

'Wow,' said Oscar in some surprise as she put them on. 'Cool. Why've you got pink glasses?'

'Dyslexia,' said Mrs Braithwaite, looking closely at the caterpillar, 'wasn't diagnosed till I was four hundred and ninety. It's a disgrace.'

'You should sue somebody,' said William admiringly.

But she shrugged. 'Not much point.'

'Why not?'

'Frankly,' said Mrs Braithwaite, eyeing him over the top of the pink specs, 'they've all snuffed it. How many people do you know who were born when Henry Tudor was on the throne? Apart from me, of course.'

Oscar and William exchanged glances. They thoroughly enjoyed this game she played, and endlessly tried to catch her out by asking which king came after which other, what year it was when the plague came to Foxbarton, what year Mackenzie Brown made the angel – but Mrs Braithwaite liked to say her memory was still perfect, and they hadn't managed to catch her out yet. In fact the whole process had led them to being better educated in English political and social history than almost any other boys of their age.

True to form, Mrs Braithwaite knew the caterpillar. 'Red admiral,' she said. 'We've not seen those around Foxbarton Woods for years. Joshua Gilfoyle and his chemical farming. In my day it was all done by hand, you know. Scythes and ploughs and horses.'

'I bet it was much more interesting round here back then,' said William wistfully, 'what with the highwaymen and plague and stuff.'

Oscar rolled his eyes. 'Well, it could hardly be less interesting than it is now, could it? This is the least exciting village in the Western world. My Uncle Edward's sock drawer is more exciting than this village, and he's only got one leg.'

'I should think that makes his sock drawer quite interesting,' said William, pedantic to the last. 'I mean, you could try to guess which leg he didn't have from the wear on his socks.'

'Oh, ha ha. It's so boring here you can live to be five hundred and six 'cos there's nothing exciting enough to give you a heart attack.'

'We had the angel stolen,' said William. 'That was exciting.'

Mrs Braithwaite nodded. 'That was the night I was ill.'

'What was wrong with you?' asked William. 'My dad said you nearly died.'

'It was my time,' said Mrs Braithwaite. 'But then the angel was stolen so I couldn't go. It was obvious I still had stuff to do.'

'Wow,' said William, 'I didn't think that stopped you dying.' It opened up a whole new realm of possibility, he felt, if you could postpone dying just by having stuff to do. You could probably cheat death for decades by simply failing to put away your clean underwear.

'Do you know who stole the angel?' asked Oscar, but Mrs Braithwaite shrugged.

'Perhaps no one stole it,' she said. 'Perhaps it was just taken. People steal for profit; people take what they can't do without.'

'It's the same thing,' said Oscar, 'isn't it?'

'Only if you think it's the same thing to fly as to be a bird.'

Oscar was puzzled. 'Why couldn't you die when the angel was stolen?'

'It's a long story and I'm off after mushrooms so I'm not going to tell it. See you later.'

She left Oscar and William staring at one another.

'What d'you suppose she meant?' asked William.

Oscar shrugged. 'I dunno. My dad says she's too old to have a working brain.'

'She must be,' said William seriously. 'Our history teacher says none of us have proper working brains 'cos they've been shrivelling up ever since we were born, and that's only eleven years ago.'

'Is that Mr Tomkins? I wouldn't worry. When I was in year six he said that to everyone who couldn't remember Henry the Eighth's wives,' said Oscar.

William rolled his eyes. 'I mean, who cares about his *wives*?' He picked the caterpillar deftly from its branch and put it in one of the many matchboxes he carried for the purpose.

'Come on,' said Oscar, 'let's go to the badger den and see if anyone's been there.'

'I was there the other night,' said William, following him, 'with Hebe and Matilda.'

'You brought *them*? God, you're sad.'

'They'd have followed me anyway,' said William, feeling slightly ashamed of his affection for Hebe in Oscar's company. 'Actually, we lost Hebe for a bit.'

'Wow. Did you call the police?'

'No, she turned up again. But what was weird – she said she was lost and an angel showed her the way back.'

Oscar rolled his eyes. 'Yes, well, this is Hebe we're talking about.'

'What do you mean?'

'Well, she's funny in the head, isn't she? My dad said she was born upside down and she probably banged her head on the way out.'

William could feel his anger rising. 'She wasn't. Your dad's talking crap. Anyway, Hebe doesn't tell lies.'

'Oh, sure,' said Oscar, 'angels in the woods.'

'She sees things other people don't see,' said William, 'that's all.'

'You're funny in the head too. My dad says being peculiar runs in families. You're all peculiar in your – ouch! You hit me! You can't do that. Ow! God! Ow! Look – there's blood coming. YOU MADE MY NOSE BLEED! You animal! I'm not staying here with you a moment longer . . .' he rushed off holding his face.

'Piss off,' shouted William after him, feeling like a volcano inside because of the meanness. 'And keep out of my bloody woods!'

'You shouldn't have hit him,' said Julia when William told her the story. 'Not really, William. You can't get rid of people's prejudice by hitting them. But thank you, anyway. I hope you don't get into trouble.'

William sniffed, then said hopefully, 'He'll tell his mother and the vicar will throw me out of the church choir.'

'I'm certain he won't,' said Julia. 'You were defending Hebe; he wouldn't throw you out for that.'

'D'you think he would if I thumped Oscar again?'

'No, but I thought you liked singing. Tell your mother you were defending a friend. Oscar's mother won't dare say anything. She was here earlier – she helped me with my washing.'

'Matilda likes singing,' said William. 'I don't. She thinks she'll win the Haverhill Festival. She thinks she's Charlotte blooming Church. Is that your washing? I wish we had a barrel like that, it would be much more fun than a stupid washing machine.'

Julia ruffled his hair. 'It is, but I've finished. Come and help me empty it.'

'Where's Hebe?'

'Someone from the education department has come to assess her. They're in the house so I came out here.'

'Why do they have to assess her at half-term? Shouldn't they assess her when it's term time?'

'It's to make sure I'm teaching her things. She doesn't

have a half-term really. Her school is at home so she's at school all the time.'

'Wow, cool. And she knows loads,' said William. 'She knows lots of trees and flowers, you know, and she saw an angel in the woods the other night.'

Julia frowned. 'What do you mean, in the woods the other night? What night?'

William clapped his hand to his mouth. 'I mean, the other day. The other day in the woods when we were playing . . .'

'When were you playing? You never asked me. I don't want her to go playing in the woods unless you're with her, and unless I know that's where you are. She'll get lost, you know what she's like.' Julia glared at him. 'Tell the truth, William. When were you in the woods with Hebe?'

'When you came to cook dinner,' confessed William. 'We went to watch badgers, me and Hebe and Matilda, but we fell asleep, and when we woke up Hebe said she'd seen an angel.' He'd leave out the bit about her wandering off and getting lost, he thought. On balance that would add nothing to the story but might risk grounding for a week. A further week, that is, than the grounding that he could feel coming upon him already.

But to his surprise Julia said nothing at all.

After he'd gone, Julia wandered to the edge of the woods herself and stared into the trees. So Hebe *was* in the woods the other night, she thought. She escaped and I didn't even know about it. Perhaps in leaving London to come here I've swapped one lot of danger for another. I can't stop her escaping into the trees from time to time. She's the escape artist of the century. Like her father really – he disappeared when I wasn't watching too. I must tie her door handle to my toe again. I should have tied him to my toe.

She walked a little way in, enjoying the green spotted sunshine on her bare arms, glad, so glad to be in the countryside where you *could* walk bare-armed into the woods, remembering the very first time Hebe spoke. She was three years old, and they had spent Christmas as always with Merrill and Simon in Foxbarton. Despite Julia's objections they had all been hauled off to church for the morning service, and Hebe had been seated near the Foxbarton Angel, then still on its plinth. It had been during the prayers before Communion that Hebe's voice had suddenly rung out clearly with the word, 'Angel!' It had sounded more an astonished exclamation than a statement, so startling the congregation that a couple of them believed to this day that she had actually seen a real one.

I was so pleased she had spoken at all, remembered Julia, that I burst into tears and cried for the rest of the service. The old vicar was terribly kind and didn't say a word, not even when Hebe went to the communion rail for a blessing with her knickers on her head. And it had been a turning point, because after that she started to speak, and turned into a difficult child you could deal with, rather than one with whom you hadn't a hope.

She wondered what the education woman was making of Hebe – it was, after all, her first review assessment here in Suffolk. *Perhaps I'd better go back and see how they're getting on* ... But when she got back to the house neither the education woman nor Hebe was there.

A few hundred yards away in the west wing of the Grange, Joshua Gilfoyle sat on a large and overstuffed sofa listening to Gilbert and Sullivan. He was not a light opera fan, but Sonja had left it on when she went out and he hadn't had the energy to turn it off again. He was feeling unwell but he wasn't going to tell her so. She'd only fuss and make him some peculiar Norwegian remedy which would almost certainly taste of herrings. He felt fuzzy-headed, oddly disorientated. Not himself at all.

Sonja was out at an English lesson. She spent a lot of time at lessons – English, Greek, art, piano ... He encouraged her to do these things, feeling at her age she shouldn't be shut up all the time with a retired man. Anyway, he needed a bit of peace – he might be at least as potent as most men in their prime (and nuts to that fool urologist who had suggested having his testicles removed to treat the bloody cancer), but sex was a little wearing on the elbow joints. Now, though, he wished she was here. It was a light and pleasant afternoon but he did not feel well enough to go out and enjoy it, nor to seek more demanding company than hers. He sighed and flicked the pages of his book without reading them. His head felt very odd. Perhaps if he just dozed off . . .

There was a voice in the distance, singing something ethereal . . . but no, it had stopped, suffocated by bloody Gilbert and Sullivan . . .

'On a tree by a river a little tom tit sang "Willow, tit willow, tit willow!" . . .' sang the speakers, two pairs, carefully placed for surround sound.

At the French window Hebe stood, suddenly still, and listened, her attention finally caught after a long run from home to the woods and then from the woods to here. She had escaped from the teacher person by dint of hopping out of the window and down the wall whilst the teacher was using the lavatory. Hebe had waited for her chance patiently – that was the secret of escape, you had to wait for the right chance. She had seen the teacher drink two cups of tea so she had understood that, sooner or later, the teacher would go into the lavatory and shut the door. That would be her chance, and she preferred the window route, partly because she liked to climb and was extremely good at it, and partly because even though downstairs was very quiet her mother might be waiting in the kitchen anticipating her next move, just as she had with that string round her bedroom doorknob that moved the little bell.

Hebe did not like teachers, disliked the questioning way they looked at her as if she was supposed to dance for them or turn a somersault – because even when she did those things they still looked at her the same way, a way that made her scream. She had tried dancing and turning somersaults this time for this teacher person but the teacher person had not seemed pleased. Hebe had screamed then, but the teacher person had frowned and jabbered with her mouth – but Hebe had not heard the words nor even tried to. Hebe knew her ears didn't work for people she didn't like so it had all sounded like sparrows chirping and, anyway, there had been lights flashing in her eyes. First the lady had worn sparkling earrings which had flashed, and then the sun had flashed at the window, and then Hebe's own temper had made even more flashes . . . and it had all got too much. So Hebe had run to the woods to look for the nice bear-man in the coloured cave who made tunes on the thing with strings, but he wasn't there so then she had run back again to the house and the windows had sparkled too and she had needed to run even faster to get away. It was all very simple if you understood – or so it seemed to Hebe, who did not know that others did not see the world as she did, as a confusing mass of bright shining objects, of teeth and chatter and things which made you eat them, and occasional still small pools of calm where her heart didn't pound and she could sit still without anyone making a noise at her.

She had found one now, a still small pool of calm. It was quiet in this place. There was warbling going on in here, but it was good warbling. Hebe liked music, because it made order out of sound, it was tidy and didn't make flashings in her head. Instead it made her feel serene and good. She had discovered that she could make noises like these warblings, and thus bring the serenity upon herself whenever she chose. The French windows to Joshua's bedroom were open and Hebe crept in and tiptoed through to the sitting room where he dozed.

She did not notice Joshua at first, she was so absorbed in the song. When Hebe concentrated there was no room for anything else and she did not want to miss a single word.

You never knew when you would hear things again and the only way to reproduce the serene feeling was to reproduce the song perfectly.

> *'. . . and if you remain callous and obdurate, I*
> *Shall perish as he did, and you will know why,*
> *Though I probably shall not exclaim as I die,*
> *'Oh, willow, tit willow, tit willow!'*

Hebe closed her eyes in pleasure. The CD began to move to the next track and she picked up the remote control and turned it off, not wanting to confuse what she had heard with anything else. Remote controls were simple things – you pressed one button and one thing happened. Hebe could cope with that. She started to sing the song she had heard, word perfect.

> *'On a tree by a river a little tom tit*
> *Sang "Willow, tit willow, tit willow!"* . . .'

Joshua Gilfoyle opened his eyes and saw her there, poised on tiptoe with her eyes closed and her hands stretched out and flapping, as if she was about to take off. He felt dreadfully sick, so much so that he thought he might vomit. There was a pain in his head that hadn't been there a moment ago, whenever a moment ago had been. His mind seemed to be whirling, not making sense. He tried to speak but no words came out. He tried to reach out towards Hebe, who was disturbing his peace and having the nerve to bring herself and her peculiar behaviour into his own private space. He didn't want her there. The very sight of her bothered him. She reminded him of things he would rather forget. She reminded him of that retarded boy in his class in the village when he was a child. The one they sent away, who was older than the others but couldn't do anything except smile stupidly and hug people. What was the point of people like that? If they were horses they'd shoot them. He wouldn't shoot them personally, perhaps, but put them away somewhere. Out of sight, out of mind . . .

He couldn't wave at Hebe. His right arm wouldn't work. He stared down at himself in alarm. It was definitely there. It was a perfectly normal arm. He could feel it, tingling, but it wouldn't move. He moved the other one across and pinched it. It hurt. It burned. With a huge effort he pulled himself forwards, startling Hebe, who had not noticed him as he was not the source of the music.

People and inanimate objects were often the same thing to Hebe, who did not credit anything with sentient thought. The very concept that other things – be they people, trees, bears, angels – actually possessed thought processes separate to her own was beyond her imagination. This was, in fact, the very essence of her problem. Not only did she not see the world as others see it, not only did she perceive all of it at once, without the selective filters that make order out of chaos, she actually did not appreciate that others saw it at all.

Joshua toppled over sideways onto the sofa, face first into the cushion. He had realised that something was very wrong with him, but his thought processes seemed incredibly slow, as if his mind were a heavily drugged sloth wading through treacle. Why wouldn't his voice come out? He struggled to shout but his mouth felt strangely slack and wet, and he realised to his disgust that he had been dribbling.

Hebe watched him fall, her dark unfathomable eyes understanding that this was sickness. Hebe had been sick and hot once and Mummy had given her pink goo on a spoon. Mummy had been sick on the grass. The snake she had found in the woods had been sick – well, it had after Mrs Braithwaite got all frightened and chopped its head off. Mrs Braithwaite had screamed at her when she had tried to touch the snake, which was when Hebe had been sick the last time. Hesitantly she moved towards Joshua.

Joshua's face was in the cushion. He couldn't breathe. He knew what this was now. His mind had cleared completely and he understood everything. A bloody stroke. Just like his father. He couldn't struggle free. He was suffocating. He was trying to inhale but the fabric would not give, his chest was hurting and his head was exploding. So this was it – he would die, useless and alone with a bloody feather cushion up his nose. Choked to death by soft furnishings, Marjorie's bloody Osborne and Little. I should have let Sonja redecorate. Dark clouds of blackness were surrounding him, swallowing him up . . .

Something was touching that useless hand, was pulling the cushion from his nose. It was all going very dark. His head felt as if it was separated from his body. His body felt as if it was twisting, floating away. He was very afraid. 'Mary,' he tried to whisper, 'Mary,' but no sound came out – at least no sound that he could hear.

In the woods, though, Mary Braithwaite, stirring green herbs in a pot and humming an old folk song long since forgotten in these parts, stood stock still and put her hand to her mouth.

'We just find her sitting with him.' Sonja was in tears and out of breath when Julia answered the phone. 'Mrs Braithwaite finds Joshua unconscious on the sofa, and Hebe just sits and holds his hand and is stroking it.'

'Is she all right?' Julia glared at the woman from Education, who had finally appeared to confess that Hebe had run off, after searching fruitlessly through the woods alone.

'She's – well, I don't know. She is quiet and her eyes are big but she will not let go of him and she does not speak to me. I am sorry, Julia, I do not know how she usually is. Will you come and fetch her, please? I must go back, I need to be with him. It is looking very . . . Now the ambulance is here . . .'

Suddenly Julia felt sorry for Sonja. She sounded genuinely distressed, even if she should have expected this the day she came to live with a man almost old enough to be her grandfather. And it must be lonely, being a good-time bimbo in Foxbarton. It wasn't exactly a centre of cosmopolitan wild times. 'How is Joshua now?'

'Not speaking,' said Sonja, 'not conscious. I must go with him. He has a stroke, they say. This seems obvious to me, I have seen it before. I don't know anything else. Will you find Simon? I have to find a toothbrush. I don't know where his pyjamas are . . . I must go back . . . Hebe doesn't want to let go –'

'Calm down, Sonja, I'm coming,' Julia said. 'And you,' she added, turning on the unfortunate woman from Education, 'had better file a favourable report on Hebe and me or I'll tell them you lost her and panicked. She's had a few daft assessments but no one else has managed to lose her.' This wasn't true, of course – but the teaching inspector wouldn't know that. Wouldn't know that Hebe escaped from virtually everyone who came to assess her, and that was how Julia and Hebe had got away with being the way they were for so long.

But Julia had no regrets. The Education woman just had to be convinced to put up with the status quo rather than trying to impose something else on her. Hebe could not be educated within the narrow confines of the national curriculum. Educating Hebe had nothing to do with maths, at which she was extremely clever anyway, or English, which she would never be able to comprehend properly even though she could read Shakespeare aloud and recite poems she had heard only once. To educate Hebe involved confidence and order, safety and trust, giving her the chance to be herself. It involved finding a way around the labyrinth that was her mysterious mind and it needed to be far more individual a programme than the Education Department could possibly allow.

Leaving the teacher trying to get a word in edgeways, Julia grabbed a cardigan for Hebe – who had doubtless gone off in something totally unsuitable (in the days when she went to school she had once escaped and appeared at home wearing a tinsel halo from the Nativity box, a pair of adult wellingtons from the caretaker's room and a swimsuit from lost property) – and raced up to the Grange, arriving just in time to see the ambulance doors closing behind Sonja and Joshua, and to find Hebe in the kitchen with Mrs Barker, who had marched in and removed her from Joshua's side and was now doing what she did with all children – trying to feed her cake.

Julia snatched her away. 'Sorry, Mrs Barker – she mustn't have icing. It makes her hyperactive. Too much sugar.'

'Well,' said Mrs Barker, grumpily, 'there's no rubbish in my cooking, I'll have you know. Children need their sugar. Without my sugar I'd have faded away long ago.'

Julia refrained from saying that Mrs Barker looked about as likely to fade away as the M25. 'Are you OK, darling?' she asked Hebe.

Hebe frowned her tiny frown. 'Grandpa was ill,' she said. 'Grandpa couldn't talk and his mouth went all twisted.'

Julia sighed. 'He's not your grandpa, sweetie, he's William and Matilda's grandpa.'

'My grandpa,' said Hebe stubbornly. 'William swapped him.'

'What do you mean, William swapped him?'

'For my butterfly,' said Hebe. 'I wanted a grandpa and William wanted a butterfly so I swapped.'

Julia was secretly rather pleased to find that Hebe had given away the butterfly, which was dead and therefore, she felt, rather gruesome despite its pretty wings. Some long-ago lepidopterist had mounted it on a board with a pin, and Hebe had found it in the attics at Foxbarton Grange during one of her escape episodes up there. 'It sounds like a bargain to me,' she said, reflecting that having Joshua Gilfoyle as a family member wouldn't be everyone's idea of a bargain, but since Hebe had no other grandpa it might partly make up for the lack of a father. No, she thought, what am I saying? Nothing can make up for her not having a father. If only he hadn't gone so quickly that morning. Who knows how things might have turned out?

'Saved him, didn't she?' said a voice at the kitchen doorway, and Julia looked up to see Mrs Barker crossing herself as a familiar figure with brown skin and a strange spiky crew cut appeared by the sink.

'Hello, Mrs Braithwaite,' she said. She noticed that Mrs Braithwaite was carrying what looked like a round green loaf. 'How do you mean?'

'She saved him – pulled his face out of the cushion. He could easily have suffocated without her.'

'Did she?' Julia stared at Hebe, who ignored her and concentrated on the cake. Julia looked at Mrs Braithwaite curiously. 'It's lucky you were here.'

Mary Braithwaite nodded at her, then glared at Mrs Barker. 'I know when I'm needed.' She thrust the loaf at Mrs Barker. 'You give him this,' she said, 'when he's back from the hospital. He always liked my sage bread. It will make him well.'

Mrs Barker opened and closed her mouth a few times. She had a hearty respect for Mrs Braithwaite, whose brews and potions had a legendary reputation in the villages around, but she didn't want her in the kitchen smelling of wood-smoke and leaf mould, thank you very much. She took the basket gingerly and peered at the green bread. Was it sage, she wondered, that made it green, or was it something far more dastardly?

'It's only sage, and you should lose some weight,' said Mrs Braithwaite, eyeing her up and down. 'I'll bring you something.'

'You're a bit personal,' said Mrs Barker, darkly. 'My Mr B likes me just the way I am.'

'I bet,' said Mrs Braithwaite. 'I'll drop it round.' She looked at Julia, her rather catlike green eyes curiously clear for a woman of her age, whatever her age was. 'How is he?'

'It looks like a stroke,' said Julia. 'Come on, Mrs Braithwaite, we'll walk back with you.'

Mrs Barker watched them go, talking to herself. 'Think I haven't tried, does she? I put on eight pounds at Slimming World and ten at Weight Watchers, and that bloody super-model video was so depressing I put on a stone. I don't eat enough to keep a flea alive, me, so I don't understand it.' And she popped another piece of cake in her mouth. Still, Mary Braithwaite was a witch – perhaps she had a potion that would work where others had failed.

Julia, Hebe and Mary Braithwaite walked slowly back towards the woods. 'How did you know he was ill?' Julia asked.

Mary shook her head. 'Birds and the bees, my dear. When you're as old as I am you get a feel for what's going on in the world.' She looked at Hebe. 'Like your grandpa, do you?'

'He's not her grandpa,' said Julia, fearing misunderstanding might easily lead to gossip. It had been bad enough when Simon and Merrill took them on holiday to France and the woman in the shop next door assumed she was the mistress and refused to sell her stamps.

'I heard she swapped a butterfly for him,' said Mrs Braithwaite, 'and she's as stubborn as he is.'

'No, she isn't.' I can do without this, thought Julia. 'This village is already entirely prepared to believe I'm Simon's other woman, come here to complete some horrible *ménage à trois*.

But Mary Braithwaite waved a finger at her. 'If the child wants him to be her grandpa then he is. It will do the both of them good,' she said, and Julia sighed and reflected that the last thing Hebe needed was a grandfather who despised the mentally ill.

'Come on, Hebe,' she said, 'we should go home. You shouldn't have run off.'

Hebe frowned. 'Grandpa's sick.'

'I know. Grandpa will be fine,' God, she thought, he might not. I shouldn't lie to her. 'Hebe, Grandpa is poorly and had to go to hospital . . .'

'Grandpa will be fine without you, child,' said Mary. 'Someone's looking after him.'

'Angel,' Hebe said, and pointed into the woods.

Mrs Braithwaite smiled and looked at Julia. 'There have always been angels in these woods, you know. What with them and the headless horsemen it can be a very busy place of a full moon.'

'Oh, don't be ridiculous,' said Julia crossly, 'you'll scare her. Hebe, why don't you show us where you saw the angel?' And Hebe led them determinedly into the trees.

Some half an hour later they emerged beside the pond where, to their mutual delight, a heron was fishing, and the angel was forgotten, at least for now.

Chapter Five

'*We are pleased to find that Hebe is making excellent progress. She will be reviewed again in six months' time when you will be invited to make further application for national curriculum material for your home classroom,*' read Hebe aloud from the letter which had arrived in the post.

'Very good, Hebe. What does it mean?'

'I don't know.' Hebe began to howl.

'You could understand it if you weren't standing on your head, Hebe,' said Matilda, 'couldn't she, Aunt Julia?'

'I don't know that it makes any difference really. Some artists stand on their heads all the time.' Perhaps I should try spending some time upside down, Julia thought. After all, if my brain got half the blood supply my other bits have been getting recently I should be turning out original art at the rate of a new exhibition every day. The angel would have been finished weeks ago. She looked rather mournfully at the row of six herons on the lawn. I ought to be able to come up with something else.

William followed her gaze out of the window. 'Why don't you make an elephant?'

Julia smiled, 'Well, I'm not sure that there's much of a market for wicker elephants.' On the other hand, she thought, it would be a change from birds. 'How is your grandfather now?' she asked William. She felt a little guilty at not taking Hebe up to the hospital to see him even once over the last couple of weeks, given that she kept referring to his sickness, but it would only end in tears if she kept calling him Grandpa. Besides, Hebe was not good with hospitals. There were too many noises and flashing lights. It was the kind of situation that brought on her worst panics. She had once been given a head scan to make sure there were no other reasons for her odd behaviour (Julia had taken 'reasons' as an oblique reference to brain tumours). There was nothing wrong with Hebe's brain, the scan had told them. Ironically, whilst the radiologist had been looking at the films and reaching this considered decision Hebe had been halfway down a drainpipe outside the window of the paediatrics ward, screaming as if she was an extra in a disaster movie whilst two paramedics desperately tried to set up a ladder to reach her without understanding that if they would only turn the blue flashing light off she would come down perfectly well by herself.

'He's a lot better,' said William, who found his grand-father's reduced capabilities deeply upsetting. 'Sonja says he's coming home next week but he's going to need a special nurse 'cos he can't speak and his hand doesn't work properly and he chucks his food all over the place.'

'You chuck your food all over the place too,' said Matilda, hiding her distress over her grandfather in provocative squabbling, 'so why haven't you got a special nurse?'

William turned his back on her so that she wouldn't see the sudden tear. There was, of course, only one tear, as real men only ever have one. Oscar had told him this, having heard it said in a film on late-night TV, and they had both felt it had a ring of the genuinely macho about it. Julia put her hand on his arm, which made another one come, and he dashed it away angrily. 'I'm going to feed my beetles,' he said in a rather gruff voice, and hurried off.

Matilda watched him go. 'Whoever heard of feeding beetles?' she said, a little limply. 'Mum says he's driving us mad with beetles. He put a caterpillar in my knickers drawer last week, and Mum says she's sure it was him that put woodlice in Sonja's wellingtons.'

'Oh dear,' said Julia, imagining poor Sonja pursued

screaming by a swarm of woodlice. 'Was she very upset?'

'Course not, she never even found them. Mrs Barker found them when they got out and hid under the onions in the pantry. Sonja never wears her wellingtons, because she hates dirt. Grandfather said Norwegians don't like mud, only snow and herrings. But Mum told William he should grow up and stop being a twit, and I said there's no chance of that happening for a good twenty years yet. That's why he put the caterpillar in my knickers.'

Julia smiled. 'I can see that would be a problem.'

'It was,' said Matilda. 'I put them on and it crawled down my leg in assembly and I screamed. Just imagine, it could have gone anywhere.'

'That wasn't very nice, William,' said Julia, spotting him still lurking by her back door.

He sniffed. 'No, I know it wasn't, and I did say sorry.'

'No you didn't.'

'Yes I did – to the caterpillar. It must have been awful for him being stuck next to your bum.'

'You're so beastly.'

'You're my twin, what's that make you?'

'Disadvantaged!'

'Oh, girls are just *so* unbearable,' and this time William was gone.

It struck Julia that bickering was what William and Matilda did to keep sane. Hebe, of course, never bickered. Hebe was always either ecstatically happy or totally and devastatingly sad. She was never merely grumpy. With Hebe you either got hugged or you got kicked. You never got bickered with.

Hebe got down off her head. 'There's a bear in the woods,' she said. 'In a red and yellow cave.'

Julia smiled. 'I love your imagination,' she told Hebe. 'D'you know, Matilda, they try to tell me she doesn't have an imagination. It just goes to show they're not right about everything, doesn't it, darling?'

Hebe frowned her tiny frown and wandered off.

'Don't go out of the garden,' Julia called after her. 'Matilda, will you keep an eye on her? Lunch is nearly ready, and after lunch I'm taking you all back up to the Grange. I've to go out somewhere with your mother.'

'Oh really, where? You never go out,' said Matilda, 'Mrs Barker says you'll never find a good man unless you go out.'

Julia grinned. 'She's probably right but you've still got to look in the right place. Good men don't grow on trees.'

Matilda giggled. 'How would you know if you found a good one? I mean, do they look different from bad ones?'

'If only they did,' said Julia, 'it would make life very simple.'

'Was Hebe's daddy good?' asked Matilda, with the thoughtlessness of one too young to realise that there are some things you just don't ask.

Julia swallowed. 'I hope so,' she said. 'I didn't get chance to know him very well. I lost him.'

'That was a bit careless,' said Matilda sadly. 'Didn't you have his address?'

'No, I didn't. I don't think he really had one.'

'But how can you have a baby with someone you don't know very well?'

'You can if you're very young and very stupid,' said Julia, thinking, Merrill will kill me if I start on this. 'Anyway,' she said, 'your mother and I are going on an artistic tour of Cambridge. I need some inspiration. So don't let Hebe go into the woods on her own. Promise?'

It had been Merrill's idea that Julia should try some gallery browsing to stimulate her dormant artistic streak, but Julia couldn't help feeling that starting at the Fitzwilliam Museum was not the best idea her sister had ever had.

'Ancient Greek pottery and Egyptology,' she said rather ungraciously, as they sat in the Fitzwilliam coffee rooms after a rather dry couple of hours staring at ancient statues and painted masks, 'don't have the essence I need to get me creating again. I mean, I know there's inspiration in the past, but a statue of a winged Anubis might go down rather badly at St Gregory's, don't you think?'

'Absolutely,' said Merrill. 'You could be responsible for the souls of Foxbarton winding up toasting for all eternity for worshipping false gods.'

Julia sighed, 'They're all false gods as far as I'm concerned. I don't believe in eternal souls and harps and bonfires – or cherubim and seraphim and all the company of Heaven.' She sighed. 'I don't know, Merrill. I don't even know how to begin to make Joshua's angel. To me an angel has no form of its own.'

'You mean it's a ghostly being?'

'No, I mean it's in people. You can't see it, but it touches you now and again and leaves you better – or safer – for it.'

'I think you're getting too metaphysical,' said Merrill. 'If it's got wings and a halo, it's an angel. How hard is that?'

'I just can't imagine that's what an angel is,' said Julia, 'something in a nightie from the school Nativity.'

'I don't see why not. It's generally children who see angels, after all, so they're far more likely to be the ones that get it right. I've told you, you saw one when you were three.'

'It's no good to me now,' said Julia, 'I've forgotten.'

'Well, get Hebe to tell you what her angel looked like.'

'She can't,' said Julia sadly. 'I've asked her. I wish she would, if only because Joshua would be horrified if he thought Hebe was designing his precious statue. There's a strange irony, don't you think, in the man who can't abide mental handicap being Hebe's saviour?'

'Even more of an irony now.' Merrill lapsed into silence and after a moment Julia said, 'Is he dying? I mean, is this all something to do with the cancer?'

'I don't know – Simon doesn't know either. Sonja sits by his bedside like the knitting women of the French Revolution, all pale face and red eyes. I think she's convinced herself that he's dying, but Simon says lots of people do well after strokes. I mean, this is Joshua. If anyone could go on for years with prostate cancer and a stroke it would be him. Simon says the longer he goes on after it without having another stroke, and the better he gets, the more chance he has that he'll last years. As long as he doesn't just give up.'

'I can't imagine that. Not him.'

'No.' Merrill had had enough conversations about Joshua to last her weeks, and wanted to talk about something else. 'D'you really think coming here has saved Hebe?'

'I know it has. London was destroying her.'

'So you're definitely staying?'

'As long as I manage this angel,' said Julia ruefully. 'I mean, it never occurred to me that I might not, but somehow, with it being an angel, it's become too important to begin until I know where I'm going.'

'I thought Joshua said you could keep the cottage even afterwards. I mean, it's not as if he needs it. That cottage was empty for years before you came – and anyway, if . . . I mean, if he doesn't make it . . . well, you could certainly keep the cottage then.' To her astonishment Merrill realised there were tears in her eyes at the thought of Joshua dying.

Julia put a hand on her arm. 'I know. He sees me as Foxbarton's permanent artist in residence. I think he's bequeathing me to the village as well as the angel, but if I don't come up with the angel he might change his mind. And we must stay. It feels right for Hebe here. She has this thing about counting stars, you know, and in London we couldn't always see them, there were so many other lights all the time, and it used to upset her. She needs things around her to be very simple. She can't deal with lots of sensory information, it makes her crazy.'

'That's a funny word for you to use,' said Merrill. 'If anyone else called her crazy you'd mince them in seconds.'

Julia smiled and finished her coffee, scooping the froth off the top with her spoon. 'I suppose I would. But I know I don't mean any harm.'

'Maybe other people don't either. It's like black people being allowed to tell racist jokes when white people aren't.'

'No it's not, it's not at all like that.'

'It is exactly like that, Julia Fitzgerald. You think because you're her mother you can say what you like, but no one else can because they haven't proved they're blessed with sensitivity and understanding.'

Julia eyed her scone thoughtfully. 'Does this have something to do with artistic expression, or are you just grabbing a chance to get at me?'

Merrill sighed. 'No, not at all, I just think you're defensive in the extreme. You've put a wall around you and Hebe. Inside it the two of you can do what you like, but outside it no one can pass comment. I mean, shout at me if you think this is too far-fetched, but don't you think maybe there's such a barrier around the two of you that nothing and nobody can get in? Including any inspiration?'

Julia stared at her. 'You're saying I'm too much of an introvert? That's rich coming from the woman who told me I was being too wild in London.'

'I mean, you won't let anything in,' said Merrill, exasperated. 'And it's years since I said that, anyway. Now I wish you'd be a little wilder. You've closed your mind to everything. Look at you. You're a beautiful woman. You have hair I'd die for and the kind of bottom that's really fashionable now –'

'Wow, thanks.'

'No really, women are having implants in their buttocks to get them like yours.'

Julia finished her scone. 'How the hell did we get from the Foxbarton angel to my buttocks in three simple sentences?'

'Sex,' said Merrill, with triumphant clarity – and the word echoed suddenly into the slightly rarified academic atmosphere of the tea room.

'Shush, people are looking. People think I'm with a mad agony aunt.'

Merrill sniffed. 'You look me in the eye and tell me I'm wrong. When did you last have sex?'

Julia ignored the hopeful eyebrow of a man in his sixties sporting a badly fitting toupee and trying to attract her attention from across the room. No chance, mate, she thought. Aloud she said to Merrill, 'You may be my sister but you can't ask me that.'

'I just did,' said Merrill. 'Go on, when?'

Julia rolled her eyes. 'Years,' she said. 'It's not that easy.'

'Exactly,' said Merrill, looking smug. 'That's where all your creative energy is, locked into your G spot. You need to let your sexual energy out.'

'Don't be ridiculous. Anyway, it's not an option. I've Hebe to consider. Look, believe me, in the years since inspiration left me I have considered that my lack of a sex life might have something to do with it.'

'So?'

'So nothing. I rejected the notion. Meaningless sex never inspired anyone. And anyway, you can't just . . . go out and have sex. There's not a line of men with suitable erections standing in the marketplace waiting to be picked, you know.'

'You could find a man,' said Merrill, 'if you wanted one.'

Julia chewed her lip and stoically avoided the searching gaze of the bewigged would-be suitor. 'It's not a good enough reason to go out and have sex. I mean, it just wouldn't be right.'

'I can remember,' said Merrill, waving at the waitress, 'when Simon and I used to joke that you had sex with almost everyone you made eye contact with.'

'I was never that bad,' said Julia.

'You were.'

'Well, maybe I was every now and again. But I learned my lesson. I mean, I conceived Hebe after an abandoned night of lust with a stranger.' What a wonderful man he was too, she thought wistfully, so gentle, so poetic, so sad . . .

'Did you honestly never find out who he was?'

Julia shook her head. 'No. I did try, when I realised I was pregnant – I thought he had the right to know there was going to be a bit of him growing up on the planet – but he disappeared.' And afterwards, when I realised, I was glad, she thought, that of all the liaisons I'd had, that was the one that ended in pregnancy. In her mind she was there again with him, that glorious sunny morning when she had suddenly felt she could do anything, that either of them could do anything.

'How could he just disappear?'

'He took some money and went out to buy croissants and never came back.'

'Croissants? He'd never have found croissants in Shepherd's Bush in those days. He's probably still looking.'

Julia sighed. 'Don't joke. I was sure he'd come back. I mean, we just kind of connected.'

'Sounds to me like you docked,' said Merrill. 'No wonder you never wanted to discuss it. Talk about gullible.'

'Don't be crude.'

'Well, honestly, Jules. It was a one-night stand. How could you just connect? Perhaps you'd been smoking something.'

'No, I hadn't. I can't explain it.'

'Someone must have known him. Where did you actually meet him?'

'He was just a sad, drunk bloke I found on the pavement one night when I was looking for a cab. Come to think of it, I'd been at your place, actually, one of your endless parties. I was looking for transport home and I just kind of fell over him somewhere near the Brompton Road. He could have been anyone. I mean – he could have been the King of Bolivia, for all I know.'

'Bolivia doesn't have a king.'

'Perhaps that's what he wants you to think so he can sneak around London shagging daft art students anonymously. Look, Merrill, it was an anonymous encounter. It happens all the time.'

'Don't you think you ought to try again to find him? I mean, doesn't Hebe have a right?'

'Not this again. Yes, she does have a right, but it doesn't mean it would be responsible of me to exercise it on her behalf. Lots of us have rights to have things that it's better or safer for us not to have. You know Hebe. The last thing she needs is disruption. She can have a tantrum for a full week if I change our brand of cornflakes. I couldn't possibly introduce some man into her life. Particularly not one who might disappear.' God, she thought, he went out to buy croissants, dammit, and never came back, and that was the first and only time I ever made love to anyone and felt I could really *love* them, that the potential was there for it to be so much more than it was. If I could have found him then it might have been something. But now it's nine years too late.

'Maybe you're protecting her too much. She's got to get used to the realities of life, Julia. I mean, people let you down, people die – if you don't prepare her for that, how will she ever cope alone?'

'She won't be alone.'

'She might be one day. And what about her singing? You can't just ignore that.'

'I've let her have the bloody lessons,' said Julia, becoming irritated. 'Why are you on about it again?'

'Because it might turn out to be the most important part of her. Just because she's . . . got a disability, that doesn't mean she can't have a talent. Mrs Peel thinks she's amazing. She's got her doing duets with Matilda.'

'You've been watching *Rain Man* again,' said Julia. 'Just because she's got her own personal brand of autism that doesn't mean she can recite phone books and play Rachmaninov without opening her eyes, you know.'

'Yes, but what if she could?'

'It always ends in disaster. Look at what happens to autistic savants. They may be gifted but it's because they're obsessed. They finish up like circus acts, paraded on documentaries. They do the thing that they're good at obsessively. There's no room in them for anything else. It makes them more abnormal, don't you see?'

'Yes, but maybe it gives them pleasure as well. Anyway, Jules, having a beautiful singing voice isn't the same thing. I mean, it's a gift, isn't it? It's not an obsessively learned skill. Not like Rachmaninov and phone books.'

'I still don't feel secure about it,' said Julia reluctantly. 'I did agree to the lessons, but I won't do anything that throws her. We'll do it a step at a time and see how it goes.'

Back in Foxbarton William and Matilda were in a giant panic. They had been playing hide and seek with Hebe at the edge of the woods, and for the last twenty minutes had been trying to convince each other that she was hiding particularly well. But she wasn't. They had finally admitted to each other that she had taken off. She wouldn't have hidden for this long, not unless she was upset about something. Mind you, she was upset – she had been upset with William for whistling with a piece of grass. She had screamed and held her ears, kicked him and run off. They had pursued her and calmed her down but she hadn't said very much – just looked at them with her strange eyes and frowned her tiny frown. And now, ten minutes after the scream, she had taken off again, and this time they had no idea where she was. Well, one idea . . .

'We'd better find her quickly,' said Matilda, deeply alarmed. 'Mum will kill us if we lose her.'

'Mrs Braithwaite's cottage. I bet she's there,' said William, and they set off at a run. He beat her narrowly, but when they got to Mrs Braithwaite's cottage, in the wood near the lake, Hebe wasn't there.

'Apple cake?' asked Mrs Braithwaite, smiling toothily at them and utterly failing to appreciate their panic.

'No thanks. We're looking for Hebe. She's run off.'

'Ah,' said Mrs Braithwaite, 'well.'

William folded his arms. 'What do you mean, "ah, well"?'

Mrs Braithwaite poked at her fire. 'I mean, that child's a changeling. You can't catch changelings. I've seen her kind before. They're never where you first look.'

'Well, we've first looked here, so that stands to reason.' William was impatient. 'Where shall we go next?'

Mrs Braithwaite raised one bushy eyebrow. 'You could look amongst the gypsies,' she said thoughtfully. 'That'd be the second place you looked then, wouldn't it?'

'Well, it depends whether you count the time we spent playing hide and –' began William, folding his arms and preparing pedantry, but Matilda shoved him.

'Shut up. Are the gypsies here then?'

'You'd have heard them yourself if you didn't talk so much,' said Mrs Braithwaite. 'Just listen.'

'I don't see what –'

'Shut up, William Gilfoyle, you're all ears and no brain . . . Listen. I can hear chinking – like horse stuff.'

'I can hear Hebe singing. That's a much better clue. Come on. Thanks, Mrs Braithwaite.'

Mrs Braithwaite watched them go, then drained the contents of her mug of tea, spun it twice, shook it out and looked inside. And smiled.

In Foxbarton Woods the gypsies had arrived early this year for the midsummer horse fair, having been moved on from several roadside stopovers more quickly than they had hoped. Their big, modern caravans were parked in the clearing they always used, dwarfing the red and yellow Romany van at the edge of the trees. Children were filling huge plastic containers from the water tap Joshua Gilfoyle had installed for them long ago. Ponies grazed the grass around the edges, some untethered, some tied to pegs in the ground. A group of small boys had lit a little bonfire and were cooking baked beans in a small saucepan whilst arguing over the relative merits of two different electronic games.

None of them found the Romany van odd. It was not uncommon, even these days, to turn up at a site and discover some bloke who fancied he had gypsy roots had set up camp in a bought and painted caravan. People like that did no harm. Actually, when the village idiots and the press turned up trying to move the travellers on, the occasional antique van was rather more photogenic than the rest, and added weight to their claims of a long and picturesque Eastern European tradition.

But you couldn't live in one of those vans. They were damp, they had no proper wiring, no cooking facilities, no satellite telly. The people who lived in them were usually pop stars and poets, their stay in the vans temporary fulfilment of an escapist dream. And this John James was OK. He obviously had money. This was evidently just his other life. After all, those old vans cost a fortune these days.

Still, they had welcomed him. For the moment he was a traveller, whatever other comfortable middle-class life he went back to in between – and, in any case, they were not poor themselves. They carried their wealth in gold knick-knacks but they also had cash ISAs in the Ipswich Building Society. They even had a reluctant admiration for John, sitting out the wetter nights on the edge of the clearing, wedged into the trees, catching his own trout and writing by candlelight late into the night. He was certainly doing it properly, given that he was doing it at all.

And today that strange, beautiful little girl with the pale hair had come to see him again. She had been around several times, the last time the other day, whilst John sat on his steps reading, and although she had not said a word she had watched him in apparent fascination and utter silence for a good ten minutes. He had smiled at her a few times but had received no answering smile, and after a while he had gone back to his writing and she had sneaked up and watched over his shoulder. Once he had finished his page he had turned it over, at which point the child had startled them all by reciting a poem which turned out to be, word for word, exactly what he had written on the now-concealed page. She had then turned tail and run, leaving John saying, 'Where did she come from? I thought she was one of yours, Tracey,' and Tracey had said, 'Don't be daft, John. Mine don't read if they don't have to.' The sheer enormity of what she had done was somehow disguised by the oddity of the child herself, and so it had passed them all by, apart from John himself, who still could not quite believe it well after she had left.

The next time she came he had sat playing his mandolin and she had watched his fingers in fascination but absolute silence for a while before some children called her in the distance and she had gone again, taking off back into the woods like a tree fairy. John had not been able to get a word out of her. He seemed rather taken with her, had said that perhaps if she turned up again he would take her home and tell whoever ought to be looking after her where she had been. The women all said he should watch it as it didn't do for single men to go befriending little girls, however innocently they did so, particularly not little girls who weren't quite all there, as this one clearly wasn't. The effing fuzz were always coming around, they said, with their truncheons and their prejudices, and if he didn't watch it he'd have a record for hitting some dim constable he'd never even set eyes on right on the bonce. It happened all the time. Billy had been in the slammer three times for just that, when he had barely touched the bobby and it had all been entirely provoked.

Unlike John, the women, whose own children ran entirely free (although they never went out of vocal range of dinner) saw nothing worrying in itself about an odd child of eight or so wandering free in the woods. Now, when Hebe turned up again, they barely looked up from their various tasks and occupations. She had been here so often she was familiar enough not to cause a ripple.

This time, though, John wasn't home. He had gone off walking somewhere, and Hebe stood, looking lone and alone, awkward and odd by the steps, watching three children play with an electric toy, not understanding what it was that made them know each other and not her. The children ignored her, having sensed something not right, in the way children do. In the doorway of one of the vans an unwashed but just about discernibly pretty young woman began to sing a folk song to the tune of an old guitar.

> *'The gypsy rover came over the hill, down through the*
> * valley so shady.*
> *He whistled and he sang till the green woods rang,*
> *And he won the heart of a la-dy . . .'*

Another voice interrupted, hoarse from too many cigarettes and too much lager: 'Oh, for Christ's sake, Tracey, shut the fuck up or sing something we all know.'

'It's bloody traditional,' shouted Tracey at the unseen voice, 'so keep your tasteless opinions to yourself, Billy Smith.'

'It's bloody crap. Do your Elton John!'

'Fuck off! If I want to sing folk songs I'll bloody well sing folk songs.' Tracey prepared her chord again – then stopped, her hand poised in midair as another voice cut in.

> *'The gypsy rover came over the hill, down through the*
> * valley so shady.*
> *He whistled and he sang till the green woods rang,*
> *And he won the heart of a la-dy . . .'*

sang Hebe, in a perfect soprano, her tremolo fine and clear and steady, her notes perfectly tuned and true.

'Bloody hell, Billy,' said Tracey in awed tones. 'Would you listen to that?'

Billy Smith emerged from the caravan behind her, wearing a string vest and a pair of jogging trousers. A cigarette hung unlit from his mouth. He stared at Hebe. They all stared at her, and she stared back and closed her mouth. There was no self-consciousness in Hebe, whose lack of appreciation that others had thoughts of their own meant that worrying about what people thought of her was an irrelevance. But she had no more to sing. She had finished.

'Get her to do that again,' said Billy. 'I've never heard anything like that out of a kid.'

Tracey held out a hand to Hebe, but a dog barked. Hebe jumped. She disliked dogs, disliked their unpredictability, hated their sudden noise and movement. She turned and ran off back into the woods.

'You should tell someone about that,' said Billy. 'Could make a bit of money out of that voice, she could.'

'Is that all you ever fucking think about? She's not right in the head, anyone can see that.'

'Well, she could do with the money then, couldn't she?' Billy retreated back into the caravan and Tracey sniffed. By the fire the children continued to play with their Pokémon Gameboy and heat their beans. They weren't interested in singing girls.

William and Matilda Gilfoyle appeared at the edge of the clearing, red-faced and breathing rapidly.

'Excuse me,' they said to the children, ignoring the adults, whom they regarded as a different species to themselves, 'have you seen a little girl with long blonde hair? We lost her a minute ago.'

One of the boys stood, wiped his nose on his hands, his hands on his trouser, walked towards them rather menacingly. 'You're trespassing,' he said.

Matilda drew herself up to full height. 'Oh no I'm not. These are my bloody woods and I'm looking for my cousin. Have you seen her?'

The boy looked taken aback at the response to his attempt to be scary. He tried to look more menacing. 'What's it worth?'

'Me not giving you a black eye,' said Matilda.

The boy looked uncertain, glanced at William, who sported a split lip and a bruise on his right cheek, due to a beetle-trapping incident that had gone wrong high in a tree about half an hour earlier.

'I should listen to her,' he said. 'Look what she did to me.'

The boy shrugged. 'She was here a few minutes ago,' he said. 'She went that way.'

They found Hebe back at Mrs Braithwaite's house, being fed apple cake and elderflower lemonade. Mrs Braithwaite was stroking her arm and Hebe's eyes were half closed in a kind of ecstatic trance. Mrs Braithwaite, though, had a tear on her cheeks.

'What's the matter?' asked Matilda in some alarm, arriving back at a fast trot and utterly relieved to have found Hebe.

'Nothing.' Mrs Braithwaite glared at them both, her eye-brows quivering. 'Why should there be?'

'You looked sad.'

'Woodsmoke,' said Mrs Braithwaite sharply. 'I haven't cried since the war.'

William nudged Matilda. 'Which war?'

Mrs Braithwaite sniffed and muttered under her breath. Matilda thought she heard, 'That bastard Cromwell's,' but she couldn't be sure.

'We lost her,' said William to Mrs Braithwaite. 'She was over by the gypsy site. Those children are really rude.'

'Makes them like most other children then,' said Mrs Braithwaite, producing more cake. 'Here.' She looked at Hebe. 'What did you go to see there?'

Hebe blinked. 'The bear in the cave.'

William rolled his eyes. 'She kept saying there's a bear in a cave. Hebe, there's no such things as bears. I mean, not here. There are bears in Canada, obviously, and India and places like that, but not here. When I go to the jungle to study anacondas and things I might see bears.'

'My bear's got a coloured cave,' said Hebe. 'On wheels, and a pony.'

'Oh,' said Matilda, 'she must mean that caravan. It is sort of like a cave, isn't it, Hebe? Have you seen it, Mrs Braithwaite? It's a proper gypsy van on wheels. I've never seen it here before.'

Mrs Braithwaite shifted tobacco around in her gum. 'No,' she said noncommittally, 'well, I've seen him once in a while.'

'D'you know whose it is, then? Is he a really handsome gypsy? With earrings and everything?'

Mrs Braithwaite spat the tobacco, sending it flying like a bullet into the undergrowth with some force, fascinating William, who found that when he spat it just went on to his chin and made him look as if he couldn't eat properly. 'I know them all,' she said. 'You should watch this child properly. She's not like you.'

'She's special,' said Matilda, 'aren't you, Hebe? She sees angels.'

'She's a changeling,' said Mary Braithwaite, and William thought he saw the tear again. 'I've seen changelings before. I know who she is. It's in the tea leaves.'

'We could have told you who she is,' said Matilda. 'She's our cousin. You can't see that in the tea leaves, can you?'

'You have to know how to look. I've learned how to look in my years here. You don't get to my age without seeing most things in Heaven and Earth.'

'Really? What about the Loch Ness monster? And have you ever seen a spider lay an egg? 'Cos I watched mine for ages and they didn't do a thing.'

'You are such a pillock,' said Matilda to William. 'Mrs Braithwaite, were all boys always pillocks when you were little or is it only William and Oscar?'

Mrs Braithwaite smiled suddenly. 'I think you'll find most things have happened before,' she said. 'Now, I'm off to gather some herbs for Mrs Padley's legs. Feel free to finish your cake.'

They watched her go.

'She talks in riddles,' said William. 'It's like something out of *Harry Potter*.'

'D'you think she really is hundreds of years old?'

'I don't know,' said William. 'Perhaps Hebe thinks Mrs Braithwaite is an angel. Perhaps that's who she really means when she says there's one in the woods. C'mon, Hebe, finish your cake.'

But Matilda was doubtful. 'She can't do. I mean, I'm sure angels can't be all warty like that. Anyway, she's got no wings. What d'you think, Hebe?'

Hebe shrugged. It wasn't the kind of question she could answer, being far too nebulous in structure and definition, so she filled her mouth as full as she could and said nothing at all.

Chapter Six

Kate Coleman stared at her calendar and sighed. Tonight she had a meeting of the Foxbarton Horse Fair committee, and for once, she couldn't face it. Next to her recent afternoons spent reading poetry with and directing longing looks at John James in his rather romantic gypsy caravan (sadly, he had so far failed to notice her increasing longings and ravish her within an inch of her life), a committee meeting looked utterly boring. She felt restless and strange. Not even the thought of Oscar's recent success at grade five violin (neither of Martin's stepchildren could play a note) buoying her up in the usual way. Her life was, she felt, a series of boring meetings upon which she was sailing like an empty ship, single-handed, towards middle age.

Yet how else could she occupy her evenings? Oscar spent most of his worthily occupied in things she had set him to do, and so Kate was generally alone. She was too attractive to be particularly welcome in the dinner party circles of the comfortably married, so she had seen her social life dissolve along with her marriage. Committees were the only place to which the halves of village couples went singly in the evenings.

Kate could never have admitted to anyone that she was lonely, least of all herself. She felt obliged to cope, so that Oscar would never have cause to let slip to Martin he was concerned about her or had seen her cry. That would be the ultimate humiliation. But today, when Martin's awful letter had arrived by way of the afternoon postman, and Kate had no one to tell, for once she felt the full burden of her alone-ness, the full price of her display of strength. So she held herself together for long enough to pick up Oscar from the school bus stop, feed him and deliver him to Haverhill tennis club for an evening tournament, before going home to down the half-bottle of red wine which remained in the fridge from Jonathan Doyle's sexually uneventful visit. Two men, she thought, gulping it defiantly, two men for whom she nurtured desires – and neither of them had even noticed. She was an abandoned woman, of course. Martin hadn't wanted her either. No one wanted her . . .

Thus mildly sloshed and very maudlin Kate went round to see Julia, the only other single woman in the village, feeling that as a likewise abandoned soul, Julia might understand her response to this latest slap in the face.

Julia, sitting in her small kitchen sketching angels and rejecting them one by one on the grounds, mainly, of lack of originality, whilst Hebe lay on the floor with her eyes shut, was surprised to find Kate tottering on the doorstep, clutching a crumpled letter and an empty wine bottle.

'Kate,' she said. 'Come in. I was just persuading Hebe to go to bed. Help yourself to Mrs Braithwaite's lethal brew.'

'I don't know. They do say that's what gave Mrs Padley her leg ulcers.'

'Rubbish. It's what keeps Mrs Padley alive. You can't smoke sixty a day for eighty-five years and grow to be the size of a minke whale without the odd leg ulcer, you know. Come on, drink some. You look stressed.'

'Do I? I'm never stressed,' said Kate, a tear running down her cheek. 'I'm just an empty woman leading an empty life.'

'You're also neither drunk enough nor sober enough for a proper conversation,' said Julia, sighing. 'So sit here and decide which way you want to go.'

So Kate sat at Julia's table and rendered herself not partially but completely inebriate whilst Julia persuaded Hebe to remove her knickers and put on her pyjamas at the same time as continuing to feign death. She called this Hebe's marble statue impression – she could keep herself completely still and lifeless to a degree that had alarmed one visiting education inspector into trying to commence CPR. Whereupon Hebe had screamed, bitten him, and retreated to an outside window ledge whilst Julia had obtained yet another favourable educational report in return for not reporting him for assaulting her daughter.

'So,' said Julia, emerging at last from the ritual, leaving Hebe still and silent beneath her quilt. 'Tell me about it, Kate.'

'About what?' Kate clutched the dandelion wine and tried to look cheerful. 'I've got a committee meeting tonight, you know.'

'I don't think you're going,' said Julia. 'I'll tell them you were sick.'

'I'm not sick,' said Kate.

'You will be,' said Julia, eyeing the bottle. 'What's that in your hand?'

'Bloody b . . . b . . . bastard,' Kate snivelled into the piece of paper in her hand. 'I married a . . . bastard.'

Julia sighed. 'That's why you're free of him now, Kate. What's happened?'

Kate sniffed. 'Martin and his bloody solicitor. Wrote a bloody unreasonable letter. I'm going to be des . . . des . . . destitute.'

Julia sighed. 'Let me see . . .' She took the paper from Kate, glanced over it. Martin's solicitor had advised, it said, that although child-support payments for his son would continue until Oscar was eighteen, the amount of ex-wife maintenance Kate would receive was to be reduced from the end of next month. Reduced substantially, rounded down, down to a very round number indeed, a very big zero. Martin's lawyer, read Julia, did not believe he should be maintaining Kate in the style she seemed to expect. She was clearly capable of work and ought to get off her fat arse and do some. Either that or find herself some other poor sod to sponge off. The letter claimed to be hers, sincerely, Martin Coleman.'

Julia sighed. 'Is this really a surprise, Kate? I mean, did you think he'd support you for ever?'

'Never said he wouldn't,' said Kate, and hiccupped, 'when he ran off with a trollop . . . in an M and S B cup. I was always a R . . . R . . . Rigby and Peller woman,' she snivelled miserably into her glass, '36D.'

'I expect he thought you'd remarry,' said Julia mildly, 'so he wouldn't have to keep paying you.'

'It's vindictive, that's what it is,' said Kate, the snivelling shifting into anger. 'He's been vindictive ever since we split up, you know, all because I told him his was the smallest penis I'd ever seen.'

'Oh dear. Was it?' Julia tried not to smile.

'Absolutely,' Kate sniffed. 'I'd never seen any others.'

'Oh, Kate, is Martin the only man you ever slept with?'

'No, of course not. I just never liked to look when I was younger. Then when I saw his it was such a disappointment – you know, compared to statues and things.'

Julia shrugged. 'Most statues are by Italians of Italians – what do you expect?'

'I know that now, but there hasn't been anyone since Martin.'

'Oh dear. Every woman needs the occasional wild fling. It doesn't matter who, just find someone and use them mercilessly.' Listen to me, she thought. Doctor Ruth. Maybe I should practise what I preach.

'It's easy for you to say,' said Kate, 'I mean, no one seems to notice me, not in that sense.'

'You have to be obvious,' said Julia. 'Men are very dense. Be forward. Make yourself crystal clear.' She wondered who Kate had her eye on. 'Tell them you need a fling and they're it.'

'I couldn't.' Kate was pink. 'Not like that.'

'Yes you could. You've nothing to lose but your inhibitions.'

Kate giggled. 'You're right, of course. Sometimes I think I could ravish the milkman.'

'You'd give him a heart attack,' said Julia, rather liking the human side of Kate, whom she had always thought rather prim, 'he's seventy-two.'

'I know. Have you got anything else to drink? Something really alcoholic, please.' Kate hiccuped and belched. 'Oops.'

Silently Julia opened her fridge and extracted a bottle of elderflower cordial, entirely alcohol-free, and tipped a measure of it into a tiny glass. 'Here,' she said, 'watch this, it's lethal.' I can't be responsible for her hangover, she thought.

'I know why he's doing this,' said Kate, downing her measure on one shot and pouring another. 'That pasty-faced wife of his has always been jealous of Oscar – he's junior chess champion, you know. They know Oscar's success depends on my being here for him. They're trying to punish him for being gifted.'

'Come on, Kate, you can't really believe that. Anyway, I don't know how you can stand to depend on him still, feeling as you do. Perhaps you should find yourself a job.'

Kate sighed. 'That's easy for you to say, you create things. But what can a woman like me do in a rural backwater about as throbbing with the hum of industry as the south face of Everest?'

Julia shrugged. 'Well, what are you good at?'

Kate frowned and thought hard, through a mind blurred by the alcohol. She was a gifted woman, a nurturer – yet her CV was empty of all but Martin. She had sacrificed herself to nurture Martin to success – and as a result had not had chance to demonstrate her talents in the world of employment. Who would want to employ her without a CV?

If only she were like Julia, a woman of reputation and skill. If only she had been to art college, won prizes, been commissioned to design potentially the most famous statue of the year, the new Foxbarton angel! Julia was such a fool. She had no idea how to market herself. She wandered around in her old trousers and tatty shirts, making things out of twigs with her big rough hands, that glorious (and obviously naturally blonde) hair totally wasted in a dangling rat's-tail down her back. Julia should look at her image, that's what. If Kate were Julia she would not waste such opportunity.

And then a revelation struck Kate, with the enormity of Handel's vision of the company of Heaven when he sat down to write something to link parts two and three of his sacred oratorio *Messiah*, and ended up writing the 'Hallelujah Chorus' in three hours flat. Kate could nurture. Julia needed someone to nurture her. There was a job that needed doing and she was perfect for it. Perfect.

'I've got it!' she said to Julia. 'I know exactly what I can do. It's a marvellous idea. I couldn't have planned it better. It's brilliant. I could work from home. Keep things local, a base in the village, contacts with galleries everywhere . . . There'll be the international travel, of course, in the end, but we could work round that. I mean, it's not as if we're going to be unimportant; we couldn't be pushed around by galleries. Oh no, this is going to be big. Julia, this is really great! You won't be sorry, I promise . . .'

Julia observed her in rising alarm, wondering if perhaps there was something more powerful than elderflower in the cordial. I wouldn't put it past Mary Braithwaite, she thought, to try and give me a high. 'Kate, what on earth are you talking about?'

But Kate's eyes were sparkling, her mind suddenly unfolding with the clarity characteristic of the fairly drunk. 'It's obvious, Julia. I'm going to relaunch you as . . . ash an . . . an artisht. I'll be your m . . . manager. We're gonna haff . . . ann . . . an . . . nnn expedishion!'

*

126

In the end Julia had to call Jonathan Doyle to help her get Kate home. There seemed no one else to ask for help, as Simon and Merrill were out, and to ask anyone else in the village would be too mortifying to poor Kate once she was sober. She could have left her on the kitchen table to sleep it off, but it didn't seem quite right to have Oscar arrive home from his tennis tournament without a mother to greet him – even one who was so inebriate as to be less useful than a jar of fish paste. So Jonathan turned up in his old Volvo and carried Kate off, leaving Julia to hope that by morning her plans would be forgotten in the inevitable surge of embarrassment.

Jonathan was a little excited at being summoned to Julia's house in the evening with a peremptory 'I need you.' It meant he had entered the exclusive circle of those whom Julia trusted well enough to telephone without apology and to demand without explanation, which must mean he was well on the first step to friendship. He was, therefore, mildly disappointed to discover that he was expected not to hear Julia's worries or concerns but to escort Kate home, a now dozing Kate who giggled with the infectious laughter of the very drunk when he lifted her into his arms and then belched quietly once and apologised loudly about twenty times.

Nevertheless, a vicar's lot is to offer himself in any guise possible for the salvation of the eternal souls of his parish, and if the way to Julia's eternal soul involved carting a drunk Kate home – well, he was prepared to give it a go.

He was rather less well prepared for the rather stirring pass Kate made at him when he deposited her onto her sofa (having decided the stairs looked too risky) some twenty minutes later. Her arms were already around his neck and as he leaned over to put her down he found her lips planted firmly upon his, a warm and determined tongue clear evidence that this was more than a polite thank you from a grateful parishioner.

Hastily he pulled back and said his goodbyes, hoping against hope that if Kate retained any memory at all of the event she would think it had been a dream of the most embarrassing kind, never to be mentioned again. What a shame she had been drunk, thought his heretical mind. Would he have been so quick to leave had she been sober? Of course he would – his reaction would have been entirely the same. After all, no vicar can take advantage of a parishioner, drunk or not. Kate would be horrified if she remembered what she had done. She was not the sort of woman to seduce or be seduced. She was a good woman, with Christian values and Christian morals. His kind of morals . . .

He left the house hastily, almost guiltily, passing Oscar, dropped off from tennis by another tennis mother, on the front path. Thank goodness he hadn't arrived a few minutes earlier.

Would Jonathan have been so quick to leave if those had been Julia Fitzgerald's lips? She, who was definitely not a parishioner, nor a Christian, and surely not off limits in the vicar-parishioner sense. The last time he had asked her about religion she had told him she did her own thing and she did not wish to participate in anyone else's. She was as wild and exciting a prospect as he could imagine, with her beautiful feet and that absolute sense of sensuality . . .

No, he was a vicar. He had no business fantasising about wild and wonderful women. And he had no business kissing Kate either. Still, if you ignored the embarrassment and inappropriateness of the situation it had been rather a nice kiss. Almost arousing, if he had been the kind of person to be aroused by a totally inappropriate kiss.

Julia sat in her kitchen after they had gone, eating a huge pile of cheese and crackers, thanking heaven her weight had never been an issue because she was going to finish this entire piece of Cheddar before bedtime, and staring crossly at Kate's empty glass. There was, she found, great solace in cheese at moments of irrational agitation.

And she was being irrational now. She was unreasonably angry with Kate, partly for being such a winge about her stupid ex-husband, who clearly hadn't been worth tuppence, and partly for thinking that she, Julia, would fall in with such a ridiculous plan. Kate, she felt, had done all her living through first her husband and then her son. Now, Julia thought, she's trying to do it through me. You can't live your whole life through someone else. You have to get on, let go of the past, do something new, start again, accept your world has changed.

Is that my problem too? she thought. Is that why I can't create anything any more – because my world changed and I'm a mother now? Can I just not accept that those wild nights – that particular wild night – are left behind, are gone for ever, are many years in the past?

Uneasily she got up and wandered into the bathroom, where she inspected herself in the mirror. Definitely not past it. Can't see the feet – best feature – but good breasts. She cupped them experimentally. Weighed at least as much as a bag of sugar. Each. Tall, big-boned, long blonde hair – I ought to cut it, really. I look as though I don't want to disturb nesting birds in that bit – green eyes. I suppose I look like Hebe – or she looks like me . . . I haven't changed much, not for years. If Hebe's father saw me now he'd probably think I hadn't changed a bit. Rotten bugger. Croissants, indeed. He probably woke up horrified, once he was sober and couldn't wait to escape.

I shouldn't have cared. After all, he might have been the inspiration for my best ever piece of work, but that didn't mean the loss of inspiration was anything to do with the loss of him. Because that would be both ridiculous and insoluble. Most of the time I was happy when they did a runner. I hated it when someone got heavy. I suppose *he* came along just at that point when I was starting to change, starting to want it to mean a bit more.

No, it wasn't him that made it important, it was me. And that would have been all there was to it, if it weren't for Hebe. Because I would just have slept with a whole series of other men, getting slightly more serious with some of them, until I found the right one. Instead of which, I've put myself on hold. No sex and no moving on. My life and my career put on hold with Hebe as the excuse. Just like Kate with Oscar.

So I need to take myself in hand. I could start by putting some inspiration into the willow. Perhaps William had a point about making an elephant. Why shouldn't I make a willow elephant? Why not use willow as art? I mean, clay isn't the only medium. There's more to life than trying to do something that you've done before. And if Kate wants to try and organise me – maybe I should let her.

Julia sighed and put her chin in her hands, feeling the shawl of her hair run rather silkily over her shoulders. What a waste of long hair, she thought, not to be able to dangle it on to someone's warm naked flesh. What is the point of hair, otherwise?

There I go again. Thinking about sex. It's the wrong time of the month now, she thought, and I could still eat Jonathan Doyle alive and spit out nothing but the hymn book. So much for theories about day fourteen – it's always day bloody fourteen in this house. It's like groundhog day: I just keep having it again and again. Definitely time for bed. Maybe I'll wake up sober – except, unfortunately, I'm not drunk.

Joshua Gilfoyle lay in his hospital bed the following morning and glared at the physiotherapist and the occupational therapist. A pair of bloody women in white tunics – he didn't have to put up with their stuff and nonsense.

'Bugger off,' he said experimentally, but it came as 'Baaaa

. . . gffff.' He screwed up his mouth at them – not difficult, in the circumstances, since it wasn't straight anyway.

I haven't lost my faculties, you silly cows. 'Fffnt . . . lshtt . . . mmy . . . fac . . . lll . . . tshh.'

It was their bloody fault they couldn't understand him. He was speaking perfect English. No education, young women these days. Whatever happened to grammar and syntax, Shakespeare and Chaucer? Probably brought up on *Blue* bloody *Peter* . . .

Joshua's thoughts ran on with relentless clarity and with a rapidity of which he had not been conscious when he could speak, perhaps because his voice had always before been able to keep up with them. He beat frustratedly on the inside of his skull with his disconnected brain and tried to will the wiring between his thoughts and his speech to reconnect instantly. It just wasn't good enough. What was the point of having a brain if it couldn't work properly? What was the point of his still having his intellect without the power to communicate? It made him no better than that child. Which child . . . the one he knew now, or the other one, long ago? They were merging into one in his dreams, both golden-haired, both beautiful . . .

'Come on, Joshua. They want to see if they can get you on your two feet.' That was Sonja. *She probably hopes I'll fall over and finish the job properly this time.*

The physiotherapist smiled at Sonja. 'Is your father always this grumpy, then, love?'

Sonja suppressed a glare. *Joshua must be hating this.* 'He is not my father, he is my husband.'

'Oh. Sorry.' The physio was slightly surprised. Nothing odd about rich old men with replacement model wives, of course, but you somehow didn't expect it with the ones who were crumbling like this one. Prostate cancer and a stroke. It was pretty bad luck, really, but then, perhaps she'd hoped he wouldn't last long. Maybe that's when the real ice-maidens gather. Ready for the reading of the will. She eyed

Sonja with new dislike. 'It might be best if you waited outside.'

'I think not,' said Sonja, with the immunity of years. 'Joshua, you stop pissing about now and stand up. In Norway we would say if you stay on your behind too long you freeze to the floor.'

Joshua sighed. At least he could do that – he had discovered a new expression in sighing. Sonja's increasing bossiness interested him with objective fascination, as if he was watching what was happening to himself from some place up on the ceiling. She had never bossed him this much when he was alive – properly alive, that is. With a shock Joshua realised he had thought of himself as dead.

Sonja and the physiotherapist were at his arms and, unwillingly, he allowed them to pull him upright, only to discover a marked list to the right as soon as their grip slackened He tried to straighten up but the right side still wasn't doing what he was telling it to do. What the hell was the good of standing if you looked like a cripple? He indicated furiously that he wanted the laptop, on which he had taken to typing thoughts and instructions with his left hand.

Sonja and the physiotherapist exchanged glances, the physiotherapist now slightly mollified by the sense of genuine concern on the younger woman's part.

'Very well, Joshua, we sit you back down and you type, but you know if you walk they let you go home.'

'Bugger off,' typed Joshua, 'and take the battle-axe with you.'

Sonja looked at the physiotherapist. 'Sorry,' she said.

'Home,' typed Joshua, 'now.' His relative clumsiness in typing with his left hand annoyed him and he jabbed at the keys.

The physiotherapist smiled at Sonja, thinking, *well, she's got her work cut out, cantankerous old sod. Thank goodness the very worst people go private. At least I'm on twenty quid an hour*

. . . 'That's all right. Perhaps he really would be better at home, you know. We can visit you every day. When it's private there's really no limit . . .'

Sonja smiled a little shakily. Money had not always been no object, and sometimes she still resented the privileges it brought, remembering her parents and how they had struggled when her father became ill, refusing the help of the state and thus finally losing the dignity they thought they were preserving. 'You may be right,' she said. 'I discuss it with Simon, his son.' She eyed the physio darkly, still resenting her earlier unspoken but nevertheless obvious thoughts. 'My stepson. He is a GP, you see. He can advise.'

'Well, of course he must come home if that's what he wants,' said Merrill resignedly, fighting the sinking sense of dread that told her that Sonja would not miss a single one of the nail, hair, skin, body and Other Personal Development appointments that so thoroughly occupied her day to the exclusion of any useful work or companionship, and that she, Merrill, would end up waiting on the old bastard hand and foot. 'He's your father and this is still his house.' She and Simon were alone in the kitchen, Simon having just returned from the hospital with Sonja.

'He's being very stubborn,' said Simon. 'He won't even try to walk, can't bear the indignity of having to lean and shuffle. The therapists think he's got more function than he shows, but his pride is getting in the way. He hates being publicly helpless. I'm hoping in the privacy of his own home he might improve. We can employ a nurse.'

Merrill felt a surge of relief that she would not be expected to attend to Joshua's bowels or feed him scrambled egg off a spoon. Even when she *was* a nurse she had always found the elderly infirm rather depressing in their acquired and hopeless helplessness. 'D'you know anyone?'

'I'll sort someone out.'

'Thank goodness for that. I can't see Sonja sick nursing. She might break a nail.'

But Sonja, presented with the opportunity for twenty-four-hour-a-day private nursing care, folded her arms and stubbornly refused it.

'I manage,' she said. 'You all think I am a bimbo – well, we shall see what the Norwegian bimbo is made of.'

An hour later she had made a list of all Joshua's requirements so complete that even Simon could not fault it, booked a night-sitting nurse, ordered a pressure mattress from a company in Derby and organised Joshua's transport home. Simon, watching her slightly covetously as she employed her carefully over-correct English to get her own way every time, was for the first time seriously impressed with his father's judgement in marrying her, rather than simply at his potency.

'I don't know how the hell she thinks she's going to manage,' Merrill grumbled to Julia later as she watched her expertly twisting willow into a series of animals of her own design (for they certainly hadn't figured in God's). 'She's no idea what she's taking on.'

Julia shrugged, feeling that Sonja was proving rather more of her worth than any of them had expected. 'Perhaps she has. I mean, you don't know much about her.'

Merrill was startled. 'What do you mean?'

'Well, I don't know. She comes from somewhere, doesn't she? She's got a past, she's someone's daughter. She might have nursed someone before.'

Merrill frowned, not liking the feeling that Julia might take Sonja's side – wasn't it enough that Simon lusted after her? 'I doubt it, not with those nails. Anyway, what on earth's that?'

'It's an emu,' said Julia blandly. 'I'm doing a series of zoo animals. William inspired me.'

Merrill raised her eyebrows. 'Now that I can believe,

given that it's weird and it looks like nothing on earth. So – I hardly dare ask – what's that?'

'A llama,' said Julia, 'obviously.'

'Even to me,' said Merrill, 'it looks like a brontosaurus, and I own a llama.'

'It's figurative,' said Julia crossly. 'I'm trying to be original. Look, that's a giraffe, and that little one over there is an antelope.'

Merrill looked at it sideways. 'I see what you mean. What about the angel?'

'Don't talk to me about the angel,' said Julia. 'I still don't know where to start. Perhaps angels really are only for Christians and children anyway.'

'Perhaps Hebe sees the same one you saw. She got it from you – you know, when you stopped believing in it.'

'Sounds to me as if you've been reading *Peter Pan*. Or are you trying to tell me the knowledge of angels is imprinted in my genes?'

'Could be. Like fear of snakes, you know, people say it's a genetic memory.'

Julia sniffed. 'That's rubbish. Fear of snakes is taught by stupid parents. Hebe's not afraid of snakes.'

'Hebe's not afraid of anything.'

'Dogs,' said Julia, 'and policemen, actually, but you're basically right.'

'I'm always – Wow, look at him. You don't see men like that in Foxbarton every week. Is he coming here?'

Julia looked up and squealed. It was so sudden and sharp a squeal that for a brief second Merrill's heart jumped into her mouth, expecting to see Hebe falling from a window or lying under a car – but then she realised Julia had squealed in delight and was running towards the approaching stranger shouting, 'Daniel! My God, after all this time! I can't believe it! How *are* you? How have you *been*?'

And Merrill watched bemused as a creature who looked like an African Brad Pitt with dreadlocks wrapped her sister

135

in a bear hug and squeezed her bottom with the kind of familiarity usually found only in those who have seen one another naked on more than one occasion.

Merrill watched them covetously, unwilling to acknowledge that beneath the sympathetic motherly concern she felt towards her sister she slightly envied her the freedom to have her bottom felt by a handsome stranger.

And then after a moment the balloon burst. 'Merrill, this is Daniel, remember, my old friend from art college who's now something in the media. Daniel, it must be over a year since I've set eyes on you. The media have whisked you away to the high life and you've forgotten your lowly origins in my flat in Shepherd's Bush.'

'Jules, Jules, how could I ever forget those nights in Shepherd's Bush. The all-pervading smell of turps and burned toast. The endless parade of used and discarded men . . .'

'And that was just your discarded men. Mine left quietly.'

Merrill sighed internally. Of course, *that* Daniel. How could she have forgotten those dreadlocks? And of course he was gay. All Julia's best friends from college were gay. What was it about artists? 'What brings you here, Daniel?'

He beamed. 'I've been meaning to come and look you up for ages – got your change-of-address card, then some extended leave came up and I just drove down. What a fantastic place you've found! It's like something out of *The Wind in the Willows*.'

'Too right,' said Julia, 'we've even got a toad in the Hall. After a fashion, anyway.' She felt suddenly guilty, being mean about Joshua now that he had had a stroke. 'Oh, but will you stay for a few days? Hebe will be so pleased to see you.'

'Darling,' said Daniel, 'I thought you'd never ask. And how is Hebe?'

'Fine, better for being here. She's asleep at the moment, actually – she doesn't sleep well at night. Counts stars until the early hours sometimes, then sleeps half the day. Come in and have some tea. Merrill, d'you want some?'

Merrill shook her head. 'I must go, Jules. Daniel, it's very nice to see you again.'

Daniel and Julia watched her go.

'Nice arse,' said Daniel, beaming his amazingly white-toothed beam as he watched her go.

'Careful,' said Julia, digging him in the ribs, 'that's my sister, and you chose your gender-preference years ago; you can't change your mind now.'

'You always were a killjoy. You know I've only ever been seriously tempted by Anthea Turner, and that was in her *Blue Peter* days. Come on, then, where's that not-a-proper-goddaughter of mine? It's been over a year too long.'

Chapter Seven

The arrival of Daniel Cutter caused something of a ripple in the normally calm waters of village life. Foxbarton was not, the older residents remarked to one another, the kind of place where you expected to see homosexual black men with earrings. Julia, overhearing one such comment in the post office, commented that you'd be lucky to find a homosexual black man *without* earrings – and then immediately regretted being the cause of the embarrassed and uncomfortable silence that followed. Still, she was glad he was visiting, especially as it was clear that he was on some sort of stress break, that his career was not going well.

'It's dog eat dog in the music industry,' he told her one lunchtime, sighing into his salad. 'I sometimes think I made all the wrong choices. I should have stuck with my art, like you.'

Julia shrugged. 'It's not done me a lot of good, Dan. I mean, apart from Hebe I've nothing at the moment but an out-of-date reputation.'

'You'll get it back Jules. You just need a bloke. You only ever worked well when you were getting it.'

'Getting what?'

'Oh, you know. Don't be coy. We used to joke that we could always tell when you'd used some handsome thing until he was a limp rag. You used to wake up, leave him collapsed under the duvet, and sculpt some amazing creation whilst the poor bloke skulked off unnoticed. I was jealous as hell.'

Julia glared at him. 'You're exaggerating.'

'I am not. Some of them never even got a cup of coffee. You were legendary. That day you made *Being*, you started when the sun rose and I swear you didn't stop till you'd finished. It must have been days. You were just inspired.'

She sighed wistfully. 'I was, wasn't I? It seems a long time ago.'

'It wasn't so long. Time is only as long as the pieces you count it by.'

'What's that supposed to mean?'

'I dunno. It was a line in the last song I promoted.'

'I've never heard it.'

'You wouldn't have. It bombed, like everything else I've done recently.'

She squeezed his hand. 'Well, you're having a rest now. Coffee?'

'Coffee.'

It was not long before Kate discovered that Daniel, whilst disappointingly disinterested in ravishing her on the kitchen table, was far more polite than Julia, and easily co-opted on to the committee for approval of the new angel. This latter group was one whose existence Julia had suspected for some time, a small gaggle of villagers who were keeping an eye on what she was doing lest she produce an unacceptable angel for the plinth in the church. Almost every day someone walked past and asked her how the angel was going. Sometimes it would be Mrs Padley or Mrs Barker, at other times Fiona, the pub landlady's daughter, or one of the series of stockbrokers' and bankers' wives who lived in the smarter of the cottages and sang in church on Sundays. The regularity of the enquiries and the fact that it was always one of the church choir or their families who made them had convinced Julia that the information thus gleaned was being shared, that the minute the angel started to look in any way unacceptable – developed horns and a trident, maybe – petitions would be signed and delegations would be waiting at her door. It would perhaps be amusing if she actually had an angel to show them. As it was, it just added to the frustrating feeling that something ought to be happening on the angel front, and wasn't.

A few days after Daniel arrived Julia was working on her willow zoo in the garden whilst he juggled endlessly for Hebe, who screamed whenever he tried to stop. It was a glorious summer's day, even though it was still early June, one of those magical blue-skied days which everyone remembers as plentiful in their childhood but which mysteriously fail to materialise ever again for the rest of their lives. There was loud Puccini coming from Julia's kitchen window to inspire her and the smell of cut grass perfumed the air. (Stewart Barlow had been by on his tractor mower that very morning and had seen, instead of a naked Julia Fitzgerald cavorting on the lawn, a naked Daniel nitrogenating it with the contents of his bladder. This had deeply upset Stewart, who felt that seeing a naked gay man in some way compromised his own sexuality and as a result the lawn was only half-mowed.)

Julia was at least enjoying the rush of progress resulting from having at last started something new and original when Kate appeared again to see if she could view progress on the commissioned angel. This time she was more direct than the usual 'How's it coming on?' questions, which were easily brushed aside.

'I just wondered about the angel, Julia. I mean, when can we expect to see some preliminary models?'

'You won't,' said Julia, carefully wrapping willow around something which was meant to be a rhinoceros. 'I don't do preliminary models, Kate. When I start modelling something I just get on with it.'

'Goodness,' said Kate, 'isn't that a little risky? I mean, it could be very expensive if it went wrong.'

'It's only clay,' said Julia, appalled at her ignorance. 'I make the statue out of clay and then it's cast and made into a bronze afterwards.' Why *should* I make it out of clay? she thought suddenly. I don't have to make it out of clay . . .

'Oh, I see . . . . So do we get to see the clay model before you cast it?'

'No,' said Julia, 'absolutely not. You might hate it.'

Kate looked alarmed and glanced uncertainly at Daniel, who was contriving to keep three balls and an orange in the air between his hands. He smiled.

'Don't worry, Katie, there's nothing obscene in Julia's potting shed, I promise you,' and Kate sighed and said she was relieved to hear it, and that she didn't have all day to stand around as she really must get on and walk the dog.

'You've been talking to her, haven't you?' said Julia crossly, after Kate had gone on her way with her enormous dog attached to her arm, looking quite unusually eager to reach the river. 'She's got you spying on me.'

'Darling Jules, I promised her I'd be her inside man,' said Daniel cheerily.

'Why?'

'Because I thought it wouldn't do any harm. And Kate likes me – someone from the media to brighten her sexually empty days. Having said that, there's a glow to her cheeks today, did you notice?'

'She's gone to see the bear,' said Hebe suddenly, and Daniel smiled.

'There's no bear in the woods, Hebe, I've told you.'

'Hairy bear,' said Hebe. 'In a red and yellow cave. Eats Auntie Kate for breakfast.'

Daniel and Julia exchanged glances. 'Hebe,' said Julia, 'who have you been spying on?'

But Hebe, as so often when pinned down, broke into song and turned her back on them. Today she was singing something Welsh which she had heard at her singing lesson from a CD which Mrs Peel, her singing teacher, had played her. Mrs Peel was, in fact, quite bemused by Hebe's singing ability. Her memory was unshakeable and even language seemed to pose no barrier. Often she could not translate what she was singing, yet she could reproduce it after hearing it only once, and she sang with a degree of expression which seemed extraordinary in a child whose control of her own basic emotions was so lacking. She had had only three lessons so far, but already, Mrs Peel had told Julia, there was evidence of something extraordinary. This was no news to Julia, who watched her daughter's fascination with her own voice in some alarm. But what could she do? Hebe was determined to sing, seemed to use it to calm herself and her world. And, after all, who could honestly say for sure whether her gift would be her nemesis or her salvation?

'Cup of tea?' asked Daniel.

'Yes, please.'

'It was a request, actually. I'm busy juggling.'

'And I'm busy making a willow thing.'

'I can see that,' said Daniel, 'which is why I suggested you made tea. It would be more useful than your willow thing by . . . well, by a whole cup of tea and a giant shapeless creature of unknown provenance.'

'Oh thanks,' said Julia, picking up the rhinoceros and hurling it as far as she could, which wasn't far. It rolled towards Hebe, picking up grass cuttings as it went, then fell head first into a dip in the lawn. Hebe looked at it.

'Angel,' she said.

Julia stared.

'I suppose it is rather angelic,' said Daniel. 'I mean, if you think angels look like Ford Granadas.'

But Julia had her eyes narrowed. 'No, she's right. I mean, why does it have to be a clay angel?'

Daniel looked quizzical. 'Well, you are an artist, dear. It's your privilege.'

'Hebe drew this angel in a tree,' she said. 'And the whole thing – I mean taken as a whole – did look a little like my rhino.'

'Rhino, is it, then?' Daniel eyed the willow. 'It's a bit small for a rhino.'

'Size isn't everything.'

'I don't know who you've been listening to, darling, but he clearly had his own reasons for lying. Believe me, bigger is always better.'

Julia stared. 'Bigger. You're right!' Her face lit up and she started to hop from one foot to another.

Daniel pulled a pouty face. 'I don't see it as that much of a revelation.'

'I'm not talking about penises, you pervert, I mean the angel. I mean, why should it be small? Why should it be small and why should it be made in clay?'

'Morning, Julia,' said Jonathan Doyle over the wall, and Julia found herself blushing, as if being caught saying penis was somehow unacceptable in front of the vicar, even though one would assume his anatomy was no different from any other man's.

'Hello, Jonathan. We were just – Would you like a cup of tea?'

'No, thanks, don't want to interrupt,' said Jonathan with slightly false cheer, since he had been listening slightly jealously to the familiar banter between Julia and Daniel. 'I've just been with Joshua. I think he's feeling in need of your angel, actually.'

'From what I hear he needs a kick up the backside,' said Daniel, who had been talking to Sonja about it. Sonja, who had been less than welcome in Joshua's family and in Joshua's village, had struck up a swift and interesting friendship with Daniel, discovering that the two obvious outsiders had more in common than was initially obvious.

Jonathan sighed. 'Is the angel making any progress?'

'Not yet,' said Julia. 'But I've done a good rhino . . .'

In the kitchen the Puccini CD finished and silence floated from the window. Hebe jumped to her feet, her hands

flapping strangely at her sides, 'Mum Mum Mum Mum . . .
listen Mum listen Mum listen . . .'

'What, darling?'

And Hebe sang, perfect Puccini, fresh from the CD, her
voice as a bird's, as effortless as a lark, as clear as the chimes
in Kate's garden . . .

> *'O mio babbino caro, mi piace è bello, bello;*
> *Vo'andare in Porta Rossa a comperar l'anello!*
> *Sì, sì, ci voglio andare e se l'amassi indarno,*
> *Andrei sul Ponte Vecchio, ma per buttarmi in Arno*
> *Mi struggo e mi tormento! O Dio, vorrei morir*
> *Babbo, pietà, pietà . . . . Babbo, pietà, pietà.'*

Once she had finished she beamed briefly at them as they
stood with their jaws slack and expressions of stupefaction
on their faces, then picked up Daniel's three juggling balls,
balanced herself as if to juggle them as perfectly as she had
sung, flung them wildly in three different directions and ran
into the house howling.

Daniel stared after her. His mind was whirling. He had
just seen something amazing. He had just seen something
that had immense value in his other life, the life he had been
at the point of abandoning owing to the slumping of his
reputation, his failure to really make it work. 'God in
heaven, the child is a genius. You could put your daughter
on the stage, Mrs Robinson,' he said in awed tones. 'You
know, if you wanted me to talk to one or two people . . . I
mean, that was . . . was . . . Jules, did you know she could do
that?' It's like listening to an angel, he thought. My God,
what an extraordinary thing. The child is a phenomenon.
The child is a winner. The child is one in a million. The deal
has to be mine . . . I could be made. The one-deal millionaire.
We all dream of it – who would have thought I'd find it on
my escape to the countryside.

Julia swallowed. 'No – no, I definitely don't want you to

talk to anyone,' she said, suddenly feeling a profound sense of threat. It was not the first time Hebe had sung something in another language; it was not the first time it had been perfect – but it was the first time she had seen so clearly demonstrated that Hebe had to hear it once – *once* – and could reproduce it so beautifully. And yet she must have no idea what she was singing. God, thought Julia, *I've* no idea what she was singing. Swallowing hard she went inside to make camomile tea to calm the sudden sense of dread that had enveloped her.

About half a mile away and deep in the woods Kate would not have heard Puccini if Pavarotti himself were singing in her ear. Such things had paled to insignificance since she had discovered the delights of being ravished by a poet in a caravan. It bothered Kate not at all that she had thrown herself at John James – Julia had been right, John had needed her to be obvious. If she hadn't he'd still be sitting on his blooming sofa reading her poems – but she had explained in graphic terms that she needed an outlet for her sexuality, and handsome gypsy lovers did not come her way often. So he had smiled and obligingly seduced her. Several times.

Kate felt wonderful for it. She had not realised how sexually unfulfilled she had been until now – including during the years with Martin. Besides, there was something rather pleasing about becoming a kind of Bohemian by absorption when she was so near to her fortieth birthday. Well, she was thirty-five, but recently that had seemed extremely near to her fortieth birthday. She had even been to see the lady GP who worked with Simon to ask if there was any risk of things seizing up with underuse. The doctor had recognised this poorly couched request for permission to use a vibrator and had said yes, bodily things can indeed seize if not regularly exercised, but Kate had still been far too inhibited to buy one (what if it affected the TV reception?) so nothing had changed.

Now, though, enjoying active intercourse of the biblical kind in a gypsy caravan with John James, a man about whom she knew little and wished to know nothing more lest it spoil the sheer outside-normal-life quality of the whole experience, Kate was able to let go of all her inhibitions. Indeed, so effectively did she do so that as the little caravan rocked slightly she uttered a loud whooping noise. Billy and Tracey outside grinned at one another, and remarked that the swans were obviously nesting early this year. Beside the caravan, Gwen the dog sat mournfully contemplating the ground and reflected doggily that she seemed to have sat in the same place several times recently, and despite the wealth of animal and people smells which had excited her here the first time, this same patch of earth was beginning to pall a little.

Afterwards Kate lay beside John as he smoked a cigarette and stared into infinity. She remembered Martin's mean letter, and felt, somehow, that she was even at last. She could have a wild passionate fling with a gypsy poet. The best he could do was his secretary.

'Do you think my bottom is too fat?' she asked John.

He smiled. 'No, Kate. You have a beautiful bottom.'

'I don't.'

'How would you know?'

'You're right. One of the mercies of womanhood is that we rarely get to see our own buttocks.' Kate stood and craned her neck, trying to see hers. She could catch a glimpse of the edge of it – a soft, pale buttock, falling over the edge of the gluteal muscle and disappearing into the shadows of the top of her thigh, rather like dough that has been left to prove and has slipped off the side of the plate to hang helplessly over the void. You certainly wouldn't use it to advertise knickers. She turned and swivelled, trying to get a better view of the other one but her neck was not as flexible as it used to be and it clicked, reminding her that she had once had a whiplash injury when Martin slammed the brakes on during a row about his driving.

John smiled. 'Vanity, thy name is Woman,' he said, and rolled onto his back, staring at the ceiling. For a while there was silence.

'What are you thinking?' Kate dared eventually, praying it would not be something terribly banal. If he said anything at all about football she would leave right now and never come back.

'I was just wondering,' he said after a brief pause to exhale a remarkably complete smoke ring, 'whether a touch of madness is essential to genius.'

Kate helped herself to a puff of the cigarette. It wasn't a real puff – she didn't smoke, had never smoked in her whole life – but right now she needed to feel as if she smoked, particularly as she believed this to be marijuana (she was in this, as in many of her assumptions regarding John, quite wrong). John smiled. She knew he was well aware of the fraud, but it didn't matter. This whole thing was fraudulent. It was fun – and for Kate, who had suddenly realised that she had never actually had any fun at all, it was a revelation of the potential that life held.

'Are you a genius, then?' she asked him.

He sighed. 'I don't know. Usually they decide after you're dead.'

Kate puffed very carefully, attempting to blow some smoke out without taking any in before handing back the cigarette. 'Are you published much?'

'I'm quite well known as a poet,' he said lightly, 'but poets are rarely much known.'

'You could be,' said Kate, 'you're brilliant.'

'I'm content enough as I am. I don't need much, Kate. I could live right here in these woods, catch my supper and write my poems and it would be enough.'

'You wouldn't catch much here now,' said Kate. 'The

foxes eat all the rabbits. That lot out there get groceries delivered on-line. I know because I passed the man from Tesco trying to work out how to find them.'

John shrugged. 'I catch fish, and of course there's always hedgehog. D'you know, if you roast them the spikes just drop off?'

'You wouldn't!'

'What d'you think those kebabs are?' he asked, indicating the remains of his lunch over on the cupboard, and Kate wrinkled her nose.

'I don't know how you could eat hedgehog. Is it legal? What's it taste like?'

'I've no idea. That's frozen pork from Sainsbury's.'

'But you said . . .'

'I didn't, it's what you heard. Anyway, you never answered my question about genius.'

Kate was gratified that her opinion seemed to count enough to be checked back into. 'It depends what you mean by genius,' she said now. 'My son is very talented. Very. But he has to work at it, and I suppose I always imagined that a genius doesn't. If that's true then there has to be something strange about them, doesn't there?'

He shrugged. 'Do you know that child in the village, the rather strange child with the extraordinary voice who plays in the woods?'

'That's Hebe. She's sort of related to the Gilfoyles.'

'Really? How's that?'

'Oh, not a blood relative. Her mother is some sort of sister-in-law.' Kate knew perfectly well what Julia's relationship was to Merrill, but instinct told her not to discuss another young and beautiful woman with this man. 'She's very odd – but I don't think she'd count as a genius. I mean, Hebe's not mad, she's supposed to be autistic, although if you ask me she's just odd. I mean, it's not as if she recites dictionaries and things. Have you met her, then?'

He shrugged, not wanting to appear too interested lest he

be thought of as unhealthy, but nevertheless oddly drawn to know more about Hebe. 'She plays in the woods and she often comes this way. I haven't heard her sing myself; the others told me – but I was a little concerned that she was out here alone.'

Kate sighed. 'Her mother's an artist. There isn't a father, and I think Hebe is difficult to keep hold of. I'll mention it to her – she's a friend of mine. D'you think she could be one, then? A genius, I mean?'

John stubbed out his cigarette. 'I don't know. I think autism is a bit different. As you say, it's not the same as madness, not quite what I meant about genius, either. I think you have to be born with the right wick for genius, and I think it burns very brightly – but if you don't take care the wick burns too fast so that the flame is unstable and easily snuffed out. Look at all the geniuses who die young: Mozart, Rupert Brooke –'

'He died of an abscess on his lip, not because he was mad. Surely that doesn't count?' Kate was slightly lost in the metaphor.

John sighed. 'If he'd lived he probably wouldn't have been regarded as a genius. He'd have been another mediocre poet living in a caravan in Foxbarton Woods, looking for inspiration like me.'

Kate stretched in the bed and reflected that with Martin she had always complained that he neglected her by failing to talk in bed. With John she just needed to make up for a little lost time. 'I'll tell you what,' she said, 'if you're looking for inspiration, why don't I inspire you a little?'

'I don't bloody want sex,' said Joshua via the keyboard to Sonja, who had walked into their bedroom stark naked and now stood in front of him. Her majestically enhanced bosoms, in that odd way common to implants, looked as if their thoughts were elsewhere.

Sonja bent over him to read what he had written and

shook her head. 'Dirty old man. Can I not be naked in my own bedroom without you thinking I want sex? If I want sex I have it with the gardener, not with a man who will make no effort to stand or speak. Look, I stand at the window and the whole world can see my breasts and desire them.'

Joshua rolled his eyes and then closed them. He knew what she was at, and somewhere inside him there was an unwilling appreciation of the effort she was making to persuade him to cast off his wheelchair and walk. But he couldn't bear it; the inevitable defeat and humiliation was far too hopeless. Here he was, his mind a fierce flame burning in the body of a decrepit old man, a man who could neither speak nor stand. At least to stay seated in the wheelchair and attempt no speech gave him his dignity. Far better that than having to stumble, fall and splutter with these enormous Brunhildes who kept turning up from the private hospital disguised as physiotherapists and trying to persuade him to try. It was like wrestling with Wagnerian sopranos – one of them had almost suffocated him in her enormous bosoms in her attempt to pull him to standing – but he had learned very easily how to resist and make himself far too heavy to move at all. There is a knack to being immovable. He had seen that loony child do it, outside on the lawn when his grandchildren wanted to take her away. She just distributed herself differently and resisted. It was very effective. Funny that he should have learned anything at all from watching that child. He remembered that she had saved him and felt guilty for insulting her in his thoughts – but then, saved him for what? A slow decrepit death whilst the woman he loved danced her beauty in front of him as if she could will him to his feet, and the ghosts of his past came back in his dreams to taunt him?

Anyway, Sonja must be barmy if she thought he'd risk attempting to have sex with her, beautiful though she was. How could she possibly want a twisted cripple? And what if he couldn't actually manage it? Others might believe

Sonja had married him for his money, and he was certainly not vain enough to imagine she had married him for his looks. But he had always been rather smugly aware that he had been more than a surprise to her in bed, and she had not been unhappy with her lot, even before the unbelievable had happened and the two of them had fallen in love. True, the urge was there, but she couldn't see that, and it would be the ultimate humiliation to fail in that area where his confidence had always been supreme. After all, the urge to speak was also there, and that part of him also would not obey the commands of his imprisoned brain.

Outside he could hear his grandchildren arguing, and was taken with a sudden wish to see them.

'Send William up here,' he wrote to Sonja, 'and take your bloody diaphragm out. You won't be needing it.'

Sonja tossed her blonde head and marched into their dressing room, put on the dungarees and checked lumber-jack shirt she knew he hated, then appeared in the doorway again. 'I might ask them to come,' she said to him angrily, 'or I might say this nasty old man does not deserve a visitor.'

Joshua shut his eyes, but not before she saw the tear appear in the corner of one. Overcome with remorse she kissed his eyelids and ran from the room, leaving Joshua annoyed that his minor eye irritation had been so mis-interpreted.

A few moments later William appeared, followed in a rather straggling fashion by Matilda and Hebe, looking at him unfathomably from whatever place it was that her mind inhabited.

For the first time Joshua found himself suddenly wondering what it felt like to be her, wondered whether, like him, she could appreciate the intense frustration he felt, of being on the outside looking in, unable to participate properly because the relevant bits were not properly assembled. But no, there was no comparison. The child was a mental case with a normal body, whilst he was completely the opposite. That boy so many years ago in his class at the village school had been a mental case too – that boy with the funny round face, golden hair and thick pebble glasses who had said very little but sometimes curled in a corner and cried. He had only been in Joshua's class for a year, because after that Joshua had moved on to his prep school in the Cotswolds and the slow, stupid boy had stayed down. You couldn't expect boys like that to go to prep school. So, thought Joshua, after you had gone to the grand prep school the smiling boy must have got his sandwiches ground into the playground dust and cried tears of bewilderment because of meanly aimed blows to the solar plexus by the boys who called him Mongol, because there was no one left to defend him. And later, when they said he'd gone to a special school for damaged boys who didn't belong with normal people, you were at last relieved of having to feel guilt for his tears.

'Forget about it,' his father had said. 'He belongs in an institution. It's nothing to do with you.'

His mother, oddly, had said nothing on the subject, and it was only a year or two after that she had disappeared from his life altogether, without explanation, without even a goodbye, her name to appear on a stone in the churchyard whilst people muttered that she had died of a broken heart. It was all during the war. A lot of people died of broken hearts and other things during the war.

'Grandfather,' said William, interrupting his reverie, 'would you like to see my maggots?'

Joshua raised his eyebrows to express revulsion. Oddly, despite the right side of his body refusing to respond to most of his commands, his right eyebrow did all he told it to, and he had found his grandchildren particularly sensitive to the nuances of eyebrow expression. Children, perhaps, are more visually aware than adults of facial expression, being slightly less inclined to concentrate properly on what's being said to them.

'I'll take that as a yes,' said William cheerfully, and Joshua, knowing full well that William had understood him to be saying, 'I'd rather be fried in walnut oil than look at your maggots,' felt his first stirring of humour since the whole disaster. Sonja had put them up to this, he was sure of it. It was a conspiracy. Bugger.

'Here,' said William, and took Joshua's useless hand and turned it palm upwards, depositing on it, to his distaste, a matchbox-load of squirming maggots. He writhed his eyebrows frantically to signal disgust whilst keeping one horrified eye fixed on the maggots, as if he could hold them there with the power of his gaze and thus prevent them from running up his arm and thence, via his external auditory canal, finding a direct pathway to his brain. Mind you, they might do a better job in there than his doctors had managed ...

William beamed. 'The advantage of having them on the arm that won't work,' he beamed, 'is that you can't accidentally jerk and throw them at Matilda.'

'You're vile,' said Matilda. It was her latest word, imported into her everyday speech from teenage TV. 'Sorry, Gramps, I'd rescue you but I can't possibly touch those. If I scream my singing voice will go and Hebe and I are going to practise our duet. William, you are the most disgusting vile piece of guinea pig excrement I've ever, *ever* had for a brother.'

'Aw,' said William smirking, 'you're only being nice to me 'cos you want something.'

Joshua made a purposeful eyebrow movement at Matilda and touched his throat with his good hand, taking his eyes off the maggots for a moment. When he looked again, to his surprise, Hebe was sweeping the maggots from him with an expression of indignation. He stared as, cupping them in her two small hands, she dumped them firmly back into William's. She said nothing.

Joshua raised his eyebrows again at Matilda, pointing this time to her mouth.

'I don't understand,' said Matilda, playing with the end of her long red ponytail and gazing at him through disingenuous blue eyes. 'Does you throat hurt?'

She knew bloody well he wanted her to sing for him, thought Joshua, enraged. Sonja had put them up to this whole thing. He understood the game. This was about his refusal to try to speak. Well, would you want to speak if it made you spit and slobber and it still came out as if you had a whole Canada goose in your mouth?

He waved his left arm at Matilda, then attempted to use his keyboard, only to find that Sonja had unplugged it before leaving the room. His eyes filled with tears of frustration, annoying him immensely since tears bring pity, and pity was the thing he feared the most.

'Sonja says we've got to be unhelpful unless you try to talk,' said William apologetically. 'Sorry.'

Joshua shrugged with his good shoulder and closed his eyes.

William and Matilda exchanged glances and tiptoed out.

'I think it's mean,' said Matilda, when they got outside. She was close to tears. 'Poor Gramps – it's bad enough that he can't speak without trying to make him lose his dignity.'

William sighed. 'Well, Sonja says he could speak if he tried to. It's like singing practice. If you don't keep making those terrible noises you call practise, you never get to make the good ones.'

'You've been making terrible noises for years,' said Matilda rudely. 'It hasn't worked for you. If aliens from Venus landed and the first thing they heard was you singing they'd be off back to the Horsehead Nebula in a shot.'

'Well, they'd be lost, then, if they were from Venus, Captain Kirk, 'cos the Horsehead Nebula is absolutely nowhere near Venus. Don't girls know anything about space?'

Matilda glared. 'That's my point. They'd be confused as well as in a total panic so they'd go back to the wrong planet.'

William sniffed. 'The Horsehead Nebula's not a planet, it's a nebula. It's all gas – like some people I know. I'm going for a biscuit.'

'Me too. Where's Hebe?'

'I dunno. You were supposed to be looking after her.'

'No, I wasn't. We both were.'

'God,' said William, 'it drives me mad that she keeps doing this.'

'She doesn't keep doing anything,' said Matilda defensively. 'She doesn't see anything wrong with wandering off. Anyway, I think she's still in with Gramps. I'll go and see.' She went back into her grandfather's sitting room, where she found Hebe cross-legged on the floor in front of him, staring at him intensely whilst pulling a series of extraordinary faces. Joshua, whilst obviously trying to ignore her, clearly could not quite bring himself to turn away, and so a strange truce had ensued, with Hebe contorting her face like a contestant in those North Yorkshire girning competitions in which toothless old men contrive to look like Popeye, and Joshua doing his utmost not to react at all.

'Sorry, Gramps,' said Matilda after a moment, unsure whether she should interfere or not, and deciding that the best course of action was to pretend she had not noticed anything unusual going on and so avoid having to address it. 'C'mon, Hebe.' She held out a hand.

Hebe took it without appearing to look round, and followed Matilda out of the room.

As the door swung partially shut behind them the evening sun came out from behind a cloud and shone brightly in through Joshua's window, casting a golden light on the dust particles that hang in the air whenever a door moves suddenly. They looked like rays from heaven, and at the same moment Joshua heard an unearthly sound, which he at once recognised as an angel calling him to account. It wasn't English. It was the language of Heaven. The words of an old hymn that he'd sung decades ago when dragooned

155

into Foxbarton church choir popped into his head: *Angel-voices, ever singing, Round Thy Throne of light . . .*

They'd arrived for him. His time had come. That sodding vicar would have been pleased to hear it, the one who'd made him learn the words of that hymn some sixty-odd years ago when he sang in the church choir. He'd see him soon. Be able to tell him he still remembered every verse. This was it. The heavenly bloody host were here at last. Bound to happen after a dirty great stroke like that. Sure that he was dying, Joshua closed his eyes to wait, hoping no one would come rushing in as he was halfway there and ruin the angel music by pounding on his chest or some such nonsense, bringing him back to a state even more impaired than the one he was leaving. He felt really rather well, for a dying man, which was surely the best way to go.

Chapter Eight

Julia was in her garden a few afternoons later, softening the large quantities of willow she now needed for her planned composition, when Matilda arrived, still in her school uniform, brandishing a letter.

'Hebe needs to be in a singing competition with me,' she announced without preamble. 'Mrs Peel says it would be good for her.'

What Mrs Peel had actually said was that maybe, just maybe, Hebe could *possibly* enter the duet section in the Haverhill Festival with Matilda, but only if Hebe's mother agreed and only if all concerned agreed she wouldn't get too stressed. Mrs Peel had already, in four short lessons, witnessed what could happen if Hebe did get stressed. (The episode when Hebe had climbed out of the window and down the wall outside upon being asked to stand on her feet rather than her head was particularly well ingrained in her memory.)

Julia stood and frowned. 'I don't know, Matilda,' she said. 'I mean, she's barely started having lessons. Maybe next year.'

'Yes, but she can do the duet with me this year. She loves it. And next year I can't be in the under twelves, so I'll be up against all the teenagers.'

'What duet is it?'

'Oh, it's all quite proper,' said Matilda anxiously and earnestly, 'honestly.'

Julia smiled. 'What can you mean, proper?'

'Well, nothing about sex or drugs, even though I am

nearly a teenager. We're doing some folk songs and "Who Will Buy?" from *Oliver*.'

'I don't know.' Julia was doubtful, feeling rather out of her depth. I never had this sort of gift, she thought. I don't know how to decide. I mean, it could be stressful – yet maybe she needs to do it. Maybe her voice is there for a reason . . .

'Please, Aunt Julia, at least let her practise with me. If she doesn't want to do it on the day then that's fine.'

'When is the day?'

'This Saturday, in Haverhill.'

'You mean the Haverhill Festival? When you said singing competition I didn't realise . . . I thought the Haverhill Festival was quite serious, full of talent spotters, you know, very competitive.'

Matilda attempted to look casual but didn't quite pull it off. 'Oh no – I mean, they do have talent spotters and things, but not for the schools' stuff, really.' Inside she was holding her breath desperately. She knew just how many girls there were wanting to be the next Charlotte Church – but a duet? No one else was doing that. They were all singing that song from *Titanic* and trying to make their voices vibrate like Celine Dion's. Her duet was different. This was her route to stardom.

'You can't deny her the chance,' said Daniel suddenly, from the kitchen window, where he was standing washing up their lunch things at the sink. 'I mean, come on, Jules. The child has the voice of an angel. We always said you should follow your dreams, remember?'

'That was at art college,' said Julia, 'when we could afford to be idealistic because we didn't mind living on beans and farting all evening. This is different.'

'How?'

'I have to make a choice for Hebe but it might be Hebe who has to live with the consequences.'

'Jules, you ought to let her try. Other people should get the chance to hear her.'

'What do you mean, "other people"? Why are you so interested?'

'Well, you know, when you have a voice like that, you can't just keep it hidden. Gifts like that should be shared, flung about like manna from Heaven.'

'Since when have you been the Voice of God? I'll do what's best for Hebe,' said Julia flatly, feeling suddenly threatened by his enthusiasm. 'Look what happened to David Helfgott, the pianist. He was so brilliant it did something to his mind.'

'Rubbish, Jules. His brilliance didn't do anything to him, it saved him. Come on, lighten up. It's just a little local singing contest. Give her a chance. If she hates it you need never let her do it again, but if she loves it – well, it could be really good for her. She should at least have the chance to find out.'

'She's only eight,' said Julia, dubiously.

Matilda winced. She was nearly a teenager. Well, as soon as she was twelve she'd be nearly thirteen. Time was running out, she was almost past it in child-star terms . . .

'And, Jules . . . ?'

'What?'

'I never farted.'

'Oh, sure, and Vlad the Impaler was vegetarian.'

'Please, Aunt Julia, we have practised ever such a lot. Let us just sing it for you.'

'Oh, all right,' said Julia uncomfortably, knowing this would be a *fait accompli* because, given Hebe's vocal quality and Matilda's long-established beautiful solo voice, they were bound to sound good.

She was not so prepared, though, to have them sound utterly stunning. It was just an unaccompanied duet, she told herself. Just a couple of folk songs. OK, one was sung impressively in Welsh, but the other was just 'Early One Morning', which Matilda said was the set piece for the competition, and which she must have heard a million times. And then 'Who Will Buy?' – well, it blew your mind and made your eyes water. She was aware of Daniel hanging out of the kitchen window with his mouth open, and of a sense of dread.

'You look like a codfish,' she said to him, in an attempt to dispel the feeling. 'Close your mouth before something flies in there and builds a nest.'

'What can you say?' said Daniel. 'You're stuffed, Jules,' and his head disappeared into the kitchen.

Julia frowned at Hebe. 'Come here, darling.' Hebe wandered over and beamed. 'Do you want to sing with Matilda in the competition?'

Hebe frowned her tiny frown. 'OK.' She looked at her mother directly, with those big dark eyes that could look into you or through you, depending on her mood.

'Do you know what a competition is, Hebe? When lots of people take turns to sing?'

Hebe shook her head. She took a deep breath and looked through her mother and then at her again, and Julia realised she was struggling to find the words for something. She realised she was holding her own breath too.

Hebe's frown turned into a big frown and she screwed her eyes shut. And then she said, 'Will angels be at the competition?' Then took Julia's cheeks between her hands and planted a firm and very prolonged kiss on one cheek. 'I love you, Mum.'

'I love you too, Hebe. I don't know if angels will be there. Did you know I have to make an angel of my own? Perhaps you could help.'

Hebe's face darkened suddenly and she pushed her nose up against Julia's. 'You can't make angels. Angels live in trees under the moon. Angels sing. Mummy . . . I want to go to the moon. Can I go to the moon?'

'You can go every night in your dreams,' said Julia, who knew better than to make any promises about the moon to

Hebe, not even of the 'maybe one day' kind, as Hebe held you to things in a very literal way.

'Can I go and see Grandpa?'

'Maybe later. Come on, it's time for your tea. Then after that I need you to help me make an impala.'

'What's an impala?'

'You'll see one soon.' Hebe has such a literal mind, she thought, if I don't show her some photos soon she'll think most of the creatures of the African plains really do look like woven-willow Ford Granadas.

Joshua Gilfoyle was, he was surprised to discover, still alive. He had completely failed to die at what he had believed to be the appointed time. He was unable to explain the heavenly voices calling him to his final rest the other day as being anything other than a dream, a dream in which he had then heard the voice of his long-lost son saying, 'Father, I'm here,' over and over again. He had thought it must mean Gabriel was dead and he would finally see him at last – but then he had woken up with a stiff neck from leaning in his chair, to find that his right foot had twice the movement it had had earlier. Wriggling it, he had actually been astonished at the improvement, and had wondered whether to ascribe it to angelic intervention.

He had considered letting Sonja know about the foot, but decided against this in the end, as a slight improvement in one foot was worse than no improvement at all. It would surely raise false hopes of a man who could still neither speak as though his mouth were not full of worms nor eat his food without spitting most of it into his lap. It was better to conceal these small gains, for they were paltry enough for a man who was accustomed to running an empire from his own two feet and eating in the best restaurants in this land.

He was, though, all the more determined that Gabriel should be found, if only to come back and apologise to him for appearing in such an unpleasant dream. He wrote several times on his laptop, 'Get my bloody son!' Each time his son Simon appeared instead, and told him off soundly for refusing to attempt to speak. They were now deliberately ignoring his written instructions. They'd even trained bloody Mrs Barker to unplug him in midsentence. Well, he'd beat them at that game. He wasn't going to give them the satisfaction of treating him like a child and pretending to be pleased when he managed to say his name. He was a bloody captain of industry. He had been at school with a boy who could barely say his name. He had seen at first-hand how the world had no place for those who couldn't take part in it. If he couldn't walk or talk he might as well be dead, and that was the end of it. Not for anything would he admit to anyone, particularly not himself, that he was actually overjoyed to be still alive.

So Joshua continued to sit slumped in his chair and refuse to take part in any effort to help him, whilst the parade of increasingly well-bosomed physiotherapists and speech therapists Sonja was hiring, in what had degenerated into an obvious attempt to make him laugh, continued unabated.

'D'you think we ought to do anything about your father?' Merrill asked Simon that evening. 'I mean, d'you think he'd make more improvement in a nursing home or something?' They were sitting together at the kitchen table, drinking coffee and reading the papers. The children had left the table and were playing wild cricket on the lawn with Oscar and Hebe. The sounds of birds singing and children laughing filled the air, together with the occasional scream of 'William Gilfoyle, that's not *fair*!' from Matilda. They were, Merrill thought suddenly, the sort of sounds she'd like to be hearing if she was old and dying.

'I don't think it would help,' said Simon. 'There's nothing you can do to make him co-operate. He's a stubborn old fool – he knows what's wanted of him and he's refusing to try. There's nothing I can say. He doesn't care about getting better. He's determined to die rather than be an invalid, but he won't lift a finger to try and recover. I'm afraid he might will himself to death, except that he desperately wants to see Gabriel before he goes.'

Joshua's recent missives had actually demanded that Gabriel be found at once and brought to him to apologise for being the cause of this current incapacity. Joshua, Simon realised now, had always expected to find his son before the eleventh hour of his life. Dying he might be, but as a man who had always kept control of absolutely everything up until now, it had not occurred to him that he might die before he was ready, nor that he would die without accomplishing exactly what he planned to. The only thing Joshua had ever failed at was getting Gabriel to become what he wanted him to be – and even that he believed he had only put on hold until he was ready to come back to it.

Merrill put a hand on Simon's arm, aware he was upset about his father's obsession with his brother, guessing at the reason. 'D'you still think it's your fault?'

Simon frowned at the newspaper, not observing that it was both yesterday's and upside down. 'How do you mean?'

'You know what I mean, Simon Gilfoyle. I'm your wife, which means you're totally transparent to my eyes. You think it's your fault he lost touch, because you didn't see him when he came to find us that night in London, that night when we were having our party. You still think if you'd seen him then he might have come back, mended the fences.'

'Of course I don't,' said Simon. 'Gabriel had decided he wanted nothing to do with Gilfoyles well before that. I know how it works, Merrill. There was no way he could stay in touch with you and me, yet not also with Father. He had to sever all ties if he wanted to escape his chosen destiny.'

'Chosen destiny? That's a bit heavy.'

Simon shrugged. 'All my father ever wanted was a son to

take on Gilfoyles, and he thought he had it. That's why I was allowed the soft option.'

'Soft option? Is that what you think?'

'Of course not, but it's what he thinks. Is that a beetle on the kitchen floor?'

'Undoubtedly,' said Merrill without looking, 'but you become inured to beetles after a certain point. The worst moment for me was the breakfast cereal incident. They looked so like raisins that I still don't know how many I ate. After that nothing could bother me.'

'D'you think Mrs Barker's calmed down yet?'

'I doubt it. She doesn't take kindly to living things in the sugar. But you're changing the subject.'

'I think I could have tried harder to find him,' Simon said. 'He's my brother.'

Merrill sighed, 'We did try, don't you remember? Perhaps he doesn't want to be found, Simon. If he did he knows where we are. I mean, didn't Mark Smythe say that people can only really disappear if they want to? I know you don't want to believe he could be dead, but –'

'He's not dead.'

'Either that, or he's changed his name. I mean, after all that time of forever turning up at the door at all hours needing a bath and a hot meal and somewhere to sober up, he seemed to disappear off the face of the earth.'

'I wonder if he was going to tell us he was leaving that night when you saw him looking in through the window. And why didn't he?'

'Well, we were having that party,' said Merrill, 'all of our friends were there. Perhaps he was embarrassed. Perhaps he was pissed, as usual. Perhaps I imagined I saw him. After all, I spent half that evening lecturing Julia about her dissolute life – I probably had the family black sheep on my mind. And sometimes you think of people, then imagine you see them. Anyway, he's had plenty of chance to find us and explain himself if he'd wanted to.'

'Maybe we should have tried harder.'

'Look,' said Merrill crossly, 'are you trying to prove that you love your father, or do you honestly think that you could have found Gabriel? Because you don't have to *prove* you love that cantankerous old bastard – but, you know, Simon, if I was Gabriel I wouldn't want to come back to be told I was only welcome if I promised not to let my children sully the Gilfoyle name with my crappy genes.'

'I know. I was going to speak to him about that. I'd been waiting for an opportunity.'

'Well, he's a captive audience now. Frankly, I think you'd have more luck if you spoke to Sonja. She's the only one with any influence over him, sex-mad old bugger.'

'Merrill!'

'No one's listening, I can say what I like. I'm going out to see what the children are doing. Are you coming?'

'In a minute. You're right. I might speak to Sonja now.'

Simon watched Merrill flounce out to find the children, aware that she liked him watching her, appreciating the flounce. If only, he thought, there was more time. We have no idea how much time we have, any of us, but Father has less than most. If only he weren't so stubborn. If only Gabriel had seen the lost old man that I now see beneath the veneer, he'd come back, I know he would. And if Father could only admit to himself that he loves his eldest son at least as much as he loves me, then he might be able to see that it's his own failure he's punishing, not Gabriel's. His own failure not to produce exactly the family line his father wanted. From what I remember of Grandfather he was the hardest kind of parent. All that rubbish about weak genes must surely have come straight from him.

How do you reconcile two people you love when they're hiding themselves so completely from one another?

Sonja was sitting with Joshua when Simon came to see him. Joshua was asleep, for once – oddly, since the stroke, he barely seemed to sleep at all – and Sonja was dozing on his chest, her fine white-blonde hair hanging about her face, the clean Nordic lines of her cheekbones catching the light of the sun shining in through the windows. She looked protective, tender, and Simon was aware of a flash of internal guilt at some of the things he had thought – and said – about her. A robin fluttered briefly against the glass outside and flew off. Simon could hear the children playing on the lawn.

'If you don't run faster than that,' William was shouting, 'evolution will overtake you and turn you into . . . into . . . Get off me. MUM!'

Wondering absently where on earth William got his vocabulary, and without properly stopping to think, Simon moved over to Sonja and stroked a strand of hair back from her cheek. She opened her eyes, which were extraordinarily blue, like something off a postcard from the Isles of Greece. They ought to be coloured contact lenses, but he knew they weren't.

Conscious suddenly that his hand was still on her cheek he pulled it back guiltily. 'Sonja . . . sorry.'

Sonja glared at him. 'You should be.'

He frowned. 'What do you mean?'

She glanced at Joshua, who was deeply asleep. 'You hate me marrying him, you think I'm not good enough, and now you creep up and touch me?'

Simon was surprised at the outburst. 'I didn't creep up. I moved your hair, that's all.'

'You hate it that he loves me.'

'I don't hate it.'

'Ah, you welcome me with the arms?'

Simon sighed. 'Open arms. I know we didn't, but did you expect us to be delighted? He's an old rich man and you're –'

'Desirable,' said Sonja, standing up and pushing her enormous breasts against him. 'Isn't that your problem?'

Simon swallowed, aware, to his mixed embarrassment and pride, that he had developed an instant and, given their proximity, very obvious erection. Sonja took hold of his tie – and stared into his eyes. 'Tell me I am not right.' She stepped back.

Outside Merrill, umpiring the children's cricket, bit her lip. Through the window she had unmistakably seen Simon and Sonja together in a clinch. It had been brief, it had been too distant to make out who had done what, if they had kissed, if it had just been a friendly hug – but as far as she knew Simon was not on friendly hug terms with Sonja.

'I . . . Of course you're an attractive woman.' Simon fought desperately to keep his cool. It was just an erection, explicable by the shock. Normal men get them every so often whether women like Sonja are pushing their breasts against them or not. 'You've proved your point – but it doesn't prove you love him.'

'I don't have to prove it to you,' said Sonja with dislike, 'only to him. Now what did you want? To tell me I am not good enough to follow your mother in some other mean way?' She sat back on Joshua's bed and turned her back on him.

Simon swallowed and blushed. 'I'm sorry, I didn't mean . . . I mean, look, of course we've all resented you a little.'

'You call me the Norwegian tart,' said Sonja, still not looking, 'and humiliate me in small things.'

'What do you mean? What small things?'

'Beetles,' said Sonja, 'living in my wellingtons just to show I do not wear them. I do not wear them because they are vile rubber bog-boots. I prefer to have the wet feet.'

'Oh, but that's not –'

'You pretend to despise me. You watch my buttock with joy yet look at my brain with derision.'

Simon could tell she was upset by the shake in her voice. 'Your bottom,' he corrected, 'and your mind.'

'My bottom and my mind. You see, you know.'

'I'm sorry. It wasn't intentional.'

Sonja sniffed. 'I go to London tomorrow. I am going to

look for Gabriel. Someone must find him and you do not try.'

Simon sighed. 'We've looked, Sonja. If it was that easy –'

'I need photographs. You know where they are. I need to see the face of the man for whom I search. And I want all Joshua's papers. There are diaries there. Your mother's diaries.'

'They're in the safe at Gilfoyles – Mark Smythe has access, although I don't think – I mean, my mother's diaries are – Have you asked Father? I don't think he would want them read.'

'It is for his own good. I look for clues to Gabriel. I do not wish to read private thoughts.'

Simon shrugged. 'Her diaries won't help you there, and I'd rather you didn't . . . Look, I can get you a photo . . . but will you do something for me?'

'I am not interested in your mother. What?'

'This rubbish about Gabriel's children. The will. It's bizarre and unfair. He'll listen to you.' It hurt Simon to say the words, but he knew they were true.

Sonja blinked. 'I think you are a good man, Simon, and I will try to do this because I think you are right.'

On the lawn Merrill, trying not to look at the window, frowned furiously and yelled 'LBW!' at Oscar, who flung his bat furiously to the ground, shouted, 'Never!' and stormed off the lawn.

William and Matilda applauded. 'Very good, that's much better. Go on, Oscar, one more go. Try it again.'

Oscar sloped back to the crease and aimed another swing at Hebe's ball.

'LBW!' they shouted in chorus.

'Bugger it!' shouted Oscar, flinging his bat to the ground again, then bowed as the others applauded, delighted at his dramatic success. 'Is that better?'

Merrill folded her arms. 'Yep, you've got almost everything it takes to be an England cricketer. Only one thing missing.'

'What's that?' asked Matilda, grinning.

'Just to be able to play cricket.'

Oscar sniffed. 'I don't have to take this abuse, you know. I got three wickets in the last house match. C'mon, Wills, let's go and see if Mrs Braithwaite's got any cake . . .'

'We're coming with you. C'mon, Hebe . . .' Matilda was in hot pursuit.

'You can't run to save your life,' William was shouting over his shoulder. 'You'll never keep up.'

'I jolly well can. Mr Williams said in sport I run like a gazelle.'

'A blooming fat one with three of its legs tied together,' shouted William. 'Girls run like big apes.'

'Come here and say that . . .'

Merrill watched them running off to the woods together with one half of her brain, whilst with the other she worried that her husband was gripped by lust for his father's wife. Wasn't that what always happened to boys whose fathers had mistresses? God, imagine. She might end up having to set up an abandoned wives' club with Kate Coleman, who had clearly spent the last few years wallowing in the self-pity of it and hoping for someone else to share her fate.

Kate Coleman had in fact made a determined decision not to wallow any longer. Martin and his shorthand-scrawling trollop were no longer the objects of any of her envy, resentments or sexual hurt. They had nothing she wanted. She had a lover and she had a purpose. They only had each other. They were no longer her concern. She was buoyed and strengthened by her new-found sexual allure, her confidence, by the fact that she had taken a gypsy lover and used him for joy and pleasure. Sex for joy and pleasure had actually been rather more of a revelation than she had expected it to be, making her realise that Martin had been even less adequate in that department than she had formerly thought. And this knowledge made her even more smug.

Still, the relationship was drawing to a close. They had both expected it to be temporary. He and she were worlds apart – one a gypsy, the other a lady . . . Well, not quite. He obviously wasn't your average gypsy – despite the romantic idea of it, Kate Coleman would never have a wild adventure with just any old gypsy. But he was, nevertheless, not a soul mate. She needed someone altogether more sensible to be her soul mate. Someone like Jonathan Doyle, silly fool, who consistently failed to notice that he had a giant target painted on his head.

Besides, the dog was starting to get bored, sitting outside the van. Soon she would start howling, which would be deeply embarrassing.

Kate also had other things on her mind, things just as important to her future development as wild romps in the woods. She had now set about her task of becoming Julia Fitzgerald's manager with her usual efficiency and had approached Simon Gilfoyle to ask if she could use one of the barns in the village. There were several empty barns, all maintained in beautiful condition by Joshua, who believed old and beautiful buildings should always be kept beautiful, and it had struck Kate one of these would be the perfect place from which to relaunch Julia.

Having been in there and admired the perfect natural light, she was working on her business plan when Oscar appeared in the kitchen doorway for a moan.

Kate didn't take much notice at first – as a mother she routinely allowed a certain amount of moaning just to wash right over her before anything started to seem out of the ordinary – but this time Oscar was fairly cheesed off.

'I just saw my violin teacher,' he complained now. 'She says you've entered me for the Haverhill Festival.'

'What's wrong with that?' asked Kate, planning that Julia

would display the new Foxbarton angel on a small plinth in the centre of the room. It would be marvellous to open the gallery with the unveiling of Julia's new collection and have the angel as the highlight. She could call it *Angels in Art*. Or even *Kate's Angels*. Well, perhaps that wouldn't really do. They were Julia's creations really, even if it needed Kate to bring them to the world. *Kate's Children*, perhaps . . .

'. . . so that's really unfair,' said Oscar.

'What was that, darling?'

'Mum, you weren't listening.'

'I was,' said Kate cheerfully. 'It just fell straight out of my head. Say it again.'

Oscar peered at her. 'What's up with you, Mum?'

'Nothing,' said Kate, 'I couldn't be better. Why?'

'That's exactly it,' said Oscar. 'You haven't been all cheerful like this for ages.' He frowned suddenly. 'Have you got a boyfriend?'

'Of course not,' said Kate, alarmed and astonished at her son's perceptive powers – but then, she thought, he will have inherited them from me. 'Whatever made you say that?'

Oscar watched her carefully, not sure if this was a good thing or a bad one. 'You know Toby Hilton in my form? His mother has one, and Toby says she's gone all dippy ever since.'

'Dippy? I am never dippy.' Kate was as red as a beetroot, and Oscar regarded her with dawning conviction.

'You have, haven't you? Who is it? I won't tell anyone. Is it the vicar?"

'Of course not – that wouldn't be proper at all.'

'Whyever not? I bet he fancies you. He ate all his olives that night he came to supper.'

Kate blushed even redder. 'He likes olives . . . Oscar, really, I don't know where you . . . The vicar is not my boyfriend. Now can we drop it?'

Oscar frowned. 'You don't know anyone else.'

Kate was indignant. 'I'm not that sad, thank you very much. I do have a few friends.'

'They're all married,' said Oscar, 'and you wouldn't. Who is it then?'

'I couldn't possibly –'

'It is the vicar, isn't it? That'd be cool, I like him. I bet he knows loads of God jokes – wait till I tell Toby. Wow, my mum shagging a vicar . . .'

'Oscar!' said Kate, appalled. 'I am not shagging the vicar, as you so dreadfully put it. I'm happy because I'm going to be Julia's manager and open an art gallery in the village.'

'What do you mean, open an art gallery?' Oscar was diverted.

'An art gallery. You know, where artists' work is put on show and people come and buy it. Come on, now, tell me again what's so unfair about you winning the Haverhill Festival and being talent spotted by the BBC.'

And Oscar forgot Kate's secret romance in his utter horror. 'I am not playing in the Haverhill Festival. It's really girlie. Matilda and Hebe are in it together . . . I mean, I do have some pride.'

Kate sighed. 'It will do you good, your violin teacher said so. Go and do some practice – I'm going to take Gwen for a walk.' She put on her wellies and left the house, thinking, just another quick romp and then we'll do the adult-to-adult talk.

Oscar stared after her in surprise, noticing both that she had not stayed to supervise his practice as she normally did, and that she had forgotten the dog.

As Kate strode through the village towards Foxbarton Woods she noticed Daniel Cutter in the phone box. That was odd. Maybe Julia's phone wasn't working. Mobiles didn't work in the village anyway – they were in a radio reception hollow, which meant that no one's mobile phone worked and no one's radio would pick up *The Archers*. People drove up the hill towards Great Wratting every day to sit at the top to listen. Kate waved at him rather furtively and hurried on towards the gypsy caravan where her confidence in herself was being so thoroughly restored.

'So why were you hugging her?' asked Merrill that night.

Simon looked uncomfortable. 'She stood near me,' he said. 'I didn't hug her.'

'That wasn't how it looked. Why are you being so shifty now if you've nothing to hide?'

'Oh, for heaven's sake, nothing happened.'

'Don't try and get cross. I never for a minute thought anything did happen. Even Silicone Sonja wouldn't do that in front of him – he could still change his will.'

'We shouldn't call her that,' said Simon, guiltily. 'She's not so bad.' It seemed to him that Sonja's love for his father was worth more than his own. He had let his brother go for all these years . . .

'What? Defending her now, are you? What is this sudden soft spot for your father's mistress?'

'Wife. She's his wife. I've realised she loves him.'

'How? Because she told you?'

'Oh, Merrill, please. You don't like Joshua so don't get all holy about her inheriting his money. You won't do so badly out of his will yourself.'

Merrill slapped him clean across the cheek. 'Bastard!'

He put his hand against the hot place. 'I didn't mean it like that. There's no need to go all Jane Austen on me.' Merrill burst into tears, and he added, 'I'm sorry. It wasn't anything. We were talking. She was feeling upset at the way we've been treating her, that's all.' Apart from the erection, of course. Best not to mention the erection.

'Treating her? We've been perfectly civil. Anyway, what does she expect, marrying a seventy-year-old man at her age? A red carpet?'

'I don't know, Merrill. She loves him. God knows how he

173

managed it, but she does. And now she's trying to find Gabriel for him. She wants to go through all the old papers, see if we've missed any clues.'

'Oh, just as if. Joshua has had people looking for Gabriel for years. What can Sonja do? Stand on the top of Nelson's column and wave her gargantuan boobs, until he just comes running along with all the other men?'

'Now you're being mean,' said Simon, and Merrill, who knew she was and couldn't seem to help it, flushed guiltily.

'I just don't see what she thinks she'll achieve.'

'She wants to go through everything again, including Mother's diaries. They're in the safe at Gilfoyles, and Sonja thinks there might be something in there. Father probably wouldn't want her to look at them – I mean, Mother probably had a few choice things to say about him . . . so I think I ought to be there with her . . .'

'Don't you dare, Simon Gilfoyle. Sonja doesn't need you with her, and Matilda's singing in a competition on Saturday. Say you'll be here or I won't let go.'

'Absolutely . . . and if you twist that any further I'll be impotent for ever. I don't know why you're so het up about it,' said Simon, knowing full well what the matter was. She was his wife. She had sensed that erection from twenty paces and through a wall by ESP. 'You're right, there's nothing more I can do.'

'What about him?' asked Merrill, feeling churlish. 'Who's going to look after Joshua whilst she's gone gallivanting off around London to give orders to the private detectives?'

'She's got a new agency nurse in full time. Started yesterday. Looks like an East German shot-putter, actually.'

'He'll hate that,' said Merrill rather petulantly, since she had been planning to refuse to do it herself and would have liked the opportunity to be difficult about being taken for granted. 'I think he rather likes the Barbara Windsor physiotherapists.'

'I think he's meant to be amused,' said Simon. 'You have to admire Sonja.'

'No, I don't. She'll probably spend the weekend having her hair done. I mean, can you see her traipsing around under Westminster Bridge with a pile of "Have you seen this man" posters?'

'Well, no, she's hardly the traipsing type, I agree – but she's barely left his side since the stroke. I think we've misjudged her, made too many assumptions. She's doing her best to make him happy.'

'Well, OK, but I still don't like you hugging her.' Merrill put her arms round him.

'Point taken.' He kissed the tip of her nose. How vile I am, he thought, to have erections at the thought of my father's wife, how vile and unrepentant. To imagine, even for a second, having her on the boardroom table in a pair of high heels and a tight little skirt . . .

The thought brought back his former physical response so that Merrill, pressed up against him, said, 'Is that a stethoscope in your pocket or are you just pleased to see me?' He was then compelled to go upstairs and make love to his wife with the erection brought on by the thought of his stepmother, in order to alleviate his guilt. It didn't work, of course. It just made it a million times worse.

Downstairs and on the other side of the house, Joshua awoke to find that it was now dark. Sonja had gone off somewhere, and that dreadful sumo-wrestling nurse whom she had left him with all day was in the next room preparing some vile tray of slop.

He opened his eyes to see Hebe staring at him through the French window which led out on to the rose garden. There she was again. She was just staring, as usual, with that look that almost didn't see him, distant, lost . . . unnerving. He glared at her and made furious eyebrow signs, but she didn't even blink. The blasted child just kept on turning up – she had been every night since he got home. She came to watch him, came to the window when it was dark and just wandered in and stared at him. Sometimes she touched him, and sometimes she sang. He had no idea what she was doing out so late – presumably the artist mother didn't know she had escaped. He supposed you couldn't watch them all the time, these subnormal children – that was why they needed to be somewhere secure. After all, the mother was bound to be drunk and dissolute, artists always were. Even if she did have fabulous breasts she probably spent every evening with a bottle of gin throwing paint at the walls. He rather hoped so, actually – he had heard that all the best artists did that.

Now Hebe was singing that song again, in her eerie sweet voice. She never said much to him, only sang, and he had become accustomed to the unearthliness of the sound. He knew now that what he had assumed to be the entire company of Heaven coming to get him had merely been Hebe singing in Welsh, and this had given him a new respect for the Welsh language which sounded, he felt, so much more appropriate for the heavenly host than Latin. Obviously if all the great composers had had the advantage of Welsh they would have been greater still.

He was sure that Hebe knew that some of his speech was returning and that his right leg was regaining its strength. He could have sworn she hadn't been there when he had lifted the leg, manipulated the hand, surreptitiously exercised his voice, yet he still was sure she knew. Sometimes she touched the wretched hand and then applauded. Sometimes she pulled at the leg, sometimes she touched his throat . . . and, he had to admit, it proved that even these subnormal children could sometimes have skills. Even so, she made him uncomfortable, and earlier, when she had come in daylight, he had asked Brunhilde, the shot-putter (her name was actually Laura, but Brunhilde suited her so much better) to chase her away, finding some relief for his own frustration in watching the importunate rage of a silent child removed from the one place that apparently fascinated her. Hebe was, it seemed to him, as trapped and helpless as he was, and watching her frustrated fighting as Brunhilde carted her off whilst screaming for Matilda or William to come and get her seemed to give power to his own.

But the night was different. In the night there was no one to read his laptop messages. He could have called for help – when Sonja was there sleeping on the Put-u-up bed (because he wouldn't have her in his bed, trying to inveigle herself on to him like some strumpet) during Hebe's nocturnal visits he could easily have woken her, but that would have meant admitting that he was seriously rattled by the presence of a child. And, of course, he wasn't bothered. Subnormal children weren't anything to be scared of.

He closed his eyes to blot Hebe out, but the singing continued, and when he could no longer see, it reminded him of other singing, in the village school when he was a boy. That strange, stupid boy had also had a sweet singing voice. A memory jumped out and surprised him of that boy cowering in a corner of the playground once when he, Joshua, had gone over to rescue him from the taunts of Jimmy Griffiths from the pub. He remembered how the boy had hugged him after he'd dispatched Jimmy to the sickroom with a bleeding lip, and then had sung a short song with surprising musicality. It had been the school hymn, 'When a knight won his spurs, in the stories of old . . .' So many years ago – the past is so lost, locked inside a memory. A tear ran, unexpected and searingly hot, down the side of his nose. Abstractly it occurred to Joshua that he had not cried for years before his stroke and now he cried at the slightest thought. And it hurt. Perhaps he was allergic to tears. Perhaps that explained why this one hurt so much as it trickled down his cheek and hung, trembling, on the end of his nose. They say tears are cleansing. Perhaps they could cleanse away his helplessness, make him the man he was before this disaster.

Yet, he asked himself angrily, what was the point in defeating this latest dreadful, sickening, helpless thing just so that he could die from the other wasting, vile, cankerous thing that was planning, plotting and growing in his bones? It was like resuscitating a man on death row who inconveniently has a heart attack three days before he goes to the chair.

And he answered himself, because, now that death looked him in the eye from possibly only a little further down the road of life, Joshua realised that he wanted those last few steps on the path. He needed those remaining weeks, months, hopefully even years, whatever remained to find his son, to love his wife, to enjoy his grandchildren, to remember his past joys and sorrows. God, how he wanted to find his son.

And when he looked at Hebe, doggedly turning up to gaze at him and sing, the strangest feeling came to him that she was keeping him alive by being there – no, even more than that: that she was willing him to recovery from Heaven's recent blow. An extraordinary revelation struck him. What if Hebe was an angel, sent to save him? She had come here because of the angel, after all. The theft of the original from Foxbarton church had, slowly but inevitably, led to her being here now. Perhaps it was all part of a cycle that was meant to be. Perhaps, he thought, angels are sent amongst us, slightly but badly disguised as normal people. Perhaps she was here to make sure he kept his bargain and replaced the lost statue before he died.

Then in an episode of that strange mental bargaining that sometimes overcomes even the most minimally superstitious people from time to time, Joshua traded in his mind with Heaven. *I offer you the angel in return for living to see my lost son*. It seemed to him that the day he handed the Foxbarton angel to St Gregory's church and completed the cycle again was the day he could expect to find Gabriel and some sort of healing of mind and body. And when Hebe stopped singing and crept over to touch his right hand, which everyone else thought did not work at all, he turned it palm up and held hers, more firmly than he expected, and smiled, less crookedly than he had feared. And Hebe, from the distant place which she often seemed to inhabit, focused suddenly on to his eyes, on what he believed to be his soul, and smiled back.

'Grandpa's happy,' she said, and for a sudden, surprising moment, Joshua realised that he was.

Chapter Nine

On the Saturday morning Matilda Gilfoyle was up at dawn practising singing her scales. Hebe Fitzgerald, on the other hand, had been up most of the night counting the stars. Every time she almost got to the end more of them appeared, and some of the ones she had seen before disappeared, and it had pleased her that this was so because she believed that the world would stop and they would all fall off when she reached the end. Stars had to be counted – for Hebe this was akin to being on a treadmill: she had to keep on counting and counting, but she would never reach the end.

So when Matilda arrived the next morning Hebe refused to wake up.

'Aunt Julia, she's lying here all still with her eyes closed,' shouted Matilda down the stairs, 'and she's supposed to come and practise. When I poke her she acts as if she's dead.'

'If you want her,' said Julia cheerfully, well aware that Hebe was listening to every word, 'you'll have to get her. And when the two of you come down, if you're quick enough, you can take some of these muesli bars with you, but if you're slow Daniel will have eaten absolutely every one of them.'

Hebe leaped from her bed as if bitten by a spider, dashed past Matilda into the bathroom, and started to brush her teeth with enormous vigour.

Daniel sauntered into the kitchen, having been strolling round the garden discussing the relative merits of electric and petrol mowers with Stewart outside. (Stewart was keen to know if Daniel had seen Julia naked, and kept engaging him in inane gardening-based conversations in the hope of steering the subject round, casually and apparently accidentally, to the colour of Julia's pubic hair.)

'Big day, today, then?'

'Apparently,' said Julia, trying not to let her nerves show. 'We're off at ten.' She looked out of the window, where the lawn, to her artist's eye, currently resembled a big game park full of willow animals – although Mrs Padley, who had passed the previous day, had peered over the wall through her thick lenses and said rather puzzlingly, 'Those people in your garden are very quiet, dear. Are they having a party?'

'I thought I might come,' said Daniel casually. 'I'd like to hear Hebe sing, and I can hold your hand if you have the vapours.'

'That's sweet of you. Mind you, it's more likely that you'll give the judges the vapours – they're all very nice ladies of a certain age. They're not used to dreadlocks in Haverhill. Nor eyebrow rings.'

'Rubbish,' said Daniel. 'The world has changed, Julia. Very nice ladies of a certain age are all on HRT now. When they see someone interesting they don't flush and palpitate, they take them away and ravish them. You may have to cover me whilst I escape through a side exit.'

'I can see,' said Julia, 'that you've never been to the Haverhill Festival.'

It was a glorious blue-skied day, one of those days that seems to carry all the promise of summer, when late St John's wort still fills the hedgerows with soft yellow, the bright rape flowers are tailing off in the meadows and zephyr breezes whisper stories of the Mediterranean into ears grown tired of the English spring. Birds twittered, rabbits chased, caravans started to form jams on the roads to the coast, and Hebe decided she was not in a singing mood.

'Hebe,' said Matilda rather desperately to her still-silent

cousin, 'we've got to practise. Aunt Julia, what if she does this when we're there?'

'Then you'll just have to sing on your own.'

'Oh, sure,' said Matilda, 'in the duet class. People will be laughing too much to hear me. Come on, Hebe, I've even got you some of William's wine gums.'

'I wouldn't eat those,' came William's lugubrious voice from the doorway. 'They're all pre-sucked.'

'William,' Julia hadn't expected him, 'you shouldn't be down here. We're going in a minute and you won't fit in Daniel's car with us: there aren't enough belts.'

'Mum says if you come up to our house we can all go together in the big car,' said William, 'although I don't see why I have to go. It's only girls singing.'

'You'll see it differently when we've won and I've got a recording contract,' said Matilda, who had high hopes. 'You'll be proud then to be brother to the next Charlotte Church.'

'I can't think of anything worse,' said William, 'apart from being eaten alive by soldier ants . . . but, no, I take it back, it would *still* be worse to have to listen to you crowing every day for the rest of my life.'

'The vicar says we should be glad for each other,' said Matilda, 'when good things happen. Weren't you listening in church last week?'

'Are you kidding?' asked William, who generally found much better things to do in the church choir stalls than actually listen to the vicar. He had been attempting for some weeks to recover a deathwatch beetle from the much-chewed pew in front of him by scraping holes in the wood with a drawing pin, unaware that the timber had been treated some years ago and there was nothing in there at all.

They walked up to the house together, Matilda holding Hebe's hand and anxiously trying to persuade her into a quick chorus of 'Who Will Buy?', but Hebe stayed silent. Merrill was waiting for them outside the house, looking frustrated because Simon was out visiting a patient even though he wasn't on call, and hadn't got back at exactly the time he'd promised.

'You're too obsessive,' said Julia fondly. 'We'll wait – we've loads of time. How's Joshua?'

'I haven't seen him this morning,' said Merrill darkly. 'The latest Brunhilde won't let me in – says he doesn't want visitors – and Sonja has gone off to London on a wild-goose chase. Look, we've got ten minutes, then we must go.'

'What was wrong with Simon's patient?'

'Dying,' said Merrill. 'They always are.'

'Oh dear . . .'

'I'm being sarcastic. Dying of something you don't die of, like earache or an ingrowing toenail.'

'Painful, though,' said Julia, wondering suddenly if something was wrong between Merrill and Simon. It struck her now that whenever Merrill mentioned him lately it was in rather derogatory tones.

The children had started the kind of chasing about and squabbling that they always seemed to embark upon when a moment's wait was required, and it was a few minutes before they realised that Hebe had taken off and was nowhere to be seen. When they did notice there was barely time for Matilda's histrionic 'Oh no!' before a dramatic scream drew them round the west wing of the house and revealed that Hebe had just removed her teeth from Brunhilde's thumb.

'I am off right now,' the nurse was shouting. 'I do my job well and I can handle cranky old men that peer at my breasts and big smelly dogs that pee on the carpet, but no one warned me that ejecting crazy children would be part of this job. This one is an animal. She bit me! An animal, I tell you!' She shook her fist at the house and stormed off to her car.

It was a moment before the noise of her revving up and driving away had died down, especially as she reversed back to shout, 'I shall expect a month's wages in lieu of constructive dismissal!' But once silence had fallen they all heard a strange noise.

'Oh my God, it sounds like choking!' shouted Merrill, and she dashed into Joshua's room, closely followed by Merrill and the children. There they found Hebe sitting at the foot of Joshua's bed with blood on her chin, and Joshua making a very good attempt at roaring with laughter.

The arrival of Simon interrupted the general fussing and rushing about which accompanied making sure Joshua was fine (he was), and making sure none of the blood on Hebe was her own (it wasn't). Matilda was growing increasingly frantic as her planned departure time was upon them, and Hebe was staring at Joshua with her strange intensity. Eventually she said, 'Grandpa's getting better.'

Joshua frowned at her furiously with both of his eyebrows. He didn't want anyone else guessing at the minor improvements in his physical abilities – it was one of the reasons he had recently banned them all from visiting him most of the time. Either he got back his full physical ability, or he would die in this chair, if Hebe would allow it, with none of them ever getting their hopes up, none of them treating him like a well-behaved child who has managed at last to take a step and stop dribbling. And then he realised, to his astonishment, that he had even qualified his thoughts with that phrase, 'if Hebe would allow it.'

He discovered they were all looking at him and shrugged with his one good shoulder. He looked again at Hebe, at her dark eyes staring at his, through him, at him again – and he understood to his astonishment that she was doing it on purpose. She was turning herself on and off to people on purpose. He winked with the eye that still could. Hebe stared back unwaveringly, but a tiny frown creased her forehead. He knew she knew he'd rumbled her. I have your secret and you have mine, he tried to say with his eyes. Then she looked through him again and he knew she had chosen not to see him at all.

'She means you,' said William helpfully, and Joshua attempted a glower. 'Mum,' he added, 'can I stay here with Grandpa now that Brunhilde has cleared off?'

'What d'you mean, cleared off?'

And then Simon had to be appraised of the injured-nurse scenario, with its inherent suing potential, and there was an argument about whether William, at eleven, could possibly be left alone with his chairbound (no one dare say disabled in Joshua's presence) grandfather. The upshot of it all was that Daniel, who had had his own reasons for wanting to hear Hebe sing at the festival, felt an enormous unspoken moral pressure to offer to stay behind. It was pressure born of his own guilt, since he had been plotting and Julia would kill him if she knew – but it meant he offered to sit with Joshua, and the rest went tearing off in the family Discovery to try to get to the festival in time. One thing had been achieved at least: Hebe had decided she was willing to sing.

Haverhill town hall was a relatively modern building at the head of the High Street. The car park behind it was full, but they squeezed the Discovery into a space which wasn't a space, argued briefly over whose fault it really was that no one had a twenty-pence piece to put in the ticket machine, then were rescued by William's discovering one in the passenger footwell – together with a half-eaten packet of crisps, half a dozen petrol receipts and a flyer from a car valeting company.

The town hall was buzzing with anticipation when they went in. The previous class, which sounded as though it was to find the most warbly women's choir, was just finishing and the audience was changing over. There were dozens of children gathering to compete, and parents and other interested parties filled almost all of the audience seats ahead of them. As a result, Merrill, Julia and Simon found themselves seated separately from one another, whilst Matilda took Hebe to the competitors' area down at the front. William found Oscar, then left him to take up the seat behind Julia so that he could whisper in her ear, 'Oscar's mum says there are people here from the BBC.'

Julia barely heard him. She had developed the most terrible butterflies in the pit of her stomach. They seemed to be wearing crampons and tackling the climb up her stomach wall with mountaineering vigour. What if Hebe should throw a wobbly in the middle of these proceedings? Hebe's wobblies were sometimes of catastrophic immensity. This was all so grimly formal and everyone looked so proper and competitive – what if Hebe bit some of *these* people? Julia swallowed hard and checked her pulse rate – fast, very fast – that couldn't be healthy, she thought. At which point, to her relief, the woman in the next chair showed herself to be a late departing warbling supporter and got up to leave, so that William slipped into the vacant space. To his utter disgust Julia took hold of his hand and squeezed it tightly.

'Let go,' he whispered furiously. 'People will see and I'll be embarrassed.'

'William,' said Julia, 'I don't give a hoot right now. Hold my hand and shut up or I'll stand up and scream and then you'll really be embarrassed.'

Kate Coleman was also in the hall, but she had arrived early to secure a good seat. She had secured an exceptionally good seat, both in terms of acoustics, of view, and of immediate neighbours, as she had Jonathan Doyle on her left and a man who introduced himself as 'an uninteresting bod from the Beeb' on the other. Kate was immensely excited. She had clearly found the rumoured talent spotter, which should accord her a most wonderful opportunity to plug Oscar's future career when the chance arose (for the moment Kate had put Oscar's future careers as heart surgeon, newspaper editor, Nobel prizewinner and grand chessmaster on hold and was concentrating on his career as internationally acclaimed violinist).

Jonathan watched her fluttering and flapping, and doing her best to prepare the man on her left for the forthcoming acoustic treat that Oscar's performance would be, for in the apparently random programming that was the festival, the under fifteens violin solo class would immediately follow the under twelve duet class. (This was widely believed to be so that anyone performing in two classes would have to make two expeditions on two separate days, and acquire two separate parking tickets in the process, rather than the single one which might result from a sensible timetable.)

Jonathan had never noticed how delicate Kate's hands were till now. She was fiddling with her rings as she spoke to the man beside her, and he wondered why she sometimes wore the wedding ring. The man she had been married to was now married to someone else, and she professed to hate him absolutely, so it was presumably respectability, then. Jonathan sighed for Kate, acutely aware of her vulnerability as he listened to her expanding on Oscar's talents to the chap on her other side – who was, he was well aware, nothing to do with television but an unemployed parishioner called Dermot Digby with a good repertoire of chat-up lines. Suddenly he did not want to see Kate hoodwinked by Dermot, harmless as it might be. He leaned around her.

'Dermot. How's the car-valeting business going?'

Dermot flushed guiltily. 'Er – not very well, actually.' He glanced apologetically at Kate. 'Difficult to valet cars when you're in and out of the studio so often.'

Kate looked puzzled. 'How do you two know –'

'Oh, Dermot is a great supporter of Haverhill church,' said Jonathan cheerfully. 'Wasn't it you who painted the walls a couple of years ago with that rather odd paint? The stuff that all had to be stripped off again because the plaster started to dissolve?'

'My, my, how time has flown. Be seeing you,' said Dermot, leaping to his feet and departing, leaving Jonathan and Kate sitting in silence. Kate was blushing painfully.

'I suppose you did that because you heard me making a fool of myself,' she said after a moment.

'I did it because I hear him telling you lies,' said Jonathan gently. 'Speaking out for your son isn't making a fool of yourself.' He put a hand on hers, without thinking, and noticed how small it felt within his. Tiny, compared to Julia's great, rough ones, Kate's nails neatly manicured whereas Julia's generally had clay or soil beneath them. His mind flashed to Julia, so big-boned and capable, needing no one. What a contrast Kate was. She smelled of Chanel – Jonathan generally preferred women to smell of fresh hay and soap, but he did like Chanel, the perfume his first girlfriend had worn for their first illicit sexual experience in a hay barn just outside Dorchester. He realised he felt deeply stirred towards Kate, and it struck him that this was not the first time he had felt this way. Perhaps, even though she was a parishioner, it would not be so terrible . . . But he had to be clear in his mind. Was it Julia he wanted, unsuitable though she was, with her rough sensual qualities, her independence and rather wild artiness – or was it delicate, vulnerable Kate, who so needed looking after and protecting?

Kate was acutely aware of Jonathan's hand on hers. Amazing, she thought, no one shows the slightest interest in me sexually for over a decade – including my own bloody husband – and the minute I jump into bed with a poet even the vicar fancies me. It felt rather nice to be cared for, though. Perhaps, now I've had wild romance in the woods, it's time for comfort and caring in the bedroom.

'It is now time for the twelve-and-under duet class,' said the rather headmistressy woman in bifocals who was running today's events. 'Now this year we have a very small class – sadly, the art of the vocal duet seems rather to have left us. Still, I'm sure our pair of entrants today will be of the very highest quality. Matilda Gilfoyle and Hebe Fitzgerald.'

And Kate, despite the fact that she was only here for Oscar and didn't want Matilda Gilfoyle stealing the show, watched Hebe walk on with that strange expression that suggested that whatever she was looking at was not of this world, and held her breath. What if Hebe got distressed? What if she screamed and ran off or lay on the floor and played dead? Kate had found her lying in her garden in the middle of the night once, and when asked to explain her presence Hebe had said, 'I was tired,' as if going to sleep in someone else's daffodils at midnight was the most normal thing in the world. Jonathan squeezed the back of Kate's hand, and she realised that he was just as nervous as she. It was as if they all had some part in Hebe now – she was part of their community and of their responsibility. What a shame we didn't manage the same for Gabriel, she thought, turning her hand palm upwards, instinctively, surprising herself and him with the sudden tingling it generated on both sides.

> 'Early one morning, just as the sun was rising
> I heard a maid sing in the valley below.
> "Oh, don't deceive me, Oh never leave me.
> How could you use a poor maiden so?"'

Julia could feel a slow flush spreading over her throat and neck. Her heart was beating so hard that she felt as if her entire left breast was bouncing up and down on her chest wall, and she glanced down at it to check that it was not noticeable. Hebe was there on stage, still and calm, her gaze fixed on some lost star a million light years away, and Julia could tell she was completely unaware of the rapt audience listening to her. Her voice filled the hall, her high notes rang effortless and pure, and she sang as if her heart would break. Matilda, beside her, sang with a serious intensity that belied her years, and although her voice did not have quite the soaring quality of Hebe's, the combination of the two was almost ethereal. Could it be genetic? Julia wondered. Could she have inherited artistic genes that allow her to express herself through music, even though she can't express herself otherwise – at least, not without screaming and climbing out of windows.

She listened in absolute silence, gripping William's hand until, as he told Oscar afterwards, he was afraid it might go green and maggotty and drop off – which would have been interesting, if painful. She had heard Hebe sing many times, of course, had seen Jonathan and Daniel stunned by the sound of her Puccini that day, but she had never before sat amongst strangers, listening, as aware of their response as of her own. Actually she would never have guessed that Hebe would be capable of performing. She had gone completely to pieces in the last school nativity play she had been involved in. During the performance she had become distressed, lain down in the middle of the stage and played dead. Mary and Joseph, improvising brilliantly, had inter-mittently said 'oh look, a marble statue,' and they had left her there for the whole scene. She had not been given a role again. Maybe it's the control, the discipline of the music that stops her losing it this time, Julia thought, gripping William's hand ever-tighter. Maybe she's just happier singing.

When they finished you could have heard a pin drop in the hall. There was around ten seconds complete and absolute silence before uproarious applause began. Matilda bowed, Hebe remained staring intently at a spot in space some million or so light years behind the audience. William shook his hand dramatically and said rather mysteriously, 'Phew, Aunt Julia, you're just like Batman.' Kate, applaud-ing with the rest, had tears in her eyes. She remembered her conversation about genius with John in his caravan and decided that Hebe did indeed have a talent that could be called genius – at least, it was a gift of genius proportions.

Perhaps Julia needed a manager for Hebe as well as for herself. She would call round and see her later. She had to give her the plans for the exhibition anyway, since its success was dependent on Julia producing pieces of artwork of the right size for the alcoves and displays Kate would be arranging . . .

All around people were saying, 'Hasn't that child got a remarkable voice?'

'Did you hear that . . .?'

'It was so effortless . . .'

'It was like listening to angels singing . . .'

'Stunning. Just stunning.'

It was no great surprise, of course, when they won the 'best in class' certificate, given that there were no other entrants. Actually it would have been rather awful, Julia thought, if anyone else had entered, so completely would they have been outclassed. It took her a while to find Hebe afterwards – in fact it took everyone a while, and the festival had to be temporarily suspended whilst the backstage area was searched. Hebe was finally found at the top of a fifteen-foot spotlight ladder pretending to be asleep, an effect spoiled only by the fact that she was hanging upside down by her knees and could therefore surely not be, and Julia had to fetch her down in a fireman's lift, an art she had perfected long ago during many similar episodes.

'Heaven help me,' she said to Merrill, 'if she's still doing this when she's eighteen.'

Hebe was silent all the way home, making a complicated aeroplane out of her winners' certificate, then, as they rounded the bend into Foxbarton, burst into a sudden chorus of 'Where the bee sucks', which seemed currently to be her favourite song.

Matilda, however, seemed to have deflated. She and William were in the rear, side-facing seats, glaring at one another.

'What's the matter, glumface?' asked William, brimful of tact.

'Nothing.'

'I'd hate to see your face when something's up then. I might turn to stone.'

'Don't be rude.' Matilda folded her arms and turned her back on him. 'Mum, he's being rude.'

Merrill, next to Simon in the front of the car, looked appealingly at Julia behind her, and Julia leaned back. 'Guys, you did brilliantly. Matilda, you can't do better than win.'

'Bound to win when you're the only one in the class,' said William.

'Is that what's wrong?' Julia sighed. 'Come on, Matilda, you know the two of you would have won if there had been a hundred others, but you'd have been so much better that the others would have felt awful. So it was great that there was only you. More like a concert than a competition.'

Matilda stared at the floor.

'It's because no one from the BBC signed her up,' said William, 'isn't it? *Charlotte Church*?'

Matilda shrugged, 'I don't want to be on the stupid BBC.'

'Ah,' said Julia, thinking: Thank God they didn't.

They got back to find Joshua asleep again, and Daniel on the phone in the kitchen whilst Mrs Barker fussed around preparing lunch and complaining that Daniel's dreadlocks were probably full of wildlife and anything could get out and bite her when he wasn't looking. William, to whom this idea had never occurred before, became immensely excited at the suggestion and spent quite some time exploring Daniel's hair for signs of unusual insects. Julia and Merrill left them to it and took Hebe into the garden to lie in the sunshine.

'It's the horse fair next weekend,' said Merrill casually, as they sipped iced lime squash and pretended, for the sake of the children, not to notice when very large wasps buzzed nearby even though they were obviously trying to decide whether or not to sting them to death. 'It's all more or less organised, you know. The various village stalls and things, I mean.'

'Oh yes?' said Julia, wondering what she was about to be asked to do.

'The face-painting woman has dropped out, though,' continued Merrill, as if she hadn't spoken. 'She just called round this morning and dropped in the face paints. Huge palette of them, all sorts of colours. I've got no skills in that direction.'

Julia sighed. 'Who's going to watch Hebe if I paint faces?'

'I'm sure William and Matilda will watch her, and you can keep an eye –'

'Have you ever painted children's faces?' demanded Julia. 'It's like climbing Everest backwards on a unicycle whilst a crowd of angry mothers complain you're not being quick enough. Back-breaking – you can't stop concentrating for a second and you don't get to look up once. You can't even take a pee because there's always a queue of children who're next.'

'Please, Jules? You know you can't live here and not be roped in to all this stuff.'

Julia sighed. 'Why don't you ask Kate if she'll do it?'

'Kate couldn't paint faces. She's about as artistic as that blooming llama.'

'Anyone can paint faces,' said Julia, watching the llama watching them over the hedge, 'and some llamas are very artistic. There was a piece at the Tate one year a llama had done.'

'Oh, come on, you're having me on.'

'No, really, there was. They splodged paint on a wall, and then the llama rubbed its nose in it and made patterns.'

Merrill looked at Brian thoughtfully. 'So you mean that snooty creature might have some use after all?'

'I doubt it. The one at the Tate got panned by the critics. They said the llama obviously didn't know its arse from its elbow.'

'Do llamas have elbows?'

'How should I know? You're the one with the llama. Go and ask it.'

'I could ask it to do the face-painting,' said Merrill rather glumly, 'if you won't. It's next on my list.'

'Fine, let the llama do it.'

'Oh, Jules, please. It spits.'

'So do I when I'm in a really bad mood. Anyway, it's not rocket science, painting faces . . . Oh, don't look at me like that. Oh God. OK, I'll paint the bloody faces. I suppose that llama's going to get away with doing nothing at all.'

'Always does,' said Merrill, eyeing the llama darkly. The llama ignored her and ate another delphinium.

Normally Julia said yes almost without thinking to these requests for face-painting, but she had been feeling a little tense about Hebe since this morning. It seemed to her that the festival had demonstrated just how unpredictably well Hebe could perform, and how absolutely unlike any other child she was underneath. One minute triumphant on stage, the next fifteen feet up, hanging like a bat from a ladder. 'One day,' she said to Merrill, 'I'm afraid Hebe will just fall from somewhere and I won't be there in time to catch her.'

'She's like a mountain goat,' said Merrill, 'she won't fall. You know she climbed out of Matilda's bedroom window when she was four.'

'She didn't! You never told me!'

'I only found out myself a few days ago. William said he found her out there in the tree because she didn't like the noise.'

'What noise?'

'I dunno.'

Julia sighed. 'She just astounds me sometimes.'

'I don't see why. Don't you remember how we used to climb things? I remember you climbing up scaffolding on a building site and hanging by your knees at the top, thirty feet above all the rubble and broken glass, just because you could, and you were only seven yourself.'

'God, I did, didn't I? Imagine what our mother would have said. She had kittens when you did handstands in the garden and she banned me from tobogganing when I came home covered in bruises because she said it would make me infertile.'

'See,' said Merrill triumphantly, 'you ascribe all Hebe's foibles to autism, but some of it is just inherited from you. Your weird genes.'

'Maybe so,' said Julia, 'but then perhaps my weird genes made her autistic too. It can be inherited, you know. I've met several people who have two autistic children.'

'Well, I don't think there's been any in our family before.' Merrill was doubtful. 'Anyway, yours aren't her only genes.'

'I know. I often think of that, that some of her must be him. I don't know where the voice comes from. I sound like a frog on speed when I try to sing anything at all.'

'I feel the same about Matilda,' said Merrill, 'and her genes. Sometimes it just comes. I could never sing a note. William has a glorious voice too, but he'd rather hunt beetles than sing.'

'Can Simon sing?'

'No, not a thing. When he sings in church it's like pipes creaking. His mother could sing, though, apparently – had a fabulous voice.'

'What happened to her?' asked Julia. 'I mean, I know it's all caught up with what happened to Gabriel, but did she really die of a broken heart?'

'No, she died of breast cancer,' said Merrill. 'Joshua blamed Gabriel, though. Gabriel had been very close to her but when he told Joshua he wanted to leave Gilfoyles Joshua told him he'd be cut off, out of the will, not welcome, all this heavy stuff – so in the end Gabriel just took off without a word and that was when Marjorie became ill.'

'Why *did* he drop out? I mean, when you got married he was running Gilfoyles, wasn't he?'

'Oh yes, but it wasn't what he wanted. It was expected of him. Joshua wanted one of his sons to run Gilfoyles, and Gabriel was so brilliant, and being the eldest . . . well, he never got to choose. He went to Harvard, then straight into the City. He was running Gilfoyles by the time he was twenty-three. So Simon got to go to medical school.'

'I remember Gabriel missed your wedding. I was supposed to sit next to him but I got the vicar.'

'Quite,' said Merrill. 'He was abroad somewhere doing some enormous deal. Marjorie was very upset, but Joshua just said the business came first.'

'Silly old sod,' said Julia. 'Still, I suppose that's why he's rich and I'm not. Why didn't Gabriel jack it in earlier?'

'I think he felt he couldn't. Everything Joshua had done, everything Gabriel had been given, was all so he'd run Gilfoyles. He was perfect for it, but it wasn't perfect for him. That's why Simon feels so guilty. If Gabriel hadn't done it Simon would have been the one forced into the company. So he feels in a way Gabriel did it for him.'

'And what about Marjorie?'

'Oh, it all blew up when the twins were babies. Gabriel didn't turn up at Gilfoyles one day, left his resignation and disappeared. When we went looking he'd already sold his flat and given the proceeds – every penny he owned – to a mental health charity. That really annoyed Joshua, of course – you can imagine.'

'He sounds quite a nice bloke,' said Julia, 'compared to his father.'

'He was, actually. Anyhow, he disappeared completely. It turned out later that he'd buzzed off to Greece and worked in a boatyard, but no one knew. Marjorie was frantic with worry, and Joshua, of course, was furious.

Anyway, it turned out that poor Marjorie had breast cancer. She didn't tell anyone about it, didn't see her doctor at all. She must have known for months, but she ignored it, so it killed her before anyone even knew she was ill. Joshua thought it was because of Gabriel, that she would have looked after herself if she hadn't been worrying about him.

'Anyway, you know about the funeral. It was really awful, Gabriel turning up so drunk and the police coming. He never came back here after that.'

'I'm not surprised. Imagine your own father having you arrested at your mother's funeral.'

Merrill shrugged. 'I know. Joshua was furious when the police told him they'd let Gabriel go.'

'Did you see Gabriel again?'

'Occasionally. He dropped out completely, slept in Hyde Park when the park warden didn't find him first, became a street bum. He often turned up at the house for a bath and to wash his clothes and he was still drinking, but he would never have any money or anything else from us. Then one day he just stopped coming. I did wonder if maybe he'd gone back to Greece, but we haven't seen or heard from him since we left London. Joshua has had people looking for him for years.'

'Wow,' said Julia, 'you married into a really dysfunctional family.'

Merrill shook her head regretfully. 'Just Joshua. He's always been so . . . unbending. I think that's why he's being so obstinate now. He has the same attitude to weakness in himself that he's always displayed to weakness in others.'

'He's a nasty old bigot,' said Julia, remembering anew his thoughts on Hebe.

'Mummy?' Hebe was at her side, her face flushed from running around, a large wasp sitting on the back of her hand. 'Look what I've found. D'you want to stroke him?'

'Er – goodness, just shake that hand, darling – that's right, he's flown off now. That was a wasp, Hebe. They can hurt you if you play with them. Oh no – oh, look, Merrill, she's got a sting. Darling, a wasp has stung your arm. Isn't it sore?'

Hebe looked at the weal on her arm, shrugged and wandered off round the side of the house. Matilda appeared from the trees and followed her at a distance.

'You know,' said Julia watching her go, 'sometimes she doesn't even seem to feel pain. And at other times the tiniest little thing completely throws her. I feel so afraid for her. Matilda, will you keep an eye on Hebe, see where she's gone? I don't want her to get stung again.'

Matilda waved and disappeared after her cousin, who was now on her way up a tree at the front of the house, so that she could hang by her ankles from a branch.

'Julia . . . tell me, have you ever thought Simon might be unfaithful to me?'

Julia stared. 'Simon? No, of course not. Why, what makes you say that?'

'I saw him hugging Sonja,' said Merrill, 'the other day. He said it was just to comfort her, and it probably was, but it's left me feeling . . . a bit rattled.'

'So what are you going to do?'

'I don't know. What do you think?'

'Well,' said Julia, 'you've got a few options really.'

'Go on?'

'Closed-circuit cameras,' said Julia, 'private detectives, an assassin – for her, I mean, superglue on her lips whilst she's asleep to see what's stuck there by the following evening –'

'Be serious.'

'I am. Or you could just accept his answer, assuming you trust him. I mean, he is a GP. They must hug people constantly.'

Merrill frowned. 'My GP never hugs me.'

'Then she's useless – get another one. Why don't you put a hex on Sonja? You could make her grow coarse hair on her upper lip just by willing it.'

Merrill started to giggle. 'Don't be silly.'

'Ah, well, deny yourself if you will. Your husband is a safe bet, I'm sure of it. He might fantasise about her boobs but he wouldn't want to lose you for her.'

'But I don't want him to fantasise about her boobs,' said Merrill miserably.

'Oh, for goodness' sake, they're not real. You could let them down with a pin if you really wanted to. All men have fantasies, Merrill. They develop them in their teens. Joshua had a string of mistresses, from what I've heard, so it's easy to see where Simon's fantasies come from. But that's all they are. Fantasies. He probably just needs to have you on the boardroom table.'

'Julia!'

'Don't be such a prude. Buy a red lipstick and take him off to London for the day. And now I'm going to make some lunch. Are you coming?'

As the sun rose to its highest point and they settled down to a light lunch in the Grange, Mrs Braithwaite was settling down to fish and chips with a guest. John James had brought the food over and the two of them were sitting on the grass outside her cottage with glasses of home-made dandelion and burdock, listening to the birdsong and the sound of the wind in the trees.

'You should know better,' said Mary Braithwaite. 'You'll hurt her.'

'She's a grown woman,' said John, 'and she makes her own decisions.'

'That's as may be, but she's in love with the vicar.'

'Ah. She never said.'

'Well, you wouldn't, would you, not whilst you were off with the raggle-taggle gypsies, oh?'

John sighed. 'OK, point taken. I'll do the right thing by Kate. So tell me about this child, Hebe.'

'Nothing much to tell. The mother is Merrill Gilfoyle's

sister. She lived in London till a few months ago, then she came here, moved into the Woodcutter's cottage. Joshua asked her to make him an angel to replace the one that went from the church.'

'And has she made one?'

'Not yet. She's unfulfilled. She needs someone, she just doesn't know it yet. And the daughter . . . They call it autism, although in my day we'd have said she was a changeling.'

'I know. But in your day you said everyone was a changeling and babies came out from under mushrooms.'

'Don't you be cheeky, young man. Just because I'm old that doesn't mean I'll take it. The child has enormous gifts, but something of her has been taken away.'

'Or perhaps it was never there.'

Mrs Braithwaite shrugged and sipped her drink. 'Perhaps. She has no fear, so she faces danger all the time, and her life is a quest. She shouldn't have been wandering in these woods alone, though. If you find her you bring her to me.'

'Her mother should watch her,' said John, suddenly angry with Julia without even knowing her.

'She does,' said Mary, 'but the child could escape from Alcatraz. You should meet the mother.'

John shook his head. 'Stop it, old woman. I'm not here looking for love. I saw an angel of my own years ago, I don't need anyone else.'

'Mortals don't fall in love with angels,' said Mary Braithwaite, 'so don't talk rubbish.'

'I did.'

'Go and write your stupid poetry, then, if you're going to come out with that rubbish. But leave that Coleman woman alone. Her destiny is elsewhere.'

John rolled his eyes. 'And where is my destiny, then?'

'Right in front of you,' said Mary Braithwaite, 'if you'd only open your eyes. Now leave me be. I'm an old woman, I need my rest.'

'Hello,' said Daniel into the telephone. He was in the call box again, near the post office. 'Well? What did they think?'

'My God, Dan,' said the voice, 'she's an absolute phenomenon. But there's some weird thing going down as well. I mean, what was all the stuff with halfway up a ladder?'

'Autistic,' said Daniel. 'You know.'

'No I don't bloody know. I'm in the music business, I leave the care in the community to others. What is it? Is she nuts?'

Daniel winced. 'Remember Dustin Hoffman in *Rain Man*?'

'Oh, the telephone directories thing?'

'That's right. That's autism. A little weird but sometimes brilliant. She doesn't have to give interviews, Carl, she just has to make records.'

'I dunno . . . Mind you, it could be a bit of a selling point, don't you think?'

'What could?'

'Her being handicapped. I mean, tastefully done, of course, and we don't want the punters thinking too weird or it puts them off. But she does have a kind of an eerie quality.'

'I don't think so,' said Daniel. 'That's tasteless, and the mother would have your testicles on toast. Trust me, this one's got big hands. She sculpts. Imagine that grasping your nadgers.'

'Ouch. You're right, of course. Are you sure the mother will buy into the whole record thing?'

'I think so,' said Daniel, 'but if you use the word handicap you're on your own, mate. This one kicked a traffic warden who told her it was a shame.'

'What was a shame?'

'That the child was like she was. It was when they lived in London. The police cautioned her for assault.'

'Bloody hell. I've wanted to kick a traffic warden a dozen times. If I'd known all you got was a caution I might have given it a go. Look, Dan, how about offering a carrot to the other child, the cousin? I mean, not the same voice, but pleasant, and she was a good foil. If we had a few duets that'd be something new.'

'Absolutely. I think she's much more likely to go for that. What are we talking about? Ball-park figure? Fifty thou? As much as that? Right, just give me the week. And Carl?'

'What?'

'I expect the usual agent's terms. Forty per cent – I found her.'

'Twenty, you didn't find her, you knew her all along.'

'Thirty – if I hadn't come here you'd never have known about her.'

'Twenty-two. It was easy, she's your friend.'

'Twenty-seven. It's my balls on the line here, Carl. If Julia Fitzgerald thought I was making deals on her daughter I'd never fancy anyone again.'

'Twenty-five, plus ten thou up front if she signs this week.'

'Done.'

Chapter 10

Kate called round to see Julia on the Monday afternoon, having spent the morning taking her mind off the latest disagreement with Martin by drawing up a variety of plans and reinspecting one of the Gilfoyles' empty barns. She was now filled with excitement and enthusiasm at her own sense of purpose, and was desperate to pass it on.

She found Julia on the lawn, where she was happily bending willow into a series of tall thin people, unaware that Kate was about to expand her future irrevocably. Beside her, Hebe, her hair catching the sun like spun gold, was dozing in a deck chair as she had been, in fact, for most of the day. Julia took this simply as further evidence of her nonconformist nature, unaware she was now exhausted due to having spent several hours of the previous night sitting with Joshua whilst he exercised his arm and leg, pulling strange gurning faces at him that he had eventually realised she intended him to copy. At first this seemed just a game – but then, incredibly, he had realised she was making him exercise the drooping side of his face, and it was working. A tingling function was gradually creeping back to the parts of him he had feared were for ever cut off from his brain. These nocturnal meetings were their secret, unknown to and undetected by anyone else, and had left them both very tired. Up at the Grange Joshua was also sleeping.

In the kitchen Daniel Cutter sat making lists on pieces of paper. The left-hand column was his current outstanding credit card bills. The right-hand column was the order in which he planned to pay them off. He just had to make sure he put this properly to Julia. His motives were sound, and Hebe could only benefit, but it was easy to see how Julia might misinterpret his actions. Perhaps a cricket box would be sensible . . . ? He resolved to ask William or Oscar if they possessed such a thing. He might even go for a stroll and meet the kids off the school bus – they should be back at any minute. He waved idly at Kate as he passed, and Kate waved back, rather impressed that she was now the kind of woman who both seduced handsome gypsies and had dreadlocked black men waving at her. The thought so enticed her that she forgot she had meant to ask Daniel if there had been something wrong with Julia's phone the other day.

'Gosh,' said Kate now, waving at Julia over the wall, 'I do like them. What's that bit you're making?'

'A penis,' said Julia bluntly. 'What else did you think it could be, protruding from the groin of a man?'

Kate turned pink. 'Oh, Julia, I'm really sorry. I didn't mean . . . that is, I thought it was a big heron.'

Julia rolled her eyes. 'Kate, I'd murder you if you weren't so honest. Look, these are arms, not wings.'

'What's that bit hanging down, then?'

'A stick. He's walking with a stick.'

'Oh yes, I see now. Why?'

'He's a shepherd.'

'Oh, goodness. What's the constipated one doing?' Kate had her hand over her mouth. I may have become a free and sensual woman, she thought, but I'm not sure I approve of a pooing shepherd.

Julia sighed. 'He's not constipated, he's just squatting. The whole set is called *Tribe*. They're people, and they go with the other set over there, which I'm calling *Safari*.'

'Oh yes, I see it. I do see it now. Is that one the Land Rover?'

'No, that one's the hippo. Honestly, you philistine,

someone should take you to Tate Modern and show you what's a penis and what's art. Come and have some tea. I need a rest from willow and I need someone to talk to before I go stir crazy. Daniel and Hebe have both been asleep virtually all day, and I'm so bored I nearly flashed my boobs at Stewart Barlow when he sailed past on the lawnmower waving his Alan Titchmarsh wave.'

Kate smiled rather nervously. She might consider herself a two-suitor woman now, but that didn't mean she was quite ready for jokes about breasts, and she would never be ready for jokes about Alan Titchmarsh. 'Listen, Julia,' she said, 'I've got some really good news – at least, I hope it is. I've checked out the barns and the biggest one is easily best. It's got a lovely ceiling. Perfect for your exhibition. So I've brought the plans to show you.'

Julia, halfway to her own kitchen door, walking along a patch of grass she had walked upon several times already that day without incident, found a pebble to trip on and fell flat on her nose. A few minutes later, holding the soft part of it to stop the bleeding whilst Kate put an ice cube in lime squash for her to drink, she said, 'Come on, now, Kate. What exhibition are you talking about?'

'I did tell you before,' said Kate, genuinely surprised. 'That evening, you know, when I was upset . . . I had that idea that I was going to be your manager, and you said . . . Well, I can't remember exactly what you said but you seemed really pleased.' She looked anxious now, and Julia frowned.

'Well, yes, but you were drunk, Kate, and you never mentioned an exhibition.'

'Drunk?' Kate was horrified. 'I wouldn't be so irresponsible. I know I was a little emotional, that night, but never drunk, not me.'

'You were out of your tree.'

'My dear Julia, I've never left my tree in my life,' said Kate, rather affronted. 'And anyway, I could never have had such a good idea if I was drunk, could I? I mean, you obviously need an exhibition.'

'Kate,' said Julia patiently, 'how old are you?'

'Thirty-five,' said Kate. 'I was a child bride, you know.'

'Well, I'm only five years younger than you, so please don't call me dear.'

'Oh.' Kate looked as though she might cry. 'I'm sorry, I didn't mean – Oh dear, this is going awfully badly. Today is going just awfully badly.'

Julia took pity on her, seeing her vulnerability. 'What's really wrong, Kate? Sit down and tell me.'

Kate sniffed, 'Oh, the usual – it's Oscar's weekend with Martin coming up, so he's missing the horse fair, and he's peeved with me, so I asked Martin if we could alter it and he's been really mean about it. He said no and he said I was t-turning Oscar against him.'

'Well, tell Oscar about it. Then he can make his own mind up.'

'I don't like to be mean to him about his father. Children can be damaged by that sort of thing.'

'You're too noble. There's nothing mean about being honest.'

Kate looked miserable. 'It just seems I try my best for everyone and everyone still thinks I'm plotting against them. I thought you'd be really pleased with the plans and you think I'm just interfering.'

'I'm sorry, Kate, I didn't mean to knock your idea. I just— You took me by surprise, that's all. Come on, show me the plans.'

'Really? You mean it? OK, well, look, it's to relaunch you, you see . . . with an exhibition of past and recent work. Simon said we could use one of the Gilfoyles' empty barns that they did up last year. Here, look, here's the diagram of the floor plan. It needs probably about thirty-six sculptures on display – they don't all have to be recent, so don't panic – and I thought perhaps some of the preliminary sketch work. Oh, I forgot, you don't sketch, do you? Well, perhaps we could hang something on the walls . . . and then right in the centre, the new Foxbarton angel. On a little plinth.' She beamed at Julia hopefully. 'We could call the whole thing *The Foxbarton Angel*, and in the press releases – which I've done sort-off rough drafts for, here . . . and here, look . . . we can tell the story of what happened to the original one four years ago.'

Julia cleared her throat and stared at the blob which she felt was rather threateningly marked 'little plinth', awaiting the as-yet unformed angel. 'Er,' she said in a voice muffled by her handkerchief, 'thirty-six?'

'Well, you must have lots of work in store,' said Kate practically. 'You had all those exhibitions years ago.'

'It all sold,' said Julia, 'or almost all. I don't really have anything in store any more.'

'Well, I'm sure we can borrow it back,' said Kate emphatically. 'Come on, Julia, people who buy art love to lend it back for exhibitions – it increases its value. Just think, it will be wonderful. You and I running our own gallery. Here, in this village, where we all live. Look, I've got a parish council meeting tonight – I'll get them to pass it, then we're on.'

Julia blinked, taken aback by Kate's enthusiasm. Where we live. Well, this *is* where we live, Hebe and I, this is home now. Well, assuming I don't get chucked out of this cottage for failing to produce a suitable angel. And Kate's idea does have a certain attraction. I could get a lot of stuff back for an exhibition, put my wicker animals and wicker people into it . . .

'When did you have in mind, Kate?' She took the hankie away from her nose and blood trickled down her chin and on to her lap. 'Whoops. Dammit.'

'When you've finished the angel,' said Kate, delighted at this cooperation. 'I mean, that would be the centrepiece. So I thought, the first week of August – that gives you ages. We could get tons of publicity. You know, all the stuff about the old angel disappearing was in the press for weeks. It's one of those things everyone has heard of. You must admit *The Foxbarton Angel*'s a good name for the exhibition. Oh, look, you need to suck that ice cube for a good five minutes.'

Julia frowned and grasped her nose more firmly, 'Kate. About the angel . . .'

'What about it?' Kate frowned, sensing a problem.

'Well, I haven't actually begun it yet. I don't know if setting a deadline is a good idea.'

Kate looked shocked. 'Not set a deadline? How can you say that when Joshua Gilfoyle is dying? How much deader a line can you get? What would he say if you were too late?'

'Oh, put some pressure on me, why don't you? D'you think I'd forget?'

Kate tried to look supportive. 'Look, Julia, I know this is mainly your commission but, well, would you like some help? There's a whole committee of people in the village who'd love to help, you know. They've had all sorts of interesting ideas. I actually have some angel ideas of my own. In fact I took the liberty of sketching a few –'

'Kate,' said Julia rather desperately, 'please don't show me a thing. I'm an artist. I have to be original. It isn't *mainly* my commission, it's *totally* my commission.'

'Oh, I understand, of course,' said Kate, slightly disappointed, 'but you'd better get a move on then, if this exhibition is to open in the first week of August. Now, I need a list of people who've bought stuff from you who might be willing to loan it for exhibition. What about the Saatchis?'

By the time Jonathan Doyle vaulted the wall to say a passing but thirsty hello, Julia realised that she had acquiesced completely in all of Kate's grand plans. It was, she realised, guilt that had done it. She could perfectly easily have refused Kate, but she was already feeling guilty at the lack of progress on the Foxbarton angel, and now that she had managed to start creating something new, even something new made of willow, there was no real excuse not to make a bit more effort on the angel front. None at all, apart from her still having no clear idea where to begin – and the beginning, she knew, was everything.

Hebe had awoken and climbed quietly out of her deck chair to find Julia. She was making tea for Kate and Jonathan whilst they chatted, oddly, shyly on the lawn. Now Hebe hung by her knees from a tree branch at the back of the cottage, some twelve feet up, and watched Matilda and William approaching along the road from the bus stop lugging their school bags, sports kit, musical instruments and tennis racquets. They reminded her of Christmas trees, all covered in stuff.

'Oh my God,' said Matilda, dropping everything and breaking into a run. 'Look at Hebe – look how *high* she is. She'll fall.'

'I don't see why,' said William, who was still not quite sure why he had had to lend Daniel his cricket box other than it was an emergency. 'Bats don't.'

But Matilda was out of earshot, having reached the tree where Hebe hung and climbed up the trunk.

'Hebe,' said Matilda, now a few feet away from her cousin and cautiously upright. 'Shall we climb down? We could go and see Grandpa. William. WILLIAM!'

'What?' He appeared at the foot of the tree.

'Will you go and tell Aunt Julia I'm up a tree with Hebe?'

'Fine,' said William, wandering down to Julia's lawn without much sense of urgency. When he got there he found Julia just emerging from the kitchen and said, 'Matilda's up a tree with Hebe,' adding, 'Matilda thought you ought to know.'

'Is she safe?' Julia had just emerged from the kitchen and had only just realised that Hebe had sneaked away. Trust

Jonathan and blooming Kate to be staring at one another.

'Absolutely,' said William, 'as a fruit bat. Why does Daniel need my cricket box for an emergency?'

'I've absolutely no idea, William. It's certainly not for cricket – he doesn't play.'

'Grandfather says you can't trust a man who doesn't play cricket,' said William. 'D'you think he's right?'

'Not in the slightest,' said Julia. 'How is your grandpa?' Not dying too soon, I hope, she thought guiltily, because it would have been really awful if his stroke had killed him without my making the angel.

William shrugged and frowned. 'He's OK. He's grumpy 'cos Sonja's not here and no one else tells him off.'

'Ah.' Sonja, Julia thought, proved more of her mettle every day, 'D'you want some squash?'

'No,' said William glumly, 'I've got maths homework and Mr Jarvis said if I didn't do it he'd hang me up by my ankles and pay the girls to kiss me.'

'Wow,' said Jonathan, smiling, 'a lot of boys would love that.'

William eyed him as one might a dinosaur. 'Maybe in your day,' he said, 'but times have changed, Vicar. We boys don't like to be kissed. We understand about bugs in saliva,' and he wandered back towards the Grange.

Up in the tree Hebe was resolutely silent. She was staring at the sky from upside down, worrying about where the stars were. They had been there the last time she looked and it had been dark then. If she could see them in the dark, why on earth couldn't she see them now? Her mother said they disappeared when the sun shone, but surely it ought to be easier to see them when it was light. Perhaps they'd really gone this time. Perhaps they'd all died and gone. A sense of horror overcame her and she closed her eyes in despair.

Matilda sighed. She knew Hebe could be silent for hours, sensed this was one of these times. If only she'd brought the latest *Harry Potter* out here – but she could hardly leave

Hebe upside down in a tree whilst she went to fetch it. 'Hebe?'

Silence.

'Hebe, shall I go and get a book and read to you?'

Silence. If she closed her eyes, Hebe thought, and then opened them, the stars would be back.

'I'll take that as a "yes", then,' said Matilda, determined not to be trapped for hours in silence. She climbed down the tree and ran as fast as she could in the direction of home. She'd be back in two minutes. As she rounded the side of Foxbarton Grange she glanced back at the tree and was pleased to see there was no movement.

Hebe liked a challenge, and forgot her despair in a second. The moment she calculated that Matilda would be completely unsighted as regards the tree, something of which she was aware with a precise mathematical ability she did not understand herself, she slid swiftly down it, filling her hair with moss and scratching the insides of her knees, and took off at a very fast pace. No one would see her go, as she had precalculated a line of escape which kept her completely out of the viewing line of either the adults in the garden, of Matilda coming back, or of anyone else who happened to look out of an upstairs window at Foxbarton Grange. She reached the trees at the edge of the woods and, once inside the green leafy coolness, she took a few even breaths, relaxed and started to walk more slowly, singing quietly, *'Where the bee sucks there suck I . . .'*

Matilda, who was wiser than Hebe had given her credit for, followed about ten yards behind. She had expected this bolt for freedom and her run for home had been well faked, a test-run to see if it really would be safe to go and fetch a book. Perhaps she might work out where Hebe went when she sneaked off into the woods all the time. Then she and William wouldn't lose her again – because they had realised that Hebe always went back to the same places. She only ever bolted somewhere new by accident. This time, though,

Hebe was skirting the woods, heading for Foxbarton Grange.

Joshua Gilfoyle wondered what Sonja was doing. A couple of days in London, she had said – but time seemed to stand still when she was away, or, at least, crawl along at such a pace as to be imperceptible. Stephen Hawking had some theories about that, didn't he? Joshua wondered now about Stephen Hawking, that enormous mind trapped in a body that utterly refused to do the things he should have been able to take for granted. How had Stephen Hawking survived it for so many years? How could he, Joshua Gilfoyle, survive it for another day?

And the indignity of it too, being left to the mercies of the Brunhildes. The one with the bitten thumb had been the worst, but at least she had gone. Doubtless she was even now drafting a letter demanding financial damages. They should pay up – it had been worth the money just to see the look on her face when Hebe bit her. The child only did to her what he would have liked to have done himself, if he wasn't so bloody helpless. He had at least pinched her behind on two occasions, just to prove he could, and it had been like pinching a blue whale, in that the main body of the woman had been so far away that it clearly took several seconds for the sensation to travel from her bottom to her brain.

He smiled slightly, then reached out with his left hand and moved his bishop. His ability to play chess, strangely, seemed not only to be intact but to have been honed and purified by his inability to do almost anything else. Simon, who had been chess champion at school, could normally beat him squarely, but this time Joshua was putting up a fight. It was, he realised suddenly, the first time he had admitted to himself that something positive had happened to him. So much had been lost with that stroke that it was hard to concede that anything could have been gained.

'You've got me,' said Simon now. 'Congratulations.' He

tipped over his king. He was hugely relieved to see his father playing chess again, delighted to be beaten. Of course he knew, with his medical mind, that his father had had a motor stroke and there was no reason why that should affect his intellectual function. But it was good truly to sense it was so. He hid his delight and shook his father's hand. Joshua moved his eyebrows to signify that this was no big deal – wouldn't want Simon getting the idea he was feeling any kind of pleasure. He wondered where Hebe had gone. It had been the most amusing thing to happen all week, her biting that nurse, stupid bag. She had called the child an animal, which was clearly ridiculous. And it had been a great relief all the same to see the nurse go storming off like that. Sour-faced Hitler she had been.

He was acquiring a certain strange sort of fondness for Hebe which he was barely prepared to acknowledge. She was clearly subnormal, of course, but she did seem to care about his incapacity, and she'd been a darn sight more use than the bloody rest of them at helping him get better. She was the only one who knew how much he had improved, because she was the only one whom he could bear to allow a glimpse of how much he was still unable to do, and how much he wanted to try. To walk, to speak, these were things he had once taken for granted, but now? Now they were the sum of his ambition. Well, and to find that good-for-nothing Gabriel, of course.

He wondered why Hebe was never at school. Weren't there truancy people to make children go to school? In his day they had gone away to school, children like that, and they never came home. Big, hard institutions they went into, with dark gates and high walls. You never saw them again. Rather horrible to think of the beautiful, golden-haired Hebe and her amazing voice disappearing into something like that. The child had some gifts, after all. She *was* a little like him, something brilliant trapped inside something totally useless. He was conscious of a growing feeling of camaraderie towards her. Which was ridiculous, of course, because she wasn't all there and he was. Ridiculous.

He wished, suddenly, that Sonja would ring – but of course she wouldn't call because he wouldn't be able to speak to her. Would he?

Simon was standing. 'I've just got to go and see if Merrill needs me for lunch, Father,' he said, 'I'll leave you with the chess set. I have to try and find you a new nurse this afternoon.'

Joshua sighed and watched him go. And once the door was firmly shut he said, 'Sonnnnn . . . ja. Sonnnnjjjja. Shonja. Sonja. Sonja. Sonja.' It was barely a whisper but it was recognisable, at least to his ears. He tried again. 'The queeeeeck braaaaown f . . . f . . . foxxx jump . . . ped . . . ooooover . . . thel . . . lashhhy d . . . d . . . dogg.'

'The quick brown fox jumped over the lazy dog,' said Hebe from the window.

Joshua looked up. 'Chsss,' he said.

Hebe frowned. Matilda appeared behind her. 'Hi, Gramps. Sorry, d'you want us to go?'

Joshua frowned at her, caught out. 'Chesss.'

Matilda's expression cleared, neither surprised nor unsurprised at his slurred attempt at speech. Children, thought Joshua, just take it as it is. 'Oh, chess. Hebe, can you play chess?'

Hebe, in answer, sat at the chessboard. Aha, thought Joshua, I bet she can. I bet she can play chess brilliantly. There must be a brilliant mind trapped inside the whole strange package. That could explain why I feel, well, almost fond of her. I couldn't be fond of a loony . . . He wondered if that backward boy he had known at school would have been any good at chess. We never gave him chance to find out . . .

Leaning forward he moved his first piece, pawn to king four, a standard opening move to test her mettle, then waited.

Hebe stared hard at the board. Her hand hovered first over her king's pawn, then the bishop's. She looked at Joshua and at Matilda. Joshua was sure her mind was working, calculating her moves several turns ahead, plotting where to begin for maximum devastation. He had heard some autistic people could compute entire games in seconds . . .

'Have you played chess before, Hebe?' asked Matilda anxiously, having been warned that any display of excessive unpredictability on Hebe's part could upset her grandfather. 'Do you know what to do?'

Hebe frowned her tiny frown, stared at the board with intense concentration, her hand hovering first over one piece, then another. She looked up. She was ready. Then she picked up Joshua's pawn, popped it into her mouth, and swallowed it in less than the blink of an eye. She stared at Joshua.

'Hebe!' said Matilda, horrified. 'What have you done?'

Hebe smiled serenely and looked Joshua in the eye. 'Taken Grandpa's pawn,' she said with some pride. She looked at Joshua. 'Your go.'

Jonathan Doyle was facing something of a quandary. It was not easy to be a single vicar, and he had long hoped that time would bring him a desirable but suitable woman with whom to share his life and his bed.

Now, after two hours spent drinking tea and eating scones with Kate and Julia he realised that he had before him in Foxbarton both a desirable and a suitable woman, but unfortunately one of each rather than a single one combining the two qualities. There was Julia, recently the object of some of his more sensual feelings (even now, with a swollen nose and a bruise developing between her eyes she was beautiful) – but of such agnosticism that she could not help but offend the bishop. And then there was Kate who, though a good and upstanding member of the church, was divorced. Still, she was the injured party. Kate would make a marvellous wife for any vicar. Recently he had felt both deeply protective and strangely stirred by her. And yet . . . marriage is a three-legged stool, and the legs are love, children and sex. It was what he said to all the would-be married couples. If one of the legs isn't screwed on properly, the whole thing falls over. And would the sex leg of the stool be strong enough with Kate? It was hard to imagine her abandoned with lust. Julia, now, Julia would probably eat me alive. Could I cope with her at all?

He imagined himself at the altar, faced with them both in full white wedding garb, his bishop standing before him booming, 'Which one, Jonathan, which one?' He sighed. It wasn't as if either one of them would say yes if he asked them.

'The festival was a great success again,' he said now. 'You must be very proud of the children.'

'Delighted,' said Kate. 'Oscar was splendid. I thought it was a shame there were no talent spotters there.'

'Heaven help us all if they had been,' said Julia.

'Why do you say that?' asked Jonathan. 'I mean, talent is a gift, and I'm sure –'

'It may be a gift,' said Julia crossly, thinking it obvious, 'but with Hebe some of her gifts are her burdens and vice versa. It's not simple. Too much talent can be a very heavy thing to carry through life.'

'What do you want for her?' asked Jonathan curiously. 'I mean, forgive me for saying this, but I've always felt that in many ways you were proud just because you have such an unusual child.'

'I am, of course I am. I wouldn't change Hebe for the world. She's made my life less ordinary,' said Julia, surprising herself with her own honesty, 'but she needs someone to look after her. She needs someone to adore her always and for ever. Someone of her own generation for after I'm gone.' I should stop being so honest and open with

Jonathan, she thought. I'll give him ideas.

'We all wish that for our children,' said Kate, thinking, *and for ourselves*. She sent a hungry look at Jonathan but he was watching Julia, admiring the way her freckles were standing out, golden, on her nose.

'Yes, but Hebe may not ever get it. She doesn't understand people,' Julia was saying. 'She may look like an angel but she doesn't understand that people have feelings. So how will she ever –'

'You worry too much,' said Jonathan. 'Hebe will be fine. She has great gifts and great friends.'

'It's my job to worry,' said Julia shortly.

Kate sighed. 'Julia and I are going into business together,' she said, wanting the subject lightened a little, and Julia looked up, startled.

'I hadn't thought of it like that.'

'Well, it is like that. We're starting a gallery. The first exhibition is called *The Foxbarton Angel* and it's going to open in August.'

'That's marvellous,' said Jonathan. 'So can one ask, how is the angel coming along?'

'No, one bloody can't,' said Julia, suddenly stressed. 'It isn't even begun, as you both well know.'

'Well,' said Kate, standing, 'I hope you won't veer too far from most people's idea of an angel. I mean, I'd hate you to do something with eight legs or something.' She eyed the safari of willow animals rather nervously.

Julia frowned. 'It's all very well you saying that, Kate, but, I mean, how do you, how does anyone know what an angel looks like? Do we just assume it or do we base it on religious art we've seen? And where did the artists get it from? Is it because most of us have actually seen angels at some point, but only the ones with the visual memory remember them?'

Kate sniffed. 'I don't have to have seen an angel to feel sure it doesn't have eight legs. I mean, surely it needs to look as people expect an angel to look, not like a . . . a tarantula or something.'

'Can we do anything?' Jonathan was anxious not to offend. 'I mean, I am no artist but if it's spiritual advice on the angel front that you need I'm sure I could –'

'No, you couldn't.' Julia had had enough of people wanting a piece of the action. 'Look, I must get on, I've got work to do.'

'Aunt Julia, Aunt Julia, come quick! Hebe's eaten three pawns and a bishop!'

'Oh bloody hell,' Julia stood up. 'OK, Matilda, how big and what were they made of?'

'About an inch and plastic,' said Matilda. 'It's William's travel chess set.'

'Is she OK?'

'Fine. Grandpa had to put the rest away 'cos she wanted to eat the knights, so she's having cake instead.'

'Oh well,' said Julia, and sat down again. 'They'll come out in the end.'

'But, Aunt Julia, you can't just leave them in her.'

Julia sighed. 'There's no alternative.'

'Grandpa says it spoiled the game.'

Julia stared. 'Is that all he cares about?'

'Oh, don't mind him,' said Jonathan anxiously. 'I'm sure he didn't say it quite that way.'

'Oh, he did,' said Matilda, 'and he meant it 'cos after she did it he ate both knights and they can't finish playing till they've all been passed, which could take days. Mrs Barker says his bowels will never be the same again.'

Up at Foxbarton Grange Joshua hadn't laughed so much since he was a boy. This was even better than the bleeding Brunhilde. He was laughing entirely on the inside of course – it wouldn't do to let anyone see that the peculiar child had made him laugh again on the outside. Laughing at people who weren't all there was like saying it was OK to have them around, and it clearly wasn't. You can't have loony children wandering around singing and eating chess sets.

He sighed. He wasn't looking forward to those chess pieces emerging from his bottom. He wondered how long it would take. Might as well ask Simon. Might as well derive some bloody benefit from having the one remaining son turn into a bloody quack, when the only one who had ever seemed to have any business capability buggered off as if there was no such thing as responsibility.

Simon, however, was less than obliging. 'With your piles, Father, I don't suppose they'll ever get out. I should write to Waddingtons if I were you, tell them there should have been something on the box to warn people not to eat the pieces. It was particularly silly of you to eat the knights.'

'Why?' typed Joshua, thinking uncomfortably of the unevenness of the horse's head on the top (was it perhaps more likely to lodge in some esoterically named bit of his duodenum than, say, a bishop?).

Simon shrugged. 'Well, I don't know about you but I could never win a game with two castles, a bishop, a king, and a queen, even if I didn't have piles.'

Some sixty miles from where Joshua laughed and transiently forgot how much he missed her, Sonja Gilfoyle sat in her husband's chair at Gilfoyles, having finally finished going through all the family paperwork the company lawyer, Mark Smythe, had given her. It was a modest chair, from which he had commanded an empire whose influence had known no boundaries. Joshua's vision had taken Gilfoyles from a small financial services company into a global network involved in almost every legal aspect of trade on the planet. Gilfoyles now had offices in all five continents – and from this small, unimposing chair, Sonja's husband had directed it all.

It amazed her, actually, how small and hard the chair

was. Joshua's enormous presence in the company had required no material embellishment. His office was sparse, only the original Hockney on the far wall giving it a splash of colour, his chair neither grand nor even comfortable. He did not, she knew, believe in excessive comfort, thought it dulled the brain.

Sonja's brain was not dull. Not without intelligence and an analytical mind she had found her route out of Tromsø and her parents' helpless situation, only to be ambushed on the way by falling deeply in love with the old man she had planned to cherish only unto his death, after which his power, freedom and money would be hers to keep. Now, instead, she would have a long life of mourning without him – but at least she could console herself with the thought that no one would deprive him of what he most wanted before his death. If Joshua wanted his son Gabriel she would find him. She rifled the mountain of papers in front of her again. Endless reports from Mark Smythe detailing his expeditions to look for Gabriel, psychologists' analyses on Gabriel and where he might go, lists of dead people who had turned out not to be him – it had taken her hours to read everything, on top of the days she had spent traipsing around London begging for information. 'And?'

'That's everything.' She had grilled Mark Smythe to within an inch of his life but he would not break.

'So that's as far as you've got? To tell me that Gabriel may possibly have left London eight years ago under false name and gone to the Greek Islands? If I want a comedian, Mr Smythe, I employ one who is actually funny.'

Mark Smythe swallowed and eyed Sonja covertly, thinking, when you looked at the package you didn't expect such balls. That hair was like spun silver. He thought wistfully that he'd give all his teeth to find out if she had more of the same on her pubes. 'I'm trying, Mrs Gilfoyle, but I've been stonewalled at every turn. Do you know how many Greek Islands there are?'

'I know you have visited a great many of them on Joshua's behalf,' said Sonja, adding icily, 'and that you found it necessary to take your wife and children with you on each occasion.'

'I hope you're not implying that I'm guilty of any irregularity,' said Mark Smythe thinking: bugger. I thought Joshua would buy that as a business expense. After all, they needed a holiday, it made sense to come with me, and the whole trip was cheaper for the four of us as a package than it would have been for Gilfoyles to pay for just one business-class ticket for me to Athens . . .

'I imply you have not done enough,' said Sonja. 'I thought you would have more to tell me.'

'Well, there is a little more. Mostly hunchwork.'

'Hunchwork? What is this hunchwork?'

'Ah,' said Mark, 'it means instinct. I've done a lot on instinct, and instinct tells me Gabriel doesn't want to be found. I think if Joshua were to –'

Sonja frowned. 'I tell you what my instinct tells me. It tells me you think I am a bimbo with artificial breasts who can be deceived because her English is not perfect. I ask for the family papers, they are not all here. You think I do not know what a bloody hunch is? Pull the other one, Mr Smythe. You may find it has jingles on.'

Mark Smythe sighed. 'Mrs Gilfoyle, everything that has any relevance to Gabriel Gilfoyle is in front of your nose. Now, I really must get back to the office. I have clients –'

'You have only one client,' said Sonja. 'My husband, as I well know, has paid you handsomely through the years. You give a poor return for his support, Mr Smythe. You take your family to Greek Islands and pretend to me that a hunch is something clever. The first Mrs Gilfoyle's diaries, please. I know you have them in the safe – my husband has told me they are there.'

'I'm sorry, Mrs Gilfoyle,' said Mark Smythe. 'I am under instruction not to look at the personal papers.'

'I do not ask you to look; I ask you to give to me these diaries.'

'I don't think Joshua wanted anyone to –'

'Mr Smythe, my husband is dying and I have enduring power of attorney.'

Mark took refuge in officiousness. 'Yes, but Joshua is still in control of his faculties. You have no power until that changes.'

'I think he will be enraged,' said Sonja, looking Mark deeply in the eyes, 'when he hears how forcefully you attempted to fondle my breast.'

Mark Smythe was shocked. 'Mrs Gilfoyle, I would never . . . I am a happily married –'

'I seem to recall the fondling lasted several seconds,' said Sonja relentlessly, 'despite my protestations. Do you understand me?'

'I'll get the diaries,' said Mark Smythe miserably. God help him if Joshua ever got wind of this. 'But I want you to note my protests.'

'Noted,' said Sonja. 'Now go, please, get them and leave. I have work to do.'

'The trouble with vicars,' said Julia to Daniel that evening, sitting at her kitchen table sharing a bottle of one of Mrs Braithwaite's more lethal concoctions, 'is that they can't help going all bloody holy on you.' Daniel drained his glass and she eyed him in some alarm. This stuff was stronger than vodka and he was drinking it as if it were wine. She had warned him, but he had poured scorn on the aspersion that he couldn't hold his drink. Now he had the disorientated look of a man who's just spent an evening floating upside down in a giant tub of jellyfish. She'd seen it before.

Daniel grinned happily. He had planned to discuss something with Jules this evening, but he couldn't for the life of him remember what. He swigged more cordial and admired her breasts with objective but disinterested approval. 'Quite right. Quite . . . quite right. I mean, Jonathan's a nice guy, but imagine if he said "Praise the Lord" at the wrong moment. Sex would never be the same again once you started thinking God might be there with you. I mean, three in a bed is all very well but . . . Jules, this stuff is very green. D'you think it could sh . . . sh . . . shtain me?'

Julia sighed. 'I'm sure it will completely ruin you. You know, Daniel, my trouble is that I'm awash with lascivious thoughts in a village where the only eligible men are either gay or men of the cloth.'

Daniel shrugged. 'Don't look at me, darling. Stopped shwinging in your direction years ago. Abesholutely. Anyway, that'sshhh . . . not your problem at all.'

'Oh, and I suppose you know what is?' Julia wondered how many more minutes it would be before he fell asleep on the table. Fewer than two, she'd wager. She cast a surreptitious eye on her watch.

'Abesholutely.'

'Go on then, enlighten me.'

''Twas that bloke,' said Daniel. 'The gorgeous one who went off for croissants and left you in the club. That's when you changed. You got fussy about lovers after that. None of them was ever good enough for you after him. You wanna know where your insp . . . inspration went? Ash . . . shk him. Took it with . . . th him, didn . . . 'tee?'

'Rubbish,' said Julia. 'That's total rubbish.'

'No itshh not. There was something I wanted to talk t'you about. Wheressh me cricket box?'

'I've no idea. What?'

But Daniel was asleep on the table. 'Forty-six seconds,' said Julia thoughtfully, and went to find him a blanket.

Up at the Grange Simon Gilfoyle put down the phone and turned to face his wife. 'Mark Smythe is in a state because

Sonja turned up and demanded Mother's diaries. He's worried he's done the wrong thing in giving them to her but it sounds as though she scared the living daylights out of him. He wanted to tell tales to Father, I think, but didn't quite dare phone him direct.'

'Well, he'd get no sense out of him if he did.'

'No, I know. I do wish he'd try to speak.' Simon adjusted his pillow, made himself comfortable. 'To see him like this . . . well, I would have put money on Father being the one who'd recover from anything that was thrown at him. He picked up malaria during his National Service, you know, and he once chaired a board meeting during an attack, when Gilfoyles was under threat. But this stroke has defeated him in a way I could never have imagined.'

'I thought he played chess with you today?'

'Yes – well, he did. There was that. For a moment I even thought he enjoyed it – but it has never struck me before how much the shame of infirmity could do to him. I honestly believe he could will himself better if he wanted to. And he could will himself to death in just the same way.'

'D'you think he would? The kids would be desolate.'

'I know. If only Gabriel would turn up, I'm sure it would help. I wondered about putting something in the paper, you know, asking him to make contact.'

Merrill shrugged. 'The last time you did that we had fourteen Gabriels and one Gabriella make contact with Mark Smythe, and every one of them assuming there was money in it.'

'It's human nature,' said Simon sadly. 'But it doesn't matter if two hundred Gabriels telephone, if one of them is the right one.' He turned out his bedside light. 'I'll talk to Mark about it, get him to run something in *The Times*. I need to pop to London anyway – I've an afternoon off and I promised Mark I'd check through the safe with him, get him off the hook.'

'Oh,' Merrill frowned, wondering where Sonja would be,

not wanting to ask.

'D'you think Gabriel would come back, then, if he knew?' Merrill asked.

'I honestly don't know. I feel there's nothing I can do to help Father now, yet all Gabriel has to do is turn up.'

'That's the prodigal son story all over, but you know it's not like that. You and the children have been his hope for the future since Gabriel went.'

'I know. I'm just frustrated that I can't make it right. I envy Sonja actually – she was so sure she could go striding off and make a difference.'

'Mincing off,' said Merrill darkly, reflecting that Sonja's name ought to be kept out of their bedroom if she was to have a hope of regaining her own sexual confidence, 'in those shoes.'

'At least she's trying to do something. I'm supposed to be a doctor.' Simon sighed. 'I'm used to whisking in, sorting it all out, and whisking out again.' And he lay there, wide-eyed, long after her even breathing told him she was asleep, reflecting sadly that all the medical knowledge in the world wasn't enough when two of the people you loved the most were a stubborn old man who couldn't seem to find it in his heart to recover and a brother who presumably couldn't find it in his heart to come home.

Chapter Eleven

❦

'Julia,' said Daniel carefully the next morning, as they sat down to toast and figs, a treat he had brought back from an unexpected foray to Sainsbury's, 'have you ever wondered about Hebe's potential?' He held his breath slightly as he was aware that this was one of those critical conversations which could end with either the prospect of considerably enhanced earnings (his) or the prospect of considerably reduced sexual prowess (also his). He was feeling sober but fragile, but time was running out and this conversation had to be had. It could go either way. Julia was an old friend, a friend from those heady days of his youth when art and principles were more important than profit and commerce – what luxury, such a view. Would she see that he was primarily making this suggestion for her welfare, not his own?

'Every day,' said Julia, cutting her fig in half and gouging out the middle with two fingers, 'but I try not to panic.' She peered at Daniel. 'Are you sure you're OK? You were drunk as a parrot last night. I've never heard snoring like it.'

Daniel smiled, ignoring the nagging headache – this was too important. 'I'm fine, absolutely fine. No, I meant her voice, Jules. It's amazing. You can't afford to ignore it. I mean that Puccini she sang for us . . . Christ, if she'd done that at the Haverhill Festival they'd have been passing out in the aisles.'

Julia frowned slightly, a frown reminiscent of Hebe's own. 'She's having singing lessons, Dan. She's taken part in a competition. I'm taking one step at a time on the singing

226

front, not tackling Mount Everest in a single leap.'

'Of course, but there are so many opportunities at her age . . .'

Julia fixed him with an intent look. 'Spit it out, Dan. What are you getting at?'

Daniel gazed for a moment into her honest, fair face. Such an open face, wide-spaced eyes, unfurrowed brow, baby hair growing around the edge of her forehead, a smattering of freckles on her nose . . . like Anne of Green bloody Gables, she was. For a moment he really disliked himself – but only for a moment. 'Look, Jules, don't do your fly-off-the-handle thing because this is just an idea, OK, that I want to run by you, you know, sound you out. But, you see, a mate of mine, a guy I know, happened to be talent spotting at the festival and he heard Hebe sing. He's in the music business and he thinks –'

Julia sucked the fig pulp from her fingers rather sensually (if Jonathan had been there he might have felt his knees give way but Daniel was not similarly affected), and frowned. 'How do you mean, a mate of yours? Why would I fly off the handle?' She wiped juice off her chin with her arm. 'These are good. Reminds me of that time we went to Morocco. D'you remember? We got standby flights and ended up sleeping in a brothel.'

'Yes, of course I remember,' said Daniel, also remembering how she had saved his bacon by telling him not to be so stupid when he had planned to bring a bit of that hashish back in his luggage for London use. She had snatched it off him on the way to the airport and chucked it into a bonfire at the side of the road, and he had been furious and called her every name under the sun, after which she had hugged him and said she knew he didn't mean it. Then they had happily sniffed the fumes for a minute before going on to catch their plane.

He shouldn't feel guilty, though – he was only trying to help; he was part of the commercial world now and bringing her the benefit of what he knew. 'A mate I know from work, Jules. Look, I've a lot of friends in the music business and one of them heard Hebe sing at the festival. He thought she was absolutely fantastic and he thinks she has recording potential. He wants to get her into a studio for . . . Jules, why are you looking at me like that?'

'What? You mean suspiciously? What mate, Daniel? How do you know what he thought of Hebe? You weren't at the festival. You were looking after Joshua after Hebe tried to eat the mad Brunhilde.' Julia had that look in her eyes, he realised, the one that meant you could be pinned to the wall by the egg whisk at any moment. Daniel mentally checked his escape route and was pleased to see he had a clear run for the door. As long as he could run with this bloody box in his underwear. (William had omitted to tell him you needed a jock strap to wear it with.) 'What exactly do you do, Daniel? I mean, you've never really said.'

'I'm . . . in promotion, a middle man, like a sort of agent. I make things happen for people, Jules, that's all. Don't look so suspicious – it's business. I've got some major clients.'

Julia could feel a dreadful lump of nerves in the pit of her stomach as she smelled the sour scent of betrayal. 'And would this be a major client of yours who's suddenly so interested in Hebe?'

'Just an old friend, Jules. Carl was at the festival and he heard Hebe, so he phoned me and –'

Julia was suddenly very alert. 'Phoned you when?'

'Well, no, I phoned him actually, we just happened to be speaking about something else and he mentioned –'

Julia was on her feet. 'Kate said she saw you in the phone box. You snake, Daniel! You've told someone about Hebe, haven't you? Got someone to come and hear her. Don't give me any more rubbish. A mate of yours? He just happened to be at the festival? D'you think I was born yesterday in a woodland clearing with all the other little wood nymphs? What have you done with Hebe? Who have you been bloody well selling her to? How long have you been plotting?'

Daniel backed off. 'Now, Jules, don't look at me like that . . . It's me, Daniel. You know I'd never do anything to upset you. I just thought she should be heard and I knew Carl Bayer was coming to the festival and –'

'Carl Bayer? The man from Bayer Records? The one with the record company and the private jet and the Caribbean island and the reputation for eating banana splits off his mistresses?'

'Have you heard of him, then?'

'Save it, Daniel. I'd have to have been entombed since the time of Christ not to have heard of him. Are you telling me Carl Bayer was at the Haverhill Festival listening to Hebe?'

'He often goes out spotting. Jules, I just happened to mention to him on the phone the other night that there was this child with a voice he ought to hear. I didn't really think he'd come himself. We were just chatting –'

'In the phone box?'

'Yes, well, I went for a walk and –'

'What was wrong with my bloody phone? You sneaky bastard! You've been trying to do a deal on Hebe behind my back, as if she were some bit of commercial property. My God, I can't believe you'd do it. Not you. Not you, Dan, after all we've been through together. How could you? How dare you?' There were tears running down her cheeks and she dashed them away angrily. 'This is not what she needs right now, Daniel Cutter. Get out of this house. Get out of my house. This is my home now and I live here and you're not welcome here any longer. And I want you to keep right away from Hebe. She's nothing to do with you.'

'Jules, it wasn't like that – I was only trying to help. Look, you don't know what she needs any more than I do. The child's a phenomenon.'

'At least I'm looking out for her interests. You're looking out for your own. You're a vulture. I can't believe it. I was *sick* on you. You were bloody sick on me, for that matter. I thought you were my *friend*.'

'I am your friend. Carl's an old mate. We were talking business. I needed to make a private call, and then it just happened to come up in conver –'

'Get out of my kitchen,' said Julia, 'right now, with your earring and your dreadlocks and your faithless personality – and you can take that hash you've put in my shoe polish drawer as well. This isn't bloody Woodstock, you know.'

'Oh, come on, Jules, how long have we been –'

'Jonathan,' said Julia, looking at the vicar, who had appeared fortuitously over Dan's shoulder, 'would you please help me get Daniel out of here before I murder him, chop his body into little pieces and feed him to the fishes? I know I don't go to church but I honestly think you'd be saving my immortal soul – and everyone else's once he comes back up the food chain and turns them all into involuntary cannibals.'

'Jules . . .'

'Go, Daniel,' said Julia, 'before you lose some part of your anatomy you value more than your wallet. If there is one. Which I doubt.'

Oh God, thought Daniel, she's looking for the egg whisk out of the corner of her eye. I've seen her do this before. He had to make her see that when chances like this came your way you had to go for it. 'Jules, Carl Bayer is coming to see you this Thursday. I thought you'd be pleased to give Hebe a chance to –'

'Bugger off right now this minute – and tell your "mate" not to bother himself with trying to give Hebe a chance. Trying to help, my foot – you've got dollar signs behind your eyelids. I can't believe you'd try to set Hebe up, Daniel. She's eight years old and she's autistic. Don't you understand what that means? It means she can't cope with becoming the means to someone else's financial success. It means she's too special to be risked for cash!'

'Jules, please, I didn't tell you I'd suggested he came to the festival because I didn't want you to be let down if he wasn't interested. It's a fantastic opportunity. I know how worried you are about her future. This way you'd make millions and she'd be secure. There's never been a child star with autism. She could make a mint.'

'If you don't go,' said Julia, picking up the rolling pin which lay conveniently on the kitchen worktop, 'I'm going to make you wish you'd been born a woman.'

'Mate,' said Jonathan in wise and vicarish tones (less likely, he had found, to get him caught in the crossfire than a normal voice), 'I think she means it.'

Daniel looked at the rolling pin. And left.

Julia was left staring across her small kitchen at Jonathan, who stared back. 'I can't believe it,' she said, beginning to cry again. 'I can't believe it. I've known him for years. We were students in the same digs. He went on anti-capitalist marches and wanted to live in an ashram. We went to Morocco to look at art. Bastard. Bloody, bloody bastard. Trying to use my poor little Hebe. He's supposed to be her not-a-proper-godfather. Bastard. Bastard. Bastard.'

Jonathan crossed the room to her. 'I heard – at least, most of it. I'm sorry, Julia, that you've been let down. I don't know what else to say. Except that she's not poor little Hebe and you know it. You shouldn't even say that.'

Julia sat back at the kitchen table with a bump. 'Carl Bayer. I mean, how bizarre is that?'

Jonathan put a cautious arm around her shoulders, aware that he was doing it with a prayer of thanks for the opportunity to be more than just a nuisance in her life. She smelled of rosemary and he wondered if she rinsed her hair with it.

Julia sounded muffled, her face in her hands. 'Oh God, what if he's right? I mean if she has a gift, maybe it's some sort of compensation for the rest. Maybe your God gave it to her in return for all the difficulties. What if I am depriving her of the chance to be financially secure, her chance to make her life fantastic, by protecting her from her chance to win through?' She looked up at Jonathan, inadvertently bringing her face within a few inches of his.

Jonathan swallowed, trying to remember his recent resolution to do nothing until he had made a decision as to which woman he wanted to make his for ever (but then, he hadn't honestly thought he stood a chance with either). 'I don't think anybody's God works like that.'

'So you think I'm right?' Her green eyes looked clear into his, making him think of the light through leaves in a woodland clearing. This could be my only chance, he thought. You don't turn down moments of bliss – I mean, maybe they're sent . . .

'I think you have to follow your best instincts,' he said rather huskily, and kissed her swiftly before he could stop himself.

Oh shit, thought Julia, opening her mouth in surprise, it's not even day fourteen. You've done it now . . . As his tongue slipped past her lips she felt everything switch on. It reminded her of those scenes in ancient mummy films when someone pushes aside the stone at the entrance of the tomb and the whole place fills instantly with light. She muttered very quietly and inhaled deeply of Jonathan's sandalwood scent.

Jonathan, horrified and enthralled at the same time, engaged himself in a furious but brief mental battle comprised entirely of arguments he had had with himself before. They ran through the unacceptability of kissing a parishioner, the observation that Julia was not technically part of his flock, the acknowledgement that the bishop would not approve of a pagan single parent artist, the acknowledgement also that even if this situation was sent from above it might be intended as a temptation to be resisted rather than a reward to be gobbled up, the fact that he was a man like any other and celibacy had not been part of the deal in the Church of England . . .

By the time Jonathan's mental argument had run this far he was following Julia up her stairs whispering, 'Where's Hebe?' and hearing the immortal response, 'Up at the Grange playing chess – she stayed the night with Matilda.'

Once in the bedroom Julia wrapped herself around him so effectively that he lost his balance, and they tumbled on to the bed in a mass of entangled limbs.

Jonathan attempted to sit up. 'Julia, I shouldn't . . . I'm taking advantage of you . . .'

Julia whipped her T-shirt off, revealing the breasts about which he had so fantasised. 'Jonathan,' she said, 'you kissed me, I know you liked it, so stop complaining and come here,' and she placed his hand firmly on her right breast and closed her eyes.

Jonathan fought himself in vain. There was no denying the fact that he was wearing his dog collar – had been wearing his dog collar, he corrected himself as it fell to the floor – and that he was therefore here as her vicar rather than as her friend . . .

Julia pushed him over and pinned him against her bed. There was, she felt, no very good reason why things should not continue, having gone this far. He was unattached, she was unattached, Hebe was at the Grange and she really, really felt like it. Obviously she was going to really regret it later, but sod later. Now was now. 'Just kiss me,' she said against his lips, 'and accept that you've got no choice.'

Jonathan decided he probably didn't have any choice now. Her hands were cupping his buttocks and he could smell the whole scent of her – rosemary, a hint of turps on the palm he had gently bitten, the faintest smell of rose cologne surprising him in the hollow of her navel . . .

Panic took him suddenly, as she slipped his underwear down and he felt her body pressed against him, skin against skin, her nipples against his chest. This was his mental boundary between heavy petting and No Going Back. With a huge effort of willpower that he regretted even as he summoned it, he whispered, 'Julia, we shouldn't . . .'

Julia looked him straight in the eye, did something with her pelvis that she had clearly done before, and impaled herself on to his erection with a ceremonious care which reminded him suddenly (and, it seemed afterwards, disgracefully) of himself lowering the Communion cup after holding it up to the altar. He was there, inside her, like a bee enticed into one of those carnivorous plants with the long, narrow, perfumed chamber full of sweet sap . . . Well, he thought, it's too late now. Technically we've done it, so . . .

Banishing even this from his mind he turned her over, needing in the glorious abandonment of it all to have her completely rather than allow himself to be had. A tiny part of himself recognised that this was a lust born of impulse and its like might not come his way again.

Julia sighed as he pushed himself deeply and satisfyingly into her soft flesh, shifting herself fluidly to urge him on. It was like making love with an African dancer, he thought suddenly, she gyrated with an extraordinary sensuality. He kissed her passionately, over and over, her lips, her neck, her breasts, and she whispered, 'Oh, that's lovely,' as her hips moved with his, bringing an intense pleasure in a rising tide so that the whole act became a battle of ecstasy with self-control, but a self-control that was as ecstatic as the moment of climax which finally shook him from top to toe, sending a great shudder through his body and leaving him gasping upon her, all his muscles turned to jelly and a cool light sweat across his shoulders and back. And for a few moments his only regret was that it had been over so quickly.

Julia gave herself up to it entirely. She did not share Jonathan's scruples about flocks and bishops, and her only real concern was that Jonathan might read more into it than she did, a concern she had decided to defer until afterwards lest it spoil her enjoyment of the best sex – the only sex – she had had since Hebe came out by that very same route. In the carefree days of her student youth it had been widely understood amongst her contemporaries that sex was sex and did not necessarily imply anything more than the enjoyable satisfaction of an impulse. In these more adult times of children and permanent settlement, a misunderstanding might be uncomfortable. Oh, but good sex – God, had she missed it! You'd think a vicar would be more inhibited . . .

I did not, she told herself firmly, do this in any way because Daniel implied that my inspiration left me when Hebe's father walked out of the door.

It was glorious to share this with someone again, like being thrown on to a raging torrent, crushed beneath a sweating, gasping man, as he poured his passion into her. Julia thoroughly enjoyed it, particularly the sweat, which she felt was a good sign of abandonment to lust. One should always be abandoned to lust, she thought. There is something faintly peculiar about a man who does not pump until he sweats. Finally, when he collapsed, shuddering on top of her, she said in matter-of-fact tones, 'Wow, Jonathan, I really, really needed that.'

Jonathan lifted his head from her neck, lifted a rope of tousled hair from across her face and peered into the green eyes.

'It's not the most romantic thing anyone's ever said to me whilst I was still inside them. You sound as if you've just had an orange lolly on a day at the seaside.'

Julia raised an eyebrow carefully, thinking, oh dear, watch your step, Jules. . . 'Romantic? Jonathan, please don't tell me you love me . . .'

He smiled ruefully and rolled off her, thinking, I was just wondering if I did, or certainly feeling that I could, given half a chance to repeat this.

'. . . because I know you don't.'

'I think you're beautiful,' he said. 'I've lusted after you

unacceptably ever since I first saw your face.' Blast, he thought. This is going to go badly.

'Unacceptably?'

'I am a vicar.'

'And I'm a single woman, not the handmaid of Satan.'

'You're a parishioner,' said Jonathan. 'I shouldn't compromise you – and the Church has a view on sex outside marriage.'

'I couldn't call it a view,' said Julia, 'I'd call it a blinkered opinion. Anyway, it's not as if you were a virgin. You're pretty good, for a vicar.'

'Oh? How many vicars have you . . . ?'

'Oh, dozens,' said Julia airily, 'and the odd bishop. Oh, don't look like that – I am joking, for goodness' sake. Anyway, you don't have to be celibate, do you?'

'No, of course not. But I actually have been since I became a vicar.'

'God, no wonder.'

'No wonder what?'

'Well, you were like a turbine. D'you think we should do it again?'

'You mean, another time?'

'No, I meant now.'

'I couldn't do it again now. I'm forty next year, you know.'

'I bet you could, old man.'

'No I couldn't. I mean, I'm just drained.'

'Just lie there, then.'

'Oh no, really, oh no, you mustn't . . . oh God, you really shouldn't . . . oh well, if you insist . . .'

It had been, Julia reflected as he left, something of a success, despite the inherent risk of expectations. She felt gloriously well oiled, imbued with energy and a glow that she had not felt in years. Who would have suspected a vicar could acquit himself so admirably?

What luck that a moment like that should arise when Hebe was spending the morning playing more chess with Joshua. Interesting chess, lacking as it did several pieces, but chess nevertheless. Even so, she must be sure that this would not make things complicated. Nice though Jonathan was, any sort of relationship would be regarded as marriage in a place like this, and she was not in love with him and had no wish to work towards changing that state of affairs. The only alternative would be to ruin his reputation, so this had to stop right here.

She wandered idly into the shower – it would not do to go up to the Grange smelling of him. Merrill would pick up the faint scent of incense he had imparted to her pubic hair and, using her big-sister ESP, would work out immediately what had happened, where, when, with whom and for how long.

Once under the gloriously rushing water she began to think with renewed vigour of the Foxbarton angel. She would be able to do it now, she was sure. Relief washed over her at the thought it was only good sex she had needed, rather than good sex with one specific, long-lost, unattainable man. And it occurred to her suddenly, as she soaped herself with rosemary-scented soap, that if Hebe saw angels in trees, but Hebe was unable to explain exactly what they looked like, then the obvious thing she should do was to ask Hebe to help her make the angel. And having already opened her mind to the idea that the angel did not have to be only eighteen inches tall, and did not have to be modelled entirely in clay, then why should it not take some of its inspiration from Hebe? Hebe was her daughter, so if Hebe had seen an angel in a tree then that was a good enough angel for anyone. And if it turned out to look like an owl – or a fruit bat – well, so be it. Why hadn't she thought of it before?

A few hundred yards away Daniel emerged from the phone box, cursing his bloody mobile which just wouldn't transmit out of Foxbarton. The whole bloody village was stuck in a time warp. He had been reduced to using a pay phone to call Carl's mobile, and, of course, calling Carl's mobile cost more change than he had in his pocket and they didn't have a bloody cardphone, did they? Not in bloody Foxbarton. He kicked the phone box with childish glee, then saw Kate Coleman watching him with distaste from across the street.

'I'm sorry,' he shouted to her across the road, 'I ran out of change.'

Kate gave him a dark look. 'It doesn't excuse petty vandalism.' She crossed the road, headed past him.

'Where are you going?' asked Daniel. He had lingered long enough at Julia's back door – hoping for a reprieve, or at least the chance to grab his stash from her drawer – to get a fair sense of the way the wind was blowing with her and that vicar. Angry though she was with him, he did recognise that her day and her mood would not be improved by the arrival of Kate whilst she was humping the vicar on the kitchen table. That sort of thing, thought Daniel, who had grown up in a village the size of this one, generally went down very badly in villages.

Kate frowned. 'What's it got to do with you?' Even I, she thought, I who am pursued by both the dark-eyed gypsy and the vicar, could not possibly be of interest to a gay black man with dreadlocks.

Daniel tossed his dreadlocks back over his shoulder. 'I thought if you were going to see Julia I'd save you the trouble. She went shopping, which is why I came out to use the phone – but I ran out of change.' He looked at Kate hopefully. 'I don't suppose I could use yours, could I? It's really immensely important.'

Kate, torn between wanting to tell him to go and boil his head and feeling unable to refuse to help a stranger (what would Jonathan say, particularly when she had so recently done the parable of the Good Samaritan with the Sunday school?) said reluctantly, 'OK, well, my house is just along here – but you'll have to be quick. I mean, I don't want to be rude, but I have to go out.'

So Daniel followed Kate to her neat, perfect house, watching the way her bottom moved as she walked up the path to her front door, and wondering if she was getting any and, if so, from whom. He'd offer himself if he hadn't decided long ago to ignore any slight heterosexual leanings that came his way from time to time – that wouldn't do at all, not in the music industry. It wasn't that they minded heteros, more that you had to be quite clear about what you were, no midlife dithering between sexual preferences.

Inside, the phone stood on a polished table under a mirror in the hall.

'There,' said Kate, wondering if she should watch him in case he was going to call Nepal and be on the phone to someone in an ashram for half an hour.

Daniel beamed at her. 'Don't worry, it's only London and, of course, I'll pay for the call.'

Kate blushed and noticed that he had nice eyes. She wondered if what they said about black men was true, then, appalled at herself, offered tea and biscuits, then went to fetch them.

'Carl?' she heard as she left the hall. 'Got you at last. Yes – as well as could be expected. It'll need a little work. Trust me – you know what they say about money talking. She'll see you on Thursday, I know Julia. She'll have to see you – for Hebe's sake. Just emphasise opportunity and minimise stress, if you get my drift. I'll see you afterwards – I'll let you know where to find me. No, I've outstayed my welcome rather, so I've got to find somewhere else to stay.'

Up at Foxbarton Grange Hebe awoke late and slowly. She was tired as she had spent the greater part of the previous night playing chess with herself, and she had now worked out how to win without eating the pieces.

Matilda was screaming in the corner of the room, and

Hebe hopped out of her bed curiously to investigate. The source of the trouble seemed to be a small family of stag beetles who had taken up residence in Matilda's pillow. They had apparently been quite comfortable in there all night – at least according to William, who was also there – but were now rather agitated because of the extraordinary noise levels. Matilda stamped on William's toe and William roared, 'Hebe, did you see what she did to me?'

Hebe frowned. She didn't like noise, particularly not when more than one person was making it at once. It confused her, and made her headache and her stomach churn, and colours flash in front of her eyes like angry stars. If noise was tidied up and turned into music then that was OK; that was properly controlled noise so it was comfortable and made her feel good. She turned her back on William and Matilda and began to sing.

> '*Early one morning just as the sun was rising*
> *I heard a couple doing it in the valley below.*
> *She got her boobies out*
> *He waved his thing about*
> *And said "Let's have a quickie 'cos I've really got to go."'*

Matilda and William stopped fighting, aghast.

'Hebe!' said Matilda. 'Where did you hear that?'

Hebe smiled serenely, glad they had stopped shouting. 'William,' she said, 'and Oscar.'

Matilda glared at William. 'You idiot. Fancy teaching Hebe something like that. Boys are just so foul, I'm so glad I'm not one.'

'So am I glad you're not one. A brother wearing Barbie knickers would be really awful.'

'I do not wear Barbie knickers.'

'Oh yes you do. Look.' William whipped a pair triumphantly out of her drawer and another small insect dropped out.

Matilda shrieked, 'You're turning my whole life into a bug house and I really hate you, William Gilfoyle. I hope you fall down a giant bug hole and get eaten by woodlice!' She stormed from the room to find a sympathetic adult to tell.

Hebe and William looked at one another. 'She's very noisy, isn't she?' said William.

Hebe gave him a dark look. 'That's your beetle in her knickers.'

'It might be,' said William. 'It's an experiment. Hebe, you mustn't sing that song again. The grown-ups will be really cross.'

Hebe blinked. 'Why?'

' 'Cos it's rude. It's not . . . Children aren't allowed to sing stuff like that.'

'You sang it with Oscar,' said Hebe, 'in the woods.'

'Have you been following us?' asked William. 'You're not supposed to go into the woods on your own.'

'Angel lives in the woods,' said Hebe. 'I'm not on my own.'

'Well, promise you won't sing it again.'

'I promise,' said Hebe dubiously. People made her promise things all the time but she had no idea what this meant. It was just something you had to say sometimes, like promising her mother she wouldn't go into the woods by herself, and promising not to climb trees or bother the Grandpa man. She grinned at William. 'I'm going to see Grandpa.'

'He's not really your –' began William, then sighed. It didn't really matter whose grandpa he was, he was still all dribbly and strange. Dad said he was getting better but he wasn't out of the woods yet. Then Mum said they had to understand that people didn't live for ever, which was stupid because obviously they knew that. If people lived for ever then Tutankhamen's pyramid would all have been pointless, wouldn't it? And what did they mean, not out of the woods? Grandpa hadn't been in the woods for years. William collected up his beetles carefully.

'Don't you dare leave any behind,' said Matilda, who had returned, also deflated from her former hysteria, her twin's mood oddly catching.

'Misunderstood,' William said mournfully to the beetles, 'you and me are misunderstood.' He remembered one of his music teachers saying that geniuses were often misunderstood. Perhaps this meant that he was a genius. He must run that by his maths teacher the next time he got told off for not doing his homework, or handing it in all muddy and crumpled.

Hebe left them and wandered through to the west wing where she found Joshua still in bed. Jackie, the latest agency nurse, was just in the process of shaving him, a process which made him only slightly less impatient than trying to do it himself – but at least this way he didn't end up covered in blood. He glanced up when Hebe came in through the French windows, expecting Jackie to shoo her out, but Jackie smiled. She had worked in a rehabilitation unit until recently where her principle aim was to get the patients riled, as she was a great believer in the restorative power of being rendered extremely cross.

'Good morning,' she said to Hebe. 'Have you come to see your grandpa?'

'Sh . . . she's n . . . n . . . not my g . . . g . . . g . . . rannndooorrrter,' said Joshua, horrified into speech by the assumption.

Jackie folded her arms and grinned at him triumphantly. 'I knew you could speak, old man,' she said. 'They told me you still hadn't said a word but I knew straight away you were faking. Well, if she's not your granddaughter then God knows why she's here to see you. I wouldn't bother.'

Joshua glared, angry at being caught out, and Hebe sidled up to him and took his nearly useless right hand between her own small cool ones. The feeling was pleasant. He was feeling too warm, stale and unwashed after a night of bad dreams in which Gabriel, shrouded and rotting, had arisen from an unmarked grave and accused him of abandonment. It was, he knew, another symptom of the strange creeping guilt that had begun to assail him.

'We could play chess,' said Hebe, 'Grandpa.'

Joshua's lips twitched, despite himself. He thought of the two knights, doubtless somewhere in his large bowel at this very moment, and wondered how Hebe was getting on with the lot she had swallowed. It struck him as rather amusing that out of the whole world only the two of them could now complete the chess set. He wriggled a brow at Hebe.

Jackie noticed the half-smile and regarded Hebe with interest. She was well aware of the child's difficulties, having been warned by Mrs Barker not to let her bother Joshua too much as he didn't like her. Still, you didn't get to be a good nurse without completely ignoring the more ridiculous requests people made, and it seemed to her that as far as Joshua was concerned, Hebe was a particularly good thing.

'Come on, Hebe,' she said, 'help me shave your grandpa.'

Joshua's eyebrows almost shot off the top of his head and he squeaked, 'S . . . she'll b . . . bllllloooooody m . . . mangle me!'

'Well, well,' said Jackie, 'your speech *is* coming on fast. Come on, Hebe, here's the razor. Here, put it on here . . . that's right . . . down that way. See, if you go the other way it will feel sore.'

'Ouwwch!' said Joshua, who had realised already that he was outflanked.

As Hebe and Jackie shaved Joshua, Sonja sat on the train home and wondered about the entry which had puzzled her in Marjorie's diary. She had really been looking for something that would tell her where Gabriel might have gone – a family contact, an old friend, some mention from Marjorie of whom he might have turned to, where he might have gone. But there had been nothing of that sort, just a prolonged and fairly graphic diatribe against Joshua – and that one strange comment, one unanswered question. She sighed. She was no nearer to Gabriel.

But finding Gabriel was imperative. Joshua needed to see his son.

She looked at the entry again now – it was one of the last.

It has been months now since we heard from Gabriel. Such a stubborn boy, you'd think Joshua would be proud of such stubbornness, but he retreats into his own anger and I hate him for it. I used to wonder how Joshua's mother had borne being married to the man who took her son away. Now history has repeated itself, and I think I know. No wonder she died young.

The man who took her son away? What could this mean? Who had been taken away? Could Joshua have a brother somewhere who had been taken away? Could Gabriel have found this long-lost uncle?

She had phoned Mark Smythe but he had insisted that there was no brother. 'There are no other family members, Mrs Gilfoyle. It's the first line of investigation I went through. The company records are clear – Joshua was an only child.'

So now Sonja was coming home. She had done all she could. She had had that one picture of Gabriel that Simon had given her blown up to A4 and copied five thousand times. In the last two days she had visited all of Gabriel's old friends in London, all sadly regretful at his disappearance but caught up in their own City jobs. She had shown his picture to policemen and prostitutes, art students and beggars. She had sat beside the statue of Eros and shown it to groups of tourists who seemed to be trying to get a sense of the real England by sitting on a traffic junction and smoking French cigarettes amongst Japanese neon signs and an old stone statue of a Greek God. None of them had seen Gabriel. Neither had the street-sleepers beneath Waterloo Bridge, the drifting World's End pot-smokers, the worn but warm-faced people who ran the soup kitchens and night hostels, the bus conductors and platform sweepers, and the Dean of St Paul's Cathedral upon whom she had chanced whilst sitting in the cathedral garden eating her sandwich.

No one could help. The picture was probably too old, Sonja thought, the leads all long since gone cold. Nevertheless she had distributed her five thousand copies as widely as she could, spacing them at ten metre intervals along the underpass at Marble Arch and charming a couple of policemen out of arresting her for illegal bill posting. Only the Dean of St Paul's had seemed to offer anything constructive, when he had said, 'Sometimes, my dear, the reason we don't get the answer is because we ask the wrong question.'

'What do you mean? I ask where is Gabriel Gilfoyle. It is a simple thing.'

'Ah,' had said the Dean, 'perhaps now, instead of "Where?" you should be asking "When?" or, even, "Why?"'

Sonja pondered on it on the train out of King's Cross. So was the better question to ask *why* did Gabriel disappear? And in what way had history repeated itself for Marjorie Gilfoyle? There was only one person she could ask, and that was Joshua himself. Oh, if only he was even a little better. If only, if only he were no worse.

Sonja had no illusions. She had seen illness before, knew that the chances of Joshua having another stroke and dying were real. The fear that he would die before she got home haunted her, and she had rung Mrs Barker several times for secret updates on his progress. Who else could she ring? Simon and Merrill believed only the worst of her – and they could very easily have been right, so it was hard to resent them too much. It had, after all, been her clear intention to marry Joshua Gilfoyle for his money. It was he, and not her own better nature, that had ambushed her. So why should they not think the worst? The children could not be expected to speak frankly and Joshua himself was apparently unable to say a word.

But Mrs Barker had been less than reassuring, telling her that Joshua would neither speak nor try to stand, that he spent most of the day asleep as if exhausted. The only thing that he seemed to respond to, Mrs Barker had said, was that odd child Hebe, who seemed to upset him no end.

Sonja looked out of the window, a pale, forlorn figure in a half-empty train. The Hertfordshire countryside flashed by, green and yellow, fertile and smiling. She remembered her life in Tromsø, her parents ill and unable to work, too proud to accept help from the state, life a constant struggle between what money they had and what they must buy . . . Working in the local supermarket where the owner would touch her thigh, but she had let him because no one else would employ an underage schoolgirl . . . Then the day she turned sixteen he had done far more than touch her thigh. Afterwards, sullied and distressed, she had told him to stuff his job, knowing that she could tell no one – how could she tell her parents the final price of that job? So she had gone to Oslo, lied about her qualifications and got a secretarial job with a big company, determined to work her way up and buy her parents a warm and comfortable home with all the roast meat they could eat for the price of a fair day's work.

She had done well, become the managing director's PA; the warm and comfortable home had seemed a possibility – and then her parents had died, one after the other, just as life seemed at last to hold some promise for them. A few weeks later, feeling alone and pointless, she had met Joshua. She had been called in to translate for a meeting between her boss and the chairman of Gilfoyles, who had been in the process of buying and asset-stripping the company for which she worked. And he had asset-stripped her very effectively that very evening and worked on her all night.

What had she thought of Joshua Gilfoyle then? That this was an old yet not unattractive man, that the return for a few years of her youth life would be security for ever, that it didn't matter any more, that she would never have to be poor again . . . that she had found a rich protector who would take nothing from her without paying what it was worth.

She had not thought it for long, but it had been there, so who could blame Simon Gilfoyle for what he thought of her? Poor man, he couldn't help fancying her – he'd probably caught his father with his secretary when he was at that formative age. It always gave them a thing about their father's women – she had read it somewhere. She sighed and rubbed her ankle, suddenly aware that one of the blisters on the back of her heel was bleeding again. So many hours on her feet these last days, traipsing around London with those posters, but it had brought Gabriel no closer. Only Marjorie's diary had offered the tiniest glimmer of something. She eyed her bag thoughtfully as the train rumbled on. After all, why would Marjorie have suggested Joshua had a brother if he did not? It was the only lead she could think of that might help. So she would follow it.

Chapter Twelve

✦

Kate smiled as she walked through the light-dappled woods. She was pleased that she had asked Daniel in to use the telephone – she had invited him to stay with her now. He had proved so charming when she had offered him tea and biscuits and had been so encouraging about her plans for Julia. And he *was* one of Julia's oldest friends. Julia was certain to regret turning him out when he was only trying to help Hebe – and then she would find him, still there at Kate's house. She was doing everyone a favour – and it was rather nice to have someone staying, and particularly nice to overhear Oscar telling Martin on the phone that 'this huge black bloke has moved in to stay. He's really cool.' He was interesting, too. Kate had been able to pump Daniel for information about the record business, the famous Carl Bayer, Hebe's prospects and, for interest, Julia herself. She needed to know all about these things if she was going to manage Julia and Hebe. She needed to be well-informed.

Things were going well, Kate felt. Julia seemed to have made an enormous number of these strange willow figures, and had given her the contact numbers of various galleries that had sold her work in the past. Several had already agreed they would ask clients who owned Julia's work to loan pieces back for Kate's exhibition. Even if the Foxbarton angel itself hadn't yet taken shape, there was no denying that Kate was making progress with the organisational side. Better still, Oscar had told his father that she had become Julia's manager. Let him put that in his pipe and smoke it, she thought. I know he thought I would phone him and beg him to support me, she thought. He was just waiting for the call.

She thought back to the Parish Council meeting last night. The council members were gratifyingly delighted when she told them of her plans for the exhibition and the permanent gallery which would eventually follow. It quite made up for their being so disgruntled about her volte-face regarding the Foxbarton Horse Fair.

'But, Kate,' Mrs Padley said, 'every year you take charge of the committee and you try to stop all those ghastly gypsies coming and camping our woods for weeks.'

But Kate had smiled and replied, 'Mrs Padley, I have come to feel that having the gypsies here is culturally enhancing. If we want to be seen as a centre for rural art then to be also known as the home of one of the longest-established traditional pony fairs in the country can only help. No, my view is that having the gypsies here each year is highly beneficial and we should try and include them.' She had smiled as she said it, thinking of the particular benefits the gypsies had brought her this year. 'In any case, the fair is less than a week away. It's far too late to stop it.'

Now Kate reached the clearing in the woods still smiling at the thought of her new-found open-mindedness. Ignoring the rather knowing smiles of the family gathered around the remains of a meal, she tied Gwen to her usual tree stump and knocked on John's door. She had come today to explain to John that with her new-found confidence as a sexual being and desirable woman, she was now going to go after the man she really wanted, the one with whom no affair would have to be surreptitious or sweetly stolen. She was fully aware that John had not hoped for love, or even planned to desire her for any longer than it took to pack up the remains of the horse fair and leave. He was her wild fling. Every woman should have a wild fling. Julia had said so and she was absolutely right. But as for permanence, well, Kate knew what she wanted for permanence. She wanted Jonathan. She clearly had Oscar's advance approval, and, as for the village – well, people were always saying what a shame it was that Jonathan hadn't found himself a nice wife. They said it so often to Kate that she was sure the words were aimed at her particularly. She would make an excellent vicar's wife, and it was only a matter of time before Jonathan Doyle saw it as clearly as she.

So she explained the way she saw things rather earnestly to John, and he was extremely gallant about it. It had been a wonderful interlude, he told her, and Kate felt this made her sound like Audrey Hepburn. She smiled rather mysteriously and wondered if perhaps she should get a smaller dog. You'd never have seen Audrey Hepburn with a wolfhound.

'I hope you find what you want, Kate,' he said to her seriously. 'But when you do, hold on to it tightly and with both hands.'

'You sound sad,' she said to him. 'I mean, have you lost someone?'

He smiled. 'Not really. I found someone special once, but she was never mine.'

'Oh. How romantic.'

'Not really. It's a bit of a cliché but she made me see myself clearly, and I realised I didn't like what I'd become.'

'Wow, how poetic.'

'Long time ago now. So, if I see you at the fair, am I allowed to say hello, or will you be on the arm of the vicar?'

'I'm not that fast,' said Kate, 'but I'll be working on it.'

'Joshua,' said Sonja from the doorway of his room, and he looked up in surprise. Hebe turned from the chess set and beamed.

'Grandpa won,' she said cheerfully, ' 'cos I had to lend him one of my horses.'

A tear of relief ran down Sonja's cheek. Joshua looked

better, she thought, much better than when she went away, even though it had been only three days, and even though he had three pieces of toilet tissue stuck to his chin. She hurried over to kiss him and several more tears followed the first.

'Yeuch,' said Hebe, 'kissing. It's really disgusting.'

'Well,' said Sonja to Hebe, wondering how her presence here tied in with the reports that she annoyed Joshua so terribly, 'perhaps you look the other way, Hebe. Look at the chess.'

Joshua had dreaded her kissing him, feared that he would dribble and appal both her and himself, dreaded the disgust she would feel against that lopsided mouth, yet in response to her warm lips he unwittingly revealed the improvement in the muscles of his face over the last few days, and the kiss was both delightful and dry.

Sonja smiled into his face. 'You are getting better. I see it. I am so happy to see you.'

'He's lots better,' said Hebe, resolutely not looking up from the chessboard. 'He ate two horses and that's why.'

'Two horses? Joshua, what did you eat? I do not understand.'

Joshua grimaced and frowned rather sheepishly, and Sonja realised to her astonishment that he was being abashed. Hebe nodded matter-of-factly.

'I ate the pawns and the bishop, then Grandpa ate the horses. Then he laughed and got better. You can walk as well, can't you, Grandpa?'

Joshua glared fiercely at Hebe. He had really thought she was not there when he hobbled gingerly across the room alone for the first time last night, even though it often seemed that when the stars were out she was there more often than she wasn't. God, she was sneaky. He shook his head angrily and reached for the laptop.

'He talks,' Hebe said to Sonja. 'He's just pretending.' The light washed in through the French windows and haloed

251

her face with white light. She folded her arms and looked first Joshua, then Sonja, square in the face.

Sonja pulled out the plug and put her hands on her hips. 'I know too you can speak,' she said. 'You can't fool me.' It struck her that Hebe and Joshua wore the same facial expression. Stubborn beyond stubbornness. It was something in the eyes, that direct, challenging stare. Perhaps those who face more than the usual difficulty develop these things. Perhaps they had bonded in their shared adversity. 'So, if you can walk and talk, Joshua Gilfoyle, then perhaps it's time you left your bedroom and we went for a walk in the gardens.'

'Grandpa won't walk,' said Hebe. 'He's too sulky.'

'Grandpa, heh? Come on, old man, on your feet.' And when Jackie, who had been on her break, smoking Marlboros in the kitchen garden with Stewart the gardener, returned to her duty, her patient had completely disappeared and she found him halfway across the lawn with his wife and his would-be granddaughter, with his commode acting as Zimmer frame to stabilise the whole caboodle.

'Well,' she said to Mrs Barker, who was pretending to clean the windows in order to spy more effectively, 'would you look at that?'

Mrs Barker sniffed. 'I don't know,' she said, 'at his age and in his state of health he should be more careful. I knew if he married that Brigitte Bardot lookalike no good would come of it.'

Jackie sighed. 'For heaven's sake,' she said, 'if you're going to live your life as if you're dead already you might as well not bother living at all.' It was her philosophy of life, and it explained why she smoked, why she drank, and why she occasionally went to Brighton for wild weekends of bingo and fumbling with Spanish waiters with names like Joaquim and Fernando whom she picked up in Cambridge bars. 'Everyone should have a fling every so often.'

Mrs Barker misunderstood. 'My Mr Barker likes me to lie still,' she said, and flounced off to tell Merrill what she had seen.

'God knows why,' muttered Jackie to herself, watching her waddle off enormously, 'I mean, it's not as if he's likely to miss.'

Merrill – and Simon, when he got home from the surgery and heard – were delighted to hear that Joshua was walking. So delighted that they even managed not to tell Sonja that they told her so when she revealed at supper that she had made no progress in finding Gabriel.

Merrill had not really wanted Sonja invited for supper. Ever since Simon had seemed so evasive about that hug she had overseen, Merrill had felt deeply uneasy about his views on Sonja. Now she felt herself watching Simon, trying to avoid the secret fantasy that Joshua would die and Simon would take on his father's wife in more ways than financially. After all, if marrying your mistress creates a vacancy, you could say the same thing about widowing your former mistress. Another vacancy arises. Leaves her needing a nice rich bloke – and where better to look than here? She wouldn't even have to move house. She eyed Sonja rather ungraciously. 'Did you find out anything new at all?'

Sonja walked rather slowly over to the window and looked out over the lawn. 'One thing I find,' she said, 'which might help. I do not know what it means. I hoped we could talk about this thing –'

And then Matilda and William came tearing in with Hebe in tow, William shouting, 'Yo, parents, what's for supper?' and Matilda shouting, 'You don't deserve any supper after what you did. That was my very, very, very best music case and now it's RUINED!'

Hebe was singing to blot out the noise, '*The gypsy rover came over the hill, down through the valley so shady . . .*'

Sonja put her hands jokingly to her ears, and Merrill noticed her wobble slightly. She glanced automatically at Sonja's ankles, expecting to see a pair of ridiculous stilettos, and was astonished to see low court shoes and a couple of large Elastoplast, one of which seemed bloodied. 'What did you do to your heels?'

Sonja flushed apologetically. 'My shoes rubbed,' she said. 'I walked a lot around London.'

'Really?' I didn't mean to sound that disbelieving, thought Merrill. She tried not to notice Simon's reproving look. 'Where did you go?'

'Oh, most places: Soho, Covent Garden, all the West End – Piccadilly, Hyde Park – Kensington, Westminster, Chelsea, Islington, World's End, the City, St Paul's . . .'

'All of those?'

'Sometimes I take a taxi,' said Sonja, 'for a while, when my feet hurt. But you cannot look for a man from a taxi.'

'You should wear something low for walking,' said Simon. 'Shall I take a look?'

'No, let me.' Merrill definitely did not want Simon looking at Sonja's ankles, medically or otherwise.

'It's perfectly OK,' said Sonja. 'I do not like ugly shoes – I am Norwegian. We like the beautiful shoes because often we must wear the fur boots. It was hot and I spent a long time handing out posters. Five thousand pictures I had, but they are all given out and posted up now. Perhaps someone will see and recognise Gabriel. Hello, Hebe, that's a nice song you sang.'

Merrill looked at Sonja's raw ankles, and flushed guiltily, feeling mean-spirited and nasty. 'We should bathe these in something. Here, sit down. We have to get the plasters off you first.' Merrill took hold of one plaster gingerly.

'I am fine. Please. I soak my own feet.' Sonja was uncomfortable with the attention.

'You won't do it properly,' said Merrill. 'You'll wince and give up. Keep still.'

'Mum,' demanded Matilda, taking advantage of the silence which followed, 'William took my best music case and made it into a den for insects.'

'It's not insects,' said William, with the patience of one much tried. 'It's two chrysalises . . .'

'Chrysalidae,' said Simon, 'I think.'

'Well, whatever, they're going to be butterflies. I thought you'd be pleased to have butterflies in your music case.'

'I don't want anything in my music case. Mum, tell him.'

'Oh, for goodness' sake,' said Merrill, exasperated, looking up again from Sonja's ankles (bugger it, she had been on her feet for three days and they didn't even smell!). 'William, how often have I asked you to keep living things out of the house? If it isn't beetles in the knickers its woodlice in the wellies, and if it isn't –'

'That was you?' asked Sonja in surprise. 'You put the woodlice in my wellingtons?'

William blushed, 'Yeah, sorry – you never used them so I thought it would be OK.'

'Liar,' said Matilda. 'He thought it would be funny to watch you scream. He likes making girls scream, don't you, William? He's really *really* good at it – AREN'T YOU, WILLIAM?'

'I'm quite good,' said William modestly, adding belatedly, 'Sorry.'

'That's OK.' Suddenly Sonja felt reassured that, far from the insect incident representing her unwelcome status here, it actually meant she was being treated just like everyone else. She beamed. 'You can have my wellingtons if you like,' she added. 'I need some with heels.'

'Wow,' said Matilda, 'can you get wellingtons with heels?'

'I try,' said Sonja. 'Then I tell you. Please, Merrill, I do my own feet. I prefer it,' and Merrill retreated at last, embarrassed.

Gabriel and the question of the lost brother were not

discussed over supper. Sonja did not bring it up, thinking Simon and Merrill might not want this aired in front of the children, and Merrill and Simon each did not mention it as they assumed she had no more of value to say. So it was only after Matilda and William had set off towards Julia's cottage to take Hebe home (via Joshua's room, where she insisted on saying good night to him even though he knew full well she would be back later) that Sonja was able to talk. She watched Simon thoughtfully before she spoke, wondering if he would know anything – but when she said it she was sure he did not.

'It was in this,' she said, producing a slim blue book, 'that I found something.'

'Sonja,' said Simon, 'that's one of my mother's diaries. You really shouldn't have it. I mean, I'm sorry, Sonja, but I thought we agreed. She was his first wife and –'

'I did not get them in order to pry,' said Sonja. 'I told you I was not interested in her and that was so. Joshua told me that I was not to have them but I told him I would make up my own mind. And when everything else revealed nothing at all, I hoped there would be a clue in here. I thought she might have heard from him.'

'Mother never heard a single word from Gabriel after he went off,' Simon said, 'but, in any case, we found out afterwards he was in Greece, bumming around. There was no one here he could turn to. Mother found that hard to bear.'

'I know,' said Sonja. She looked Simon in the eye. 'You feel my presence here insults her.'

Simon flushed, taken aback. 'I don't feel that. I'm sorry you think it.'

Sonja shrugged. 'So. Here is the entry. See what she says about history repeating itself.'

Simon took the diary from her rather gingerly, read it aloud.

It has been months now since we heard from Gabriel. Such a stubborn boy, you'd think Joshua would be proud of such stubbornness, but he retreats into his own anger and I hate him for it. I used to wonder how Joshua's mother had borne being married to the man who took her son away. Now history has repeated itself, and I think I know. No wonder she died young.

'My God, she was dead herself not three months after she wrote this.'

'Yes, but what does she mean?' asked Merrill. '*The man who took her son away*?'

'I suppose she means Father going away to school,' said Simon. 'I mean, he was boarding at nine, you know.'

'Do you think she would say he was taken away, though, if that was what she meant? I mean, she would have expected him to go away to school. Joshua always tells me your children are the first Gilfoyles to stay home.'

'Well, I see your point, but what else can she mean?' asked Simon.

Sonja sighed, crushingly disappointed. 'I am so sorry. I did not think of boarding school. I took it to mean Joshua's mother had another son, taken away from her. I thought that was what she meant about history repeating itself.'

'Why should anyone take away her son?' Merrill frowned. 'Unless he died.'

Sonja frowned. 'Perhaps, I thought, he had a different father. These things sometimes happen in grand families. I thought that Gabriel might have found him.'

Simon shook his head, 'There was no other brother, and certainly no scandal of that sort. I would know. But look, Sonja, you've obviously tried really hard. Thank you, from all of us.'

'Don't thank me,' said Sonja. 'I did it for him, not you,' and she left the room with a toss of her blonde head, limping slightly as the shoes rubbed the sore places on her heels.

Simon and Merrill looked at one another.

'She really doesn't like us, does she?' said Simon.

'Well, are you surprised? We've not been very welcoming. It must have been lonely, coming here at her age and having us all calling her the Norwegian tart. I feel really guilty now. She looks as if she's walked miles.'

'So do I.' Simon rubbed the back of his neck. 'I just didn't see why he had to marry her – he never married any of the others.'

'You should feel bad,' said Merrill, 'you're twice as bad as me. At least I don't fancy her.'

'Of course I don't fancy her,' said Simon, 'she's my father's wife.'

'I know she is, and that's bloody classic. Loads of men fancy their stepmothers. I bet you walked in on your father with one of his other women when you were a teenager. That's how it always starts.'

'Oh, yes?' Simon hid his guilt in anger, startled at the accuracy of the assessment, remembering vividly the time he had found his father with his temporary secretary spread-eagled on the boardroom table beneath him one sultry July day when he had skived school and taken a surprise trip to London. 'And how would you know? Half-baked psychology part of general nursing training now, is it?'

'Don't be such a pompous, arrogant idiot,' shouted Merrill. 'OK, so I was a nurse and you were a doctor but it doesn't stop me noticing when my husband's got an erection that's nothing to DO WITH ME!' She stormed out of the room and slammed the door. After she had gone Simon paced guiltily up and down in front of the fireplace a few times, wondering if he was supposed to follow her or if he was supposed not to (you'd think after thirteen years of marriage he'd know, but he never seemed to get it right) then stamped out of the French windows and marched off to the woods to cool off.

Hebe was sitting amongst the trees, trying to explain to

her mother once again what an angel looked like – 'bright and shiny, high in the trees and it sings' – when she saw Simon coming towards them with a face like thunder. She did not like angry people, as she had found from experience that they tended to make a noise, so she jumped to her feet and fled for the house, leaving Julia to face Simon alone.

'Hi,' said Julia, surprised to see him looking so rattled. 'Is everything OK?'

'Fine. I'm just going for a walk in the woods,' said Simon, hovering, not at all sure he wanted a walk in the woods but feeling too foolish to turn back.

'Come and have a glass of dandelion wine,' said Julia, sensing marital friction, 'and tell me all about it.'

Back at the Grange, Merrill had, after pacing the living room for a while and getting William to remove all stag beetles from her wardrobe on pain of seeing his pregnant spiders evicted, gone to find Sonja.

'Hello,' she said cautiously when Sonja sat her down on one of the sofas in the small living room in the west wing. 'I came to apologise.'

'For what?'

'For being so hard on you.' Merrill sighed. 'We were all set against you when he married you. You have to understand, you were so young and beautiful, you seemed so obviously to be a . . .'

'Mistress? Gold-digger?' Sonja smiled sadly. 'I don't blame you for this. I think there was an element of it when I first met him, but I fell in love with him. I want to find his son for him. He wants him back.'

'I know. I'm sorry I've hated you.'

'Why would you hate me? Joshua is not your father.'

Merrill flushed. 'No, but I suppose I did it out of duty to Simon. And also,' she swallowed painfully, 'you're so beautiful, I was always afraid that Simon would want you himself.'

'Now you are ridiculous,' said Sonja, suddenly cold. 'Am I a toy woman who, if desired, will merely capitulate to my lover's son like an apple to be eaten?'

'No, I didn't mean that. Don't you see, it wouldn't matter whether you capitulated or not. It's the thought that he wants you at all. You're his stepmother, for God's sake, and you've got a body better than I ever had.'

Sonja sighed. 'Simon doesn't want me. This you know, Merrill. Oh, I agree he probably has thoughts of that fantasy, you know, where young men find their father with the mistress? I know this happens, but that is not the same as wanting.'

'I knew it,' said Merrill triumphantly. 'I thought that was what caused it. Did Joshua tell you?'

'No, of course not. I read it in a magazine.'

'Oh. It must have been the same one I read.' She was silent for a moment, then said, 'I'm glad Joshua's getting better.'

'That child makes him better,' said Sonja. 'She is there watching him all the time. I think he sees something of himself in her.'

'Strange,' said Merrill, 'given his feelings about mental illness. Not that Hebe's ill, but you know what I mean.'

'Why does he feel like this?' Sonja frowned. 'He is very extreme about Gabriel.'

'You mean the business about Gabriel's children? He thinks there's weakness in Gabriel's genes.'

'Exactly so, yet why should he think this when Gabriel was surely sad and low because of the death of his mother? When my mother died I thought my world ended.'

'Prejudice,' said Merrill, realising that she had no idea if Sonja had any family at all. 'I know you love him but he's still a prejudiced old fart. Sorry . . .' she hiccuped twice, 'sorry – it's my wine talking.'

Sonja smiled. 'Your wine is very honest. I must go and sit with him now. Actually, between you and me, I am hoping there will be sex.'

So was I, thought Merrill gloomily, but after bringing up the thorny issue of Simon's erections there's probably no chance of that at all.

'So you do fancy her?' said Julia matter-of-factly, pouring Simon another glass of Mrs Braithwaite's best dandelion brew (one hundred per cent proof and takes no prisoners).

Simon screwed up his face and tried to speak clearly lest Julia should think he was drunk – which he wasn't obviously; a man of his capacity did not get drunk on a couple of glasses of home-made dandelion cordial. 'I don't know. She . . . I find myself watching her and then I get this huge erection when I think of her. I shouldn't be telling you this . . .'

'It's the wine talking,' said Julia. 'Don't worry, you won't remember a thing in the morning. Come on, Simon, you're a doctor. You know erections just happen. It doesn't have to mean anything.'

'I got one when I hugged her,' said Simon miserably, swigging wine. 'I've always fancied my father's mistresses. I caught him with one once, and I've never forgotten it. She was blonde too; her name was Penelope.'

Julia smiled. 'What happened?'

'They were on the boardroom table. The truth is, I've had recurring fantasies ever since of having my father's mistress on that boardroom table.'

'Sonja's his wife, not his mistress,' said Julia. 'Does she still count?'

'She looks like a mistress,' said Simon miserably. 'God, what is this stuff? It's like drinking the bottom of the pond.'

'Dandelion wine,' said Julia. 'Don't worry, it's harmless. How does she look like a mistress?'

'High heels,' said Simon, 'and that long blonde hair. He always went for blondes. Liked to do that gimmick where they undo it and it all falls down. God, I feel peculiar. Are you sure this stuff is harmless? I really feel quite . . .'

*

'He's passed out on my kitchen table,' said Julia cheerfully to Merrill, on the telephone. 'D'you want to leave him here till morning? I don't think he'll be much use tonight.'

'He's on call tomorrow,' said Merrill dubiously, 'from seven in the morning. I think he'd better come back.'

In the end he had to stay put, since it proved impossible for the two of them to get him shifted and there was really no one they could ask for help. Merrill suggested Jonathan, but Julia was reluctant, fearing that he might read too much into it, so they left Simon asleep on the kitchen table with a blanket around his shoulders and his mobile phone next to his left ear, so that when the patients started ringing in the morning he would be sure to hear.

Deep in the woods on the caravan site they were awake much later. It was two in the morning but it was Midsummer Night and they had no real reason to go to bed particularly early. The gypsies, most of whom actually spent most of the year in tidy brick homes on the outskirts of Peterborough and Milton Keynes, were listening to Simon and Garfunkel, and dancing impromptu steps in the flickering shadows. From the edge of the trees Hebe watched briefly, fascinated, listening to the music before wandering over to look for John James. She found him particularly interesting although she could not say why.

As she watched, someone stopped the CD and John began to sing to his mandolin. Hebe liked the sound, and gradually as he played she crept out of the shadow and into the firelight, her eyes never leaving the strings of the instrument.

The gypsy children watched her approach without curiosity. They had become accustomed to her turning up and watching them, and now took her extraordinary voice for granted, just as they accepted the peculiar way she stood on tiptoe flapping her hands or stared straight through them. 'Hebe's here,' they said to John, and he looked up in surprise, shocked that she was out so late. He smiled at her carefully, not wanting to scare her off.

'Hello, Hebe,' he said, taking his hand off the mandolin. 'How are you?'

'I'm strange,' said Hebe, taking the question literally. 'Grandpa says I'm retarded.'

John winced. 'Who's your grandpa?'

'Grandpa,' said Hebe, 'in the big house.' She put her hand on John's shoulder. 'You've got a hairy face, and I can shave. I shaved Grandpa.'

John stared at her, puzzled by a connection he couldn't understand. 'Joshua Gilfoyle is your grandpa?'

'Now he is – William gave him to me for a dead butterfly.' Hebe found this exciting. She began to hop from one foot to the other, flapping her hands beside her.

John suppressed a smile. I wish I'd seen the old bugger's face when he heard that, he thought. 'Oh, I see. And you shaved him?'

'Oh yes. I didn't make blood but the nurse did.'

John suppressed another smile. 'I bet he enjoyed that.'

'He did,' said Hebe, hopping and flapping more violently. 'Then he learned to walk again. I showed him. The nurse says I made him better.'

'I bet you did,' said John. 'You're a star.'

'No,' Hebe stopped hopping and frowned, 'not a star. I'm a girl. Hebe Fitzgerald, born April the twenty-fourth, nineteen ninety-three at the Whittington hospital, child benefit number nine-oh-one-one—'

'I don't want to know your child benefit number,' said John hastily, aware that one of the gypsy children was scratching it in the dust and that such information was easily traded for cash in certain North London bars. 'Shouldn't you be in bed, Hebe? You shouldn't be out here on your own.'

'I like the moon,' said Hebe. 'And angels. I like that thing. Will you play it?'

'It's a mandolin. I'll play it if you like, but after that we must take you home, because it's very late and if you're a girl you should be in bed.'

'Angels aren't in bed,' said Hebe.

'I know one who should be. Do you want to sing?'

'OK,' Hebe shrugged slightly but her hands started to flap again, a sign, he had quickly realised, of excited pleasure.

'You choose,' said John. 'Are you ready? What shall we do?' he strummed a simple A major chord.

Hebe frowned, explored her mental music bank briefly, flapped her hands a few more times and then remembered something she had sung a week or two ago, which had begun exactly with this chord. She went still, defocused, and launched into perfect Italian . . .

'O mio babbino caro, mi piace è bello, bello;
Vo'andare in Porta Rossa a comperar l'anello!
Sì, sì, ci voglio andare e se l'amassi indarno,
Andrei sul Ponte Vecchio, ma per buttarmi in Arno
Mi struggo e mi tormento! O Dio, vorrei morir
Babbo, pietà, pietà, Babbo, pietà, pietà.'

She stopped and closed her mouth. Into the absolute silence which had fallen on the whole camp, Billy Smith said, 'Fuck me.'

John swallowed hard. He had kind of kept up with the chords, but how the hell did she know the words? It was one thing for a child to have an amazing voice . . . What a gift she had, if indeed it was right to call it a gift. It is possible to be too extraordinary.

'Hebe,' he said, 'do you have lessons?'

'Yes,' said Hebe, 'with Mrs Peel and Matilda.'

'Did they teach you to sing that?'

'Heard it on the CD,' said Hebe, who saw no difference between singing 'The Gypsy Rover' in English and turning

264

out perfect Puccini in Italian. She had never needed to understand what she was singing in order to do it.

'What does it mean?'

Hebe shrugged. 'Nothing.' She did it for the moment, for the way it made her feel. That was all.

'How many times have you heard it?'

Hebe shrugged. 'Don't know. Do you have mandolin lessons?'

'I did a long time ago. Hebe, does your mum know you're out here?'

Hebe shook her head. 'No, she's asleep, and Uncle Simon is on the kitchen table.'

John wondered if Hebe's mother was aware of the extent of her child's gift, of how difficult it can be to be the best at something. It reminded him of his conversation with Kate about madness and genius. Hebe was not mad, of course, but perhaps her incredible ability was in some way born out of all the things she couldn't do. Perhaps, he thought, I am a successful poet only because I failed so miserably in the rest of my life. 'You should be asleep too. You shouldn't come out here on your own,' he said to Hebe.

'I don't sleep much,' said Hebe, genuinely surprised. 'I have to count stars, and an angel lives in the woods. Then I see Grandpa.'

'Ah. What does the angel look like?'

Hebe frowned. 'Shiny. High in the trees.'

'I see. Hebe, I think we should take you home now.' John was aware that Hebe's mother might not appreciate a strange man turning up at her door in the middle of the night with her eight-year-old daughter. He could do without the police being called and asking questions – that really might put the cat amongst the pigeons. He had come here for the solitude, not for trouble and drama. The weeks in the caravan were usually his best creative time. 'Tracey, would you come with us?'

'Sure, John.' Tracey clambered to her feet, 'C'mon, Hebe, bedtime.'

It didn't take them long to walk through the woods. Julia's cottage stood open, as Hebe had left the front door unlatched. Often – most usually – she used the window, but tonight she had crept downstairs to see Uncle Simon on the kitchen table and had then impulsively let herself out through the door.

'D'you want a cup of tea?' she asked John and Tracey as they came to the door, 'and some scones? My mum makes lots of scones.'

John smiled. 'That's very kind, Hebe, but I think it's very late for scones. Here, in you go and I'll close up after you.'

'They're really good scones,' said Hebe. 'We have them with chocolate spread.'

'You do?'

'Mm,' said Hebe, 'they're yummy with chocolate spread.'

'I know,' said John. 'In you go.'

'OK,' said Hebe cheerfully. 'Night-night.' She crept through the kitchen past her sleeping uncle and up to her bed. John watched her go, glanced thoughtfully at the hunched figure of the sleeping Simon, and closed the door firmly.

'Come on,' he said to Tracey, 'let's go.'

'OK,' she said. 'What's up? You look as if you've seen a ghost.'

'Not at all,' he smiled. 'I was just remembering someone I once knew.'

'God,' said Tracey, 'I hope I'm not as sad as you when I'm your age. Come on, let's get back before the others finish all the lager.'

Mrs Braithwaite also watched Hebe approach the house with John and Tracey, just as she had watched her go through the woods to the gypsy clearing and sing for John. She felt specially responsible for Hebe, because Hebe was

266

not the first changeling she had met. She was sure of this, and equally sure that she had failed the first one. So when Hebe crept past her cottage in the darkness she had followed her into the woods. She had done this several times in the last few nights, as for several nights Hebe had followed the same ritual of creeping into the woods, climbing a tree, counting stars, then making her way to Joshua's window. Mrs Braithwaite had therefore seen a few things that astounded her, but as long as there was no danger she generally pursued a policy of not interfering too much. It wouldn't be right, given that at her age she shouldn't be here at all. Anyway, she had been seeing angels in the tea leaves for several weeks now, so she had known something was afoot.

'You know,' she said to John James, surprising him out of the shadows just after he settled back down on his caravan steps with his mandolin, 'you should be looking after that child.'

He frowned, accustomed to her appearing suddenly, not at all bothered by her assumption that he would listen to her advice. 'She's not mine, Mary. I can't look after her.'

'You should talk to the mother about it.'

'I've never even met the mother.'

'Then it's time you did.'

John sighed. 'Mary, I appreciate you trying to match me up with someone else, but you know I don't want to get involved in this village and its inhabitants. I just came here to be in the woods. It helps me write.'

'You can't come here and live in these woods and not bear any responsibility, young man,' said Mary sharply. 'This is your home.'

'Only for one month of the year,' said John, equally sharply. 'Then I shall go back to where I live for the other eleven months. Then this is no longer my home.'

'You can't discard the past as easily as that,' said Mary crossly. 'I haven't lived to see my five hundredth year without knowing that. It always comes back to you in the end, if you live long enough, and it's coming back to find you, John James, mark my words.' She turned and walked away, disappearing into the shadows as quickly as she had come.

'She's really weird, that one,' said Tracey, who had been holding her breath so as not to miss any of the exchange, and who now felt quite light-headed. 'She can't have been here five hundred years, yet when you look at her you could almost believe it.'

'She believes it herself,' John said, 'but she means well, and I'm very fond of her. She's looked after me more than once.'

'Are you from round here then? I mean, we've not seen you here before.'

'No,' said John, 'I'm not. I travel.'

'I mean originally,' she insisted. 'Where were you when you were born?'

'I was born twice,' he said, 'and only the second time counts.'

'Where was that, then?'

'London,' he said, and began to strum on the mandolin again, successfully blocking any more attempts at questioning and thinking perhaps it was time to leave. Old Mary was clearly after a man for that child's mother. Well, he could understand her feeling responsible, bearing in mind the sadness in her own past. But that didn't make it his problem. He had his own life to lead. Hebe was very sweet and absolutely fascinating but it didn't do to get involved, however much Mary Braithwaite insisted that the tea leaves said she was written into his destiny. He had nothing to give in that respect – he gave it long ago and never got it back. He had taken enough of a chance coming here and behaving so badly with Kate Coleman. It was definitely time to pack up and go home. He would leave straight after the fair.

Chapter Thirteen

Julia awoke a couple of days later knowing that it was Thursday and feeling happier than she had for a while. Since making love with Jonathan she felt somehow restored. OK, she wasn't rushing outside naked to begin sculpting, but her confidence was returning. She could feel it. Daniel had been wrong to suggest that one man held the key to her inspiration. She had done lots of good work before she ever met Hebe's father.

Now, too, she had a fair idea what the new Foxbarton angel was going to look like. She had had several long conversations with Hebe, who was still asleep this morning, had sketched some thoughts which Hebe had approved of – and since Matilda and William were at school there was nothing to stop her from starting straight away. Pulling on her T-shirt she hurried into the garden, full of joy and energy – and almost fell over Daniel Cutter lying on her doorstep.

'Oh bugger,' she said to him, 'and I was just feeling good about today.'

Daniel sat up, rubbing his left shoulder where she had inadvertently kicked him. 'Look, Jules, I had to come over and see you. Carl Bayer is coming over today and we do need to discuss it.'

Julia folded her arms implacably. 'Daniel, Hebe and her voice are nothing to do with you. Whether I talk to Carl Bayer or not is nothing to do with you. So please go away. You are not my friend.'

'Jules, I'm here to help. Carl's a businessman. He's here because he wants Hebe's voice. I understand the industry. I can look after you. You need someone like me on your side, to make sure she gets a good deal.'

'On my side? Why the hell should I imagine you're on my side?'

'Because I am, Jules. I know you think I've sold my artistic soul, gone over to the bad guys, and maybe you're right, but I care about you and I know how the music industry can be. I don't want to see you shafted by some bloke with a clever contract.'

'Daniel, it seems to me you wouldn't know an artistic soul if it came labelled and you'd only want one if you got it at a discount. Contracts? I don't even want to see this person, I'm certainly not going to discuss contracts.'

'Well, that's fine, Jules, but he is coming and he'll want you to discuss contracts. You can't close your eyes to it – she sings Puccini, for God's sake. You need someone like me, someone who speaks Carl's language. I can control the whole thing.'

'You started this whole thing, Daniel. I don't trust you any more.'

'OK, so you don't trust me – but if you tell me to fuck off who else is there who can help?'

'Daniel,' said Julia, 'fuck off.'

He stood up, suddenly angry. 'Don't you talk to me like that, Julia Fitzgerald. I've known you since you arrived at art school as green as grass. I've held your head when you vomited your guts up. I've –'

'Changed, Dan. You've changed.'

'Don't brush me off, Jules. This is my deal; I deserve to be here.'

'Bog off, Daniel, or I'll poke you in the eye.'

Daniel sighed, stepped out of range. 'It'll be difficult without me, Julia.'

'Are you threatening me?' Julia could hardly believe her ears. 'Because if you are you'd better be wearing that bloody box.'

'No, I'm telling you,' said Daniel, rather regretting that he had given it back to William, who had needed it for a school match – but it had proved rather uncomfortable, having slipped in his underwear and trapped one of his more delicate parts rather suddenly. 'You need me, or someone like me. There's big money involved here.'

'How much is your share, Dan? Thirty per cent? Forty per cent? I rather think I need you like I need a purple giraffe with a hole in the head.'

'Mummy, who is it?'

'It's Daniel, darling. He's just going.'

'Oh, is Daniel the one who's got a bent willy?'

'Hebe!'

'That's what William said,' said Hebe. She looked at Daniel. 'Did someone bend it? Can I see?'

Daniel turned on his heel and stormed out of the garden. The encounter left Julia feeling uneasy, her impulse to start work on the angel gone.

'Come along, darling,' she said, 'let's walk up to the Hall and see your aunt. I think I need to blow away the cobwebs.'

'OK,' said Hebe, 'but I've got no knickers on.'

'Well, we'll find knickers first,' said Julia.

'Only blue ones. Can I see Grandpa?'

'Sure,' Julia sighed. She herself had not seen Joshua since his stroke, despite Hebe's frequent visits. In truth she had rather been avoiding him, sure that he would want news of her progress with the angel after this dramatic reminder of his mortality – but at least she now knew where to start. She could honestly tell him that the angel was under way.

They found Merrill in the kitchen, Simon just leaving for work.

'Ugh,' said Hebe, 'they're snogging.' She looked around for a chess set to stare at but, this being the kitchen, there was none so she frowned and stared at the floor.

Julia smiled, wondering if Merrill had taken her advice. Certainly she was aware from Matilda and William that the two of them had gone off to London yesterday. Was it too ridiculous to imagine that, whilst there, they had availed themselves of Joshua's boardroom table, a stick of lipstick and a pair of stilettos?

'Morning, Simon,' she said to him as he passed her on his way out. 'How's the head?'

'Absolutely fine,' he said. 'I'm so sorry I passed out in your kitchen the other night.'

'You don't have to apologise again. Four times was enough.'

'Well, I'm off. Sick people to heal, the world to put right, the NHS to prop up, the Government to maintain in power through acting as professional scapegoat for all ills, both human and bureaucratic.'

'What time will you be home?' asked Merrill.

'Early,' he said, 'my early day today. I'll pick up the kids from the school bus. You paint your nails or something.'

Merrill fluttered her eyelashes. ''Bye then.'

'No need to ask what you've been up to,' said Julia after he had gone.

Merrill looked arch. 'We're fine. We sorted it out. It was stupid, really. What brings you up here so early?'

'Hiding, actually,' said Julia. 'Hebe wants to see Joshua, and I don't want to be around the house.'

'Really? Why?'

'I'll tell you over coffee. OK, Hebe, you can go and see Grandpa. I'll come and find you in a little while.' She watched Merrill brewing tea. 'How is he?'

'Simon? Well, you saw.'

'No, I mean Joshua. Hebe seems to have a real thing about him.'

'I know. It's rather sweet. I think he likes her coming round.'

Julia sniffed. 'I doubt it, given his attitudes to mental health. But then she hasn't got any other grandpas, has she?'

'I don't know, Jules, you tell me.'

272

Julia looked defensive. 'I did try to find her father, I told you. I wouldn't know where to start looking now.'

'It's like Sonja, looking for Gabriel,' said Merrill, slightly guiltily. 'Do you know she spent days tramping around London in her stupid shoes handing out posters? She had five thousand made and she didn't stop till she'd handed out every single one.'

'Well, I'm not about to do the same. But look, that's not why I'm here. Daniel's music business mate, Carl Bayer, will be here some time this morning. I want to lie low.'

'What? Carl Bayer? The Carl Bayer? The one with the jet and the banana split thing?'

'Exactly. He's coming to hear Hebe – thanks to my so-called old pal Daniel, who has so recently been revealed as a snake. And I don't want him to. It will upset her terribly and to no purpose.'

'Golly, Jules, are you sure?'

'Yes, I'm sure. She couldn't make records, Merrill. She can't even dress herself properly. She wouldn't wear any knickers that weren't blue today. It took us ages to find an acceptable pair, and when we did they were mine. I'm surprised they're not round her ankles.'

'So buy her some blue knickers. At least her requirements are specific. Matilda won't wear anything she doesn't like, and what she doesn't like changes daily – which is far more frustrating, believe me.'

'You know what I mean. Hebe can't deal with things.'

'Hebe can climb out of windows better than a squirrel and she's got the voice of an angel.'

'It's no good if you can't deal with it. She sings because it makes order out of noise. I don't want to put her in danger.'

'Well, it's your decision.' Merrill sighed. 'I wish you'd told me about this before.'

'I couldn't,' said Julia. 'I knew you'd talk me into it, and Matilda would have heard and wanted to come along too.'

'What would I have wanted to come to?' Matilda

appeared at the kitchen door in her school uniform. 'Sorry, Mum, we missed the bus.'

'Damn. Well, I'll run you to school . . . Hang on a minute, the bus hasn't gone yet.'

'Yes it has, it's half-past . . . Oh. OK, it hasn't, but I need to be here today. Look Mum, Daniel was here and he told me about this man who's coming. He wants me to sing the duet with Hebe.'

'Oh, for goodness' sake,' said Julia furiously, 'no one's going to be singing for him.'

Matilda stared. 'But, Aunt Julia,' she wailed, 'this is my one chance. I'm at least as good as Charlotte Church, and I can sing in German.'

'School,' said her mother, without much hope of being obeyed, 'now,' and Matilda left the kitchen.

William edged in. 'Can I listen?'

'You what?' asked his mother.

'To Matilda making a twit of herself for the record guy. I can sing in German too, you know, and Dad's always saying if I want to go to the Amazon I've got to think about funding.'

'I know,' said Merrill, 'and you can go to school as well.'

'D'you think they'll go?' asked Julia as he also disappeared.

'I dunno,' said Merrill gloomily, 'but I very much doubt it. You may have to let Hebe sing, just to get my lot out of this poor guy's hair.'

'Whatever else he is,' said Julia, 'he's not a poor guy. I'm going to see what Hebe's up to.'

She found Hebe playing chess with Joshua, whilst Sonja tidied around them and watched out of a corner of her eye. The lost chess pieces had been declared permanently lost by now, and a new set purchased. With equality of both sides Hebe was now surprisingly good at holding her own. Joshua, despite his determination not to be seen using his right hand until he could use it properly, found he was tending to use it more and more, and every so often he muttered, 'Dammit,' proving that he was also regaining his power of speech.

'Morning,' said Julia awkwardly, standing in the doorway. He was not as bad as she had been led to believe – in fact, he looked to her very much like the same old Joshua. 'I see you've got Hebe under control.'

'Angel,' said Joshua very clearly. 'My angel.'

Golly, she thought. He has changed his views. 'Well, I wouldn't go that far, although she is a beautiful –'

'Where's . . . my . . . bloody . . . an . . . gel?'

'Oh. It's coming. It's begun. It should be ready in a few weeks,' said Julia, adding hastily, 'as long as they can cast it as soon as it's ready.'

Joshua nodded and went back to his chess, but Hebe patted his hand. 'It's time for Grandpa's walk. Come on.'

Sonja produced a Zimmer frame and to Julia's astonishment the two of them helped him to his feet and Joshua set off determinedly through the French windows and into the garden with Hebe as his guide. Julia stared after them with tears in her eyes.

'Blimey,' she said to Sonja, 'this is the man that said she should be put away and didn't belong in the village. I didn't know they were friends.'

'They are,' said Sonja. 'More than friends. Hebe has been good for him. Julia, he makes huge improvement. May I – Do you mind if I ask you about Hebe?'

'No. What?' Julia shared Merrill's guilt about her misjudgement of Sonja; felt that she herself had been equally at fault. She stared at Sonja, marvelling at the amazing silver-blonde hair, the startlingly blue eyes, wondering if they all looked like Sonja in her part of Norway.

'What is her problem? I mean, I know there is something.'

'It's called autism,' said Julia, 'although in Hebe's case it's relatively mild. She's what's called high-functioning autistic. It means –'

'Ah, I have heard this word before. So why does she not go to school?'

'She can't. They wanted to pack her off to a special school miles away, but I couldn't bear it so I teach her at home and every so often someone comes to check up on us to make sure I'm really doing it.'

'You do it very well. What is a special school? You mean a mental institution?'

'Well, not exactly. Not any more. It was like that years ago. Handicapped children were taken away to institutions for their whole lives. Was it the same in Norway?'

'I don't know. What do you mean by "taken away"?' Sonja frowned.

'Sent to big mental hospitals to live,' said Julia. 'They were usually huge and isolated, and people just disappeared into them for ever. Lost from society as if they didn't really exist. They're all gone now, those places, thank God.' She looked at Hebe.

'Taken away for ever?' Sonja was looking thoughtful. 'The rest of their life?'

'Often,' said Julia. 'Why?'

Sonja looked out of the window at Joshua, walking slowly and lopsidedly across the lawn with Hebe. 'Joshua knew a boy at school who was not normal. He says this to me one day. Then his first wife's diary makes reference to his mother having a son taken away. Simon thinks this means boarding school but I am not so sure. When you say taken away also, I wonder if there could be some connection.'

Julia frowned. 'I can't imagine what.'

Sonja frowned. 'If Joshua knew a boy who was not normal, it would surely not have been at his boarding school.'

'No, I wouldn't have thought so. That is, I presume Joshua went to some grand public school. They wouldn't take handicapped children.'

'Then how would he know a handicapped boy at school?'

'I don't know.' Julia frowned. She had not heard the brother theory; could not understand the importance of this to Sonja. 'Why?'

Sonja looked thoughtful. 'Joshua went to the village school when he was small. What if it was his brother who was not normal? Could he have been sent away?'

Julia shook her head. 'I don't know. People had strange views about mental handicap in those days – especially rich families. You should just ask him.'

'I will ask,' said Sonja. 'It may be a clue.'

In the garden Hebe and Joshua continued their walk to a seat on the far side of the lawn where he sat to rest and she kneeled on the grass picking daisies. There was a fresh smell of cut grass and birds were singing in the trees. A song thrush made a particularly pretty sound and Hebe copied it on 'ah', then drifted into the song he had heard her sing before.

> *'On a tree by a river a little tom tit*
> *Sang "Willow, tit willow, tit willow!"* . . .'

Kate heard Hebe singing as she walked past the wall of the Grange on her way to the vicarage. There was no denying that the child had the most amazing voice. It forced you to realise that the other voices, Matilda's sweet soprano and Oscar's now-broken chorister treble, were merely foils by comparison. Still, Oscar had many other talents. Really, it was just a matter of which he would excel at the very most.

She frowned at herself uncharacteristically. There I go again, she thought, worrying about Oscar's future when today I'm going to tackle my own. Today I'm going to start my campaign to woo and win Jonathan Doyle. He needs me; I just have to make him see it. She patted the basket that she carried. No man can resist me, she thought, not when I bring him my cheese scones.

'Good morning.'

277

Kate almost jumped out of her skin, so lost had she been in her reverie, and was mildly discomfited to see old Mary Braithwaite standing behind her.

'Hello, Mrs Braithwaite, how are you?'

'Not bad,' said Mrs Braithwaite, emitting what was, in Kate's view, a decidedly witch-like cackle, 'for my age. Off to see the Reverend, are you?'

'Actually,' said Kate, 'I'm taking him some cheese scones I happened to have left over.'

Mary Braithwaite eyed her thoughtfully. 'I could help you, if you like. He could do with a good woman like you.'

Kate flushed painfully. 'I'm sure I don't know what you mean.'

'Of course you do. I'm very experienced in matters of love.'

Kate regarded Mrs Braithwaite's wrinkled brown skin and strange, cropped black hair with unease. Stories of Mrs Braithwaite's skills as a white witch had dominated her years in the village, and although that sort of thing was obviously a load of old rubbish it wouldn't do to annoy someone who could very possibly put a hex on you. 'I don't think I ought to –'

'Rubbish, woman. Take a tip from me. The way to a man's heart may be through his stomach but if you give him cheese all will be lost.'

'What are you talking about? I make the best cheese scones in the village.'

'Take it from me,' said Mrs Braithwaite archly, 'you win them with apples and lose them with cheese. I seem to remember from the last village fête that your apple pie is excellent,' she winked. 'Don't you have one in your freezer?'

Kate hesitated, torn between wanting to see Jonathan now, whilst she felt ready to make a start on her campaign to win him, and wondering whether Mrs Braithwaite might have a point. After all, Oscar had recently told her with resounding indelicacy that, wonderful though her cheese scones were, if he had more than two he farted all evening. It would not do to make Jonathan fart – aside from being uncomfortable for him it could really spoil a romantic moment.

'I am off to see him myself,' said Mrs Braithwaite. 'I won't be long, but I'm sure it gives you time to pop home for a pie.'

'I do have one in the freezer,' said Kate, feeling slightly bewitched herself. Old Mrs Padley said that Mrs Braithwaite had been Joshua Gilfoyle's nanny. If it was true that would make her about a hundred years old.

'I knew you would have. Well, you go and get it, dear, whilst I have a word with him.' And Mrs Braithwaite hurried off, leaving Kate wondering how she could possibly have known about the apple pie, far too ready to credit Mrs Braithwaite with supernatural powers to guess that it was because she had asked Oscar to check the previous evening.

So Mrs Braithwaite knocked at the door of the vicarage unfettered by Kate's presence, determined to right what she felt was a simple imbalance of people, and when Jonathan Doyle let her in she explained something very secret to him, in strictest confidence, something which would make sure he dropped any thoughts of romancing Julia Fitzgerald completely and concentrated his efforts elsewhere.

It was just before lunch when the limousine arrived. It was long and white, as a limousine should be when really designed to impress, but it was so long that it was completely unable to negotiate the sharp turn into Julia's tiny drive, so the chauffeur had to park it next to the post office, where a gang of pensioners at once gathered to admire the paintwork and make assumptions about what the owner got up to behind the tinted glass in the back.

From it Carl Bayer, record company director and impresario, famous for being a giant in the music business and for having a particular appreciation of banana splits, emerged wearing jeans and a casual jacket, popped a pair of

279

dark glasses over his eyes and sauntered over to shake Daniel's hand.

In the garden at the Grange Hebe was hanging from a tree branch somewhere above Joshua's head, singing 'Where the bee sucks, there suck I' whilst Merrill, Sonja and Julia drank tea on the grass ten feet away, each wondering what would become of her. At the far side of the lawn Joshua dozed in a garden seat, having shoed them all away to allow him a nap in the dappled shade of a pear tree.

Daniel and Carl Bayer simply followed the sound of Hebe's voice, and listened to her for a few minutes before interrupting the gathering.

Julia was tense, wishing now that she had asked Daniel what time this friend of his was likely to turn up, or that she had agreed a time to meet him so that she at least didn't have to feel at a disadvantage when he found her, as he was certain to do. So when two figures set out towards them across the lawn Julia stood first, realising that the dreaded meeting was about to take place, but already resigned to the fact that simply avoiding it was not a solution and relieved that she could stop worrying, at least, about when.

'Hi there,' said Carl Bayer, 'ladies. I'm Carl Bayer.'

Julia took a deep breath. Sonja blinked and smiled, and Merrill frowned and said rather critically, 'Did Mrs Barker let you in? She really ought to have told us you were here.'

Daniel beamed charmingly. He had always had a good line in charming beams, thought Julia cynically. 'Sorry, we bypassed your lady and just followed the sound of Hebe singing. Carl – this is Julia, Merrill, Sonja . . . Mrs Gilfoyle.'

Sonja smiled cautiously. 'Hello. Would you like tea?'

'I don't know if we have anything to talk about,' said Julia coolly, brushing her long hair back from her face and suddenly wishing she didn't look like a hippy. Carl Bayer was bound to think she could be trodden on. 'It might not be worth making it.'

Carl Bayer shrugged pleasantly, 'Well, tea would be very

welcome either way. Thank you.' He watched appreciatively as Sonja took her slim hips daintily across the lawn to ask Mrs Barker for a fresh pot and more cups. Merrill noticed that although she was wearing flatter shoes she still had a slight limp, and that Mrs Barker was already watching them through the living-room window.

The appearance of Matilda and William as they all sat down together was really no surprise, Merrill thought, reflecting that Carl Bayer looked like quite a nice bloke, considering his reputation.

'Why are you two not at school?' she asked them crossly.

Matilda flushed and glanced pointedly at Daniel. 'Oh, Mum, you know I had lots of SINGING STUFF to do today.'

Daniel took his cue, 'I'm so sorry, Merrill. It was my fault. You see, Carl was really keen on the two of them as a duet, and he was hoping to hear them sing together again.'

Carl removed his sunglasses. He had, Julia noticed, surprisingly candid grey eyes. She began to wonder if she had misjudged him by his tabloid reputation, rather as they had all misjudged Sonja. Still, nice eyes are simply not enough.

'Miss Fitzgerald,' he said to her frankly, 'I know you don't welcome this intrusion from me, and if, when all's said and done, you don't want to go ahead, that's fine – but from what I heard the other day your daughter could be the next Charlotte Church. Not only that, Dan here tells me she has an extraordinary memory.'

Julia raised her eyebrows. 'Did he tell you she has autism?'

'Well, yes, he did. But that can mean a whole range of ability. I understand it's largely socio-communicative in Hebe's case, and that she's OK with very specifically tailored tasks as long as there's not too much information coming in.'

Julia bit her lip. 'How do you know all that?'

'I'm not completely ignorant, even though I am a music producer.'

'I'm sorry,' she looked at the floor, 'I don't know that Hebe could cope with all this. I'm really not sure I want to explore it.' She was aware of Matilda sucking air in between her teeth and holding it there, and William trying not to choke.

'Well, look. I'll tell you what all this involves and then you can decide. Is that a reasonable deal?'

Julia glanced at Matilda, who was hopping from one foot to the other, and William, who looked as if he had ants in his pants (mind you, on his usual form he probably did), and then at Merrill, who was trying to look unbiased and failing by a factor of a million.

'I suppose,' she said after a pause, 'I have nothing to lose by listening.'

'Yippee!' shouted Matilda, and ran across the grass towards Hebe, shouting, 'Come on down. We're going to sing together,' whilst William pointedly cleared his throat and wondered aloud if his Anthony Way impression might get an airing, since having just one record go to gold could finance years of tarantula expeditions in Amazonia.

The Anthony Way impression was, sadly, turned down without a hearing on the basis, Carl explained kindly, that boys should always follow their first love (his was presumably bananas, Julia thought) and if that meant arachnids in Amazonia, well, so be it. Much mollified at being understood, William wandered off to fetch Hebe from her tree. Then they drank tea and ate scones with chocolate spread, a delicacy Julia had invented, whilst Hebe and Matilda repeated their duet from the Haverhill Festival. After this, on prompting from Matilda, Hebe sang 'The Gypsy Rover', 'Where the bee sucks', and, as a finale, her Puccini. As she sang this last, Joshua got up gingerly from his seat on the other side of the lawn, and Sonja hurried over to help him.

Carl Bayer watched him out of the corner of his eye as he told Julia that Hebe was every bit as wonderful as he had thought, and that he would like to arrange to show them the studio the coming weekend. 'I need to hear them sing under studio conditions, and then you can all see what's involved,' he said. 'We'll do it on Saturday.'

'We can't – it's the Foxbarton Horse Fair on Saturday,' said Julia, as Matilda danced round and round them. 'I'm painting faces.' She felt this was a little out of control already.

'On horses?' Daniel beamed disingenuously.

Julia delivered him a withering look. 'On children.'

'Can you get out of it?' That was Carl, smiling.

'Absolutely not,' said Merrill. 'This is a village. It's take part or die. Seriously.'

'Sunday, then,' said Carl Bayer, 'at my studio in Soho. I'll send a car.'

Hebe planted herself in front of him. 'Excuse me, man.'

'My name's Carl. What can I do for you, young lady?'

'Have you got a bent willy too?'

Behind him Joshua, who had just finished crossing the lawn, made a choking sound. Merrill held her breath, whilst Julia merely smiled slightly and said, 'Sorry. She comes out with some choice stuff. Hebe, that's not a polite thing to ask. You don't say willy to people.'

Hebe frowned, social niceties being something that had always passed her by. She could accept that she was not allowed to say willy, but the subtleties of why would always elude her, and next time she would simply say penis instead. The problem with Hebe was giving her specific enough instructions on dealing with other people without handicapping her conversation completely by forbidding half the words in the English language.

'That's OK,' said Carl Bayer cheerfully. 'I've been accused many times of having no balls; it's refreshing to hear a variation. Well, look, thank you for seeing me – Julia, Merrill. It was nice to meet you, Mrs Gilfoyle, and . . . er, Mr Gilfoyle.'

He had hoped to avoid talking to Joshua, did not like physical impairment. His smile widened suddenly. Unless it was attached to someone very rich, of course. 'Say, are you *the* Gilfoyle? Of Gilfoyles? Wow, I'm impressed – I have shares in your company. Great interim figures; I was impressed. Well, thank you all for your hospitality. I must get back to London. See you very soon.'

As the limousine drove away Daniel smiled hopefully at Julia. 'Well, Jules, he wasn't so bad, was he?'

'At least he's honest,' said Julia, and turned her back on him. She felt uneasy, pushed along by other people's nice-ness and enthusiasm, her gut feeling that this whole thing was a very bad idea not relieved by Carl Bayer's normality or the fact that he seemed to know something about autism. After all, anyone could read it in a book.

In the limousine Carl Bayer leaned back against his leather seat and opened the bar.

'How did it go?' asked his chauffeur.

'Piece of cake, Jack. The kid has a great voice, kind of a fairy quality. She's coming down to the studio on Sunday.'

'Really? Have they signed?'

'Not yet. I didn't want to push it. One thing at a time. She could be the next Charlotte Church, Jack. I could retire on this one, but the mother's a bit jumpy.'

'I thought jumpy women were your speciality.'

'Absolutely, Jack, you just have to know what makes them tick. In this case, I knew the child was weird so I read a book about autism on the way down here. Weird stuff, I tell you, but meant it went like a dream. You're working with the maestro, mate.'

Kate passed the limousine, which was just leaving when she returned to the vicarage with the apple pie Mary Braithwaite had recommended. Jonathan Doyle was some-what stunned when he opened the door to see her there, holding it. It seemed to be his day for being stunned. Mary

Braithwaite had left him stunned on several levels. I mean, he could accept what she had told him about Kate – but the rest? Was it just an old woman's imagination?

She was, though, right at least in one respect: Julia was not for him. Whether, as according to Mary Braithwaite, she was already destined for someone else, he wasn't sure, but he wasn't going to argue either.

Jonathan was very fond of Mary Braithwaite. She might have some odd ideas about metaphysics (headless highwaymen, for example) but sometimes he got the feeling she was watching over them all. He remembered what his predecessor had told him about the night Mary had nearly died, the night the angel was stolen. 'She was fading, Jonathan. I'd seen it before. Smiling and at peace with her life, nearly gone for hours – and then at two in the morning she sat straight up in her bed and said, "Bugger, I've got work to do after all." And that was it, she was up brewing tea. Fitter than I am.'

So Jonathan listened to Mary, and when she told him Julia was not his soul mate he knew she was right. Actually, he had always known Julia wasn't for him – too independent. Too atheist. He had been agonising ever since that wonderful morning they had shared. It *had* been wonderful, but it should never have happened. He didn't love her, nor she him, and whilst her view that sex was something physical that you partook of when you felt like it was understandable, it was not one he could afford to share. He needed the kind of woman who would also need him – to be nurtured by him, to nurture him back, the kind who would worry about his late nights and poor eating habits and bake apple pies for him just to show that she cared. Someone like Kate Coleman, as Mary had observed, had much more in common with him at soul level.

Not surprisingly, then, Kate's arrival with an apple pie borne aloft seemed fortuitous in the least, and it struck him forcibly that removing Julia from his mental field of contenders left Kate with a very clear field. An empty field, in fact.

'Jonathan, I hoped you could find a use for this. I know you barely sleep and hardly eat. I've been baking and I had some spare,' said Kate, adding, pink-cheeked, 'besides, I wanted to make you something to say thank you.'

'Thank me for what? Do come in.'

Kate smiled, and a pair of dimples he had never noticed before appeared on either side of her mouth. 'Well, actually, I'm thanking you in advance. I'm going to need some help with this art exhibition I'm organising for Julia, and I was hoping I could count on you. There's no one else I could turn to.'

Jonathan smiled, taking the pie from her, and as he did so their hands touched for slightly longer than was necessary. 'You can always count on me, Kate,' he said, looking into her eyes and noticing what an honest and sensitive shade of grey they were, 'you know that. Why don't you come and sit down and we can talk about your plans? Tea?'

'Let me make it,' said Kate. 'Just show me where everything is.' Get into the kitchen, Mrs Braithwaite had said, and you get into the heart. It may be the back route but it's better than shoving on the front door when he's forgotten to unlock it. She pottered around Jonathan's kitchen, opening cupboards and rooting out bits and pieces, whilst he leaned against the cooker and reflected that she really looked rather at home there. Yes, if he were going to attempt some sensible and serious courting, with riotous lovemaking as the hoped-for end point rather than the opening gambit, then Kate would be a fine choice. And if Mary Braithwaite was right about everything else, she might be right about Kate too. There are, after all, few things more romantic than being told by an old friend, in deepest confidence, that a woman such as Kate, whom you rather admire, has been secretly falling in love with you right under your very nose. Yes, helping her on this

286

exhibition would provide an opportunity to grow a little closer. Then, well, who knew . . . ?

'Who is Mary?' asked Sonja. They were sitting on the terrace outside his bedroom window, she and Joshua, Hebe occupying the third seat at the table, a chess set between them. Hebe was singing softly. Julia and Merrill had gone indoors to cook supper and argue about recording contracts.

Joshua frowned at her. 'Don't know any Mary,' he said slowly and carefully, without looking at Sonja. Those huge blue eyes of hers were far too clear and penetrating. He'd known managing directors in their fifties who couldn't spot when he wasn't telling them everything, but Sonja, at twenty-eight, saw through him as if he were glass. So he concentrated hard on his diction, rather smugly aware that he was doing awfully well.

'Grandpa does know Mary,' said Hebe, who was carefully contemplating her next move. Dishonesty and deception were foreign to her as she dealt in straight fact. 'She's his grandma. Check.'

Joshua sighed. 'My nanny,' he said, 'was called Mary. Very . . . long . . . timago. Why?'

'You call her name in your dreams last night.'

'Rubbish.'

'You do. I was jealous of this Mary.'

'Well, don't be. I d . . . dreamed of her last night.'

'Mary lives in the woods,' said Hebe, and Joshua glared at her.

'Don't be s . . . silly.'

'She does,' said Hebe, 'so there.' She glared at Joshua, remembering Pinocchio. 'You shouldn't tell lies. They make your nose grow so long that leaves grow out of the end and little birds come and sit on it.'

Joshua sniffed. 'Been w . . . watching Dis . . . ney.' He peered at the chessboard. 'Damn.'

'Indeed she has, old man, and I know you watch it with her. You watch *Pocahontas* yesterday.'

'Cobblers.'

'You enjoyed it. Just because I am from Norway this does not mean you can pull the wool over my eyes. Joshua, I have to ask you a question.'

'What?'

'Your wife's diaries. Now don't look at me like that, I am trying to find Gabriel and I make no apology . . .'

Joshua closed his eyes. He had learned the hard way that, despite his improved vocal control, real anger was still impossible to express and resulted in undignified spluttering and confusion.

'Grandpa's upset,' said Hebe.

'Not your grandpa,' said Joshua, barely audibly.

Hebe folded her arms. 'You are too my grandpa. I got you, and William got a butterfly.'

'Ah,' Sonja was intrigued. ' Was this a rare and valuable butterfly?'

'It was dead,' said Hebe. 'Mum said it was disgusting. It's still your go.'

Sonja suppressed a smile. 'Joshua?'

'I won't discuss that d . . . diary, you had . . . no bus . . . iness.'

'I had every business, you stubborn old man. You knew a boy who was handicapped. You have told me this.'

Joshua frowned. 'L . . . ong time. At school. I'm thirsty.'

'You change the subject. Where? In the village or in your grand school for bullying and buggery where the English send their sons?'

Joshua glared. 'Village school. Another cup of . . . tea.'

'So. We have more tea when I have finished my interrogation. Was he your brother?'

Joshua dropped his tea cup, and it clattered noisily into the saucer. 'W . . . w . . . w . . . what?'

'A brother, Joshua. You know, one of those family

288

members like sister but male.'

'B . . . bloody qu . . . questions. What's this . . . s about?'

'Why did your mother talk about her son being sent away?'

'My mother? How sh . . . should I know? Bugger off! Gowan cook summm-thing.'

Sonja smiled, glad that he was so near to being normal again. She looked at Hebe. 'I'll find out, Joshua Gilfoyle.' Joshua shrugged, and she stood and folded her arms. 'Shall I tell you what I think? I think you have a brother. Is that the problem you have with looking in my eye? Maybe Gabriel found him – two black sheep together.'

Joshua flung his right arm across the chessboard, sending pieces scattering on to the lawn and making Hebe jump and back away. 'Don't be sh . . . show bloody shtupid . . . couldn't be more . . . wr . . . wrong.'

Sonja sighed. 'Joshua,' she put her hand on his arm, 'I know there's something. I just want to help.'

Joshua sniffed, annoyed with his vocal slurring. 'Then leeeave it. N . . . no brother.'

'Well then, if you're so sure, there is one other thing.'

'Checkmate. I won.' Hebe jumped to her feet and began to run around the lawn with her arms out like an aeroplane.

'P . . . Pyrrhic,' said Joshua, 'wasn't conc . . . conc . . . n . . . trating.'

'Joshua, I ask you for truth. Why do you ban Gabriel from giving his children your name?'

This time Joshua glared right at her. 'Weak . . . genes.'

'They tell me Gabriel was a depressed boy. This is not passed on.'

'You know nothing, woman. Nothing at all. Gabriel gave . . . up. He threw in his j . . . job and d . . . drowned his sorr . . . rows. Weakness breeds weakness . . . Don't want any more'f it in th'Gilfoyles. You don't know anything, sshhh . . . tupid cow. Go'nd paint your nails or s . . . something.'

'Then tell me, Joshua. Tell me what I don't know.'

'N'thing t' tell.'

'Are you sure about that? Then look at that child, running across the lawn. Look at her, Joshua.' Unwillingly Joshua turned his gaze upon Hebe. The light caught her hair, her pixie face intent on some inner game she was playing, and as he watched she stopped and fell flat on her back, her arms and legs outstretched, and sang at the top of her voice, '*Swing low, sweet chariot, coming for to carry me ho-o-o-ome . . .*'

'Well?' said Sonja.

'*Swi-ing low, sweet chariot, coming for to carry me home . . .*'

'What are you getting at?'

'You detested that child, you thought she was subnormal, tainted. You were angry when she came near. It is all the same thing, you say to us all – to be weak or ill or mad is all the same to you. She is one of those you would put away. But you were wrong about her – she has looked after you.'

'So?'

'So maybe you are wrong about your son also. When you say your son should not have children you deny also this child her right to live. You thought she had no value but now you could not do without her. You love her like she is your granddaughter.'

Joshua started to dribble. 'Rubbish. You're talking rubbish.'

A few feet away Hebe began to sing, oblivious to the discord,

> '*I looked over Jordan, and what did I see*
> *Coming for to carry me home?*
> *A band of angels coming after me –*
> *Coming for to carry me home . . .*'

'You love her,' said Sonja, 'admit it.'

'Crap and d . . . double crap.' Joshua beckoned Hebe over. 'Go away. Bugger off!'

Hebe stopped singing, stared at him for a moment with big blank eyes, then turned and fled.

'You stupid old fool,' said Sonja. 'You had no right.'

Joshua shrugged to demonstrate how little he cared, but a tear ran, unexpected, out of his right eye and down his cheek – at least, it might have been a tear, but his eyes did tend to water at the moment, anyway.

'You are a stubborn old man,' said Sonja, wiping his mouth and then his eye, 'but I will get to the bottom of this. You'll see.'

'Leave me alone.'

'Fine. I go. And find nicer company than a selfish mean old man who does not know when he is blessed.'

Julia found Hebe watching the stars again that night, singing something very mournful whilst tears ran down her face and dripped off her chin.

'Hebe-jebe, what are you doing?'

'Too many to count.' Hebe began to howl.

'Sshhh.' Julia held her. 'Don't make that horrible noise, Hebe.'

'Grandpa hates me. Everybody hates me.'

'No, they don't, Hebe. Grandpa is poorly. What did he say to you?'

'Go-away-Bugger-off,' said Hebe. 'I hate Grandpa.' She howled even louder.

'No, you don't.' Let me at him, thought Julia, mean old bastard. 'You don't hate Grandpa.'

'I hate Grandpa. I want my angel.'

'Tell me about your angel.'

'In the tree,' said Hebe, and the tears stopped at once. 'Angel shines at the moon.'

'What's the angel's name?'

Hebe frowned. 'Angel.'

'And does it speak?'

'It sings,' said Hebe.

'What does it sing?'

And to her astonishment Hebe hummed a familiar tune on 'la'.

'But you know the words to that, Hebe. That's "Waltzing Matilda".'

'Yes, but Angel doesn't know the words,' said Hebe.

Julia put her arms around her. 'Perhaps the angel would rather listen to you. I'll tell you what, you can sing it to Grandpa later. And don't you worry about him being rude to you. Mummy will sort him out.'

Chapter Fourteen

'Joshua Gilfoyle, what did you say to Hebe, you mean old bugger?'

'Julia, I think you shouldn't shout at him. You'll upset him.' Jackie appeared at the window.

'Upset him? I'd like to bloody strangle him. Where are you, you nasty old man? Come out and defend yourself!'

Jackie opened the window and behind her Julia could see Joshua sitting on his wheelchair, looking as ill as she had ever seen him. He hadn't slept all night, largely because something which couldn't possibly have been guilt – but nevertheless felt awfully like it – had churned in his stomach and prevented him from getting any peace. He had waited for the child to appear and stare at him so that he could tell her he was sorry, but she hadn't come.

Now it was no surprise to see the mother, raging at his window like Boudicca on amphetamines. In many ways it was a relief, since no one had spoken a word to him since Sonja turned on her heel and strode out the previous evening. The reappearance of Jackie, whose services had not been required very much since Sonja got back from London, only served to underline the contempt with which he seemed to be regarded this morning.

And it was all because he had told a child who didn't understand anything to bugger off. They were all stupid to make such a fuss over it. But Joshua felt a weight of awfulness that he privately suspected was only partly to do with his rejection of Hebe.

'Good morning t'you t . . . too,' he said, squinting up at

Julia and still appreciating the way her breasts moved under her T-shirt, his speech a little slurred compared to the recent improvements.

'You don't deserve to have her visiting you,' shouted Julia. 'What were you thinking of? Telling her to bugger off!? She loves you, you silly old fool, God only knows why, but she loves you and you tell her to bugger off. How d'you think that makes her feel? Or did you think she didn't have feelings?' She strode into Joshua's room and kicked the wheel of his chair. 'Ow! Bugger!'

Jackie moved forward in alarm, concerned that her charge was about to be beaten up. 'Julia, perhaps you should –'

'Keep out of this! Joshua Gilfoyle, you apologise to Hebe or I'll make sure she never comes to see you again. And as for your bloody angel – well, you can stick it up your mean old arse. I don't know if I can be bothered to make it. Anyway, I think a devil might be a bit more appropriate as a memorial to you, don't you? Or a gargoyle. A really miserable mean-faced gargoyle with G-I-T tattooed on its forehead!'

Joshua blinked. She was impressive in a rage. 'I'm sorry.'

Julia, her mouth open to start another tirade, had let out a few of the words before the apology registered: 'And another thing, the next time you – what?'

'I said I'm bloody sorry. You can st . . . stop defending her. I'm s . . . sorry.'

'Stop defending her? I'll defend her to my dying breath. Which is what you should be doing with your lost son, the one whose children you hope will never exist.' And she turned on her heel and was gone, leaving Joshua wondering when or even if he would see Hebe again, and realising it was actually rather important to him that he did. He wondered where Sonja was. Probably doing her bloody nails. She could find Hebe for him. If she would . . .

*

294

Julia stopped in the kitchen on her way home, and found Merrill trying to persuade Mrs Barker to make cakes to sell at the horse fair.

'Mrs B, please say you will – I'm a hopeless cook, and Mrs Padley is going to be making one of her marmalade and peanut cakes so I think we really need something that we can be sure won't make anyone sick.'

'I don't know, Mrs Gilfoyle, I've got enough to do, what with Mr Barker's ingrowing toenail. Your husband said it needs antibiotics to stop it festering . . .'

'Morning, Merrill.'

'Hi. What are you doing here?'

'Came for a shout at your father-in-law, actually,' said Julia cheerfully. 'Been there, done that, going home.'

'Oh? Tea? You can tell me all about it.'

'I can't stop – I left Hebe asleep and Jonathan Doyle guarding the door in case she woke and made a bid for freedom.'

'The vicar? What was he doing round so early?'

Julia darted a pointed glance at Mrs Barker, who was well known to have a mouth the size of Felixstowe harbour when it came to gossip. 'Just passing, actually.' In fact Jonathan had turned up hoping to clear the air between them but had not had chance to work up to it as she had handed him a mug of tea as he stepped in through the door, then told him to kindly sit in the kitchen without moving and guard Hebe until she got back.

'Oh. I'm sorry – I heard Joshua upset Hebe. Sonja told us.'

'He wants to apologise to her.'

'He doesn't!'

'He does.'

'Is she OK? Matilda was worried about it when she went off to school.'

'She's fine. She was upset last night but you know how she is – everything's forgotten a moment later. She veers from ecstatic to distraught like some people do from smiling

295

to frowning. I must get back. Tell Sonja I upset him, won't you? I mean, I did shout.'

'Serves him right, if you ask me,' said Merrill, 'but I'll find Sonja later. She's probably still wrapped in a silk negligé with a face mask on.'

'Oh, come on. I thought you'd stopped all that.'

'I have. I can still be jealous that she looks like Beauty whilst I look more like the Beast.'

'Looks aren't everything,' said Mrs Barker cheerfully from over by the sink. 'My Frank says you never judge a book by its cover.'

Now there's a man who practised what he preached, thought Merrill, watching Julia leave and reflecting that her sister looked particularly beautiful at the moment. There was a glow about her, a spring in her step. She's obviously had sex with someone, thought Merrill. I wonder who. Oh well, just as long as it wasn't the vicar. Kate would die.

Sonja was not still in bed, nor doing her nails, she was in the woods, picking her way through the undergrowth in her delicate, strappy sandals, knocking on Mrs Braithwaite's door. It had not taken her long to find out that the Mary in the woods and Joshua's nanny were one and the same.

'I knew you'd come,' said Mrs Braithwaite, opening it and surveying the beautiful blonde woman hesitating on the step. 'Come in.'

Sonja followed her into the dark interior of the cottage, her eyes adjusting gradually to a hard earth floor, a couple of soft chairs with shabby, faded covers that might once have been decorated with roses, or might simply be plain but very badly stained, a table, a sink, a fireplace with, incredibly, a large black cauldron hanging from a hook over the charred remains of a fire, and a broom made of twigs leaning beside it. Mrs Braithwaite was pouring two cups of tea.

'You shouldn't be here like this,' Sonja said. 'Do you not have electric light and Hoovers?'

'I live as I wish to live,' said Mary Braithwaite, folding her arms. 'I'm immune to germs, you know, that's the secret of my longevity. This place is what keeps me alive. It keeps my skin thick and my heart beating.'

Sonja stared at her in some awe, the tobacco-coloured skin, wrinkled and tough, the strange crew cut dark hair that stood up in tufts from the top of her head, the walnut eyes that still sparkled like a bird's. 'Were you really Joshua's nanny? You must be a hundred years old.'

'I'm older than I look, dear. But I'm pleased to meet you.'

'Why does he not say to me that you were his nanny?'

'Oh, dear girl, it was a long time ago. People don't remember these things so much. I was only his nanny for a few years, and he's seventy. But that isn't why you're here.'

'You know why I'm here?'

'Of course,' said Mary Braithwaite. 'I have the tea leaves to tell me.'

'Oh?' Sonja did not understand. 'What is this tea leaves?' She peered into her cup.

'You know what tea leaves are; they must have them in Norway. Tea bags are marvellous, my dear, to save on trouble in the U-bend, but when I want to know something I use leaf tea. I look at the bottom of the cup and it tells me what to expect. I've found in life a little warning often comes in helpful, although there are rarely any surprises, not at my age.'

Sonja sighed, still not really understanding. She had wound her hair in two long plaits around her head today, so now she could rub the back of her neck freely, a gesture she relied upon at times of stress. 'You must know the whole truth about the Gilfoyles, then. About my husband and his stubbornness.'

'I know a lot of things,' said Mary Braithwaite, 'but the whole truth? I doubt anyone on earth knows it. You ask away.'

'OK, I ask two big questions only. The first, where is

Gabriel Gilfoyle, and the second, did Joshua have a brother who was taken away?'

Mrs Braithwaite smiled painfully. 'Big questions indeed. Well, as to Gabriel, I can't tell you that.'

'Can't? But you know?'

'I don't know where he is,' said Mary Braithwaite, thinking, it's how you phrase the answer, 'but as to the second, yes, of course, Joshua had a brother once. His name was David. He was the most beautiful child I ever saw, curly hair and the face of an angel.'

'Was he older?'

'Than Joshua? Yes, by two years.'

She lapsed into silence and eventually Sonja said, in a small voice, 'Where is he now?'

Mary Braithwaite swallowed. 'He was sent away,' she said, 'when he was just eleven years old. He was taken away from here screaming, and he never came home.' A tear ran down her cheek. 'I have often asked myself what I should have done. He was slow and strange and this bothered people. You see, he wasn't terrible, and he wasn't mad, but he didn't understand the world, and the world didn't like that. People said he was a changeling child, lost from us at birth. They used to call it mongolism. Now it has another name.'

'Downs syndrome. I wondered if it was this. So they sent him away? To one of these places where the mentally sick were sent? Big and dark?'

Mary Braithwaite nodded. 'Yes. I went there to see him. It was a huge place, and there were other children like him. They were lost and they cried, and he was not happy. I wanted him to come home but Joshua's father . . . he said this was not his son, that this was not a Gilfoyle.'

'He rejected his son? That's terrible.'

'He was the eldest. Gilfoyles is a dynasty, my dear. They have owned and run this land for generations. To admit that his eldest child was handicapped . . . Joshua's father could not do so. People had strange attitudes then. The eldest brother must inherit. And handicap was common in all families, not just the wealthy ones. Joshua's father had a distant cousin in the asylum – he did not want people to say madness ran in the Gilfoyles. It was his greatest fear.'

'But this was not madness. David was not mad.'

'They were ignorant and prejudiced,' said Mary Braithwaite. 'So was the whole world. It has at least grown a little better, if only a little, through the years I have watched it.'

'Did Joshua know all this?'

'Of course. Joshua was away at school, so for him it was not so odd that his brother should be sent away also. But afterwards his father told him David was no Gilfoyle, that he must forget about him. He was told David had gone away to be looked after properly, that this happened to those who were born damaged and who had no proper place in the world, and no place at all in the family. Joshua was to be the eldest son, the only son. He was told this only on the telephone, then it must not be spoken of again. David must not be mentioned ever again, people must not know there had been this difficulty in the Gilfoyles.'

'And what happened to David?'

Mary wiped away a tear. 'He died that winter. There was a flu epidemic. It was during Hitler's war, you know. He was never strong – these children are not strong – and he had pneumonia. There was no penicillin then, you understand. It was reserved for the fighting men, and these children would perhaps not have been given it in any case. So David died, in a place far from those who loved him, because the Gilfoyles could not have madness in their family. You have to understand how they feared it. They thought it was a curse that would destroy the family name. Joshua's father made him promise this would not happen.'

'This is why he so fears mental illness?'

'Of course. Yet David was not ill, he was just . . . different.

He was like an angel, that child, with his golden hair. He was always smiling.'

'And Joshua's mother?'

'She never got over it. She was dead herself within a year. Never a strong woman. Joshua was away at school then too, of course. There were difficult times during the war, many things not spoken of again.'

'This story, this makes him what he is. And now there is Hebe,' said Sonja sadly. 'Perhaps it is not so strange that she should be so important to him.'

'The circle has a way of turning,' said Mary Braithwaite. 'Joshua Gilfoyle loved his brother, however little he chooses to remember that it was so.'

Sonja swallowed. 'Does Simon know this?'

'No.'

'Why?'

'He has never asked,' said Mary Braithwaite. 'These are old and painful secrets. To bring them out and air them is not always a good thing.'

'Then why do you tell me?'

'Because you did ask. I knew you would have good reason.'

'I'm looking for Gabriel. Did he ask also?'

Mary Braithwaite smiled. 'Yes, he did. Gabriel heard it all, on the day after his mother's funeral.'

'Aha,' said Sonja, leaping to her feet and waving her arms dramatically, 'so he came here. You *do* know where Gabriel is, don't you?'

'No,' said Mary Braithwaite, 'I do not, and I'll say no more about Gabriel.'

'But you must. I must find him. Joshua needs to make peace.'

'To make peace and tell him that, whilst he is welcome, his children are to be denied his name in case they are defective? Do you think a son would want to hear this?'

'No, of course not. How did you know about that?'

'I have my sources. You know, I am just an old woman but it seems to me that Joshua can either welcome his son back truly as his son or not at all.'

'You're right,' said Sonja sadly, 'but he's so stubborn.'

'The Gilfoyles have always been stubborn,' said Mary Braithwaite. 'It is their greatest strength and their greatest weakness.'

'Couldn't you talk to Joshua, Mrs Braithwaite? He might listen to you.'

'Joshua Gilfoyle and I have not spoken since the day he drove his son away,' said Mary Braithwaite, 'and we will not speak again until the day he welcomes him back. Even if that means never.'

'But you were his nanny. Don't you care that he is dying?'

'We're all dying,' said Mary Braithwaite. 'Some of us are doing it faster than others, that's all. Now, if you'll excuse me I have sick people to visit,' and she disappeared out of the door before Sonja could gather her wits. When she did, eventually, move hesitantly outside, Mary Braithwaite was nowhere to be seen, lost in the greenwoods as if she were a part of them.

Trying to swallow the lump in her throat Sonja made her way soberly back towards Foxbarton Grange, wondering when she should tell Joshua what she knew. But as she approached the Woodcutter's Cottage she was diverted by the sound of Hebe singing lustily, and wandered onto the lawn to find Julia, back from the Grange, weaving something huge out of willow, whilst Hebe danced around and sang,

'And his ghost may be heard as you pass by that billabong,
"You'll come a-waltzing Matilda with me."'

'Hello, Sonja, how are – Oh dear, you've been crying, what's the matter? Is it Joshua? Has he upset you too?' Julia let go of a willow strand and it whipped back and struck her on one cheek. 'Bugger!'

'Oh no, you're bleeding. I am so sorry, I did not mean to distract you . . .'

'Aaaargh!' screamed Hebe, like Lady Macbeth at the height of her infamy, 'There's blood! There's blood!' She flung herself to the ground and closed her eyes.

'Take no notice,' said Julia, as Sonja looked on in alarm, 'she's a drama queen. It wasn't your fault.' She pressed her hand against her cheek. 'I shouldn't have let go. I've been doing it for long enough.'

'What is it?' Sonja stared up at the mountainous construction. 'It's very tall.'

'It's the Foxbarton angel,' said Julia. 'Not that he deserves it, but Hebe wanted to start it and so we have.'

'But I thought you were making a bronze statue?'

'I am, you'll see. Hebe, fetch us a nice drink of something.'

'No,' said Hebe, 'I can't.'

'No, Hebe, that's right. You're never to go in the kitchen and you mustn't get me a nice drink of elderflower water because if you do I might scream and cry.'

Hebe disappeared into the kitchen.

'Psychology,' said Sonja. 'I see it.'

'Absolutely. But what's wrong? You've come dashing out of the wood like a ghost.'

'I feel I've seen one. I visit Mrs Braithwaite,' said Sonja, thinking she could tell Julia. 'I go to see her – she tells me the whole truth. That Joshua had a brother who was handicapped, that he thinks this runs in the family.'

'How did you . . .? No. Go on.'

Hebe brought drinks as they sat, then proceeded to walk around the lawn on her hands as Sonja told Julia the story of Joshua's brother. 'So she says he loved this brother . . . Perhaps, then, he is full of regret.'

'So he should be. What a sad story. I suppose it fits with the way people saw things then. I mean, did you know during the war children died of meningitis because the penicillin was saved for soldiers? And people thought that was right.'

Sonja frowned. 'Mrs Braithwaite says it is full circle.'

'Perhaps it is. You know, fate.'

'That is, like God deciding?'

'I don't know about that. But perhaps it's all for a reason.'

'Poor Joshua.'

'Poor *Joshua*? What about his poor brother?'

'Oh, I know, but Joshua was a little boy. Imagine being told by his father that this boy he loved was not his brother, that this terrible thing he must reject and forget, that even the memory of this sad child did not belong to him. It's horrible.'

Julia looked at Hebe. 'It's unbearable. But it was a long time ago. What are you going to do about it now? What difference can it make?'

'I don't know. I asked these questions because I thought there was a brother still alive. I did not expect to hear this tale. I just want to find Gabriel. Joshua needs to see Gabriel, but he believes he is mentally defective and that this will again damage the family name.'

'But he knows that's ridiculous. Gabriel had a breakdown, that's all. When you consider what he'd been through it's hardly surprising. Merrill says he was a gentle man.'

'I know, but Joshua does not see reason. You have to understand, Julia, he is a proud man. For him to accept that he has been wrong all his days, and that his father was also wrong . . . Imagine, a brother sent away to die who should have lived . . . Joshua cannot say this. It is Martian to his nature.'

'Alien,' said Julia, smiling suddenly. 'Alien to his nature.'

'As you say. But, Julia, I think Mrs Braithwaite knows where Gabriel is. I think if Joshua were to stop his nonsense about children –'

'Can I go and see Grandpa?' asked Hebe.

'No, darling, not now. I'm busy.'

'She can take me,' said Hebe, pointing at Sonja. 'What's a tart?'

'Hebe, honestly! Sonja, I'm sorry, she doesn't mean to be rude. She just says the first thing that –'

'It's OK. It is what Joshua calls me. It is our joke. I must leave you, Julia. Would you like me to take her up to the Grange?'

'No, I'll be up later.' He's not having it that easy, thought Julia. Bugger off indeed. 'Hebe, I need your help with the angel. Sonja, if there's anything you want me to do . . .?'

'No. I think I have to deal with this,' said Sonja. 'But if I need Hebe, I ask you?'

'Of course.'

As Sonja headed home, Mary Braithwaite made her way with a determined stride through the woods to the clearing where the gypsy vans were gathered. Several more had now arrived ready for the fair, and there were now a couple of dozen children running through the woods, laughing and playing. John James was sitting on the steps of his van, writing. He looked far more like a gypsy than the gypsies themselves.

'Morning.'

'Morning, Mary. How are you this fine day?'

'Fed up with you, young man. It's time we had a talk.'

'Kate Coleman has finished with me. I promise she has ceased her unsuitable liaison. Isn't that what you wanted?'

'Good. But it's only part of what I wanted.'

John put down his pen, scratched his beard. 'D'you know what you remind me of?'

'No, but I'm sure you're going to tell me. Just remember respect for your elders, young man. It's what I taught all my charges in the years I was a nurse to children like you.'

'Respect for the young might not have gone astray,' said John.

'What was that?'

'Oh, nothing. You're make me think of the Fates, Mary Braithwaite, stirring and plotting and deciding who should be with whom, when, where and for how long.'

Mary Braithwaite sniffed. 'Someone's got to do it.'

'You should be relaxing, at your age.'

'That's what they always say. If I relaxed I'd be dead. You don't live to five hundred and six by sitting on your fat arse drinking tea and sucking fish paste sandwiches without the crust on. Tobacco?'

'I don't know how you can chew that stuff. So, what do you want to talk about?'

'Angels,' said Mary obscurely. 'Come on. I want to walk.'

'Oh, very well.' John stood up and stepped down his caravan steps, putting his pen and paper down.

They strolled together into the woods, heading deeper into the trees, the green and dappled shade stretching on for ever. Rustles in the bushes told of startled birds, of shrews and voles fighting for survival, of creatures mating and eating and dying. Mary said nothing.

After a while John said, 'Am I supposed to guess?'

'You could try,' said Mary Braithwaite. 'Suppose I give you a clue? Suppose I tell you it's time Gabriel Gilfoyle went to see his father?'

'What, to receive his highly qualified acceptance? Hi there, oh my long-lost son, great to see you. Come back to the life you hated and you can win yourself a fortune. Oh, but don't pollute the family with children of your own. They might turn out like you.'

Mary Braithwaite sighed. 'He is changing. That child has changed him.'

'Not fast enough. Dammit, Mary, did you know he even sent the police to look for me when the angel was stolen?'

She frowned. 'Well, he has been trying to find you ever since you left, as you well know. The disappearance of the angel was an excuse to get the police looking too. Anyway, you did take it, didn't you, so what did you expect?'

'Of course I bloody well didn't take it. Is that what you think of me?'

'Language, young man. And yes, I did think you had taken it. You were here that night, weren't you? Not in Greece at all.'

'I came to see you, because you were ill, not to steal the angel.'

'No one else could have got in. He locked the church, that old vicar. Only you and I knew about the old tunnel. I thought that had to be how you got to it.'

'Well, it wasn't and I didn't. The old tunnel collapsed years ago, as you'd know if you'd ever actually looked. It's blocked off a few feet in.'

'Climb in that hole? You must be joking. The last time I went in there was to retrieve your father and David after they were caught dynamiting the fish in the lake.'

'Really? Father did that?'

'Absolutely. Him and his brother and five hundred dead fish floating. I've never seen two more red-handed boys in all my born days. Tried to pretend the wrath of God had just struck the lake. He was a bright boy, if you could see it.' She lapsed into thought and Gabriel knew she did not mean Joshua.

'I wish I'd been there. But no one could have got in to the church down that passageway. Look, Mary, you know I'll always be grateful to you for looking after me when I needed it after mother died, but –'

'I don't want your gratitude, I want you to make up with your father. Forget his stupid will. It's not what matters.'

'Of course it's what matters. That's the whole point.'

'Why? Do you want to have a child?'

'No, of course not. I haven't even got a woman, and I don't want one now. I missed my chance on that front. You only get to see your angel once.'

'Rubbish,' said Mary Braithwaite, 'I know that for a fact.'

'Sorry, I was forgetting you're five hundred and six and know everything. But my father rejected his brother and then his son, and now he wants to reject his grandchild, even before he has one. And if I go to see him and forgive him I allow that to be OK.'

'Then convince him otherwise.'

'I can't.'

Mary Braithwaite stamped her foot. 'You're as stubborn as he is. You know, I always thought you had the angel. I hoped you'd give it back.'

'Well, I don't so I can't. I wish I had taken it, actually, but I didn't.'

'Mind you,' continued Mary, as if he hadn't spoken, 'he doesn't really need the angel any more. He's got another one.'

'You mean the sculptress's statue? Has she finished it yet?'

'She's working on it – but no, I meant that child. She saved him, made him get up and walk when he wanted to give up and die. He'd have done it, too, if it weren't for her. I've seen them together.'

'I thought you didn't see him.'

'I see him – he just doesn't see me. She calls him Grandpa, you know. Ironic, isn't it, he accepts the artist's changeling daughter given that he doesn't want children of yours?' Mary Braithwaite spat a wodge of tobacco into the undergrowth.

'It certainly is. But he can accept that child because she's *not* his granddaughter. If she was it would be different.'

'Show him it can be different. Show him how you've put your life back together, what you are. For goodness' sake, Gabriel, you're a famous poet, a success in anyone's terms.'

'You think that's going to impress him? He wanted a boardroom whizz who would scythe through other people's lives and livelihoods with the ruthlessness of Lucifer in the name of profit. I tried to do it. I thought I could be what he wanted – but it wasn't me. I hated that life, it had no soul. I had to leave and I knew he wouldn't forgive me so I went away – and then when Mother died I fell apart, drowned my sorrows. You know. He can't forgive me for not being able to take it.'

'He's an old man, Gabriel. Give it a chance – for both of your sakes.'

Gabriel shook his head. 'I'm leaving here the day after the fair, Mary. I'll not be back till next year.'

'He won't still be here.'

'I don't care.'

'I don't believe that, Gabriel Gilfoyle,' she said, 'and, anyway, you have a brother too, and a niece and nephew. What about them?'

'They don't need me. I cut my ties, Mary. You can't go back.'

'And what about the child?'

'What about her?' He did not need to ask which child.

'She likes you. She's been visiting you. I've seen her. She'll miss you.'

'Oh, don't talk rot. She barely knows me.'

'She may need your help,' said Mary. 'There are forces massed against her.'

'Oh, don't start your soothsaying. I'm not a teenager you can impress with that mumbling about headless highwaymen now, you know.'

'I really don't know,' said Mary Braithwaite, 'how you ended up so rude.'

'It's in my genes,' said Gabriel. 'Ask him.' And she had no need to ask who he meant.

Hebe did not see Joshua that day, because she was roped in on the production of the Foxbarton angel. Julia had become so absorbed in the work that she didn't even object when Kate Coleman turned up to discuss exhibits, and insisted on looking at it with a puzzled and slightly concerned air from all three hundred and sixty degrees.

'I don't think I really get it,' she said eventually,

'That's because it's not finished,' said Julia, twisting

willow quickly, 'or possibly because you're artistically blind and wouldn't recognise a piece of art if it had a gilt frame and Leonardo da Vinci's signature across the bottom. I should choose the first option if I were you.'

'Honestly, Julia,' said Kate, sidling around Hebe, who was carefully selecting pieces of willow of equal bore and laying them in rows, 'sometimes you're just so abrasive. What did you do to your cheek?'

'Self-flagellation,' said Julia cheerfully. 'All artists do it. I thought it gave me an attractively piratical air. What did you want?'

'Oh, I'm just getting things ready for the fair.'

'Have you sorted things out with Oscar?'

Kate nodded. 'He's been lovely; said he didn't mind missing the fair if it would stop his father from getting at me and he's going to tell him off, man to man. I took your advice, Julia – we had a talk. Oscar has been marvellous. He's going to help us with the exhibition. And his piano teacher said his grade five piano went so well that he can do grade six straight away. He got the top distinction in Suffolk, you know.'

'Good for him.' Julia was glad to see Kate was back on form; noticed suddenly that she was more than usually made up, with a warm pink lipstick on her lips and a lot of mascara on her lashes.

'I've done a floor plan,' said Kate, unaware that her subtle touches with the contents of her make-up drawer were so noticeable, 'and a programme. I hoped you'd do me an illustration for the front so I thought I'd drop it off and see how you were, and I have to call in on Jonathan about the fair.'

'Ah,' said Julia thoughtfully.

Kate blushed, adding hastily, '. . . And I've got a list here of the exhibits which have been offered back on loan. Several people sent photos of your stuff. Julia, I'm not so sure we ought to use this one.'

'Why not?' Actually, thought Julia, it's obvious. Kate and Jonathan. How perfect. It's a good job she doesn't know we . . .

Kate eyed the photo. 'The Saatchis got into trouble for obscenity again last week, and this one appears to be a penis, Julia.'

'No, it's not. It's called *Male*. Anyway, what's a penis-Julia?'

'Don't be silly. It looks awfully like a penis to me,' said Kate dubiously.

'Art,' said Julia, 'is in the eye of the beholder.'

'What's that supposed to mean?'

'That if you think that's a penis it says more about you than me.'

'So what do you think it is?'

'It was from a series,' said Julia. 'They were all variations on flower parts, if you must know. It's a stamen. Or a stigma – I forget. You know what they say, "Who needs sex when they've got natural history?"'

Kate blushed. 'Oh. I – er – didn't know, actually. Would you like a cup of tea?'

'Aren't I supposed to ask you that?'

'I can make it,' said Kate, adding huffily, 'or I'll just go away, if you prefer.'

'Don't be daft. Of course I'd like tea,' Julia sighed. 'Hebe will have some lime cordial,' and that was how Kate came to be pottering around in Julia's kitchen and found a discarded dog collar in the cupboard by the sink.

It was a couple of hours before Julia remembered that Kate was supposed to have been making tea, and then when she went indoors to look for her, wondering if she had perhaps fallen asleep on the kitchen table, found Jonathan's dog collar lying there like an admission of guilt. Next to it, rather sinisterly, was an empty bottle of Mrs Braithwaite's hawthorn wine. And it had been half full earlier.

'Dammit,' said Julia to the dog collar. 'That's enough to

put a lumberjack under the table. How the hell did I manage to let that happen? And why the hell did I never properly take in that she was really in love with him before now? Now I suppose she'll crawl off into a hole and weep and that will be the end of that. Dammit.'

She couldn't have been more wrong. The new, assertive Kate was not going to take this lying down. She had found Jonathan Doyle's dog collar in Kate's kitchen and she bloody well wanted to know why. And by the time he opened the door of the vicarage to her and said, 'Kate, how nice to see you wanting to see me,' and smiled in what he hoped was a charmingly endearing fashion, she had worked up such a head of hawthorn-wine-fuelled fury that she positively exploded on the doorstep.

'You bet I want to see you, Jonathan Doyle! I thought you and I were friends. I thought you and I might be more than friends. What was all that stuff about finding soul mates you spun at me the other night? What was all that business about admiring me and making the best apple pie you'd ever had? You were leading me on, Jonathan Doyle, and just because you're a vicar that doesn't mean I won't sock you one.' And she swung at him with her hand.

Jonathan dodged it easily – Kate was not built for attack; she had never been any good at rounders as she could only bowl underarm. She flew past him into the corridor and landed in a heap on the floor. Jonathan closed the door behind her, lest anyone else should witness this demise of her dignity, and attempted to help her up. Tears were now streaming down her cheeks and she dashed them roughly away.

'Get off me you . . . you vile betrayer! You were leading me up the garden path. Do you sleep with all the women in the village or only the ones you fancy?'

Jonathan stared and his cheeks flushed with guilt. 'Kate, I –'

'I found your dog collar in Julia's kitchen,' she said. 'It obviously didn't drop off spontaneously. Are you going to tell me it just fell on the floor as you were trying to persuade her to send Hebe to Sunday school?'

'No, I – Kate, you're overwrought. I . . . I'm sorry . . .'

Kate wasn't listening. 'If you wanted to put it about like a . . . a common Lothario,' she shouted furiously, 'why couldn't you have put it about with me?'

Jonathan swallowed. 'Kate, I –'

'I've loved you for ages, Jonathan Doyle. I've loved you and I thought you were too busy being c . . . celibate to want me. I had no idea you were a womanising . . . a womanising . . . Oh God, it's just like *The Thorn Birds*. Any minute now you'll go off and be Pope.' She wiped more tears away with the back of her arm and started to hiccup. I even slept with John, she thought, to prove to myself I was still a woman. If Jonathan hadn't been so busy chasing Julia I wouldn't have needed to prove anything.

'Kate,' Jonathan took her by the shoulders, 'this is nothing like *The Thorn Birds*. I am not a Catholic cardinal and no one is pregnant.'

Kate drew a steadying breath. 'Are you in love with her?'

'No, of course not.' He hauled her to her feet, noticing the beautiful way her tears sparkled on her eyelashes.

'Then why did you sleep with her?'

'Kate, it just happened. Once. Then I realised I'd been silly. Julia isn't for me.' He brushed her eyelashes, touching the tears.

'And you're not for me either, are you? No, don't say anything . . . Oh God, I'm making such a fool of myself. People will think me such a f . . . fool.'

'No, you're not, you're lovely. I think you're lovely.'

Kate looked at his face, such a short distance from her. Assert yourself, Kate, she thought hazily. This is your chance. You've proved you're wonderful in the bed department. You've seduced the gypsy rover, and he looked like

Che Guevara. Now seduce the man you love, put up a fight for him, for heaven's sake. Determinedly she planted her lips on his.

Jonathan was, briefly, too taken aback to react. Then he thought frantically of his plan to woo her first, and progress to the sex only when he was sure she was completely won and would not object to the suggestion. It seemed fairly clear that she wouldn't object to the suggestion now – indeed, she seemed to be making the suggestion. But she was drunk. He couldn't take advantage of a woman who was drunk. Particularly not when he was teaching a confirmation class in thirty minutes and her son, Oscar, would be in it. It wouldn't be right. There wouldn't be time.

Carefully he lifted Kate and carried her, lips still on his, through to his sofa, where he deposited her gently. As he put her down she was already out for the count. He frowned. He'd better go and have that clearing-the-air word with Julia.

Julia was slightly worried when she saw Jonathan bearing down on her like, she felt, the Wrath of God.

'It's the vicar,' said Hebe unnecessarily, 'with pink on his cheek.'

Jonathan stopped and flushed, and Julia was intrigued to see that he did indeed have a smudge of pink lipstick on his cheek and his collar. Very much the shade of pink Kate had been wearing only recently, if she wasn't mistaken.

'Julia,' he said.

'Hello, Jonathan. How are you?'

'Julia, I have to talk to you.'

'Fine,' said Julia, folding her arms, adding, as he looked pointedly at Hebe, 'you'll find if you open your mouth and start exhaling the words will just come out.'

'OK. I just . . . Kate is very upset . . . and *very* drunk. Julia, look, I don't know how to say this . . .'

313

'You regret what happened between us and hope we could put it behind us?'

'Yes. Yes, exactly that.' He took her hand. 'I mean, I know you didn't mean it to go any further, and I hate to bring my reputation into this as it's none of your concern . . . but the things is, I'm rather fond of Kate, and I don't want to see her hurt. I actually entertained some hopes that –'

'I'm sorry, Jonathan, I didn't tell her. Look, I thought we'd already sorted this out. I didn't even realise your dog collar was there.'

'Oh. I see, I'm sorry, I didn't mean to accuse you.'

'You didn't, and it's OK. I'm sorry too. What happened between us was just an impulse, and we genuinely thought it was harmless at the time. At least, I did. I didn't realise that you and Kate –'

'Neither did I.'

'I'm sure it's not too late,' said Julia. 'Just tell her the truth. It's generally best.'

'Well, look, that's very . . . generous of you. I'm glad we've spoken. I'd wanted to clear this up.'

'Well, that's good. Really,' said Julia, thinking: another good man snapped up. Perhaps I should have a better look at those boys on the motor mower . . .

'Is this the angel?' Jonathan's eye was caught by the willow, a large block of clay now beside it.

'It will be.'

'It looks like a giant haystack,' said Jonathan dubiously.

'Oh ye of little faith,' said Julia. 'Trust me, I'm an artist. And anyway, Hebe has told me what to do. It'll be fine.'

Chapter Fifteen

The morning of the horse fair dawned in glorious sunshine. Julia and Hebe arrived at the Grange early, as there was still a lot of preparation to be done, even though they seemed to have spent the whole of the previous day preparing. Besides, Daniel had been at the front door again, trying to endear himself to them again by turning up with figs and chocolate spread, and Julia had really felt she had to get away.

'We've got chocolate spread,' she had said to him, 'and I've gone off figs. They remind me of a friend who once betrayed me.'

Now she leaned against Merrill's rather lovely cream and granite kitchen units drinking coffee, and tried not to remember his hurt expression, since it was entirely fake and therefore no more worth getting worked up about than a plastic tragedy mask. At the table Hebe was having an eating day – she could survive for days, apparently, on air and the occasional biscuit, then every so often came a day when she ate for England. She was currently on her third bowl of Rice Krispies.

Beside her Merrill hummed tunelessly as she pottered about the kitchen, filling Thermoses to sustain them all through the day's toil. 'What is that song?' she asked Julia, 'the one I keep humming?'

'I don't know. It sounds like a tone-deaf guru meditating.'

'"Waltzing Matilda," said Hebe, and carried on with her Rice Krispies.

Julia grinned. 'Hebe. You're amazing. You heard that in the noise she was making?'

Merrill kissed Hebe. 'You're an angel. You appreciate me.'

Hebe finished her cereal and wandered from the kitchen in search of Joshua.

Julia drained her cup. 'Did you know Hebe's angel in the woods sings "Waltzing Matilda"?'

'Well, it doesn't surprise me that it would sing *something*, given that it's Hebe's angel.'

'I know, but the odd thing was, she seemed so sure. She's so certain that she sees an angel, and so certain that it sings "Waltzing Matilda". It's quite uncanny.'

'So you're in danger of being converted?'

'I almost was,' said Julia. 'She was pretty convincing – but an angel singing "up jumped the swagman and sprang into the billabong" . . . I don't know. Will you run me some water into a bottle for face painting?'

'Of course. Actually I think it's a nice tune, for an angel,' said Merrill, beginning to hum it again.

Simon appeared with his arms full of bunting. 'We used to have a music box that played that. D'you remember? It was one of Matilda's christening presents. Pretty wooden thing, lived on the window ledge.'

'Oh yes, I remember. I wonder what happened to it.'

'Haven't seen it for years,' said Simon. 'I expect someone broke it and chucked it away without telling. What d'you think of this? I thought I'd string it up over the entrance to the field.'

'What on earth is it?'

'Bunting.'

'Bunting? It looks like bits of old knickers on a string. It'll scare the horses.'

'Horses aren't scared of bunting.'

'Horses can be very funny,' said Merrill. 'They're like men. Sometimes you just can't get them going, but other times they're off at the slightest signal. No logic, and anybody's for a bucket of oats.'

'Come here, you . . .' Simon grabbed her round the waist, dropping the bunting in a heap on the floor.

'Honestly, Mother, I come down for breakfast and I find my own parents procreating on the kitchen floor in a pile of old underwear.' That was William, appearing in search of breakfast. 'You set a bad example to wildlife. At least they wait till they're fertile.'

'Oh, for goodness' sake, we were not procreating,' said Merrill crossly, as Simon muttered, 'Long bloody wait, then,' and Julia sniggered quietly into her coffee, 'Where do you get these words?'

'David Attenborough,' said William loftily, 'and he says at least animals do it for a reason. People just do it to look stupid.'

'He did not say that.'

'No, well, Oscar Coleman said that bit.'

'William, do not repeat things Oscar says just because you think they're witty, or you could end up being the first boy ever to find himself pegged out on the lawn to be eaten alive by a llama.' Merrill fetched him a bowl and spoon.

'Brian wouldn't eat me,' said William. 'He's my friend.'

'Don't you believe it. That llama takes no prisoners. Have some breakfast, young man, and then go and feed him. He's looking particularly snooty this morning.'

'He's learned it from Matilda,' said William. 'She was a llama in another life, you know.'

'Now, William. Where is your sister, by the way? She should be down here by now.'

'Pretending to be Charlotte Church in front of the mirror,' said William. 'Did you know there's a bat in her bedroom?'

'No, of course I didn't . . .'

'Neither does she,' said William, and beamed at the sound of Matilda's shriek as she came tearing down the stairs. 'You'll hurt your voice doing that.'

Matilda seized her own throat and swallowed carefully. She was supposed to be preparing for her recording

317

tomorrow. 'Hi, Aunt Julia,' she said, summoning her dignity reserves. 'Where's Hebe?'

'With your Grandpa.' Julia wondered how the reunion had gone, unaware that Hebe had already spent half the previous night playing chess with Joshua and had been utterly disinterested in his muttered, 'Sorry', having completely forgotten that he had ever upset her.

'Oh,' Matilda helped herself to toast and cast William a dignified look. 'William, go and get your bat out of my curtains. It was looking at me.'

'Bats can't see.' William reached for the breakfast cereal and proceeded, by an amazing act of balance, to fill the bowl twice over, add milk and still have the whole thing hold together like an iceberg.

'Now, William,' said his mother reprovingly, 'I don't think it's right to use animals like that.'

'Oh, for goodness' sake, it's not real. It's a fake bat. I got it from the joke shop place on the Internet. Girls are so gullible.'

Matilda retreated into scornful dignity. 'Animal,' she said, to no one in particular.

'You're such a sissy,' said William. 'Mum, where's the apples?'

'You ate them all yesterday. D'you think perhaps you were a fruit bat in a previous incarnation?'

'They're for Brian. Can I go out now? I want to watch them bring the horses to the fair.'

'I suppose so. Be there at eleven, though. You and Matilda have to watch Hebe because Aunt Julia's painting faces.'

'Oh wow – will you paint mine? I could be an advert.'

'I'm not sure what for,' said Julia drily. 'What d'you want to be?'

'Make him into an insect,' said Matilda, and was unsurprised when William jumped at the idea of acquiring a green face and feelers.

*

Joshua had had no intention of attending the horse fair, which was a big occasion in Foxbarton's life, attracting people from miles around in addition to the locals, gypsies and assorted pressmen and photographers who came to enjoy a fine traditional day out. He did not want to be seen in his current physical state. OK, he could just about walk, and could speak now without spluttering, but he still looked infirm, was still clearly a damaged human being. He didn't want his estate workers and the incoming middle classes of the village seeing him like this. This was not how the head of the Gilfoyles should be remembered. So he steadfastly refused to be moved when Sonja and Jackie told him it was time to go. Truth was, he sensed Sonja was still punishing him, even though he had apologised to Hebe for sending her away in that mean fashion, and even though he continued to punish himself for it far more than Sonja could possibly manage in a lifetime (particularly his lifetime). After all, if she wasn't punishing him then why was Jackie still here?

'Well,' said Sonja, appearing before him as a vision in chiffon and stilettos, 'I'm going.'

'It's a horse fair, woman, not bloody Ascot.'

'And I'm a Norwegian, not a bloody cowgirl. What do you expect?'

'You're trying to make me jealous. It won't work.'

'No,' said Sonja, 'nothing works with you, does it? You are an impossible old man.' And she stomped out. She hadn't been able to tell him that she knew about his brother, couldn't yet bear to see his face when she brought it up again. Whenever he got upset his face drooped and his voice slurred and she hated the thought that she was doing that to him. Yet what if the key to finding Gabriel lay with David's story? What was it that the Dean of St Paul's had said to her? Ask why, where and when. She knew when David had died, so where was he to be found now? Where had they put him? She paced her sitting room, wondering if it would help to find out . . .

In the bedroom Joshua dozed off, propped up against his pillows. When he slept the sagging of his face was more pronounced, and he snored through one side of his mouth. His right arm still hung a little oddly and Jackie, covering all possibilities, had put bed guards on both sides of his bed to prevent disaster. Now as she pottered about folding clean sheets and putting together shaving equipment so that Hebe could shave him (she was becoming rather good) she glanced up and thought for a moment she saw the shadow of a man, standing staring in through the French windows. But it was only there for a moment, and when she went to look properly there was no one there.

A few hours later the horse fair was well under way. The auction of ponies was going on in a corner of the field, attracting a large crowd of onlookers, together with the fiercely competitive men in trench coats and wellingtons who were actually bidding for the ponies. No one seemed to know exactly what they wanted them for, but this was not the point. It was traditional.

Elsewhere, ice-cream vans plied their trade, an assortment of cars attempted to sell the contents of their garages from their car boots (it was amazing, Merrill said, how the contents of these ordinary people's garages looked suspiciously like market stalls) and a large group of village-hall-supporting stalls sold cakes, plants, books and home-made wine. In a gaudy tent in one corner of the field Mrs Braithwaite read the palms of those hoping to hear that a handsome prince carrying his weight in gold in a couple of carrier bags was imminently coming to propose. This was actually a very serious tent – Mrs Braithwaite had told fortunes at the horse fair for longer than anyone could remember (even Mrs Padley's mother, who was ninety-four, remembered an old fortune-teller at the horse fair whom she swore was Mrs Braithwaite). A small tombola attempted to raise funds for the church, but it did a poor trade as it was staffed by Kate and Jonathan Doyle, and whenever anyone went to buy a ticket they seemed to be so deep in conversation with one another that people felt it rude to interrupt.

Kate was on cloud nine. This was partly because when Martin had arrived to collect Oscar he had been visibly stunned to be met at the door by Daniel, wearing a pink silk dressing gown, partly because Oscar had hugged her firmly and said, 'Don't worry, Mum, I'll be back tomorrow,' but also because a glorious sense of mutual anticipation was steadily building between herself and Jonathan. All the misunderstandings were out of the way. They had talked on the telephone late into the night and she was now sure he was well on the way to feeling about her as she did about him. She felt like a teenager again. Actually Kate had never, she realised, really felt like a teenager when she actually was one, so this was marvellous.

Julia was deeply absorbed in painting her twelfth bat-face of the day, this one on a small blonde child named Poppy, when Matilda sidled up and said, 'Aunt Julia? Can Hebe sing with me?'

'What do you mean?' Carefully Julia applied thick black face paint to obscure almost all of Poppy's features whilst her mother stood behind her saying weakly, 'That's nice, Poppy dear, how pretty,' then whispering to Julia, 'I thought she'd want to be a nice pink flower like her sister.'

'Well,' said Matilda, 'they're doing karaoke over there and I thought it would be good practice for tomorrow.'

Julia glanced up. She could see a small wooden stage outside the sports pavilion. 'Don't you think it might cause a stampede if you sing over there?' she asked.

'Of people?' Matilda was flattered.

'No, of horses, silly.'

'Well, he isn't causing one,' said Matilda, indicating the village's Elvis impersonator, who was currently putting his whole hips into a rendition of 'Love me Tender'. 'And there's not much more chance to do it before the band comes on.'

Julia shrugged. 'OK, but don't get her stressed.' She sat back. 'There,' she said to Poppy, 'you're a bat-girl.'

Poppy stared at her indignantly, then screamed, 'I DON'T WANT TO BE BAT-GIRL, I WANT TO BE A BLOODY BAT!'

From a four-year-old it was quite impressive, particularly one who looked like a young Shirley Temple.

'That's what I meant,' said Julia hastily, 'look.' She waved the mirror and her customer left, satisfied, towing the obviously cowed mother behind her and demanding, 'Now I want ice cream with two flakes and then I want a hot dog with no onions and lots and lots of tomato sauce.'

'So we can? I thought we'd do our duet.'

'Well . . .' Julia eyed her next client who said, 'Vampire, please,' and waited expectantly. 'I can't take a break, Matilda. I'm trusting you.'

So Matilda ran back to where she had left Hebe and William counting the number of maggots in the plastic pot he had just bought off Ben Diamond, whose dad was a fisherman. (Ben's dad was slightly less pleased later that day when he got to the river, set up his rod, opened his plastic pot and discovered that it contained his son Ben's packed lunch, astutely swapped that morning.)

'Come on,' she said to Hebe, 'we're going to sing.'

Hebe followed her obediently. She had no great desire to sing, but she had no great desire not to sing either. She coped with situations like this, where people and activity and noise surrounded her, by keeping her focus very tight. If she allowed herself to look all around at the field, at all the people, she would be assailed by light and noise, everything would tip and tilt and scream at her, and she would have to run as fast as she could to make it all go away. But she had learned from experience that if she imagined herself in a tunnel and just watched the person in front of her very carefully she could blot out all the rest. The secret was not to look to right or left.

So she followed Matilda towards the small stage, holding her hand. And when Matilda said, 'We're next,' and jumped up onto the wooden platform, she followed her up there too.

'Are you ready, Hebe? Yes?'

Hebe stood on the podium and stared around into the distance. She could see a coloured tent about twenty yards away with 'Fortune-teller' written over the top of it on a banner. Sonja was just ducking inside. She could see her mother, painting colours on faces. She could see the horses over the far side – that was where her hairy bear-man with the earring would be. Matilda nudged her.

> *'Early one morning, just as the sun was rising,*
> *I heard a maid sing in the valley below: . . .'*

A small group had gathered to make jolly around the karaoke machine, and it was something of a surprise to them to hear two children start singing without it. There was some muttering and a drunk boy called Ian said, 'Where's yer backing groups, girls . . .?' He was swiftly nudged into silence by the crowd as they all noticed what others had noticed before.

Hebe's voice soared effortlessly, her tremolo on the higher notes purer than any boy soprano.

'Wow,' said Ian's mate, who actually quite fancied Lesley Garrett and was something of a closet classical music fan. 'Listen – that's amazing.'

'Bugger me,' said Ian, 'you're right, mate. D'you think it's really her singing?'

His mate shrugged. 'She's probably miming.'

'What's she miming to then?'

> *'Thus sang the poor maiden, her sorrows bewailing,*
> *Thus sang the poor maid in the valley below . . .'*

The girls continued on towards the final chorus, Hebe rising gently into the descant Mrs Peel had created for them, her concentration absolute and keeping her safe from the chaos out there.

> *'Oh don't deceive me, oh never leave me*
> *How could you use a poor maiden so?'*

There was a brief silence, then the assembled audience broke into tumultuous and rowdy applause. Ian whistled and hooted and several of the boys shouted, 'MORE!'

Hebe stared. For her, noise and light were often the same thing, and now it seemed to her that light was exploding in noisy flashes in front of her eyes. She blinked and her world began to disintegrate. Directly in front of her line of vision two young men, their faces beaming, were clapping their hands together loudly and rhythmically. There were people all around her. There was just one tiny gap at the back . . . The people were smiling and their teeth made her think of wolves. All around were teeth and clapping hands. Someone whistled to round her up for the wolves. There were people everywhere. There were wolves everywhere.

Matilda beamed and bowed, then straightened up to realise that Hebe was frozen to her spot, her eyes glassy, her hands over her ears.

'Hebe . . .' Matilda tried to take her arm. 'It's OK,' she whispered, 'they're only clapping. They clapped before, remember, when we sang?' But as she remembered it herself she recalled the quiet and genteel applause at the Haverhill Arts Centre, and even then Hebe had finished up fifteen feet up a gantry.

And then Hebe took off, like a hare across the field. She tore through the gap in the startled crowd, who parted and then closed up again and thus impeded Matilda's pursuing path, taking a straight route directly through the centre of the display of morris dancing, which was just beginning in the centre of the field. As a direct result of her rapid passage two of the men, in the process of leaping into the air and banging their sticks together, managed instead to bang their sticks on one another's noses and ended up flat on the floor shouting, 'Hey.'

By the time Matilda caught up with her Hebe was standing between two ponies in the middle of the gypsy contingent, whose sale was now concluded, with her hands over her eyes whilst a rather blowsy girl Matilda thought was called Tracey said, 'Oy, Billy? Where's John. There's something up with Hebe.'

'It's OK,' said Matilda, catching her breath as she came to a halt. 'She just got scared of the noise and took off. She's OK.'

Tracey took no notice, 'John? Your little friend's upset.'

Matilda looked up at the man who had come to rescue Hebe and thought he looked rather romantic – tall, dark, bearded, wearing an earring, he looked like a real gypsy.

'Hello,' she held out her hand, 'I'm Matilda Gilfoyle.'

'John James.' He shook it quickly, looked at her hard, nodded. 'Hebe? What's wrong? Were you scared?' Hebe was breathing quickly, eyes dilated, focus somewhere far away. He squatted, placing himself directly in front of her eyes. 'Hebe? Look at me.'

'It was wolves,' said Hebe obscurely.

Matilda frowned. 'She sees things differently,' she explained to John. 'Sometimes she runs.'

In the distance the brass band from Hadstock began to play 'The Floral Dance', and Hebe put her hands over her ears and closed her eyes.

'She can't help it,' said Matilda. 'She's always doing it. Once, when we were all little, Aunt Julia took us to the Natural History Museum, and this big mechanical dinosaur by the door roared. Hebe ran out of the entrance and all the way back to the statue of Peter Pan where we had had our picnic. All the way, across roads and everything – it was miles. Aunt Julia went bananas and called the police and the police went inside to search the museum. Aunt Julia was so mad with them for being so stupid when we knew Hebe had run out of the door that she kicked a police car and nearly got arrested. The sergeant said he'd take her name if she ever did it again.'

'How did you find her?'

'You have to go back to where she was,' said Matilda. 'It's what she does. It's called autism.'

'I know.' John looked at Hebe, who had crawled under one of the ponies with her hands over her eyes. 'Where's her mother now?'

'Painting faces. Right over there.'

John squinted. In the distance Julia, her long blonde hair hanging in a ponytail over her shoulder and catching the breeze, was deeply absorbed in the finishing touches of transforming a small boy into Spiderman. Behind him a small queue had formed and were picking their noses and standing on one leg.

'I think you should take her home,' he said to Matilda, 'and I'll go and tell her mum where you've gone.'

'OK,' said Matilda, 'thanks.' She would tell Aunt Julia that Hebe had just got a bit upset at all the noise. Best not to mention that it was anything to do with the singing. Not with the most important day of her life due to happen tomorrow.

As Matilda made her way home, holding Hebe's hand extra tightly in case she should make another run for it, John made his way carefully across the field, putting on his hat as he did so, trying to avoid seeing anyone who might recognise Gabriel Gilfoyle in this older, bearded stranger. It was unlikely, he felt, for people see what they expect to see, and it had been nearly ten years since he had last been here – openly, at least. He was thinner now, his beard gave him a longer face, and, in any case, there was no one left that he would know well – apart from Simon, of course; he'd have to keep a lookout for Simon. His little brother would not understand why he hadn't been back and made his peace – but a new life was a new life. You couldn't buy back into just a few bits of the old life and expect to keep the new intact.

As he passed Mary Braithwaite's tent Sonja emerged and strode purposefully off towards Foxbarton Grange, but she didn't see him and he didn't notice her. It did not occur to him that she might have known his face from an old photograph. And so he was still glancing all around watchfully for familiar faces when he reached the face-painting queue, which had by now grown ever longer.

'I shouldn't bother,' said a disgruntled mother at the back. 'It's a bloody disgrace, this service. We've been stood here ten minutes and there's still three in front of us.'

A small child looked up at him. 'You've got a hairy face. She might do you for fifty pee 'cos it'll be less paint.'

The mother smiled at John rather flirtatiously. 'Don't mind him. He looks like a boy but he's really a vampire, aren't you, Darren?'

John smiled politely and looked at the head of the queue. He saw a young woman, steady-handed, brows drawn together in concentration, painting whiskers on a small but ferocious lion whilst its sister, a butterfly, leaped up and down in delight shouting, 'Look at Ptolemy, Mummy. He looks like a teddy bear!'

She had, the paintress, remarkably clear green eyes. She had full lips, beautiful bones, a fine-arched brow. Not the sort of face you would forget in a hurry. She was completely absorbed, completely sure of her task, and for just one dangerous moment he longed to make contact with her, to *have* a piece of her, this beautiful artist with the incredible child.

He stared at her for a minute or two, before he realised the danger he was in. This woman was a part of Foxbarton, of his father and his brother and the angel . . . and he had decided his ship sailed alone from now. The thing with Kate had been one thing, the kind of harmless, mutually pleasing fling which he had had occasionally through the years – but if he lingered here now his life would change again for ever. He knew it as surely as he knew her name was Julia Fitzgerald . . .

Gabriel turned and walked back through the crowd. On his way he fortuitously found William, complete with maggots, and instructed him to tell his Aunt Julia where Hebe had gone. Then he made his way back to his caravan as fast as he could. For him, he felt, the carnival was definitely over.

Julia had actually been rather irritated with the horse fair, coming as it did just when she had really got started on the angel. She hoped to have it finished in another couple of days, ready for casting, but you never knew how your artistic flow might be interrupted by having to make up a whole series of six-year-olds to look like dogs, cats, tigers, tropical islands, vampires and, her particular dislike, foot-ball supporters. Still, the day had gone very well, and although Hebe had got tired early on and gone home with Matilda, she had apparently had a good time and had even sung on the podium. That had to bode well for tomorrow – after all, if she could sing before the motley crowd at Foxbarton Horse Fair, she ought to be able to manage a studio. The only downside of the day was that Julia now felt as if every muscle in her body had seized up simultaneously.

'Five hours,' she moaned to Merrill in the kitchen at the Grange, 'without a single break. I couldn't even go to the loo without getting complaints.'

Merrill rolled her eyes. 'At least you were sitting down. I had to spend the whole afternoon trying to sell raffle tickets to help support the church to people who wouldn't help support the church if the church was just about to fall on their granny. Simon did nothing but sell beer to pissed villagers. His was the easy ride, I tell you.'

'What did Sonja do?'

'Just buggered off.'

'Oh, well, I suppose it's not really her thing.'

'No, I mean, really buggered off. She's taken a car and gone off somewhere. Told Jackie she won't be back till very late. I don't know what she's up to now.'

Julia shrugged. 'It's not really our business.'

'Well, no, actually, I felt a bit worried. Kate saw her come out of Mary Braithwaite's tent and go charging off as if there was a wasp in her knickers. You know what that old witch can be like with her prophecies of doom. I hope she didn't say anything awful.'

'You shouldn't call her an old witch, you'll be one yourself one day. You've got the power. I've seen you put hexes on people.'

'Oh, come on, there you go again, on about that woman Simon interviewed for a partnership.'

'Well you can't deny it. She positively faded out of contention after she met you.'

'She had spots,' said Merrill meanly.

'I know she did – but only after she met you.'

'Honestly, Julia,' Merrill started to giggle, 'you're really bad for me.'

'Nonsense. I show you your inner self, that's all. Now I must get Hebe home – big day tomorrow.'

'I know. Did you hear her sing with Matilda today?'

'No, I was too wrapped up.'

'So was I – but someone said she ran off.'

'Oh?' Julia frowned. 'You mean, really did a runner?'

'I don't know. Perhaps we should ask Matilda.'

But Matilda, when questioned, said no, Hebe had been brilliant, and William could only add that some bloke with an earring had told him that Hebe and Matilda had gone home early.

As Julia and Merrill sat down for a quiet cup of tea, Kate was whooping with laughter. She hadn't laughed like this for years. As Jonathan pushed himself firmly and warmly into her she let all of her joy sing forth. This man, whom she had loved for months and months, if not years, was in her, was possessing and possessed by her, was known to her in the most biblical fashion of all. And it made the years of her nights with Martin seem as insignificant as washing up water. It made even the brief halcyon days with John, her gypsy lover, seem like a warm-up for the real thing. For although he had made her feel like a woman, he had not made her feel loved.

Jonathan was dumbfounded. He had heard there were women who laughed during sex, but he had never realised there were any who laughed quite this much. Actually, it was rather infectious. And she was really rather wonderful. He rolled on to his back, pulling her on top of him, and took hold of her rather slim hips – Julia had been rather too hippy, by comparison, he reflected, beautiful though she was – and pulled her hard down on to him. Kate threw herself forwards.

'Tell me I'm the best,' she whispered, 'and kiss my breasts.'

'You're the best. There.'

She lifted herself off him, tantalising. 'Best of all?'

Jonathan was astonished – who would have thought Kate would turn out to be so bold, so tantalising . . . so adorable? 'Come back here . . . Oh, that's really very good. Best of all . . .'

'Better than Julia?'

He groaned. 'Stop it, you're driving me crazy. Yes, yes, better than Julia.'

'What was she like? Did she do this? And this? And thi-i-is . . .?'

'Stop teasing me, woman, or I'll ravish you senseless.'

'Now there's an idea,' said Kate, rolling over and pulling him on top of her, adding, 'Do you know, you're very rude, for a vicar?'

'You've seen nothing yet.'

'Oh, Jonathan, I've wanted to do this for ages but I'd no idea it would be so much fun.'

They had gone straight home together from the fair, after staying right to the end for the sake of decorum. Kate had been clearing up, as this was clearly her duty as the main co-ordinator of all village events, with absolute responsibility for everything. Jonathan was also helping, as a vicar would. Nevertheless, she was constantly conscious that he was watching her as she moved around amongst the now-empty stalls, picking up litter and tidying away lost property. There he was, clearing up horse dung with a bucket and shovel and making the task look truly manly. There he was, folding up the gypsy tent with those strong, manly hands. Hands which would soon be touching her, if she had any say in the matter. She did a rapid mental calculation and concluded that she did not need her diaphragm. Oscar wasn't home, Daniel could look after himself . . . No need to go home first. Tonight, Jonathan Doyle, you're mine.

When things seemed to be nearly clear and the last and most tireless of the organisers were downing tools and heading for the pub – a pub in which Kate was always welcome, as she had organised and spear-headed the campaign to keep it as the Fox and Hound and prevent it being taken over by a large chain who wanted to turn it into a tapas bar and call it, inexplicably, the Toad and Gherkin – Kate glanced at Jonathan.

'Kate? Want to come over to the Fox for a drink? Vicar, you too, of course . . .' That was Frank Barker, Mrs Barker's immense but likeable husband. He spent most evenings in the pub, maintaining to Simon Gilfoyle (who was his GP) that he couldn't possibly cut down on the beer and crisps as it took a constant effort to keep him the size that he was and if he got any smaller the missus might suffocate him.

'No, I think I should call it a day,' said Jonathan. 'Up early tomorrow, you know, Sunday.' He avoided looking at Kate.

'Oh, absolutely. See you at morning service. Kate?'

'I'm bushed,' said Kate, 'sorry. Time for bed,' she smiled apologetically at Frank, suggestively at Jonathan (who blushed scarlet in surprise and anticipation) and watched them as they all headed out of the field towards the pub. They would find out about her and Jonathan soon enough, and then the gossip would start – but first she was hoping to give them something to really gossip about. Because I'm proud that I love him, thought Kate, so they can gossip as much as they like.

The vicarage lay the other way, her own home in the direction of the pub.

'Cup of tea on your way home?' asked Jonathan, for the show of it, as it was perfectly obvious to both of them that Kate didn't want tea.

'That would be lovely,' said Kate. 'Shall we?'

They walked arm in arm to the vicarage, slowly, enjoying a sense of anticipation poorly concealed by a long and intense discussion on relationships between clergy and parishioners and how really sex was something that ought to be kept inside marriage – or at least committed relationships. As soon as they got inside the door, though, Kate wrapped her arms around Jonathan's neck and said, 'I'm ready to commit right now.'

He gasped, 'Kate . . . I mean, I wouldn't want you to think I'm loose . . .'

'I hope you're loose tonight,' said Kate, sliding her hands round behind his head and caressing the nape of his neck, 'because I'm about to be incredibly loose . . .'

Jonathan gulped, 'Kate, I . . . what we were just saying . . . you know I can only have serious relationships, in my position.'

Kate pressed herself firmly against his groin. 'Is that a bible in your pocket or are you just pleased to . . . Oh, Jonathan, I do understand, of course I do, but I'm not loose either. I'd adore a serious relationship with you more than anything in the world. I've adored you for years, wanted you for years. Why do you think I've taken the beastly church minutes for so long? My darling Jonathan, where is the bedroom?'

'First up the stairs on the right.' He swallowed. 'Are you sure you know what you're –'

Kate took his hand. 'Don't tell me where it is, you idiot, take me there! I'm about to show you that you may have had fun with Julia Fitzgerald, but you haven't lived till you've had me. Come this way . . .'

That had been nearly an hour ago. Now, completely abandoned to their mutual pleasure, their sighs and whispers punctuated by Kate's whoops of laughter, they were gloriously unaware that the bedroom window was wide open and that those teenaged members of the village who hung around by the bridge in the evenings to smoke had wandered up the road to listen.

'It sounds like seals mating,' said one. 'D'you think all vicars do it like that or is it only the Church of England?'

'I dunno. D'you think he's tickling her?'

'I dunno. I've never heard my parents make that much noise.'

'I've never heard hyenas make that much noise. It's like King Kong meets Godzilla.'

'I s'pose you don't get much when you're a vicar.'

'Well, I think it's quite cool. It's a shame for the vicar, not being married.'

'He'll have to get married now though, won't he? Otherwise he'll be excommunicated for sin.'

'What's excommunicated?'

'I dunno. I think they nail you to the cathedral door.'

Kate and Jonathan, had they but known it, had set standards for this small group of teenagers so high that it would take them years to achieve, rendering uncomfortable couplings behind bus shelters almost worse than pointless.

Sonja got back to Foxbarton late that night, and was surprised to find Hebe in Joshua's room asleep at the foot of his bed and Joshua himself slumped forwards over a clearly unfinished game of chess. Moving the chess set away from his hands she carefully set him back against his pillows, pulled the quilt up to his chest and kissed his lips. Then, with a strength that belied her rather fragile appearance, she lifted Hebe and carried her out to Simon and Merrill's sitting room, where she found Julia and Merrill drinking wine and giggling.

Julia stood when she came in. 'Had she sneaked downstairs again? She was supposed to be asleep in with Matilda.'

'She has been playing chess,' said Sonja, 'with Joshua.' She looked at Hebe's sleeping face, the child's expression in repose rather mournful. 'Do you think she knows?' she asked Julia.

Julia stood, took Hebe from her. 'You mean that he's ill?'

'No, I mean that she's autistic.'

Julia sighed. 'Not really. I mean, she's not severely autistic. They call it the autistic spectrum. These days you can have sprinklings of autism without going the whole hog.'

'The hog? Where is this pig?'

'Just an expression. Hebe will probably never quite gel with the rest of the world, but she'll never truly understand why. It's hard to grow up with knowing you're different when you can't see what the difference is – but then fifty years ago they'd just have put her somewhere to regress. She probably wouldn't have got a shot at normal life at all.'

334

'I found David,' said Sonja, sitting down and removing her shoes wearily.

Julia stared. 'What?'

'Oh, no, not as you think, I did not mean . . . David is dead. I found his grave.'

'How on earth . . . ?'

'Mary Braithwaite knew the name of the place,' said Sonja, 'where he was sent. It was in Norfolk, near the sea. So I went there, and there is one church. Tiny. And I looked until I found him.'

Merrill frowned, looking from one to another, feeling slightly miffed that Sonja and her sister seemed to share some language of which she was unaware. 'Would you two mind telling me what you're talking about? Who is David?'

'Hang on, Merrill. Sonja, was there anything else? I mean, does anyone visit the grave? Could Gabriel have been there?'

'No,' Sonja shook her head, 'at least, not recently. No one goes there. This trail does not lead to Gabriel.'

And just then Simon Gilfoyle, who had been sharing an evening's self-congratulation with some of his patients in the Fox and Hound, walked in and said, 'Did I hear someone say Gabriel?'

Chapter Sixteen

Sunday morning was grey and overcast, with a chilly spitting rain. It seemed as if the weather gods had just managed to hold off their wrath for the fête itself, but now had to cough over East Anglia like bronchitic old men to make up for it. There was a definite sense of thunder about to rumble, lightning about to flash, and all over Foxbarton people were preparing to leave.

In the woods the gypsy contingent were attaching their caravans to the Foxbarton estate tractor, driven by Stewart Barlow, which would tow them out as far as the road. Once there, connection of their ugly mobile homes to their ugly lorries could be established, after which they would all drive cheerfully back to their comfortable semis, brick-built with barbecues in their gardens to remind themselves once in a while that they were real gypsies for at least a part of the year.

John James, formerly Gabriel Gilfoyle, was fastening down the loose objects in his brightly coloured van and preparing his pony for its caravan-towing task, although he did not have far to go, as the caravan belonged to a friend near Cambridge and he merely had to deliver it back there before flying back to Greece. He fastened up slowly, only half of him wanting to be away from here now that he had seen those he had come to see, even though they had not seen him. The other half of him hoped that Hebe might come by before he left. He wanted to say goodbye to her yet feared adding some sort of weighty resonance to the situation by seeking her out just for that. The trees waved mournfully, the breeze, carried by a weather front moving in from the Atlantic brought whispers of sea spray to the landlocked fields around Foxbarton, but Hebe did not appear, and he would not have found her if he had gone looking, for she would soon be on her way to London with her mother and cousins.

Simon Gilfoyle was also planning a trip out of Foxbarton. Despite the entreaties of his daughter, Matilda, who felt she was shortly to be on her way to fame and fortune via a Soho recording studio, he felt there was something else he had to do today, and even though it had waited over sixty years to be done it could not wait another day. The shock of hearing the story of his dead uncle, of the secret his father had carried for his whole life, had left him stunned and quiet. He and Joshua were sharing a sober breakfast in Joshua's room, after a conversation with Sonja that had enlightened both of them more painfully than they had ever expected to be enlightened.

'Yes, I missed my br . . . rother. My father did what he thought was right,' said Joshua, his speach now slow but only very occasionally slurred. 'He was told it was the best thing. You know, things were different then. Mental illness was mental illness: it was incurable and it was a dis . . . aster. We didn't divide it up and give it fancy names, we just took care of it in suitable places.'

'God,' Simon rolled his eyes, 'listen to yourself. Suitable places? How would he have known that it was suitable?'

'He trusted the system,' said Joshua. 'That was what was provided. I went aw . . . ay too. It was how things were done.'

Sonja sighed. 'In Norway too we had large institutions at one time, Simon. It was the time. We do not like it now.'

He ran a hand through his hair, 'I know. It just – Never to see him again? Mary Braithwaite went to see him. Did you know that?'

Joshua winced, pain showing on his face. 'I know.'

'But you didn't go?'

'For God's sake, s . . . son,' Joshua was distressed and his speech showed the stroke a little, 'I was nine years old, halfway across the country, away at school. We were in the middle of a war. You d . . . didn't just get on the bus.'

'Couldn't you have asked to see him?'

Then, to their dismay, Joshua's face crumpled. 'You think I didn't care? He was my *brother*, for God's s . . . sake,' and he began to cry, great sobs which racked his body from top to toe whilst tears poured out of his right eye and down his cheek in a small stream. Long-suppressed memories of the village school, of the sweet, golden, smiling boy who had been his brother assailed him, of the fights he had been in to defend him, of the bloody nose and the chipped front tooth he had sustained in defence of David's inability to join in, of the thick round glasses that had been the subject of mean taunts, his puzzled smiles, his hopeless weeping when pushed over by mean older boys who stole his packed lunch, always so much better than theirs. He remembered walking home with David, watching his joy at seeing the river, holding his hand to stop him jumping into it because danger meant nothing to David. He remembered the time he let go by accident and then had to go in after him, struggling to pull him out of the weir below the ford whilst the meaner boys from the year above laughed and threw sticks. He remembered the whole lot of them being caned in a howling, satisfying row by one of their fathers when he told the head gamekeeper what they'd done. He remembered kicking the teacher who administered a caning to David for refusing to take his thumb out of his mouth, and a second one for David's distraught howling after the first. He remembered wondering what would happen to him at that school after he, Joshua, went off to the smart place in the Cotswolds where he would have the education that a Gilfoyle needed in order to take his place in the dynasty. Sonja had been right about that school, too. Buggery and bullying, not to mention slop for breakfast. It was supposed to make a man out of you.

There were better memories too. He remembered dynamiting the lake in the woods with David, who had laughed in delight when the lake flew roaring into the air and rained dead fish around them, and hiding in that old passageway when the gamekeeper came looking for them with a voice like thunder . . . hiding in trees from the village kids, playing with train sets and cricket bats, reading *King Solomon's Mines* aloud, chapter after chapter, in their secret den whilst they ate toffees Nanny had made them, and David squealing in delight when the heroes were put in a pot by cannibals who planned to boil them alive. Remembered his relief at hearing on one of those first rationed wartime trunk calls, when the operator cut you off after you'd had your time, that David would not be going back to the village school alone, that a safe place had been found for him where there would be other children just like him. Remembered feeling stunned. Never having realised before that there were children like David, or that he was 'like' anything. Coming home once for a weekend leave to say goodbye – David screaming and howling and refusing to look at anyone as they put him in the car. Mary Braithwaite weeping all that day and then handing in her notice and retreating to the cottage in the woods, refusing to speak to his father ever again. Knowing his father must be right, because his father was always right – never being free to be sorry or to want his brother back. And the next time he came home, no brother to run through the woods, just the village boys laughing, and the lonely den with its stash of toffees and its half-read book, and his mother pale and sad.

'The war, Simon. I was away at boarding school – phone calls of two minutes, petrol rationing, loss . . . There was so much going on. People gathered around radios. Boys lost their fathers – missing, not heard of for months, dead . . . I couldn't whine about my brother. You got on with it. There was . . . no bloody bereavement counselling then.'

Simon tried not to be consumed by the pain of something long past, tried not to imagine the child David, alone and forlorn. He scratched his head, stood. 'Well, come on. We have a journey to make. You do want to go, don't you, Father?'

Sonja frowned, looking at Joshua's grey face, 'Simon, maybe we postpone till he is more himself?'

'If he's more himself,' said Simon darkly, 'we won't go at all.' This couldn't wait, not for himself, he knew, and not for his father either. His father, who might have years, now that he seemed to have got some of his old fighting spirit back, or still might have no time at all, had to make his peace with this. Finding Gabriel, Simon felt with a conviction he could not explain, could only lie on the other side of today. You have to make peace with the past before you can hope to tackle the present. 'It's not the ends of the earth, you know. It's only Norfolk.'

'You know what they say about Norfolk,' said Joshua, with a flash of his old self.

'What?'

'If you go too far you just fall off.'

'I'll drive carefully.'

Julia eyed the spitting rain out of her window with a feeling of trepidation. She had brought Hebe home for a change of clothes before they left for London, and had found Daniel waiting for her on the doorstep, wanting to know what was happening. She'd told him he could go to hell.

'I'm leaving Foxbarton now, Jules,' he'd said, 'I just wanted to say I'm sorry if I've upset you. I was only trying to help.'

'Huh,' Julia had said. 'We all know who you were trying to help.'

Daniel had sighed. 'Jules, please, please phone me if you need me. I'll be home all day – here's my number. I'm still your friend even if you don't see me that way. The record business can be tricky.' And she had shut the door on him, then torn up the number and flung it away.

She shivered now, very worried about this studio session, particularly given the weather – but a car was being sent, Matilda was almost orbiting the world in her excitement, and to cancel now would have been almost impossible. Still, she looked wistfully at the tarpaulin which covered the evolving Foxbarton angel and wished they could just stay at home and have an ordinary, comfortable day. Or as comfortable a day as you could possibly have with Hebe when it was stormy, because electrical weather had a profound effect on her, almost as if she was directly connected to the charge in the sky.

Hebe appeared at the top of the stairs wearing a sparkling bikini top after the style of Disney's Little Mermaid, and a pair of Matilda's old trousers which came up almost to her armpits.

'Mummy,' she wailed, 'I've got no socks.'

'Yes, you have got socks, Hebe. Just look in the sock drawer.'

'I haven't, I haven't!' wailed Hebe, collapsing on the floor and howling as if her heart would break. 'I've got no socks. There aren't any socks. They're a-a-a-a-ll go-o-o-ne . . .'

Julia sighed, climbing the stairs, wondering if Hebe would ever, ever learn to look in a drawer. 'Come with me.' She took Hebe's hand.

'No,' Hebe sank to the floor, made herself exceptionally heavy, spread her limbs, 'leave me alone.'

'Come along.' Julia hauled her along the floor. 'Look. Sock drawer. What are those?'

'Don't know.'

'Open your eyes, Hebe. What are those?'

'Socks.' Hebe seized a pair, put them on, as suddenly detached from her previous tantrum as she had been from all reason whilst she was having it.

'Hebe,' said Julia, 'are you going to sing for the man?' She produced a suitable T-shirt and slipped it over Hebe's head.

'OK,' said Hebe in her sing-song voice. 'Fine, Hebe sing for the man, Hebe sing for the man manmanman . . .

'Once a jolly swagman camped by a billabong
Under the shade of a coolibah tree.'

'Fine.' Julia squatted beside her daughter, stared into the dark eyes which looked right through her – such an effective ruse to detach herself from people who tried to force her attention upon themselves. 'Hebe, are you sure you want to sing today?'

Hebe shrugged and continued her song:

'And he sang as he watched and waited till his billy boiled,
You'll come a-waltzing, Matilda, with me.'

I've got such a bad feeling about this, thought Julia. It's going to thunder and she's in one of her funny moods. Well, in as much as she ever has moods which aren't funny. She heard a horn outside and hurried Hebe downstairs, as the cottage had no windows on the roadside and they could not see out that way.

The astonishingly ostentatious white stretch limousine awaited them and Hebe rushed to join Matilda, who was leaning out of the tinted back window, waving wildly. Beside her sat William, trying to look as though he really didn't mind that his sister was about to be the next Charlotte Church.

'Whew,' said Julia to Merrill as she got in, 'this is a bit over the top.'

'Isn't it?' said Merrill. 'Look, it's got a TV in the back of the front seat.'

Lord, thought Julia, remembering whose limousine it was, I hope it's not tuned to porn.

Simon drove his father and Sonja to Norfolk. It seemed a long way, as each was lost in his or her own thoughts for much of the journey.

Joshua was absorbed in thoughts of the brother he had once had and the father he had enormously admired. Had his father callously abandoned his brother to an untimely death, or had he really believed it was the only thing to do? Should he, nine years old and in the middle of the war, have asked more questions, demanded more answers? What had his mother really felt about it all? If only he could turn the clock back and be with his brother once more on that playground in the village school, the one that was now converted into an elegant middle-class home occupied by Kate Coleman, the school yard where he had once fought and played given over to Kate's herb garden, the old railings where they had fastened their bikes pulled up for the war effort in 1940 and now replaced by a hawthorn hedge.

Sonja held his hand, wondering what was going through his mind. She herself had had no siblings, her only remaining family distant cousins. She wondered what it must have been like to have a brother and then to not have a brother. Perhaps in those days it was easier, when children died so much more randomly than today. Today casual infectious disease rarely strikes and everything is always someone's fault. She wondered how Joshua's mother had felt, giving up her son to a place where she could not even see him, a son who was not a blessing to his father, a son for whom, perhaps, she felt herself to blame.

Simon drove carefully, watching the cars, the traffic lights, the road. He wasn't really thinking very much at all. To discover that he had had an uncle – except that he had never had an uncle because his father's brother had died a child nearly thirty years before he was born – had a strange almost unemotional impact. In his working life he heard stories like these often. How many times would an elderly lady break down in surgery, only to tell him it was the anniversary of the death of the child she lost in another life, before she was old, when you did not speak of these things? How often had he heard stories of banished relatives with mental illness, who disappeared into the places once known as asylums, only to emerge institutionalised and bewildered decades later when care in the community became the phrase of the reformists and the gates of their old homes closed for ever? The lost David Gilfoyle was now as nebulous as a name on a family tree, yet he was somehow quite stunned by it. He hoped this strange conviction he felt was right, that there was something to be gained by this trip today, and that it might bring his father's reconciliation with Mary Braithwaite, and then with Gabriel, a little closer – because a day so emotionally wearing could easily also bring his father closer to death. But if Sonja was right, and Mary Braithwaite did know where Gabriel was, perhaps then this strange pilgrimage of penance would help. Simon didn't know how, but it seemed to be something they had to do.

As they approached the town they could hear the cry of gulls. Sonja had dozed in the back and Simon had to wake her to ask the way to the church. His father was silent, lost in thought.

'We should have brought umbrellas,' she said as she rubbed her eyes and tried to orientate herself to a place she had already seen once in the last twenty-four hours. 'There are dark clouds over there.'

'We won't be out of the car for long,' said Simon, and was startled when Sonja said, 'Stop, Simon, just pull up here.'

A moment later she disappeared into a florist's shop and came out with a bunch of delphiniums. 'Go on. That is the way.'

The church stood alone, square grey flint behind a low stone wall, low and squat to face the sea winds. Simon was startled to see a fairly large congregation in the churchyard chatting amongst themselves; in all the suddenness of this he had rather forgotten it was Sunday. He was supposed to have read in church today.

The vicar was up by the church door – he could see the white chasuble flapping in the wind – and, of course, there was nowhere to park because there were worshippers' cars parked up and down the length of the graveyard. Why did they never think to build car parks, he thought, irritated, then immediately realised how ridiculous it was, expecting quite that level of forward planning from the people who erected this building some five hundred or so years ago.

In the end they had to drive to the end of the road, which led towards the sea and towards that feeling you get along the Norfolk coast of being on the very edge of the world. Finding a spot, he and Sonja got out, helped Joshua, began to unfold the wheelchair.

'I can walk,' said Joshua, after watching Simon engage in a battle with it which rather resembled a squid fighting an octopus.

Simon glared at his father over the top of the contraption. 'I'm not going to be defeated by a bloody wheelchair.'

'Please yourself,' Joshua shrugged, and began to walk anyway, holding Sonja's arm perhaps slightly more than he needed to. Suddenly, powerfully, he wished Hebe was there with him, holding his other arm. I need her for balance, he thought, even though I never put any weight on her at all.

Simon watched them go, following with the wheelchair, oddly forlorn in its empty state, and with Sonja's enormous bunch of delphiniums across his arm. Ahead was a green churchyard, manicured and pretty, a mixture of old and new graves leaning slightly into the wind, as if whoever erected them had tried to compensate for a sea breeze that had not turned out to be as strong as they expected. The grass was striped by one of those mowers that people use when they want their lawn to look like their living-room carpet. This was, Simon felt, oddly inappropriate for a churchyard. Even so, it was comfortable, serene, peaceful. He watched Sonja guiding his father to a grave at the side of the churchyard, in a row with several others of similar age, the stones moss-covered and short.

Simon followed them very slowly, feeling that his father should be there first, and so was last to come upon the stone, with its simple engraving.

'David Gilfoyle,' it said, 'elder son of William of the Foxbarton Gilfoyles. Born May 20th 1929. Died November 20th 1940 aged 11 years.'

They stood there for a little while, as the last of the congregation left the church and walked slowly down the path, and the vicar wandered over to say hello. No, he was new and had little idea of the history of the graves, although there had once been a large mental hospital over on the other side of town, and it was likely that those who died there would have been buried here. He could look at the old parish registers if they would like . . . ?

But Joshua shook his head. There was a lump in his throat and he did not trust himself to speak. My brother, he thought. My brother, David. I wonder who chose the words. It must have been my father. No one else would have had 'the Foxbarton Gilfoyles' put on the stone. He was claimed by his family in death as we rejected him in life. As I have rejected my own elder son, repeating history in my stupidity. How easily I could have been travelling today to look at Gabriel's grave. If he is still alive it's through no good grace on my part.

How I have missed my son. How I long to see him again, to welcome him home – on any terms. My father never admitted his mistake to anyone, but I can. I will.

He watched Sonja lay the delphiniums on the gravel in front of the stone.

'We could have him moved to Foxbarton,' she said, 'if you wanted to.'

Joshua shook his head, his diction the clearest yet. 'No. He's here now. A corner of a foreign field and all that . . .'

And then there was the loudest crack of thunder they had ever heard, and the heavens opened and poured out their tears on Joshua Gilfoyle, which seemed to him an entirely just punishment for managing to pretend he had never had a brother for sixty-one years.

Hebe and Matilda stood in the studio, isolated from those with them by glass walls and earphones. There were no distractions, Julia realised, to upset Hebe. No people, no noise, nothing to startle her. The only difficulty was that Hebe herself would not take instructions down the microphone. The disembodied voice seemed to bother her, but they had overcome this problem by giving all instructions to Matilda, who passed them on.

So Hebe and Matilda sang their duets and their solos, each rendered perfect to Julia's ears as she and Merrill watched. Over and over they had to redo things, but once Carl Bayer had understood that Hebe would simply not repeat part of anything – she either went back to the beginning or didn't do it at all – there was nothing she was unable to do. She sang high, low, soft, loud, up a key, down a key . . .

Carl had greeted them when they arrived, explained to Julia and Merrill that he would need both girls in the soundproof room for an hour or two, that if Hebe looked even slightly upset there was no problem, the door could be opened, that a lot of repeating and mixing would go on and the end result would be a short demonstration tape. After this, if everyone was happy they would 'discuss terms' – and then, if Julia and Merrill were still happy, they would sign to say he could use the demo tape and take things from there. He was not a record producer himself, they understood, he was a promoter and publicist, and would use the tape they made today to promote them to a record company. Only the right company, of course – one that could handle a special child like Hebe with sensitivity and care.

Now Julia, watching from the control room where Carl Bayer gave his technicians occasional instructions on what to do, was impressed at Hebe's instinctive technical skill. She was less impressed with what Carl was doing. He seemed to be mixing in bits of synthetic this and synthetic that, until to the untutored ear Matilda's voice at one point disappeared entirely. He added a bass, and even a drum beat at one point, and although the finished sound was still definitely a duet it sounded to Julia as if all the humanity had been polished out of it. She was worried about the time it was taking. Although Hebe was still singing beautifully, the occasional flapping of her hands, the way she stood on tiptoe, spoke of tension. It could have been excitement and happiness, but it could also be the edge of normality. You never could tell with Hebe, not until she went off at the deep end – or not. But I've got to let her try, Julia thought. I can't pull her out of life every time she flaps her hands, because sometimes she's just happy.

'He's certainly a perfectionist,' remarked Merrill, not noticing anything wrong. 'I'd love to see one of his banana splits.'

But Julia was still uneasy. 'Why's he getting them to do it again?' she asked Merrill at one point. 'It sounds lovely.'

Merrill shrugged. 'I guess he's the expert on what he does.'

'He's no expert on Hebe,' said Julia, rather mutinously. She watched Hebe's pixie face and slender frame carefully for signs of distress. But Hebe seemed completely detached, not looking at her mother or even at anyone else. 'How did I,' said Julia softly, 'me, a self-indulgent hippy with hands like spades and a voice like a frog, how did I give birth to a fairy? There's nothing elfin about me. I'm as elfin as Attila the Hun.'

'Ah, said Merrill, 'that'll be the Elf King Attila, then?'

'I'm serious. I look at her and I think, you're wonderful, but who allocated you to me?'

'Sounds as if you've got religion to me,' said Merrill.

'Don't be daft. Mrs Braithwaite has a theory about changeling children, you know. That the fairies occasionally snatch one of ours and replace them with something more ethereal.'

'So you believe in fairies?'

'Maybe,' said Julia, frowning at Carl Bayer and fingering her hair thoughtfully.

'Well then. Fairies, angels, all the same thing. Hebe believes in them.'

'She sees them all the time,' said Julia. 'It worries me sometimes. It makes me feel she's not quite of this world.'

Merrill shrugged. 'You're letting Mrs Braithwaite get to you. Sometimes I think *she's* not quite of this world.'

William watched his sister and his cousin half in envy and half in boredom. He didn't think much to what they had to do – singing things over and over was really boring – but he did rather fancy making millions because then he could study tarantulas for as long as he liked without his dad saying, 'William, that's not a job – you have to secure funding.' He wandered around by himself and noticed that Carl Bayer had an electronic diary, one of those he very much wanted himself, with a metal pointer and a little black case. He stroked it longingly and Carl said, 'Feel free to look, son.' William took him at his word and examined the contents of Carl's average day with interest. Most of it was actually not very interesting at all. 'Belinda,' said one page, 'Annabel,' said another and, intriguingly, 'Annabel and Belinda,' said a third. He wondered if Annabel and Belinda were both Carl Bayer's girlfriends. You probably got more than one girlfriend in the record business – another very good reason to have nothing to do with it, in addition to all the singing. He looked up today's date and saw, 'Hebe

Fitzgerald, 11 a.m.' No mention of Matilda. He frowned. Matilda wouldn't like that.

Eventually, after what seemed like hours, Carl seemed to feel he had a perfect recording both of the duet and of Hebe singing 'Waltzing Matilda'. He must check whether there'd be any royalties due on that. Old song, probably traditional, should be fine to use it . . . 'Another half an hour and we're through.'

'Actually, I think Hebe's tired,' said Julia. 'Maybe we can call it a day now, or at least take a –'

'Twenty minutes, then we stop for coffee and chocolate croissants.'

Julia watched Hebe flapping and dancing. 'I think we should stop now.'

'We're nearly through. I'll tell you what, love, why don't you pop out and fetch supplies whilst I finish up?'

But Julia did not want to leave Hebe, increasingly annoyed now that Carl was not so willing to stop at her first uneasy instinct as he had promised, so Merrill set out alone to procure coffee, lemonade and chocolate croissants at exorbitant cost from somewhere very fashionable and French just along the road. She felt not slightly but exactly like a country bumpkin in her jeans and sweatshirt, surrounded by the cultural élite of Soho on a Sunday morning, and was only slightly mollified when it started to rain and all the Beautiful People relaxing on the pavement got their Gauloises wet and had to run indoors like lemmings for fear of damaging their perfect hair-dos.

When she got back to the studio Carl Bayer had had a call to be somewhere else and was apparently wrapping things up. Hebe was dancing around the room on tiptoe with her arms stretched down by her sides and her hands opening and closing rapidly beside her hips and Julia was looking worried and angry.

'I asked him to stop,' she said to Merrill, 'but we had to finish the tape, and now look at her. Hebe, come here.'

'Oh, Jules, she's absolutely fine. It was only another ten minutes,' said Carl. 'We couldn't have given up with only ten minutes to go, and actually I think that flapping thing is rather charming, don't you?'

'Ten minutes may be nothing to you, but Hebe's tired, and I think we should have –'

'Hebe's great,' Carl interrupted, not really hearing. 'I think we've really got something here. She could earn a fortune, you know, Jules – I mean, a real fortune. It could turn it around for you. There are these places in the States, you know, cost a bomb but you could take her, get her cured . . . I think the next stage will be to work out what goes on the launch CD, decide what exposure we can get through the press. Get her on live kids TV. That's always good publicity.'

'I don't think that would be a good idea,' said Julia, reaching for Hebe. 'And we're not looking for a cure. She hasn't got a disease. There isn't a cure. I think we've had enough. Stand still, Hebe. Look, we need to go home and think about it. You're going too fast.'

'She'll be fine. Look, darling, there will have to be a couple of live appearances. You can't expect a good launch without that, but we'll keep it to a minimum – and *Blue Peter* are very good with child stars . . .'

'Er,' said Julia, 'you're not listening, Carl. I don't know about this. I have to do what's best for Hebe.'

Merrill cleared her throat. 'I'm back,' she said, unnecessarily.

'Jules, of course you do. Thanks for the coffee, Mary.'

'Merrill,' said Merrill.

'Sure. You know, this isn't only about money, this is about realising potential. Hebe is really something . . .' Carl Bayer rubbed his hands and Julia noticed the huge diamond he wore on his little finger. This is definitely about money for you, she thought. '. . . Look at her, she's charming. I do love that funny little dance she's doing.'

'Funny little dance?' Julia looked as if she were about to thump him. 'That's not a funny little dance. She's not doing it to be funny.'

Carl didn't notice her expression. 'You know, after what I'd read up about autism I expected her to be much worse. I'm surprised we've not had one like her in the industry before. I mean, some of them are so gifted.'

'How do you mean?' Julia had frozen.

'You know – autistic kids. Still, as a marketing ploy it probably only works for the first one you find. Lucky for you we've found her first.'

Julia was staring at Carl as if he'd grown another head and she was going to sever it with her bare hands, and Merrill intervened, hastily. 'Ahem – er – are you talking about just Hebe here, or is Matilda involved?'

'Well,' Carl frowned, looked thoughtful, 'I think the duet thing is a nice idea but, you know, the potential really is best for solo careers. Hebe has a gift that should be shared. I mean, don't take this the wrong way, but the autistic thing is potentially a great selling point. People know all about autism these days. You know, Dustin Hoffman in *Rain Man*, telephone directories, that pianist – what was his name – Helfgott – wish I'd signed him . . . Now, Julia, this is a standard contract. I want you to have a quick look at it.'

'I don't need to look at it. You can't *use* her autism to market her.' Julia couldn't believe she was hearing this. 'It's no one's business but hers.'

'My dear Jules,' Carl Bayer took her arm, 'in the rat-infested marketplace that is the modern music business you use your every advantage. Hebe's autism is part of what makes her adorable. Look at that, she's so cute when she flaps her hands.'

Julia stood, towering over him. 'It's not a bloody advantage and it's not bloody cute. It's called posturing. She postures when she's getting stressed.'

'Oh, dear. Calm down. Look, I've said we can include a

few duets in the deal.' He glanced at Merrill as if she were slightly less important than the disposable stirrer in his cappuccino. 'Just sign the paper and we'll add that in later. I've got to get to another appointment shortly but we can talk tomorrow.'

'You prepared this earlier,' said Merrill, looking at the contract over Julia's shoulder. 'It doesn't mention duets, it just says Hebe.'

'It can always be altered,' Carl nodded at Merrill. 'You'll have to sign it too, of course, if you want Miranda in on it.'

'Matilda,' said Matilda, hating him intensely.

Merrill was uneasy. 'Julia, can I have a word with you?'

Carl Bayer looked slightly disbelieving. 'Is this a big problem, ladies? Because, you know, we have invested some time in this morning, and if you're not serious – I mean, time is money, if you get my drift . . .'

'I'm not sure that you're serious yourself,' said Julia. 'Hebe's not for sale. Her . . . disability is not on offer either. Merrill, I think we're ready for home. Hebe, give me your hand.'

'And for the record,' added Merrill, 'Matilda's mother feels the same.'

'OK, OK, I understand,' said Carl, perceiving a minor hitch. They'd come round. You could always suck them in with the promise of the money. After all, whatever else anyone said, the child's voice was just incredible and she was just *so* weird it was sure to be saleable. 'You're both tired and you need to regroup. If you'd sign this now we can at least get the cash rolling, then we can alter the details of the contract later.'

'I may live in the country,' said Julia angrily, 'but I didn't evolve straight out of a funny-shaped turnip, you know. I'm not signing anything.'

Hebe hopped on one foot and looked at Carl. She sensed there was going to be some noise. She didn't like the way he was looking at her mother. She looked at Matilda, who appeared mildly upset, and Merrill, who was clearly furious, and William, who had his hands on his hips like Sir Walter Raleigh on the poop deck of his flagship in the days when he had both arms. Hebe had seen a picture of Nelson on the poop deck of his flagship. She didn't know who Sir Walter Raleigh was or what a flagship was, but she knew he stood just like that. The ring on Carl Bayer's finger flashed and she blinked. Now that she and Matilda had left the soundproofed confines of the recording room she could hear the storm outside. She frowned, then she sidled up to Carl's chair and stared at him from very close quarters, inches from his nose.

Carl Bayer glanced at her sideways, then returned to Julia, realising she was far more bristly than he had bargained for. Bloody artists, they were all the same.

'Look, I'll tell you what, I'll get my people to draw up a whole new contract and we can sign over lunch. I can cancel my next appointment . . .' Hebe sidestepped right into his line of vision and he put a hand on her shoulders and moved her gently out of the way. She moved again. He moved her again. 'If you need more time we can – What on earth's she doing?' He peered at Hebe.

'She's looking at you,' said Julia, thinking, that's it, we're out of here. She stood and looked around for her coat, her bag, a pen.

Hebe pushed her face in front of Carl's again. 'Hello,' she said. 'You smell funny,' and she cackled like a hyena.

Carl moved her firmly aside, losing his cool slightly. Daniel hadn't warned him about this. 'Now she's being a little weird,' he said, slightly distastefully. 'You'd be crazy to turn down her chance at big money. She could use a cure.'

Hebe stared, her little frown appearing between her eyebrows. She looked at her mother, at Matilda, at Carl, back at her mother again. 'What's crazy, Mummy?'

'God,' said Carl, 'she's no idea, has she? You're a kooky, darling, but you sing like an angel. People will love it. Sweet but damaged – what a package.' He straightened up and saw Julia's face. Oops, he thought. Oops oops.

'I don't think so,' said Julia. If she had been a firework she would just have been going off. 'Thanks very much. You can keep this morning's recording. It's a bloody present . . . there.'

'What's that?'

'I've written it on your newspaper. Across the breasts on page three. "Carl Bayer can keep this morning's recording but otherwise he can get stuffed." That's it, that's your contract. We're off.'

'I don't think you realise . . . Let's be clear about this –'

'She doesn't want to sign with you,' said Merrill, 'and we don't want lunch. Is that clear enough?' She hoped Matilda would get over this one, although a sideways glance at her suggested this was not likely, at least not in this lifetime.

Carl looked stunned. 'I don't think you realise how much is on offer –'

'Actually,' said Julia, 'you're offering nothing at all that we want. You're upsetting Hebe.'

'Rubbish. Wake up and smell the roses, woman. Your daughter's not going to get an offer like this every day of her life. How many record producers would risk signing a handicapped child? I'm doing Hebe a huge favour here. Don't throw it away.'

Matilda stared. Merrill held her breath. Hebe frowned.

Julia tipped her coffee very carefully into Carl Bayer's lap. She was pleased to notice that the froth on the top settled comfortably on his groin like snow.

'Well,' she said, 'we'll be off.'

She grabbed Hebe and they left in shocked and stony silence.

'Well,' said Merrill when they got outside and into the rain, 'am I correct in assuming none of us liked him?'

'He was a worm,' said Julia. 'Matilda, I'm really sorry, but he wasn't nice. He wanted to buy Hebe. He didn't think she was a person – he didn't think either of you were people. Just things to be sold. I couldn't have that.'

Matilda sighed. She understood perfectly. It had been very clear to her, in the way it is always very clear to children, that she hadn't been important in Carl Bayer's scheme of things at all. 'D'you think that means we won't get to go home in that car?'

'I think we've got slightly more chance of being carried home piggyback by the Wombles. We'll be taking the train . . .'

The journey home degenerated into a nightmare. Crossing London to get to King's Cross station Hebe became progressively more and more terrified. First it was the thunder, then it was the lightning. There were hardly any taxis and they tried the underground, but Hebe became utterly hysterical at the sound of an approaching train and they had to leave again. Julia hung on to her hand throughout, feeling Hebe pull away every time she panicked, knowing she could take off and it would be hours before they found her, if they found her at all. Eventually, soaked and shivering, they reached King's Cross just in time to jump on the Cambridge train, where Hebe finally consented to sit still and be held. And then, as they chugged north, Matilda began to cry.

'Come on, darling,' said Merrill, putting an arm round her. 'You can't cry over what we never had. That was a horrible man. He just wanted to make money. He wasn't interested in music, or in you or Hebe. He just thought making music was a game for making money. To him you were just part of that game.'

'I know,' wept Matilda, 'but I so wanted to be like Charlotte Church. I wanted everyone to listen to me and to sing Welsh songs for the Pope.'

William opened his mouth and Merrill nudged him hastily with her foot, knowing a gem of schoolboy logic was not going to help at the moment. But William was not easily silenced. 'You could always be an air hostess,' he said brightly, 'that was your other plan. Then you could sing in the aisles and if you worked for Vatican Air you could sing for the Pope all the time.'

'I hate you,' said Matilda, between sobs, and William sighed the sigh of the much misunderstood.

Hebe, meanwhile, stared silently and unblinkingly out of the window, as the Hertfordshire countryside flashed past and Merrill rang Mrs Barker to ask if Mr Barker could please pick them up from Cambridge station. Outside the carriage the rain poured in a torrent down the glass, the storm pursuing them north into East Anglia like a Roald Dahl monster, and Julia wished she had never let herself be persuaded to go to London. This weather was the final straw.

The final straw for Hebe, however, turned out to be nothing to do with her day in London at all. As Mr Barker drove them the last few miles along the road to Foxbarton beneath thunderous skies, and through torrential rain they passed a red and yellow gypsy caravan being pulled by a horse in the opposite direction, the driver wrapped in oilskins, the horse dripping and quiet.

'Look, look,' shouted Matilda, 'it's that man going home from the horse fair, the one with the lovely van. Look, Hebe, it's your hairy bear!' But Hebe, after one initial glance, squeezed her eyes tightly shut and would not look. Instead she set up a low howling which continued for all the rest of the way home and a long time into the night, and there seemed nothing at all Julia could do to console her.

Chapter Seventeen

⁕

Joshua awoke next morning feeling more at peace with the world than he had felt for many years. The storm had passed, heading north to throw grey seas at a despairingly eroding coast, but the air in Foxbarton still felt thick and stifling. As he stirred he was conscious of a weight beside him, and found Sonja, nestled in the curve of his arm, her blonde hair tousled, her usually pale skin a little flushed by sleep. How did I find someone like her, he wondered, at my time of life?

And then the morning was shattered by his daughter-in-law, bursting into his bedroom as if he had no right to privacy at all in his own home. Still, the minute you have children privacy is never the same again. The day they come home from the hospital wrapped in a fluffy blanket is inescapably the direct precursor to the day their spouse charges unannounced into your bedroom whilst you, aged seventy, are considering attempting conjugal relations with your wife.

'Joshua, I'm sorry to – Is Hebe in here with you? She's lost . . . been gone from her bed for hours.'

He frowned. 'No. Haven't seen her.' He had slept like a log all night, he realised, for the first time in weeks. Guilt grabbed him. What if Hebe had come up here to see him during the night in her usual way? The windows had been locked against the storm. He had been asleep. Surely that damn artist wouldn't have let her daughter out on a night like that? Bloody irresponsible hippy . . . A child like that needed looking after . . .

Merrill had gone tearing off again and he roused Sonja from sleep, quickly.

'Sonja?' He was annoyed to find his voice slurring again. It had come on so much and yet, when he was distressed, the control seemed to go.

'Mmm?'

'Sonja, Hebe – she's mishing. We've got to help.'

'Joshua? Are you all right?'

'Fine. Get up. Start looking.'

Julia had awoken early to find Hebe gone, alarmed to find the bed cold. She rang the Grange first, and Merrill rang her back and told her that no, Hebe was not there, and because the storm had been so heavy Joshua's windows had been bolted shut so –

'What do you mean, Joshua's windows?'

'Apparently she's been sneaking up here in the night and to see him,' said Merrill. 'The French windows are usually open and she's been coming in and playing chess – but not last night because of the storm – and Matilda and William haven't seen her either.'

'Oh God. Chess? What – you mean she's been sneaking past me at night? God, I even tied her doorknob to my bedside lamp. I was going to tie it to my toe.'

'I'm sorry, Jules, I didn't know till now either. Look, she's probably just in the woods. You stay there and I'll call –'

'I'm not staying here. I'm going to look for her. Get the police, Merrill, call them for me quickly. I'm scared. Yesterday was so stressful. She hated London and she really hates storms. I should have known something was brewing with her . . . Dammit, I thought she'd stopped doing this since we came here . . . Why the hell didn't he tell me she'd been wandering at night? Bloody stupid old man,' and Julia dropped the phone and ran outside, shouting, 'Hebe! Hebe!' She fought down panic as she shouted. Please God, she found herself saying, let that so-called angel of hers have looked after her this time.

Within twenty minutes word had spread from house to house and the whole of Foxbarton was mobilising. Matilda and William were out and searching, Stewart Barlow and other men from the estate were out, Jonathan Doyle and a slightly embarrassed Kate had been awoken from a rumpled bed in the Old School House, Oscar, home from his father's, stopped from boarding the school bus and hauled back to join the hunt.

Julia was way ahead of them, already deep in the woods at Mrs Braithwaite's cottage – but Mrs Braithwaite had not seen Hebe. She was also concerned. 'It was a bad night,' she said to Julia. 'You should check the gypsy site, she liked to go there.'

'Liked to go there? What do you mean? How did you know? Did every bloody person in this village know Hebe has been wandering around all alone except me?'

'It was only now and again, when she was playing in the woods with her cousins,' said Mary Braithwaite, who thought it no bad thing that Hebe had found Gabriel Gilfoyle – but who thought it best not to mention Hebe's occasional nocturnal ramblings now. 'She was interested in the coloured Romany van. Why don't you go and look? I'll go towards the lake.' But at the mention of the word 'lake', Julia took off like a frightened rabbit in the direction of the water and so Mrs Braithwaite, a worried frown on her face, made her way towards the gypsy site at a fast pace.

There was only one van left. Billy and Tracey had stayed for an extra night's peace and quiet, but they hadn't seen or heard Hebe. 'We were inside last night,' said Billy, 'bloody awful weather. If she did come we probably wouldn't have heard her.'

Tracey was pulling her wellingtons on. 'Come on, we'll help you look. Out, you kids, we're on a manhunt.'

Julia was at the lake, staring at the rain making millions of mini-pools on the surface, trying not to imagine that Hebe was at the bottom of it. But Hebe hates water, she told herself, wondering if the police were going to drag the River Stour, hates getting wet, will do anything to avoid even wetting her shoes. It's one of the reasons she hates storms – she can't bear water dripping down her face. She won't be in the lake . . .

'Hebe! Hebe, where are you?'

Her voice failed to echo back, dulled by the water and the trees, the echoes snatched away in their prime. Feeling as though she was wrapped in cotton wool by the dead, post-thunderstorm air, Julia pressed on. God, she thought, these woods go on for miles. And Hebe could be anywhere – including a mere ten feet away from me refusing to answer, with her hands over her ears and her eyes shut. Where do I start? How do I start?

By lunchtime the whole village was out, together with all the policemen who could be mustered in West Suffolk – which turned out to be a surprisingly large number. Even in these days of police shortages and stress in the force, they all come back from their off-duty when a child goes missing, and the village was full of police cars.

Julia was sitting in Woodcutter's Cottage by now, being questioned repeatedly by a friendly policewoman, who was making her feel considerably worse.

'Would she go with a stranger?'

'Yes. Yes, she probably would. She doesn't have any fear of strangers. Oh God, what if she's gone off with someone?'

'Calm down, Miss Fitzgerald. It doesn't help to imagine things. Most children who disappear are found very quickly. Just think. Did she ever go off on her own before?'

'All the time. She's like Houdini, forever escaping.'

'What's different about this time?'

'How do you mean?' Julia frowned.

'Well, you've called us in this time. If she's gone missing before then why not call us on those occasions?'

'Oh, I see. I have called before, but not here. The police helped look for her several times in London. But she'd been better here, more predictable, more settled. Then yesterday she got very rattled – a combination of things went wrong: we had a stressful day, and then there was the storm. That may be why she's taken off, but we usually find her fairly quickly. When she gets stressed she goes somewhere she knows. Often she goes back to the same places over and over. She never goes anywhere completely new.'

'And had she particular places she went to round here?'

Julia swallowed. 'Apparently more places than I realised. She's been getting out of the bedroom window at night.'

'That window? How would she get down from there?'

'She can climb down walls. She's very good. She's been visiting the Grange, and Mrs Braithwaite's cottage in the woods.'

'Would she have gone near the river?'

'I don't think so. She hates water.'

'Where is her father?'

'I don't bloody know.'

'Could he have taken her?'

'No, he doesn't know she exists.'

'Is there anywhere else you can think of? The gypsy site?'

'Yes, she's been there. But there's no one left apart from one van and they didn't see her.'

And then, horribly: 'Do you have anything of hers we can give to the police dogs? They may be able to pick up a scent. Ma'am – don't cry. I'm not saying anything, but in the woods it may be the best way to find her. She may be hiding, cold, hungry. She might have hurt herself. There are lots of reasons why she wouldn't answer us when we called.'

'I know, I know.' Julia shivered. 'She doesn't like dogs.'

'Is there anyone else she goes to, ma'am? Anyone else she's mentioned to you?'

'No – well, there is her angel.'

'Angel, ma'am?'

'She sees angels. Well, one angel. In the woods. It sings "Waltzing Matilda",' Julia managed a watery smile, 'but it doesn't know the words.'

'Do you think this could be a person, ma'am?'

'Oh no. I'm sure not. She sees it all the time. But she sees things differently from us. It doesn't mean there's anyone there.'

'Well, if you think of anything else . . .'

'I need to go out and look for her,' said Julia, suddenly unable to keep still for another second. She pulled on her cagoule, seeing Hebe's untouched on the hook and shuddering at the thought that she might be wet, cold, injured, afraid. 'I have to go and look for her angel.'

'Ma'am, it's best if someone stays here.'

'You're here, aren't you?' And she was out of the door, finding, to her astonishment, Sonja just outside it in the process of wheeling Joshua in to see her.

'What can we do?'

Julia glared at him. 'Why didn't you tell me she'd been watching you? What the hell did you think she was doing, wandering around in the middle of the night?'

He frowned. 'I'm s . . . sorry. It didn't occur to me . . . At first I th . . . thought I was dreaming, then I just got used to her b . . . being there. I w . . . w . . . wanted her to come. I just thought you were stupid to let her g . . . get out.'

'You silly sod.'

'I'm sorry, Julia,' said Sonja. 'I did not know of this – it was when he could not speak.'

'I c . . . could speak,' said Joshua, 'I just didn't w . . . want to, God help me.'

'I've got to go and look for her.' Julia hurried past them, back towards the trees. 'I have to find Hebe's angel. I've got to find the place where she goes and sees it. It's somewhere in the woods, and it's the only other place she might be – if only I knew where she goes.'

'What can we do?' Sonja called after her.

'Just help look,' Julia's voice echoed back, blunted by the strange, dense air, and she was over the wall and gone.

'The woods,' said Sonja to Joshua. 'They're all searching the woods.'

'I know the woods,' said Joshua, 'as well as anyone.'

'We'll never get your wheelchair in there.'

'Then I'll walk. Or I'll crawl. Come, woman, stop messing about. That way.'

The police put a newsflash out on national radio very early. No one wanted to say it to Julia, but some of these children who disappeared so suddenly – well, they didn't just go, they were taken – so you needed people looking out for them much further away than just in the woods behind their homes.

Gabriel Gilfoyle was just leaving the house of the Cambridge friend from whom he had borrowed the horse and carriage when he heard the presenter tell the world that an eight-year-old autistic girl called Hebe Fitzgerald had disappeared from her home in Foxbarton and police were currently combing the woods behind her home in a search involving over a hundred officers. They were anxious for any other sightings of her. Hebe was described – her long blonde hair, her dark eyes, the clothes she was probably wearing, the last time she was seen . . . This was the stuff of nightmares.

Without thinking about it Gabriel got straight into his car and drove back to Foxbarton, telling himself when the question occurred to him some twenty minutes later that it wasn't that he felt any particular responsibility for her, or for any of them, but he had to go straight back, didn't he? I mean, for a start if they thought she had been abducted he'd be one of the suspects. It was reason enough to go tearing back. Anyone half decent would do the same. It wasn't as if he and Hebe meant anything particularly to one another. She had visited him a few times, that was all.

And as he drove he tuned in to Classic FM to calm his pulse and keep his driving sensible and legal, and he was astonished to hear the presenter say, 'And now here is a tape that was just brought in to us of an unknown child duet, recorded yesterday in a studio in London. We played it earlier this afternoon and have been inundated with requests, so here again by popular demand . . .' And Gabriel had the bizarre experience of hearing the lost child everyone was hunting singing 'Early One Morning' as he drove to the far side of Foxbarton Woods to find her.

Daniel Cutter also heard the news and also jumped immediately into his car. There was no doubt in his mind that his actions had led to this. This was something to do with that recording session yesterday. Carl had rung him in a very bad mood the previous evening and told him that the next time he discovered a mental case child star could he manage one whose bloody mother was at least tame? Daniel had realised from his account that Hebe had clearly been upset, and he had tried to ring Julia, who had hung up on him. Now Hebe had run off.

It had obviously been a disaster and it was down to him. He had persuaded Carl Bayer to listen to Hebe, he had persuaded Julia to let Hebe sing, and this was the end result. It had all gone horribly wrong and he had to make it right again if it was the last thing he ever did. He drove up the M11 like a man possessed, and arrived at Foxbarton behind a vanload of what looked alarmingly like police dogs. He hoped they weren't trained to sniff out anything other than people, then decided it didn't matter if they were – finding Hebe was far more important than worrying about his own miserable skin. She was his godchild, for heaven's sake, and it had never seemed more of a responsiblity. 'Make it all right,' he prayed silently to an unnamed god as he stumbled randomly into the woodland and started shouting her name. 'Make it all right and I'll make it up to her. I'll make it up to all of them, I promise.'

The afternoon stretched on, punctuated only by the arrival of the dogs, who seemed to detect Hebe's scent absolutely everywhere that she wasn't. Julia, rendered distraught at the sight of a police frogman in the river when she emerged briefly from the trees, had returned to the woods, where she had found Joshua labouring impressively through the undergrowth on Sonja's arm, and had taken his other arm as it gave her something to do.

It took him a very long time to get to where he was going, past the hide William and Oscar had made to watch badgers. There they collected William and Matilda, wandering anxiously, near to tears and calling Hebe's name, past Mary Braithwaite's cottage where they found Oscar up on the roof, shouting Hebe's name; and around the lake where another frogman was just appearing and shaking his head. They went through the gypsy site, where Billy and Tracey's caravan stood abandoned as they searched the outskirts of the village, and came eventually to the place where Joshua and his lost brother had played as boys, the place he had been determined to reach.

Here the woods were thick, uncoppiced, the trees tall and mossy, the undergrowth dense and scratchy, but from it, like a mini Hindu temple, arose a strange heap of stones. It was not a natural mound, although age and grass and moss made it look exactly that. It was the mound of rock that remained from the excavation of the church passage some five hundred years ago, when a secret route out of the church and into the woods had seemed like a good idea, religious differences being what they were at the time. Joshua was not at all surprised to see Mary Braithwaite there already.

She had heard them coming. Actually, you could have heard them a mile off. She remembered men in the old days who could creep through the woods without a sound, hunting deer – they would be so close that the first noise the chosen creature heard was the arrow that killed it. But the world had changed. She would be glad to leave it, actually – had been all ready to leave it once before, but she hadn't quite managed it, had turned out to have another task to complete. Now that was nearly over, and with a bit of luck it was time for some rest.

'Mary Braithwaite,' said Joshua, 'it's been a long time.'

'Hello, Joshua. What are you doing here?'

'Looking f . . . for Hebe. I thought she might have come to the den.'

'She's not there,' said Mary Braithwaite. 'Did you think I wouldn't have thought of it? It's not been touched for years.'

Julia frowned. 'What den? What's the significance of here?'

Mary pushed away the leaf mould and leaf layer with her feet, revealing an old wooden manhole cover. 'The old passage to the church,' she said. 'The passage collapsed some years ago, I'm told, but there's still a little cave down there. No one here knows but me and him,' she nodded at Joshua, 'but it's undisturbed. I wondered if Hebe might have hidden there. It was somewhere to try.'

Julia stared at the wooden lid. 'We should lift it anyway, have a look . . .'

It was not so difficult to lift when she and Sonja and Mary were all pulling on it, and it moved aside to show a hole in the ground, a wooden ladder down to the floor a few feet beneath, which, whilst clearly not five hundred years old, was not new either.

Julia had lowered herself in before anyone could stop her or warn her not to break her legs on the ladder, whispering, 'Hebe? Are you here?' But her voice echoed into dank silence. The passage was obviously empty.

It was also pitch-dark. 'I don't suppose anyone has a torch or anything?'

As Julia peered into the darkness, William, being both a boy and a reader of Enid Blyton's Famous Five adventures, produced both torch and matches from his voluminous pockets. After a brief mix-up when Julia discovered that the torch didn't work and flicked open the matchbox to reveal a rather puzzled centipede, the right matchbox was found and Julia lit up, to discover she was looking at the remains of a boys' den, a den that had not been used for, well, probably since the war.

'Wow,' said William, peering in from the top. 'What a fantastic place for a den. Whose is it, d'you suppose?'

'Is your aunt OK?' Oscar had found another torch, shone it in after Julia. 'I'm coming after you.' He slid down the hole after her.

'Let me down,' said Joshua, pulling away from Sonja. 'Help me.'

'Joshua, you are ridiculous. How can you possibly –'

'She's not here,' came Julia's voice. 'There's no proper passageway. As you say, it looks as if it's been blocked off for years. There are some ancient cushions down here, and a book.'

'*King Solomon's Mines*,' said Joshua.

'*King Solomon's Mines*,' said Julia, picking it up and squinting at the fly leaf. "Joshua and David Gilfoyle, March 3rd 1940",' and then, more quietly, 'Gosh.' She looked at Oscar in the torchlight. Oscar stared back.

'Who's David Gilfoyle?'

Joshua had tears on his face. 'I want to go down there.'

'He's not there, Joshua,' said Sonja, 'and you're not up to scrambling down holes, you know that.'

'I want to go down there. I lost my brother s . . . sixty years ago. It's the closest I can ever be to him now. Dammit woman, this was our d . . . den. If you won't help me I'll j . . . just jump.' He stepped forwards, determined.

'Joshua Gilfoyle,' said Mary Braithwaite, blocking his path, 'I was forever telling you to keep out of that blooming hole sixty years ago.'

'I didn't listen then, and I'm n . . . not listening now.'

'Oh yes you are, young man. David's not down there, Joshua. Not any more. It's Hebe we're looking for, remember.'

Joshua took a deep breath and glared at her. Then his shoulders sagged. 'God,' he said in a whisper, 'I'm so useless. I can't even climb down a b . . . blasted hole. I should be put down. If I was a horse they'd b . . . bloody shoot me. This is all my fault.'

'Don't be silly. How is it your fault?'

'She came to see me, Sonja. I should have t . . . told someone. Told you.' He looked at Julia, who was scrambling back out of the hole. 'I'm so sorry. I didn't want her to stop coming. I n . . . needed her to come.' A tear ran down his cheek and the side of his face sagged badly, as it did when he was tired. 'I looked forward to seeing her, she m . . . made it all right.'

Julia touched his arm, suddenly sorry for him. 'It's not your fault she escaped. She's always escaping. She thought you were her grandpa; she wanted to come and see you.'

'He is her grandpa,' said Matilda. 'William gave him to her.'

William frowned anxiously. 'It's not that I didn't want you, Grandpa. I figured you would still be my grandpa really.'

'That's all right,' said Joshua, who understood sneaky deals very well. 'I wish she was my granddaughter. I'd give anything to find her.' He sat down heavily, suddenly exhausted, leaned back awkwardly against the mossy stone, toppled over . . . and looked up to see a newly arrived man looking down at him, a man with a face like Jesus Christ, haunted, dark eyes, a beard . . .

'Hello, Father,' said Gabriel.

Hebe watched them from her hiding place in the oak tree. She had found this tree years and years ago, on a night when the house had got all noisy with people and she had climbed out of the window to escape and find an angel. This was her star counting tree, and it was also her angel tree. She had been here lots of times when the stars needed counting. They had needed counting badly last night after the caravan-music-man called John had taken his van away just when she had wanted to go and see him. This had been one more thing to be sad about, and whenever Hebe got too much sadness her head hurt and she had to count stars.

But she hadn't been able to see the stars last night. She had looked from her window and the stars had obviously all died. So she had climbed out and down the wall and run through the storm, which she hated because it flashed and banged. She had run to see Grandpa, as she had so wanted to see him before the world ended, but his window had been locked and the curtains closed so Hebe had known for sure that the storm had got him. So then she had run as fast as she could through the darkness for her angel tree, and had been still and silent up there ever since, waiting for the end of the world, which it must be with the stars all gone. A man on TV had once said one day the stars would all go and the world would end, and Hebe knew this must therefore be imminent. She had come here to mourn and be as quiet as she possibly could, because that way she could at least hear the angel singing at the end of the world.

It was not too wet, as the tree provided a good canopy, and although she was probably very cold and her arms were all pimply, being cold wasn't the kind of thing she really noticed.

But something was odd, extraordinary, even. Because even though the stars had gone and even though she was in the angel tree she could see Grandpa now. How strange that he should be here when the storm had already got him. And she could see Sonja, and William and Matilda, Mrs Braithwaite, and the caravan-music-man called John, who had gone away and made her sad. They had all come back. Perhaps this was the way it was at the end of the world . . .

She observed the old man being helped to his feet and hugging the caravan-music-man. Then Oscar came up head first out of a hole. Now she could see her mother too. Why had Oscar been in a hole? Now her mother was shouting at the caravan-music-man. Why was her mother shouting at the man? Hebe didn't like the shouting. She didn't like the dogs barking and she didn't like the whistles blowing. She was tired and thirsty but she didn't mind either of those things – they were not the kind of things she noticed. But noise, shouting, people being cross . . . she needed to make the cross noise go away . . . If her angel would sing then she wouldn't have to hear the shouting. Singing drowned out the chaos of the world . . .

Down below her perch in the oak tree Julia was screaming at Gabriel Gilfoyle.

'Do you know how long I looked for you? You and your . . . your *fucking* croissants! Was the most beautiful night of our lives just not bloody good enough in the end? Do you know how I searched for you to tell you we were having a child? You *must* have known who I was – my sister was your sister-in-law, for God's sake . . . How could you not have known who I was?'

'I didn't know. I had no idea who you were, Julia,' he was saying. 'You don't look like Merrill, you don't have the same name, it never occurred to me that it was any more than coincidence that the gutter you found me in wasn't a million miles from their house. There were people everywhere. I'd gone to see them that night, but when I saw there was a party I couldn't go in. I couldn't face it. I was drunk, dirty, I'd been living rough in a squat with no one I even knew . . . and then you came out of nowhere. You picked me up and took me home. You fed me scones with chocolate spread and told me I was a poet. It was the most beautiful night I had ever had – but I knew I couldn't *have* you. It was the wrong time for me. I was a wreck. I wasn't good enough. I had to leave the mess I had made and start again, try to be what I wanted to be, what you had said I could be. You were like a dream, an angel. You turned it round for me.'

'Oh great. And what do you think *you* did? I'm not a bloody convenient life-changing dream,' shouted Julia, 'I'm a woman. And I seem to recall we had a bonk. Remember that? It was shortly before you went out for croissants and did a runner. Oh, I'm sorry, Mrs Braithwaite, I didn't mean –'

'I know, I know. You were so clean, so beautiful . . . I had to leave. You had pulled me out of the gutter and I took advantage of you. I was so ashamed of myself, of what I had let myself become, so I left. I had no way of knowing then –'

'Knowing what?'

'That I had already had the best there would ever be.'

She blinked. 'And you never tried to find me.'

'No. I had no right.'

'My God, I don't know how to start to take this in . . . The father of my child is Gabriel Gilfoyle. You're Hebe's father. No wonder . . .'

'Are you my long-lost Uncle Gabriel?' asked Matilda.

'Yes. Sorry,' he shook her hand hurriedly, 'Julia, I didn't know you had a child. D'you think I wouldn't have found you if I'd known?'

'It's clearly no bloody surprise to you today,' Julia stared at him hard, 'so when did you find out?'

'I saw you at the horse fair. I saw you and I'd already met Hebe, and suddenly I just knew. It was obvious.'

'How? She could have been anybody's. I had other lovers, you know. I had jolly well hundreds of them.'

William held out his hand. 'Hello, Uncle. I'm William.'

'Er – and I'm Oscar Coleman, William's friend. Pleased to meet you. Better weather today, isn't it?' Oscar held out his.

His mother had told him you should always introduce yourself and make conversation as soon as you meet people.

'Hello – William, Oscar, yes it is . . . Julia, I know – you told me at the time.'

'I didn't want you to feel bad,' said Julia, 'at the time. Now I hope you feel a total worm. How could you know she was yours?'

'It all made sense. Mary had said something, and I already felt . . . Her voice, the way she is – my mother had a fantastic voice, and there was something about her . . .'

'Hebe is m . . . my granddaughter,' said Joshua, somewhat unnecessarily.

'For goodness' sake, shouldn't we all be looking for –' began Sonja, and then said, 'What's that noise? I can hear music.'

'Dogs,' said Oscar.

'Whistles,' said Matilda.

'It sound like wind chimes,' said Julia, straining to catch the sound.

'It sounds like a music box,' said Gabriel, 'playing "Waltzing Matilda".' They all fell silent for a moment, concentrating.

'You should cup your ears,' said William. 'That's how rabbits can tell when foxes are after them.'

Matilda offered him a quelling look but cupped hers anyway. 'I think it's coming from that tree.'

'My God,' said Sonja, looking up into the greenery and suddenly seeing Hebe peering over at them from twelve feet up. 'She is up there. Julia, she is up there. She is alive and she is right there in the tree!' She burst into tears and sat on the floor in a heap.

When they had persuaded Hebe down from the tree, and everyone had stopped crying (although Julia kept starting again, so it was difficult to say precisely when that was) William scrambled back up the tree to see where Hebe had been. And there he found an old wooden music box, still working, tucked into the hollow of the trunk and playing a rousing chorus of 'Waltzing Matilda', whilst in an alcove above it formed by a knot in the trunk was lodged a small statue, a gold statue of an angel that was about eighteen inches high and absolutely irreplaceable.

The discovery of the Foxbarton angel overshadowed even the discovery of the lost Hebe – who had, after all, not been missing for all that long in the end. The TV and radio news were rife with rehashes of the story of its disappearance, and theories abounded as to how it could have got into an oak tree in Foxbarton Woods.

Julia thought she knew. Sitting in the kitchen at the Grange with Merrill, after Hebe had been warmed in front of the Aga and checked over by a stunned Simon, they went over the night it disappeared again, and decided that they knew exactly who took the angel. Hebe had been unaccounted for that night. The police – who had interviewed virtually everyone else – had had absolutely no chance of interviewing a four-year-old child who, at that stage, did not speak an intelligible word, just screamed and howled and stood on her head for hours on end – a child who escaped from everywhere she was ever shut into and climbed up and down walls with the skill of a small spider.

Hebe had been upstairs in the Grange during Merrill's party – supposedly asleep, but in a room whose window she had since proved more than able to get out of. The church was only a short distance away, the tiny vestry window had been open, and climbing the cobbled wall was an easy task for Hebe. She had loved that angel, when she first saw it earlier that same day, the day she said her first word in church. So she had gone to get it.

'It's Matilda's music box that clinches it,' Julia told Merrill. 'Finding it with the angel. Hebe was the only possible link between those two things. The music box from the window sill at the Grange and the angel from the church.

Kate appeared in the kitchen, one of a constant stream of people arriving both to tell Julia how happy they were that Hebe was found and to have a look at the lost angel themselves. She gazed at it with some reverence.

'It's lovely, isn't it? Poor Jonathan will have to insure it again.'

Merrill smiled. 'I think my father-in-law will cover that. You know, he couldn't leave a better legacy, really. To have the angel found again.'

'All that time she was telling us,' Julia looked at Hebe, 'an angel in the tree that was shiny and that played "Waltzing Matilda".' And it never occurred to me that this might be it. I was imagining something far more . . . metaphysical.'

'How about your angel, Jules? I mean, the one you're making? Will you still do it?'

'Oh, I'll have it ready, don't worry. I had concerns about how it was going to fit on the plinth in church anyway. It is rather large.'

'You're telling me,' said Kate comfortably. 'I know I'm no art critic but I thought it was a yeti.'

'Thanks very much. How are things with you and Jonathan, by the way?'

'Oh,' said Kate, blushing, 'how did you know –?'

'Kate,' said Julia, 'this is a village.' It would be rather mean she felt, to point out to Kate that, given the noises they'd made, they probably already knew in Bury St Edmunds.

Julia had had to put any further conversation with Gabriel Gilfoyle on hold, as he currently had a lot to say to his father and brother, and this was going on quietly in another room. The shock of discovering that the man she had been looking for all this time was also the man that everyone else had been looking for too – and that rather than the down-and-out she had expected he was now a successful poet who had not touched a drop of alcohol in years – was enormous. But she would overcome it, because he was very keen to be Hebe's father, to try to make up to her by his presence now for the years of absence.

There would be time enough for them to talk later, years and years of time, and in the meantime she was storing up an awful lot of things to say. His conversation elsewhere was giving her chance to rank her cutting comments in order of choice and make sure she got in absolutely everything she wanted to say to him. She put her arms more tightly around Hebe, who sat on her knee, unaware of the level of distress she had caused, carefully unravelling a scarf someone had given her. They were all blissfully unaware that by this time the Matilda/Hebe duet had been played on Classic FM so many times that people were starting to ring the radio station asking where they could buy a copy. It was not the sort of thing that would have worried them anyway, even had they known, because they were all, every one of them, safely home.

Very much later that evening, as dusk fell, an exhausted Daniel Cutter found himself outside Mary Braithwaite's cottage where he collapsed in a heap on the woodland floor and wept. He had been far, far into the woods, wandering through the trees for hours, shouting for Hebe, and now he realised that he could no longer hear dogs barking, nor whistles, and perhaps the search had been called off.

'Young man,' Mary said, emerging, 'you seem tired.'

He looked at her through weary, tear-filled eyes. 'Mrs Braithwaite, you're back . . . Have they found her?'

'They have, and she's fine. You are the last of the search party. Here, I've made you some tea.'

'How did you know I was on my way?' He was very ready to credit her with magic powers, his sense of the eerie magic of the woodlands at dusk allowing him, really, to believe whatever his imagination suggested. Anyway Kate had told him she was said to be a witch. He eyed her with respect.

'Because you sound like a rhinoceros, crashing through those trees. Here, this will help.'

He took the tea gratefully, sipped it, gasped. 'What in heaven's name is it?'

'Borage,' said Mary Braithwaite comfortably, 'for guilt.'

'Oh.' He sat, shoulders slumped, sipping the tea, thinking it tasted like well-brewed socks. 'It won't take the guilt away.'

'Well, young man,' she said, 'nothing does that but your own actions. Borage just does away with the indigestion. After all, I think you promised to make it up to her if she was found.'

'I did,' said Daniel. 'How did you know?'

Mary Braithwaite shrugged. 'You don't get to be my age without knowing more than others give you credit for,' she said.

He smiled. 'How do you get to be so old? What's the secret?'

'There's no secret,' she said, smiling. 'You just have to have a little faith.'

Chapter Eighteen

The fuss about the girls' duet died down over the next few days. After the coverage of their demonstration tape on the radio, enhanced by the press discovering that the once-missing child was the one who was singing (earning Carl Bayer another diamond ring in the process), Julia had come under renewed pressure from Carl himself to take things further. She refused him – eventually using words of such clarity that even he could not fail to understand them. Then the hourly phone calls had stopped at last. She was not sure whether this was a good or a bad thing. Carl himself was clearly a bad thing, but the idea that Hebe might one day do something formally with that voice – well, maybe there was something in that. After all, Hebe still continued to sing, and there was an argument for helping her use her gift constructively. It could be, after all, as Merrill said, her salvation. Most people go through life with no particular gifts at all, and they manage. Hebe started off at a disadvantage – yet with her voice she could have the greatest advantage of all.

All this was revolving in Julia's head whilst Daniel camped out on her doorstep for a whole week begging forgiveness and Kate delivered him sandwiches, flasks of tea, clean underwear and silent sympathy three times a day.

'Please, Jules, please forgive me. I don't want the money, I want Hebe to have every penny, I should never have done it. Please believe me. I was at a low point in my career; it was a chance to get back in. Please, Jules, I've a lot of money here. Carl gets something every time that tape is played and a quarter of it's mine.'

'You,' said Julia eventually, stepping over him to do her laundry for the second time, 'can take your guilt money and smoke the whole blooming lot of it. You're not buying me back that easily, and Hebe's not for sale at all. She's beyond price.' And she left him there again and slammed the door, as Merrill winced and whispered, 'Oh, Jules, he looks really sad.'

It was about ten minutes later that she smelled pot and cigarette smoke, wafting in through the kitchen window on a gentle breeze.

'Did you know,' said William, appearing at the door, 'that Daniel's smoking money in your garden,' and Julia dashed out to see him doing exactly that, rolling it up and smoking it a note at a time, augmented by a considerable quantity of tobacco and a smaller quantity of something resinish which really should not have been smoked in Foxbarton, nor anywhere else for that matter.

'Oh, for goodness' sake, Daniel,' she said, exasperated, 'you'd better come in before you get us all arrested. Put that away and, for God's sake, don't burn any more of it. It's obscene. But don't think this means I've forgiven you. It's not that easy, not even nearly.'

'He looks forgiven to me,' said Merrill, watching from the kitchen table as Daniel followed her sheepishly in.

'He's not. I just draw the line at having to climb over a tragic but high fallen-friend figure every time I want to wash my knickers, and I can't bear to watch real money being burned at a rate of ten pounds per joint.'

'Oh, come on, Jules,' said Merrill. 'He did hunt for hours the day we lost Hebe. And you know Mary Braithwaite has been feeding him.' And Julia had to agree that if he had Mary's blessing then he must be worth forgiving.

'OK,' she said grudgingly to Daniel, 'you can go and say sorry to Hebe.'

So Daniel found Hebe halfway up a tree in the gardens of the Grange whilst Matilda read *The Lord of the Rings* at the foot of it, and offered her anything, anything she wanted, if she would forgive him. Hebe, demonstrating unusual understanding of the concept, climbed down the tree with her usual agility and opted for one of his dreadlocks, which she cut off with William's Swiss army knife and bore home in triumph.

Julia was very impressed, aware this was a greater sacrifice than Daniel had ever made for any woman, so he was finally absolved of all guilt. Later, perhaps, she and Merrill had agreed, they might let him look into Hebe and Matilda recording a few songs, straight, just as they came out, with no mixing and no funny synthesisers. Something that could be done in an afternoon in a small studio in Norwich under the auspices of a nice man Kate had found in Yellow Pages who usually recorded school choirs. The kind of place where Hebe would be allowed to sing whilst hanging upside down by her knees from a small ladder, should she feel like doing so on the day. Possibly.

Julia's exhibition opened four weeks later, to an extraordinary level of press interest, which she felt modestly was far more due to the presence of the real Foxbartoñ angel on a plinth in the centre of the room (surrounded by a state-of-the art security system which even Hebe had not been able to breech) than to her own efforts. There had been the added bit of publicity, when the profligate Brown family, relatives of Mackenzie, turned up and shouted that the statue ought now to be theirs since it had not been on public display at all times in accordance with the will – but they were rapidly quashed by a clever lawyer who pointed out that the angel *had* remained on display in the village, in a different and in fact very much more public place than the one Mackenzie Brown had envisaged in her will.

The exhibition was, the art critics agreed, a triumph,

finally delivering an answer to all those voices who had for so long asked what had happened to Julia Fitzgerald, confirming the promise in her earlier work.

Kate was as proud as punch. She held court at the opening party wearing her new engagement ring like Elizabeth Taylor in Hollywood. The party was, she knew, a professional and personal triumph, even though Oscar resolutely refused to stand on a plinth and play his violin for it. Martin, her former husband, swallowed quite painfully when he arrived to gloat at the mess she would surely have made of things and discovered her in a dramatic black dress with a cleavage he definitely didn't remember, and with the vicar attached to her non-bejewelled arm in a very possessive fashion. She was able to greet members of the press with an air of authority, direct people not only to Julia's older works, including *Being*, loaned by the Tate Modern for the duration, but also to the newer series of willow creatures. She had, she felt, found her forte, her niche in life, at last. Now she was not only Oscar's mother, she had achieved something for herself. She was a woman, both a professional woman and a sensual one. She was at last complete. Even the discovery that her former gypsy lover was none other than Gabriel Gilfoyle himself had not rattled her. No one need ever know, and it added to her personal sense of her own womanly mystery, giving her an added glow.

The new sculptures were attracting great interest. *Tribe* and *Safari* were under offer from several galleries already, but the crowning glory, *Foxbarton Angel II* was of course not for sale. It had delighted the critics and the village alike, pleasing even the village statue censorship committee. But it was widely felt to be more extraordinary than that. People said Julia had shown skills of prediction, since the sculpture could be construed as showing an angel hidden in a tree. They said that the sculpture had something magical about it. The fact that it was viewed to the sound of 'Waltzing

Matilda' played on an old wooden musical box was, people said, mysterious and deep, but it was more than that too. The angel had an aura about it, some people said, a sense of being something more than bronze. An aura maybe, of faith. Other people said that was nonsense, because the artist was an atheist, and anyway angels weren't solely the property of the Christian Church any more. But whether they were right or they were wrong, they weren't able to find a better word for it.

The sculpture began at the base as a tree of willow, branches reaching to each side – but higher up the tree morphed from willow to clay, now both depicted in bronze, so that the torso of the angel arose out of the tree-willow structure like a chimera. Its wings hung down its back, covered not with feathers but with leaves. Only its arms had been difficult, as Julia had not wanted to depict the angel praying. The original Foxbarton angel was praying, but Julia had wanted this one not to be an angel asking for help but an angel who had already received it. So, despite her wish to avoid imbuing the angel with too much religious significance (difficult, with angels) she had shown its arms reaching up to Heaven, as an angel's should. It was, everyone said, her finest work, and although Julia felt that wasn't saying much, given that she'd made next to nothing for years, she was still rather flattered and very pleased.

It was, of course, enormous. Joshua, who had had to foot the bill for the casting, had laughed hysterically when presented with the invoice from the foundry, and had suggested that she take the shirt off his back whilst she was at it – but then it's not often that a private individual commissions an eight-foot high bronze, particularly not when he thought he had commissioned something small enough to sit on a four-inch plinth in the church of St Gregory.

Mrs Braithwaite was very taken with the angel. She had been watching its progress over the last few weeks, and

Julia had become gradually aware that as the angel grew more formed and, eventually, emerged from its casting, Mrs Braithwaite grew weaker, seeming to fade before their eyes. A week after the exhibition opened she took to her bed. She was, she said, simply feeling worn out, but Joshua Gilfoyle spent a long time with her that day, and it seemed that a sadness came to hang over the village like a gentle and sympathetic cloud.

'How is Mary?' Julia asked a few days later as she shared a coffee in her house with Gabriel, who had called round to see Hebe, to begin, as he put it, to get on with trying to be her father.

He shook his head sadly. 'She hasn't got long. I can't imagine this place without her.'

Over in the woods Mary Braithwaite smiled at Jonathan. She was fading fast. She knew it, he knew it – everyone knew it. A series of people had stayed with her so that she wouldn't be alone, even though she told them, insisted to them, that she was not alone at all. Kate kept making cups of tea and offering lashings of worry; both Julia and Gabriel came twice a day and did the things people do when they care, like sweeping up and making a fuss about the dirty cups, and Hebe had, Julia knew, spent the previous night curled up asleep on Mary's bed.

'It's my time, dear,' she said now to Jonathan, 'don't you worry. There are people here already to guide me on my journey. You may not see them keeping an eye on me, but I see them myself more clearly with every minute. There'll be others like them – like me – along to keep an eye on all of you too. There always are.'

Jonathan smiled. He had sat with her all day now, was conscious of a peace descending. Simon had been in and out; Merrill had briefly agitated for a trip to hospital, but in the end they had all agreed that if Mary wanted to stay exactly where she was then that was the right thing, the best thing to do.

'What can you mean?' Jonathan asked her. 'They don't make them like you any more.'

'No they don't,' said Mary Braithwaite. 'They use a different mould. Warts and wrinkles aren't so popular with them up there these days, you know.' Jonathan thought she must be rambling. He touched her hand and after a moment she said, 'You know, it's a bloody funny world, but I'm proud to have been one of its guardians.'

'Guardians? You've certainly looked after people here well. And for a long time, Mary. What year were you born?'

Mary Braithwaite smiled. 'You'd not believe me, dear, if I told you. Do you know, vicars never see what's under their noses? They're too consumed with faith to put any weight in proof. But then, I've never much liked the word angel. At my age, the word guardian has a lot more dignity . . .'

Epilogue

⟨⟩

Julia awoke smiling a full year later, and it took her a moment to remember exactly where she was. Then, sensing the unfamiliar weight on the mattress beside her she remembered. Gabriel. The night. The dandelion wine.

There was a fresh, dewy smell to the air. Outside the window she could hear the shouts of the men from the estate clearing leaves and old bracken from the edge of the lawn. She blew gently and saw her breath in front of her face.

The house was silent. Gabriel was fast asleep. She studied his face for a while – he reminded her of those Botticellian pictures of Jesus looking dark and haunted. Artistically speaking he was really quite beautiful.

A snore caught her attention and she sat up. There, curled up on the foot of the bed, wearing socks, wellingtons and a faerie costume that Joshua had just bought her, was Hebe, her long blonde hair spread all over her face, her eyes moving a little beneath the lids. One hand was screwed up close to her face, as if she had meant to suck her thumb but changed her mind. In the other she held the carved wooden angel that Gabriel had given her to replace the one that now sat again on the plinth in the church.

Julia remembered the conversation she had had with Hebe the other night.

'My angel looked after me in the tree,' Hebe had said, looking at the moon.

'Of course, darling, but that angel is standing in the church now, remember?' Julia had replied, wondering if this was heading towards unwanted religious conversion.

Jonathan would be pleased. Or perhaps not – Hebe could be a mixed blessing in church. She had attended Jonathan and Kate's wedding as smallest bridesmaid, and insisted on singing 'Waltzing Matilda' from start to finish during the signing of the register when the plan had been for an equally gorgeous but rather more subtle performance of 'Panis Angelicus' in duet with Matilda.

'No,' Hebe had been insistent. 'Don't be silly, not that angel. That's just a statue. My angel has a green dress, and comes from the moon. My angel sings.'

'What do you mean?' Julia had asked, looking up at the sky. 'Is it there now?'

Hebe had gazed at the moon for a moment, her eyes, as so often, seeming to make contact with the unseen. 'Oh yes,' she had said. 'Definitely.'

Julia smiled now at her sleeping daughter; grateful that she had a child who saw angels where others see only the moon, sure at last that wherever this angel came from it had been with her before.

Outside a cock crowed, and she heard William's llama, which was currently grazing her lawn, make that peculiar whinnying-clicking noise that llamas make. It was a lovely morning.

Julia felt a rush of elation. Suddenly it was imperative that there was absolutely no delay, not even a second. She leaped from the bed, ran down the stairs and out of the front door, taking a huge breath of the fresh, damp grass-scented air. There was dew on the ground, daisies crept between her toes and the birds were singing lustily. She could feel a rush of inspiration surging through her veins like champagne. There was fresh clay in her shed. She had to get in there and start on something new, straight away. There was no time to be lost. She had felt like this every morning since . . . well, since she found Gabriel again so unexpectedly, but she wasn't going to lie around and take it for granted, not for a second.

On the far side of the lawn down by the shed the three undergardeners, Stewart, Charlie and Matt, who had gathered to mutter about the llama (which was, they felt, doing them out of a job) looked up when they heard the door open, all prepared to wave cheerily, more in hope than expectation. And they all saw her. They saw Julia Fitzgerald come dashing across the lawn towards them, a great big smile on her face, her hair flying about her head, one arm outstretched, her feet flying across the grass almost as if she had wings. And she was stark, staring naked.

For a split second they gazed in awed terror at the statuesque curves, the huge and gloriously bouncing breasts (you couldn't have called them tits, said Stewart afterwards, they just weren't tits, they were breasts), the firm stomach, the light but perceptible tan, the mass of curly blonde stuff in the vee of her thighs . . . and then, overcome by an embarrassment that was as total as it was overwhelming, they turned tail and fled.